Trying
Times

First published by David James Publishing in 2013
Copyright © 2013 Janice Donnelly

First David James Publishing edition 2013
Cover Design: Copyright © Jacqueline Stokes

A CIP catalogue record for this book is available from the British Library
ISBN: 978-0-9575610-7-6

Acknowledgements

Special thanks to Sean McMahon for his much appreciated encouragement and support, Patricia Gormley and Marj McRae for proof reading, and on points of accuracy, Brendan Graham of Invest N.I. and the staff of Foyle Women's Aid and Francis McCrory for his amazing cover image, from his painting 'Citybound.' http://francismccrory.com/

This project is supported by the Arts Council of Northern Ireland.

Dedication

For my husband, Terry,
and my daughters, Lauren and Gina.

Trying Times

by

Janice Donnelly

DAVID JAMES PUBLISHING

Part One

January Blues

'January sick and tired
you've been hanging on me...'
Pilot

Chapter 1

Saturday, 24th January

THE BLOND, LEGGY SHOP ASSISTANT strutted ahead of Cassie along the short length of corridor, to the door marked Personal Shopper. Her shiny black leggings clung to her, accentuating her firm, tiny rear. She flung the door open, holding it aloft with the entire length of one arm. A ceremonious sweep of the other invited Cassie to enter. Cassie smiled her thanks.

The girl returned it, her wide open mouth revealing a gleaming set of perfect white even teeth. She looked familiar, Cassie thought, for all the world like the blonde one from that girl band she'd seen on TV last night. The door closed with a soft, slooping sound.

Inside the room she was greeted by Gok Wan. He shook her hand vigorously and indicated for Cass to have a seat on one of two red sofas placed opposite each other. A woman was sitting on one of them, flicking casually through a magazine.

As Cassie approached, the woman rose to be introduced by Gok. It was Lorraine Kelly from GMTV.

"Hellooo Cassie, lovely to meet you," gushed Lorraine.

Cassie returned her greeting, thinking how much like herself Lorraine looked in real life. Gok, who had stepped into a side room, was coming toward her with an armload of clothes.

"Let's get started, hen night first. Wha'd'ya think Cassie? The midnight blue, or the sienna for starters? Or maybe the little black number, always perfect for any occasion?"

He held each dress out in turn, dramatically, for Cassie's approval, swinging them enticingly from their hangers.

"Ach for goodness sake, Gok, you'll have the poor wooman's head boiled, try them all on Cassie," Lorraine encouraged.

Cassie walked toward the screened changing area and did as she was told, shy at first, but increasingly, loving the attention, as Gok and Lorraine enthused over each garment she modelled for them, commenting on each one individually.

"No, that shade's all wrong for your skin tones, Cass," said Gok.

"The black's lovely on you Cassie, maybe a bit titty, but then it is a hen night," Lorraine giggled.

Eventually they all decided on the midnight blue for the night out.

"It really brings out the blue of your eyes," Gok complimented.

Lorraine nodded her agreement as Cassie did a twirl for them.

"Perfect."

Cassie also chose a dozen or so others with Gok and Lorraine's help. She was just getting her credit card out to pay the assistant, her keen stylists encouraging her to buy a few more, when the news jingle rang out. The voice of the newsreader interrupted Gok and Lorraine mid flow, waking Cassie up.

"Good Morning; it's six o'clock. I'm ..."

Cassie rubbed her eyes and swung her legs out of bed, before she realised it was Saturday. And then she remembered. She'd been so excited about her £500,000 scratch card win she'd gone to bed without cancelling the alarm that woke her for work every weekday. Gok Wan and Lorraine Kelly? It wasn't as though she watched breakfast TV religiously in her robe, but it was on in the background in the building society offices she cleaned each morning.

She liked Lorraine though. Thought she'd be a good laugh, one of the girls. And as for Gok, well her daughter Lara thought he was God. Cassie only had two decent dresses, the black one she'd bought herself for Christmas, exactly like the one Lorraine had deemed, '...a bit titty...' and a midnight blue one that she'd bought in the sale on Boxing Day, the one that Gok and Lorraine had given their seal of approval to in her dream.

Before going to bed, Cassie had been agonising over which one to wear for the night out. She hadn't got the cheque in her hand yet, so couldn't afford a new one, despite her good fortune. *Well done team, I'll wear the blue!*

She reached for the remote to lower the volume of the radio, at the same time pulling on her robe with the other arm. She half walked, half tiptoed as she made her way across the landing to the bathroom; she didn't want to wake her son, although the likelihood of that was slim at this hour.

In the bathroom, she smiled wryly at her reflection in the mirror, hair tousled, wearing her cosy chain store pyjamas. *If ever a woman needed a personal shopper*, she thought.

After flushing the toilet, she lifted the bleach bottle from under the sink, and poured the thick liquid generously round the bowl, in preparation for the clean-up she did every Saturday morning; starting with the bathroom and systematically working her way through the small house, finishing in the kitchen. She'd keep to her routine throughout the weekend, start the week as usual, tell no one until she had the cheque safely lodged in her bank account.

Back in the bedroom she snuggled under the duvet and lay listening to the radio, resetting the alarm for seven thirty, her normal waking time on Saturdays. She hit the snooze button until eight. She was too wired to sleep, so she let her mind wander as she planned how she would spend her £500,000.

A shopping trip would be lovely, but it was an indulgence she couldn't allow herself to afford. Not yet. Cassie had been a cleaner for seventeen years, hard back breaking work on low pay, with little chance of advancement.

She'd often thought of what she'd do if fortune ever shone on her. How she'd seize the chance to change her life once and for all. £500,000, although a fortune to her, wasn't a lot by today's standards.

Her mind went back to a newspaper article she'd read recently about a woman in England who'd won just over a million in the lottery. She worked as a cook in a local fire station, and after the initial excitement had died down, decided to keep her job on. Cass had read the article with interest as the winner was around her own age.

The woman had planned out each year's income for the next twenty years, with the help of a financial advisor, and whilst it certainly was enough to provide her with a comfortable existence, when the figures were laid out, it wasn't enough to retire on, not nowadays. Cass knew a half a million would be easy to spend, give her a luxurious couple of years, but then what? She wasn't even forty yet so she'd have to make this money work for her. It would be more than enough to give her the lift she needed. She'd make sure of that.

Her brain ticked over as the radio played quietly in the background. She would use these few days to think her plans through, until the cheque was hers. Maybe ask Gail to set her up with an appointment with her manager for some sound financial advice.

She thought of her experience in her own branch yesterday, of the assistant Shiralee's disdainful expression. And she knew she couldn't miss out on seeing her face as she presented the cheque.

Yesterday, as Cassie stood at customer service, fidgeting and embarrassed, it had only been by chance that Shiralee had attended her, although stating that it was she who looked after Cassie's current account. No, she'd ring; ask for her by name before lodging. What had her badge said? 'Shiralee North, Relationship Banker.' Yeah, that was it, Relationship Banker. She'd make an appointment, allow herself the satisfaction of seeing Shiralee's perfectly made-up jaw drop onto her bony little chest as she read the amount. Double checking the zeros. Cassie grinned to herself as she rolled out of bed. Who said money can't buy happiness?

Showering quickly, she dried herself and pulled on jeans and a T shirt. That was the Saturday routine. Quick wake up shower, coffee, and cereal, clean the house until around twelve, then a long indulgent shower and hair wash before her daughter Lara and her three year old Mia arrived for lunch. By that time Dean, her eighteen year old son, may just have made it downstairs.

Lara at twenty-one was on her own with her daughter. Pregnant at seventeen and in the middle of her 'A' levels, when she'd announced her news to Cassie. Cassie couldn't believe the words her ears were receiving, but she bit her tongue as her brain digested the information. Almost the exact age she herself had been when she'd delivered the same news to her own mother.

Her mother's response still rang in her ears, "I thought you lot had all that sussed, our generation were supposed to be the last of the stupid ones."

It was the recollection of the shame and hurt those words had caused her that had goaded Cassie to reply, "Have you told Jake yet?"

Lara's boyfriend Jake was, in Cassie's estimation, a monosyllabic moron with the personality of a cockroach, but she had kept her opinion to herself. Lara nodded, relieved her mother hadn't blown her stack as she'd expected.

"Yeah, he's shocked too, but we're planning on setting up

together before the baby's born…well I mean we're both still reeling…"

Lara had burst into tears and fallen into her mother's arms. Cassie had left all the questions hanging:

Do you love him?

Does he love you?

How far on are you?

Are ye sure you want to go through with it?

They had cried together in the silence of Cassie's living room, as the rain outside battered the windows, replicating their tears.

Now, to Mia, Jake was merely a distant memory, head over heels in love with the idea of being a Daddy but not so keen on the reality of dirty nappies and sleepless nights. Shortly after Mia's birth, he'd legged it back to his ma's and his nights out with the mates, while Lara grew up more or less overnight. They lived only streets away, so on Saturdays Cassie looked after Mia to give Lara a break. She occasionally met up with some of her old school friends, but mostly Lara shopped alone, while Cassie indulged her granddaughter with walks in the park or bus trips to town.

Dean, Cassie's son was eighteen and had gained three 'A' levels last year, but had had absolutely no luck in finding a job that would enable him to further his ambitions of becoming a Graphic Designer. She'd lost count of the arguments they'd had about lowering his aspirations until the economy picked up; he was resolute, he wouldn't be flicking burgers in any fast food outlet. That was "…*for losers…*"

Meanwhile, he slept all day and drank coffee all night, while she pulled her hair out worrying about him. If she was honest, part of her thought he was probably right; how good would it look on a CV? But then again how good did endless months of unemployment look? Cassie wondered if he'd have been so unemployable with a professional father in residence, someone to provide him with introductions and a leg up the ladder.

Maybe she was just becoming bitter and twisted. A lot of young ones were out of work. He'd gone to a good school, she'd done her best by him and it broke her heart to see him throwing his life away watching night-time TV after all the hopes she'd had for him.

Lara was due any minute. She poured herself more coffee and turned the bacon in the pan just as Dean's head appeared around the kitchen door.

"Hey Ma, any chance?"

His look indicated the cafetiere. She hugged him and poured a cup for him, careful not to appear too chirpy, although inside she was dancing.

"Well, Dino how's it goin', get that call from Sir Al yet?"

He grabbed a slice of toast and sat down at the table.

"I wouldn't work for that asshole if he paid me a hundred grand a year."

"I think that is the idea, son."

He grinned lazily and bit into the toast as his mother pushed the coffee toward him. The door swung open and Lara's voice rang up the hall, "Mmmmm, bacon!"

Mia ran ahead of her, hurling herself toward her grandmother full force.

"Hey Strawberry Shortcake, how's you?"

Cassie hoisted her up, smelling the sweet baby scent as she buried her face in her granddaughter's hair.

Her eyes began to fill with tears as she thought about what this win could mean for her family. Quickly she put the child down, swept around, and hugged her daughter with her head lowered.

She turned to attend the bacon as her daughter and son bantered each other - business as usual. As she cooked the lunch she steadied her emotions saying to herself, *Easy does it, Cass, keep it cool. You've still to see the colour of the money, girl.*

The day was calm and mild. Cassie sat on the bus holding her granddaughter firmly on her knee. The child chattered incessantly, playing with Cassie's hair and smiling into her face. Every now and then she'd repeat the nursery rhyme Cass had taught her last week. Applauding herself as she reached the finale, Cassie praised her efforts.

"Good girl!"

A woman seated beside them clapped along with Mia. The child laughed at her admirer, throwing her head back, delighted with herself. As the City Hall came into view Cassie rose with Mia in her arms, and gathered the buggy from the front of the bus. She pushed through the Saturday shoppers toward New Look, in pursuit of much needed work shoes. Her pay was in the bank okay, she'd checked her balance online earlier - then sat with her statement at the kitchen table, sorting out her direct debits and outstanding bills.

As usual there was just about enough to keep the wolf from the door. Again Cassie's heart soared as she thought of her win and the difference it would make. She tried on a few pairs of shoes before selecting a sturdy black pair, resisting the temptation to try on a glamorous blue strappy pair that would have been perfect for the dress she was wearing that night. Although she knew she could afford them, now that the windfall was coming her way, superstition made her stop.

She couldn't allow herself to tempt fate, couldn't allow herself to believe her days of penny-pinching were really over. She hugged her secret to herself, smiling at the wee blond girl at the pay point as she handed over the bag with the sensible shoes inside. The pair Lara had bought her at Christmas to go with the black dress were still fine for tonight. She'd buy a new lipstick to treat herself. Not much of a celebration by a lot of women's standards, but an indulgence to Cassie. She'd been scraping out the remains of her favourite one with a lip brush for too long; couldn't even remember when she'd bought it. Yeah, a lipstick would be a luxury.

As she headed towards Boots, pushing Mia in the buggy, the child sang out her favourite song and Cassie joined in, their voices lost in the hum of the traffic and city noise.

Mia sat at the table colouring, while Cassie handed the child crayons on demand. Mia took her colouring very seriously. Dean had gone over to a mate's house to stay the night, and Lara would be back any minute to collect Mia.

Cassie was relaxed and happy; with no dinner to prepare she'd have time to enjoy getting ready for her night out. The child jumped up as her mother entered the room.

"Hey Gorgeous, givvus a kiss!" Lara scooped her daughter up and hugged her.

"Good day, love?" Cassie asked.

"Not bad, I bought a new top."

Lara opened the bag and held her purchase against her body, modelling it for her mother's approval.

"Nice. You suit that colour."

Lara nodded, pleased with herself.

"Nikki texted me, they're all going into the town tonight, she asked me to go. Any chance?" she nodded toward her daughter.

Lara didn't go out often, but if the opportunity arose it was normally on a Saturday night and Cassie babysat for her happily. She rarely went out herself, maybe round to Gail's or one of her other mates, with a bottle of wine the odd night. But Saturday nights usually found her with her feet up in front of the TV exhausted from her week's work, more often than not shouting abuse at the participants on whatever reality talent show was being aired at the time. There was always one on. No sooner had one finished than another one hit the screens. Dean laughed at her antics, "You can change the channels, ya know."

Cass enjoyed it. It gave her a chance to vent her frustrations, kept her sane, stopped her from punching her boss on Monday morning. She was looking forward to going out tonight, though.

"Sorry love, I'm going out, remember the hen night, Helena's daughter?"

Lara looked disappointed.

"I thought you said you couldn't afford it."

They'd discussed it the previous week.

"I can't, but I'll be a long time dead. Cup o'tea?"

Cassie turned to fill the kettle, trying hard to stop herself from smiling at the shocked look on her daughter's face, thinking, *You ain't seen nothing yet!*

Lara recovered herself enough to ask where they were going. Cassie told her a meal and on to club. "We're meeting at Victoria Centre; we'll decide where we're headin' from there. I wasn't goin' to bother, but I missed the credit union this week, just paid the interest. Helena's been a mate since school and she asked me months ago, I didn't want to let her down."

Cassie didn't want to arouse Lara's suspicions. She wouldn't tell her about the win yet, maybe not even when she got the cheque.

£500,000 was a fortune to Cassie, but would seem even more so to her twenty-one year old daughter, living on state benefits. Lara would see it in terms of clothes for herself and endless pretty dresses for Mia, and the holiday she could never afford for herself and her child. Cassie couldn't tell her and not give her share, when she so desperately needed cash.

She wouldn't tell her, not yet. She wouldn't tell anyone yet, until she'd had time to consider what that amount of money could do for all of them - if she was smart.

Lara finished her tea and gathered up Mia's things, all disappointment about her own plans forgotten. She kissed her mother.

"You enjoy yourself Mum, watch out for bad men."

"Are there any other kind?"

Cassie hadn't so much as looked at a man since the day she'd thrown Gerry Gallagher out, literally. The suitcases had followed him out the door and landed with a thud on the pavement. Ma Riley, the nosey neighbour cleaning her windows, had nearly broken her neck to crane a better view as Cassie slammed the door after him with a bang that almost shattered the inlaid pane of glass.

Ever the wag he'd gathered his cases and his composure and strolled down the street, out of their lives forever, calling across to the street gossip as she vigorously rubbed the chamois over the pane of glass, "Hey Ma, ye missed a bit!"

Cassie ran the bath and examined her make-up free face in the mirror. It was tired and dry from lack of a decent moisturiser and from neglect. All too often she was too exhausted to bother removing the day's make-up, too stressed worrying how she was going to cope with whatever crisis the day presented.

And every day presented one.

Dean needed a new school blazer (thank God those days were over) the hot water tank had sprung a leak, the washing machine was on the blink, the oil tank was empty and she hadn't enough credit in her account to top up; one bloody thing after the other.

She sank into the bath. The bath bomb fizzed around her feet as she wiggled her toes in the water. Her legs still ached, but not half as much as usual. The thought of the money coming her way had changed her life already; she felt younger, despite the face reflected back at her. Her muscles relaxed in the scented suds. She'd read a sign in a beauty salon window in the town today, 'Chase those Winter Blues away with a Pamper Package.'

She'd glanced down the list of treatments - Indian head massage, facial, manicure, pedicure, full body massage, aromatherapy session…Her mind boggled at the price, as she thought of her meagre wages. She decided to go for it when the money was in the bank. A luxury no one else would see, but one which would mean the world to her.

She'd use the treatment to get her head together as well as her body; her future success depended on her head and her capacity to keep it. This once in a lifetime chance was going to turn everything around. She didn't know how yet, but she was sure of it.

Cassie was going to make her good fortune work for her.

Chapter 2

AS THEY DROVE TOWARD THE town in the Saturday night traffic the taxi driver sang along to the disco show on the radio. Naomi sitting alongside him, joined in. Cassie and Gail sat in the back talking animatedly. When he cruised to a stop in Victoria Street, Naomi paid the fare as the others stepped onto the pavement. She had chatted with him as he drove, telling him they were on a hen night.

"Have a good time girls," he called after them, "there'll be some damage done the night!"

They walked toward the restaurant. The others were inside and Danielle and her mates had already started on the cocktails. Cassie was looking forward to a glass of wine but was determined not to have too much in case her tongue loosened. She'd give the cocktails a miss. She couldn't cope with hangovers these days; she was out of practice.

The waiter brought the menus and the young ones ordered quickly, wanting to get the process of eating out the way, and down to some serious clubbing.

Cassie had no idea where they were going. All of this nightlife was new to the city; the shopping centre with entertainment complex had only opened in the past year. Of course she had walked through on her way to work, but this buzz of cinema goers and clubbers was an eye-opener.

Another world from her sofa and TV screen, it was a delight to see after the years of 'the troubles' when Belfast had been a ghost town after six o' clock any night.

In the toilets they touched up their make-up before moving on. Cassie scrutinised Gail's sombre expression. She sensed Gail wasn't in good form, she'd become quieter since reaching the restaurant, although she was doing her best to join in.

"Everything alright Gail, you're a bit quiet?"

"Ach, I'm fine, the girls were at each others' throats as I left, y'know what teenagers are like, put my blood pressure up a bit," she replied as she began reapplying her lipstick.

"Forget them, sure y'know they'll be the best of friends as soon as you've walked down the front path."

"Exactly. We're out to enjoy ourselves and by God I intend to!"

She threw the lipstick into her make-up bag and clasped it shut with a snap.

Gail sounded slightly tipsy already. Cassie grinned at her in the mirror.

"We've a whole night to get through remember, these young ones are fit for it, you and me are most definitely not. Don't be fallin' by the wayside before we get to the dance floor."

Gail danced to the exit.

"Oh I won't be fallin' anywhere; I'm up for anything tonight!"

Cassie danced after her and as they made their way back to the table they giggled like teenagers.

Leaving the restaurant, they passed the multiplex cinema next door. Cassie glanced in out of curiosity. She hadn't been there either, although Lara had. She said it was massive, better than the one she and her mates usually went to.

All along the foyer walls, outside each screen, stood a team of women in blue uniforms, lined up ready to enter as the movie ended. *Cleaners,* thought Cassie. *God love them. Even at this time on a Saturday night some poor soul has to clean up somebody else's mess.*

After the initial hint of a melancholy mood, Gail perked up and they all enjoyed the night, none more than Cassie who did her best 'Shania' impression for them on the dance floor, to all of their amusement.

On leaving the club, they passed the cinema again. She thought of the cleaners who'd lined the walls earlier. Recession or not, there was always plenty of work for cleaners, salt of the earth, like her.

Plenty of work for cleaners.

She thought of the invoices she'd read as she cleaned one of the offices the other morning, and the extortionate fee the client paid the cleaning company compared to the pittance she got.

That's it! I'll start my own cleaning company!

She'd use the money to work for her by starting a business. Cassie had drunk more than her fair share of wine, but her head could not have been clearer. All around her the voices of the girls babbling, drunkenly, interrupted her thoughts; she'd think it through, tell no one until she'd done her homework.

One of them started to sing, *"When the workin' day is done…"* They all joined in, Cassie's voice ringing out louder and clearer than the rest, *"… girls just wanna have fu un, oh ohh, girls just wanna have fu un!"*

Chapter 3

ORLA SIPPED HER ORANGE AND mango smoothie as she leafed through the glossy Sunday supplement, not really reading it. Her eyes scanned the pictures, taking in the images, but her mind had little interest in the stories or articles they represented.

She was sitting at her kitchen table, watching Seamus scatter muesli into a bowl at the work surface opposite. His back was tense as he reached into the fridge for milk. Grabbing a spoon, he proceeded to eat where he stood in silence; a silence that had pervaded the apartment more or less since midnight on Friday.

He had lain around the apartment for most of Saturday, only leaving in the early evening to buy a paper. They hadn't rowed on Friday night. He'd slept on the sofa until daybreak, then risen to go to the bathroom. She'd woken to the sound of him rifling through the bathroom cabinet, presumably for a hangover cure, his mood over the weekend in direct contrast to the 'hale fellow well met' attitude of Friday night, when he'd had an audience to perform to.

Orla was aware that this ritual increasingly formed a pattern to the life they shared. Her husband, the exuberant, extrovert, bursting with stories and jokes for his friends and colleagues (she had long since realised the people he surrounded himself with were of his choosing, not hers) holding the floor, entertaining all and sundry - in stark contrast to the silent, sullen, withdrawn man she was left to live with when the front door closed on the rest of the world.

She set the magazine down and made to rise to her feet to leave the room, the glass still in hand. The sudden blow to the side of her head caused the smoothie to form a somersault, her body following the curve of the orangey-yellow liquid, over and down. Glass still in hand, miraculously unbroken. The sound of his flying cereal bowl impacted on the wall with an ear-splitting crash, porcelain meeting ceramic. His voice echoing in her ringing ears as she lay sprawled, across the kitchen floor, "I told ye before, I don't like this shite."

He reached for the cereal, flinging box and contents furiously into the sink, then reached for the box and jerkily shook the remaining contents out, covering the sink and surrounding areas.

"Shite, shite, shite…"

His voice was low, almost calm – an exasperated adult, admonishing an uncomprehending child. Orla peered through half open eyes, her hair netted in a visor across her brow. She saw him lift his car keys and reach for his jacket, she heard his feet walk down the length of the hall and pause. The swish of leather against fabric told her he'd stopped to pick up his golf clubs. The door closed behind him with a soft click, and she heard the bleating noise of the lift as its doors opened and closed. Then silence.

All the while she lay where he'd landed her looking at the blue wall spattered with the splashes of orange and mango smoothie. In only seconds her mind processed the scene: muesli and milk merged to form another splash on the wall adjacent to the stainless steel work surface where he'd stood eating only minutes before. She thought of the shade card they'd pored over for hours, choosing exactly the right colours for their dream apartment, every room coordinating with the other to create the perfect ambience for their perfect life. What was that blue they'd decided on? *Blissful Blue* - that was it. Underneath the radiator she noticed a whole strip of wall that was still the mushroomy colour of the plaster, the painter must have missed it. Funny how she didn't notice it before. Funny how she didn't usually lie on the kitchen floor with her face hugging the tiles.

She tasted a metallicy liquid and realised it was blood. Running her tongue across her teeth she felt a chip on one of her right back teeth. The blood was starting to drip onto the tiles. She rose to her feet, spitting the piece of tooth onto a tissue, wrapping it up and pushing it into her pocket. Like she was going to roll into her dentist's practice with the piece in hand and say, "Can you stick this back on please?"

She ripped off a wad of kitchen roll and held it to her lip, to stop the flow of blood. Perversely her mind recalled the article she'd been scanning in the Sunday supplement, 'Ten Ways to While Away a Winter Sunday', then the list. Had this been on it?

Making her way to the window to look into the courtyard car

24

park, holding onto the cool stainless steel, she observed the resident parking area, careful to remain out of sight should he look up. His silver BMW was still there. One of the neighbours was getting into his four wheel drive. Seamus approached. Orla held her breath; she had to see him leave. The neighbour turned to greet him. She could hear their voices chatting, just a normal Sunday morning exchange. The neighbour was laughing; so was Seamus and they parted with a congenial wave. As Seamus tossed the golf clubs into the boot the neighbour's words rang in the air, calling out to Seamus, still laughing, "I'll have to remember that one. Have a good game, Seamus, see ya later. Keep yer high hand low!"

The neighbour's vehicle left the courtyard, followed by Seamus's. He'd been telling their neighbour a joke, a friendly exchange between neighbours. This above all else, this scene, this normal Sunday morning scene beneath their window, was the final straw. Not the black eyes, nor the punches to the ribs or jaw - this image of her husband sharing a joke with a neighbour, after he'd abused her, made her realise it was over. She'd almost waited too long.

Orla looked at her hand. She'd instinctively reached out for a cloth to clean up the mess. Her brain went into overload as she threw the cloth into the sink and raced to the bedroom. Thank God she was dressed. What if he had only gone around the block to fool her? What if he came back? She knew she had to move fast.

She opened her wardrobe and grabbed the largest suitcase she could see and hurled it onto the bed and began tossing armfuls of clothes into it. Trying to think, underwear, shoes and coats, she gathered up her jewellery, passport, bankcards, any documents she thought she may need, checked her bag for her phone, as her shaking fingers found her keys. Double checking the wardrobe, she saw the little mirrored picture frame her sister Aine had given her for Christmas. It had a prayer written on it, beside the photo of Aine and herself: smiling, happy girls at fifteen and sixteen. Seamus called Aine 'The Earth Mother.'

One year younger than Orla, she had four children and a bearded husband, Rory. They lived in an old rambling house in the heart of the Wicklow Mountains, where Rory painted landscapes and Aine practised Reiki. Orla had loved the gift, but she'd hidden it away in her wardrobe, out of sight of Seamus and his ridiculing eyes. He would have laughed at it, called it naff, tacky.

She quickly lifted it and wrapped it in a T shirt, closing the case with a fast pull of the zipper. She caught her reflection in the hall mirror. Her lip was still bleeding but she couldn't take the time to go to the bathroom to see to it. Racing back to the kitchen, she grabbed a whole kitchen roll and a cold bottle of water from the fridge and shoved them into the case. She had to get out now. She reached for the handle and walked into the hall, pulling the door shut behind her without a backward glance. Her legs shook as she waited for the lift, praying that no one would be in it as the light indicated its arrival. It was empty. She swallowed hard, thinking, *Oh Christ, what if he's in the hallway, or the car park?*

Her head ached, and she felt dizzy. She said aloud, "What if I pass out? Fuck oh fuck, oh fuck, fuck, fuck!"

She remembered the prayer on the photo frame. She'd memorised it. What was it? She thought of Aine. Had her sister known? The words flowed; she recited them inwardly to herself as she walked to her car gripping her keys in her sweating hand, the other struggling with the weight of the case.

'God grant me the serenity
To accept the things
I cannot change,
Courage
To change the things
I can,
And wisdom
To know the difference.'

She was crying as she slid into the driver's seat and started up the engine but willed herself to stop. Safe in her car she began the prayer again, this time aloud. Over and over again she repeated the words, until they became a chant. Her heart slowed and her tears dried on her cheeks. The Sunday morning traffic was quiet as she made her way toward the motorway. Unknowing, uncaring where she was bound, she was safe; she'd left and she wasn't going back.

The motorway lane stretched before her. She read the signs as she passed, driving on and on, following the white lines. It didn't matter where she went, so long as she left Hillsborough far, far behind. She'd turn off at the next exit, to give herself time to think where she could go.

She pushed the button on the radio for company, listening to the chirpy presenter read out requests: *"Happy Birthday to Sally who reaches the Big 40 today, sure yer only a young whippersnapper, Desi loves ya to bits, as do the ankle-biters Jason and Jenny, here's your song..."*

The strains of a familiar old song played out as Orla indicated for the next turn off, Love Affair, 'Everlasting Love.' She drove into the town's quiet main street and stopped, switching off the radio so that she could gather her thoughts. She took out her phone and scanned the contacts, checking the time. 11.16a.m. *Who do you call at this time on a Sunday morning?* Orla thought.

Her family all lived in Dublin, but even if they had been at close proximity she knew she could never bring herself to let any of them see her in this state. She was too ashamed.

She surveyed her face in the rear view mirror. The blood was beginning to dry on her lip. It would bruise, she was sure of it. She read through her list. Jo lived alone with her son but she couldn't land in on her on a Sunday morning.

Orla thought back to their conversation on Friday, Jo was having family over for dinner today. No, that wasn't an option then. Gail was an ex colleague who she got on well with, but she'd a family, she couldn't just arrive on her doorstep. Ellen was also an ex colleague; they'd been good friends in her days in the bank.

Both young and free and single, they'd had some good nights and Orla felt guilty realising she'd rarely seen her since. She rarely saw any of her old friends. That was how Seamus liked it. Ellen lived alone in a small house in the east of the city. Orla was sure she would put her up for a few days, until she got her head sorted. But she couldn't just ring her out of the blue after all this time, not on a Sunday morning. Ellen could have a partner by now, or if not, she'd be heading out. Going shopping, or to the cinema, relaxing; doing what most people did on Sundays.

She needed to think. She set the phone on the seat beside her and rummaged in her bag for her bank card wallet, pulled out a recent withdrawal receipt and checked the balance. She had plenty to see her through. She silently thanked God she had a sole account as well as their joint account. Replacing the wallet, she stared out the windscreen at the street. Typical small town: primary school, community centre, convenience store, post office, three hairdressers, one of them with beauty salon. To the right of her a ladies' clothes shop, its fluorescent, curvy-lettered blue and yellow sign above the plate-glass display window, yelling out, 'Faye's Fashions', and just to her left, the library and health centre. The security screens were pulled down; through the holes in them she could see the windows full of public information posters.

Her mind cast back to the shopping mall on Friday, the poster in the toilets, '...*it could be you...*' The number of the domestic violence helpline had jumped out at her in huge green digits, followed by the words, *'Don't suffer in silence'*.

She was scrutinising her appearance before her business meeting with one of her suppliers, a meeting she couldn't reshuffle at such short notice, checking her foundation, especially around the eye area. It had taken twenty five minutes to apply that morning before she left home, but the time had been well spent. There was no indication at all of the heavy bruising surrounding her right eye. She had carefully built the foundation up, layer after layer, allowing each one to dry, before re-applying; giving a dense coverage without a clogged, heavy look. The effect was perfect.

She was a well-dressed, young woman about town. No one looking at her would ever suspect the beating she'd taken from her husband the previous night.

The number, she'd written it down, where? Pulling the make-up bag out of her handbag, she pushed the clasp open to find the lipstick holder. Toppling the lipstick out, she flicked the piece of paper open with her thumb and forefinger. There it was. Her trembling fingers dialled the number and waited. It was answered on the third ring.

"Hello, how can I help?"

These simple words were too much. The tears began to flow again. The woman's voice was soft and comforting, with a homely country lilt. Orla instantly thought of her mother.

"Take your time, can you tell me your name?"

Orla whispered her name like a child on her first day at school.

"It's okay Orla I'm here for you, just calm yourself to give me a few details, are you in direct danger at the minute?"

Orla sniffed back the tears and whispered a barely audible "No."

The exchange became easier as the woman encouraged her with the soft voice to give her the information she required to help her.

Orla told her of the episode in the apartment that morning. How she needed somewhere to stay until she could contact her friend tomorrow. The woman told her she could offer her a place in one of their refuges if she wanted it. Orla wanted it. She quickly wrote down the address, with directions, and the name of a worker to ask for on arrival.

The woman finished the exchange with the words, "You've made the first move Orla, don't panic, you can call us back if you've any bother finding the house. Are you sure you're okay to drive?"

Orla assured her she was, thanking her. She finished the call, noticing her hands had almost stopped shaking. Turning the key in the ignition, she left the small town behind her, making for the road again; the road that would lead her to her new life.

She didn't know the area but the directions were clear and easy to follow. Seamus had Sat Nav but she'd never bothered. The street looked quiet and well kept. Orla tried to control the butterflies that were whizzing around her insides. Her mouth was dry. She reached for the bottle of water she'd grabbed from the fridge as she left the apartment and she slugged it down greedily. Wiping the escaping droplets with her hand, she winced as her hand made contact with her open wound, dabbing the area with a tissue. The blood had almost dried.

On her arrival at the house, Orla was greeted by a smiling girl in a coral coloured smock top and leggings. Orla introduced herself nervously, giving the girl the name of the worker the woman on the helpline had told her to ask for.

The girl, held her hand out.

"That's me, c'mon ahead. I've your room ready for ya."

Orla was surprised. The girl, who was all bright eyes and sunny disposition, looked more like she belonged on a magazine cover than in a place like this. The girl led her along a hallway toward the staircase, chatting easily as they walked. Orla took in her surroundings. Noting that they were surprisingly bright and well presented.

"That's the playroom in there…"

She nodded to a room on the left decorated in primary colours with cartoon characters on the walls. Orla could make out Sponge Bob and his Pineapple House. A half dozen or so children were gathered around in a semi-circle. A woman sat in the centre telling them a story. None of the children noticed her.

Orla was relieved. She was conscious of her blood encrusted

lip and wild appearance; she hadn't even stopped to brush her hair. The woman gave her a casual nod and went on reading to the children.

"...the kitchen's through there, but we'll get you settled first, then I'll give you the grand tour."

The girl - what was her name? Carmel, that was it - opened a door to a small lilac and mauve room, interspersed with pale shades of green. The single bed, in the centre of the room, was covered in a mauve and lilac floral country print throw, with green trim. The windows had matching curtains. The centre of the pane of glass was draped in an ivory voile for privacy. Beside the bed was a little white table with a white orchid cube-style light sitting on top, a matching chest of drawers to the left of it, and on the other side of the bed a matching chair. The room was basic and functional, but fresh and clean. The muted greens and mauves presented an aura of calm.

Orla was relieved and grateful for the small oasis; she was sure she'd be at ease here, sure she would find the peace to do the thinking that was necessary for her future. Her eyes welled up again.

"I'll get you some cotton wool and antiseptic lotion," Carmel said, "do you need to call a doctor, do ya think?"

Orla's hand went to her face, her fingers tracing the area of bruising.

"No no, the cotton wool and antiseptic will be fine, thanks."

"I'll not be a minute, sit yerself down take the weight of your feet Orla, don't worry, no one will come in."

She closed the door behind her and Orla listened to the sound of Carmel's feet skipping along the landing and down the stairs. In the distance a door banged and a TV boomed out the afternoon news. She recognised the jingle of the UTV channel. The announcer was a woman; she knew the voice but couldn't put a face to her. Carmel seemed lovely, but she looked more like she should be at home, putting the finishing touches to her Art GCSE final piece, rather than working in a place like this. A place like what, though?

The house wasn't at all what she'd expected. Orla didn't know really what she'd expected, but it wasn't this. It was all so bright and airy, so fresh. In her mind's eye she saw grey walls, bare floors, cold, depressing dark rooms, like a Victorian asylum perhaps. She shivered at the image.

Only minutes later the door knocked. Orla had to think for a second before she replied. This was her room. It all seemed like a dream. A few hours ago she'd woken up in her white linen bed with Seamus beside her. And now here she was in another world entirely. Despite her feelings of shock...she was overwhelmingly relieved, thankful that she'd seen the poster and had the foresight to look the number up on Friday night. It had been something she'd done with the future in mind. The temper rages were usually spaced out in terms of four to six week intervals. The break in the pattern had taken her completely by surprise. She was so grateful to the softly spoken woman who'd been her first point of contact; so grateful to the girl standing before her, handing her supplies from a first aid kit.

Carmel said she'd leave her to get unpacked.

"I'll be in the front room, on the other side of the hall from the playroom, come down when yer ready then I'll show ya round, introduce you."

Orla must have looked alarmed. Carmel patted her hand gently.

"No worries, everybody's in the same boat, no one's going to judge you Orla, I'll leave you in peace."

For the second time Carmel left the room. On closer scrutiny Orla realised Carmel was more likely to be closer to her own age of twenty nine than the teenager she'd at first perceived her to be. She probably had qualifications as long as your arm. Orla felt at ease with her.

Her knees were shaking and she could feel her right eye jumping with nerves as she sat on the bed looking out over the unknown rooftops, the enormity of the day's events engulfing her. She knew she'd made the right decision, knew she was in safe hands. It would take a while to get back on her feet again, although she would, she'd no doubt. She was a strong woman. But right now she needed to know there were helping hands waiting to catch her if she stumbled and fell along the way.

She felt shy standing at the doorway to the downstairs front room where Carmel had said she would be.

Carmel noticed her right away and waved her in.

"C'mon and have a seat, Orla, we're just getting organised for teatime."

Two women with coats on, purses in hand, were standing by

one of the sofas. A smaller, red haired one was writing a list. Carmel introduced them and the other three women sitting around the television.

"What do you need, Orla, Carol-Anne and Maggie are goin' to the shop?"

Orla couldn't think what she needed.

"For tea, to eat, we've a microwave so if you fancy a ready meal they've a good range across the road," Carmel explained.

Orla hadn't thought of eating.

"What about a baked potato with grated cheese and a bit o' ham?" the one called Maggie encouraged.

"Yeah, that'll do thanks, I'll get my purse."

Orla ran up the stairs and plucked a note from her purse. She offered it to Maggie, who tucked it in into her own purse and wrote the amount she'd given her down on the shopping list.

"Will we get you some juice and cereal for the mornin'?"

Maggie kept her gaze away from Orla's lip and bruised face, understanding it would be a day or two before she'd be ready to face the world. She nodded her thanks. Carmel had been right; no one batted an eyelid at her appearance. The women headed down the garden path into the street, chatting easily, while the others argued over which TV programme they were going to watch next.

"I'll give you a quick look round now, before everybody hits the kitchen at once. It's survival of the fittest in here, Orla, you'll learn that fast," said Carmel, smiling at her.

They left the room, the remaining women running around the sofa, two of them in hot pursuit of the one with the remote control, giggling like school girls fighting over the last sweetie in the bag.

Chapter 4

SUNDAY EVENING FOUND ORLA SITTING in the big front room watching television. The group of women around her were all residents of the house, apart from one worker.

Orla, not a great one for TV, had no idea what the programme was - some sort of ice skating reality show. She wanted to leave the room, to go upstairs. But she knew all of the women present in the house were downstairs and she'd didn't wanted to appear ungrateful, aloof. She must have looked disconnected or bored because the woman sitting to the left of her whispered to her, "It doesn't do it for me either, fancy a cup o' tea?"

Orla nodded, although she didn't really want to leave the group to drink tea with this woman she didn't know, but she was too polite to decline. In the kitchen the woman introduced herself as Anne Marie. She recognised the name. Anne Marie was the singer from earlier. As they'd sat watching the news in the front room, loud singing had reached them from down the hall; a rousing, infectious song that Orla recognised from the radio, 'This is the Life,' by the Scottish girl with the beautiful, blue eyes. What was her name, Amy something or other?

The kitchen singer was giving it her heartfelt all. She carried the tune well, the voice sweet and melodic. The women had laughed at her enthusiasm. Someone had said her name, "Anne Marie's in quare form the day."

Oh no, she sighed inwardly; she was sitting in a refuge house with a woman who sang loudly to herself when all she wanted to do was go to her room, to go to bed, to sleep. To wake up and find the events of this morning had never happened. But she was sitting here watching the kitchen singer pour them both tea. Orla thought she'd rather stick needles in her eyes. She cursed her mother for bringing her up so well.

Why couldn't she just have said, "No thanks, I'm going to bed."

Subconsciously her hand went to her lip, fingering the crusty wound. The swelling had gone down a bit since Carmel had given her a cold pack and she'd lain on the bed while it did its work.

"No, 'Dancin' on Ice' doesn't do it for me, either. I like the 'X Factor,' though, ya get a laugh at the eejits auditionin', the ones without a note in their heads. You'd think somebody would tell them before they get that far, wouldn't ye? Do y'take milk and sugar, Orla?"

"Just milk, thanks."

They sat at the table facing each other. Anne Marie sipped her tea.

"I've biscuits in m'cupboard, Chocolate Hobnobs, do ye want one?"

Orla was about to say no, but Anne Marie was already across the room, rummaging behind one of the unit doors. She found the unopened packet and pulled the tag, unleashing the length of stringy plastic toward her and presented the packet to Orla. Three biscuits peeked out of the top of the blue sheath. She nodded as Orla dithered; since she'd gone to the bother of opening them it would have been rude not to take one. Orla nibbled the edge of her biscuit as Anne Marie dunked hers in her tea, eating it with relish. Grabbing another from the packet, she looked across the table at Orla nibbling like a rabbit.

"For God's sake woman, what way's that to eat a Hobnob? Dunk it!"

She watched her struggle to swallow. It was too dry. Orla could hardly get the crumbs down her throat. She drank a mouthful of tea and dunked the rest of the biscuit. Anne Marie was right, it was lovely - moist and creamy and chocolaty. She looked up. Anne Marie was licking the melted chocolate from her fingers.

"Sorry I know it's not polite, but y'can't waste chocolate, have another one, go ahead."

Anne Marie smiled her approval as Orla took the second biscuit. She felt her guard slip as she savoured it; she'd buy a packet when she was out tomorrow and share them with the woman. The thought went through her head that she'd reached a decision; she was okay here, safe. Carmel was right; everyone was in the same boat.

As if reading her thoughts Anne Marie said, "It gets easier, I'm here two months."

Orla lifted her head and looked into the woman's face. She hadn't realised any one would stay that long, have to stay that long.

"It's all down to location, if you're prepared to take anything they offer ya (she meant the Housing Authority) you could be out of here in the mornin', but I want to be close to my family, on the other side of the town from him. Have you a good solicitor?"

Orla nodded. She didn't speak, didn't tell her she wouldn't be needing housing authority accommodation. Saying that she was going to rent privately would alienate her from this woman who had held out the hand of friendship to her, make her look uppish in the woman's eyes.

"Make sure you ring for an appointment first thing in the mornin', you're not goin' back I take it?"

"No. I've never left before, but no, I'm not going back."

Orla said the words quietly. She knew it was true, had known it from the moment she grabbed her suitcase that morning. Her marriage was over, but it still felt strange to be discussing her life with this stranger.

Anne Marie nodded her approval, sensing Orla's reticence. She didn't question her further, but went on to share her own experience. She'd been with her husband three years, the same as Orla. Weirdly his name was Seamus, too.

"Mine's Seamus, too."

"Don't think the Seamus' have the monopoly though, there's plenty more of them out there. Psycho bastards. Some of the stories I've heard since I've been in here…" She went on to relate her story.

Seamus had started hitting her on their wedding night. He'd accused her of flirting with the best man at the after wedding dance. Anne Marie had woken to her first day of married life with a black eye and a heavy heart. He'd apologised, put it down to drink, saying it was just a slap. And the pattern had started.

They'd been happy at first, despite his temper flare ups every now and again, maybe every four to six weeks. Anne Marie said she'd marked a kind of a calendar in her head, so she'd know when to expect the next episode. Orla's hands made fists under the table. She dug her thumb nails into her forefingers, the mental calendar another similarity to her own story.

Anne Marie went on to tell her she'd left him once before, last year, but he'd pleaded with her, said he couldn't live without her, threatened suicide if she didn't take him back. She had, and after a while she'd found herself to be three months pregnant.

Delighted, Anne Marie had planned for the baby, painted the nursery, bought blankets and baby clothes. *"Only white, y'can't tempt fate..."*

She smiled at the memory. Seamus had been happy, really pleased with himself. She was sure they were going to be okay. The baby would change things, his outbursts would stop and they'd be happy all the time. Then one Friday teatime, he'd come home drunk in one of his rages, picked a fight because his favourite shirt wasn't clean for going out that night. Anne Marie had tried to mollify him. Said she'd put it into the washing machine and have it dried and ironed in no time flat. She'd been reaching into the laundry basket to pull the shirt out, when he'd grabbed her from behind and tossed her down the stairs like a rag doll.

Orla heard herself gasp as Anne Marie continued telling her tale, relating it like someone giving an incident report, detached, emotionless. How her husband had stormed out of the house, slamming the door behind him as he went, leaving her lying at the bottom of the stairs, the blood oozing from between her legs, forming a pool of red, viscous liquid screaming out in stark contrast to the cream shades of the carpet. With the life inside her draining out of her, she managed to get to the phone to ring an ambulance, but lost the baby on her way to the hospital. She left him for good that night.

Orla felt the salty taste of tears stinging the corner of her cut mouth, reminding her yet again why she was sitting here.

Anne Marie rose and filled the kettle. Orla followed her across the large kitchen. She washed their mugs and dried them as Anne Marie made more tea. They worked in silence.

As they sat at the table facing each other, the mugs of hot tea sent wafts of steam into the air. Orla began to tell her story. All of it. Words she'd never uttered to a living soul. When she reached the part about the hyperventilating, the paper bags under the bathroom sink, her heart began to thud and her breathing quickened. Panicking that it was going to start again she stopped talking.

Anne Marie, sensing her distress, reached across the table and patted her arm.

"Easy…"

Orla took deep breaths and gathered herself to finish her tale, right up to the events of that morning. This time Orla was dry eyed, and it was Anne Marie who wept. Afterwards, they sat in silence.

Orla broke it, asking the question she had to ask, "Why did you put up with it for so long?"

Anne Marie stared at her empty mug for a moment and replied with one word.

"Hope."

Anne Marie asked the next question of Orla, "Why did you?"

Orla sat head down, thinking. She raised her eyes to meet her new found friend's and spoke.

"Hope."

Orla tossed and turned, waiting for sleep to carry her through the night, the image of Anne Marie lying at the bottom of her own staircase in a pool of blood haunting her thoughts.

She reflected on her initial reaction to Anne Marie's singing, the women's laughter, thinking them all a bit dense. Who could sing and laugh in a place like this? Her assumption, on arrival in the small car park, that all of the vehicles must belong to the staff as surely homeless women wouldn't have cars. Then later in the afternoon, when one of the women in the front room had risen from her chair and said she was taking her children out to visit her parents, Orla watched as the woman had piled her three children into a new, and expensive looking people carrier. Another had gone to visit a friend; she too, owned one of the vehicles outside the window.

Carmel had introduced her to all of the women; early in the afternoon one of them had left to go up to her room, saying she had to prepare for a business presentation she was giving the next day. Orla's preconceived notions had been knocked sideways. She could tell already from the conversations she'd overheard that this house was a mix of women of all ages, from mixed backgrounds. She thought of her own family home, her mother's kindness as she ministered to their every need, her father's outbursts when one of the children disturbed him in his study as he marked yet another homework.

He'd been a teacher of history, dedicated, enthusiastic; he was often despairing of his pupils' lack of interest in his passion.Working long into the night on his lesson preparation, he left the children and the day to day running of the house to his wife. But he'd been a good man, taking them out on weekends for walks, visits to museums. If her mother's presence was a constant throughout the week, their father was their constant companion on his days off.

Orla had had a happy childhood; she hadn't been reared to be beaten, but nor is any woman. She remembered her thoughts last Friday as she'd read the 'Domestic Violence' poster - that it didn't apply to women like her. It happened to a different type of woman, not stupid exactly, but not women like her. She felt ashamed of her own naivety.

Her sleep that night was fitful and erratic, her dreams peppered with demons, all wearing masks of Seamus's face.

Late that same Sunday night in Derry, Deirdre and Geraldine were in their old home. The two sisters, curled up in the cosy chairs around the hearth, curled up like commas, their mother was fast asleep in her bed.

The light from the fire glowed orange and red, the flames dancing and weaving patterns across the walls. Deirdre reached for the bottle of wine and topped their glasses up. They were relaxed, happy in each other's company talking animatedly in bursts, then sitting quietly staring into the fire, lulling to the rhythms on the late night radio. Deirdre had almost forgotten why she was there. It felt like any other visit, the two of them sharing a couple of bottles of wine, catching up on all the gossip, almost, only almost.

Her mind went over their phone conversation of Friday lunchtime. Ger had been expressing her concern over their mother.

"Would it help if I came up for a few days, Ger?"

"No, Deirdre, that's not what I'm sayin', she's just…a bit lost y'know? She's not copin' so well at times…it's hard to put into words, y'have to be here to see it."

Their mother, Mary Devlin, didn't do "…not coping…"

Deirdre had remained silent. More and more over the years, she was getting the guilt trip laid on her from Ger. Deirdre had left their home area to pursue her career in nursing in Belfast, married Benny, had his children and despite the pleas from home to "come back here and get out of that God forsaken hole", they'd stayed. Stayed in the city that was now their home. Geraldine, her sister, had remained in the small County Londonderry townland. Married Liam, reared their children and, inevitably, looked after their parents in their older years.

Their father had died a year ago, now their mother was alone on the family farm. Ger's nose was twitching like a rabbit's caught in the car headlights. She couldn't see it, but Deirdre knew it was happening in her mind's eye. It was an emotional trait, only recognised by close family members. Geraldine was close to tears. Deirdre could hear it in her voice and her heart went out to her.

"Oh Jesus, I didn't mean it like that, there's nothing any of us can do, Dee, she just wants her life back, and we all know that's gone for good."

Deirdre had taken a deep breath and asked the question she didn't want to hear the answer to.

"What's goin' on, Ger, ye'll have t'tell me sooner or later?" There was a brief pause, "The other night…"

In-between muffled sobs, Geraldine began to tell Deirdre the story. Finally, breaking down as she finished relating the incident, her cries resounded through the phone line into Deirdre's ear.

Ger had walked in late one night during the week, unexpectedly, and found their mother beside the fire in her chair, opposite their father's, with both of their slippers warming in the middle of the hearth, and two full mugs of hot, drinking chocolate on the coffee table. Ger had asked her what she was doing, and she had replied, "We're just gettin' ready for bed, love."

Deirdre hadn't hesitated, saying, "That's it, Geraldine, I'm coming up. Never mind Mum, you need a break. Don't say a word, and don't start panicking about making beds, it's my home too, remember. Don't do a thing. I'll be there in a few hours. I'll bring takeaway and wine, loads of it. Tell Liam he's on duty for the next few days, you're having a break."

And now it was Sunday night, the third night of her stay. They'd managed to avoid the problem they were all facing, up to this point in the weekend, partly intentionally, partly due to circumstances. Despite her age and ailing health, Mary Devlin could still hear the grass grow. Deirdre knew they had to deal with it, as did Geraldine. It was there between them, like the elephant in the room, whichever way they looked.

Although dreading what she was driving up to, Deirdre had been relieved to find her mother smiling in her kitchen, happy to have her daughter stay for a while. Of course, Geraldine had prepared her for Deirdre's visit; it may have been a totally different scenario if she'd walked in on her unannounced. There were no obvious signs of her deteriorating health over the past few days, apart from her confusion over names. That was nothing new though. Their mother had always called her Geraldine, likewise Geraldine was Deirdre, and her brothers exchanged all of the male names in the family until she hit it right. Since childhood it had been a standing joke with them all.

Deirdre sipped her wine and came back to the moment, "So what do you think, do we call the doctor in the mornin'?"

Geraldine looked up sleepily. It had been arranged that she would stay the night rather than bring Liam out onto the roads at a late hour.

"I suppose we have to, I should have done it months ago, but I kept on foolin' myself, trying to believe it was all part of the grievin' process."

"Do we do it tomorrow then?" Deirdre's voice was quiet; she didn't want her sister to think she was breezing in, taking over, then heading back to her own life again. She went on, "If it is dementia, we won't go for a care home, will we?"

"No, it would kill 'er," Geraldine replied, the tears not far away.

"I don't mean I expect you to take her home, we'll share the care," Deirdre said.

Geraldine tilted her head, "Yous'll come back home?"

"I couldn't, Geraldine. It would break Benny's heart to leave the kids, their wains. What if we had her with us, say three or four months at a time, then you and Liam had her for the same?"

"She'd never settle in Belfast, she loves her house, y'know that Deirdre."

"Let's wait and see what the doctor says, if it's as bad as we think, she'll not be able to be left alone here for much longer, I mean I know you're only up the road, but she'll not be capable of cookin' for herself as time goes by…"

Deirdre broke off realising Geraldine was actually crying, she sobbed through her tears, "She hasn't been capable for months. I came in unexpectedly one day, found her burning the potatoes, she'd three rings going unattended and the pot was boiled dry while she sat watchin' 'Deal or No Deal' in this very chair, I've been making her

40

meals every day since…"

Deirdre reached for her sister's hand, "Oh Ger, why didn't ye tell me?"

"It was only after Daddy died, you'd enough on yer plate."

"And you hadn't? All this time you've been carrying that on yer own, while I'm doing voluntary work for Activity Age? You must be exhausted Ger, we'll have to get Benny up, get him and Liam round the table, we need to sort this out this week, assessment or no assessment."

"It'll kill her to leave this house, what do we tell her?"

"It'll kill her to stay in it. We don't have to sell, we'll think of something, if she believes it's a temporary arrangement she'll fall in with the plans. It's too late to talk clearly now, we'll talk to Benny and Liam, get it sorted tomorrow, yeah?"

"The house'll fall into bad repair, it's old and crumblin' it needs to be lived in to keep it dry and warm, it'll break 'er heart…"

"We're both too emotional now to think straight, let's have another glass of wine and sleep on it. It'll all be clearer in the mornin'. There's a way round this, we just have to find it, that's all."

Deirdre filled their glasses up. Talked out, they sat drinking in shared companionship in the glow of the dying fire, the still unasked questions and unspoken answers, hanging over them like a heavy cloak. The flickering lights of the radio dial shone out in the corner, the words of an old familiar refrain filling the room. Deirdre listened, mouthing them to herself: her mother's all time favourite song 'Love Letters Straight from Your Heart.'

The tears rolled down her cheeks as she looked over at Geraldine who was sitting, head down, staring into her glass of wine. She couldn't see her sister's face in the dark, but Deirdre knew she was crying, too. Deirdre continued to mouth the words to the song in silence; she didn't trust her voice to speak.

Chapter 5

ORLA WAS GLAD TO OPEN her eyes to see daylight on Monday morning. She had decided to phone her solicitor first thing. She lifted the phone from her bag; it had been switched off from the previous night because of Seamus's constant texting. She ignored the numerous unopened messages and searched to make sure the solicitor's number was in her contacts. It was.

Checking the time, she'd realised it was only seven fifteen, still too early to call. She switched the phone off. Already Seamus and the apartment in Hillsborough seemed like another world. She had no desire to speak to him, not now. She needed her strength to get her through this first day, to make the calls and decisions she had to make for the sake of her sanity.

In the kitchen, people were already having breakfast, mostly still in pyjamas and robes. At the large circular table stood a young woman whose name she hadn't caught. The woman's children were sitting gathered around her at the table as she handed bananas to one of the older children, a blonde, curly haired girl. She instructed the girl to slice the fruit into their bowls of cereal. In the woman's arms was a baby, about a year old. She fed the child a bottle as she watched her children eat their breakfast quietly, four blond haired, well mannered children. It could have been a cereal advertisement.

Carmel entered the kitchen. The post had just arrived but Orla knew there'd be none for her. She poured the milk onto her cereal, watching as the women were presented with their mail. Maggie, the shopper from the previous day, took the rectangular brown envelope from Carmel, her face hopeful as she read the sender's address stamped along the top. Carmel looked on. The others followed her gaze.

Orla wondered what the fascination could be for someone else's post.

She glanced at Carmel, who mouthed silently, "A house offer."

Maggie ripped the envelope open and pulled the letter out, taking in the words at a glance. Her face fell.

"Another disappointment, Maggie?" Carmel asked, her eyes gentle, feeling the woman's mood.

"Aye, my points are up, I'm movin' up the ladder, but I'm not there yet."

She returned the letter to its envelope and folded it, stuffing it into the pocket of her robe.

Carmel turned to Orla, "Did you sleep alright Orla?"

Orla shook her hand to indicate *dodgy*.

"So-so."

"It'll get better. You'll be fine once you start getting things moving."

She'd confided to Carmel the day before, that she was going to contact her solicitor in the morning.

Carmel headed toward the door of the kitchen.

"We'll be in the office if you need anything, Orla. Sue and I are on 'til twelve, I'll introduce you to the other two, when they arrive for the shift change. If you're short of credit on your phone, you can use the office one, just give me a shout."

Orla thanked her and she disappeared down the hall. She looked at the wall clock as she ate, feeling she was outside looking in. It was all so surreal. This time yesterday she'd been flicking through the Sunday paper waiting for her toast to pop up, and here she was, twenty four hours later, in a room full of women and children, strangers to her only one day before.

Despite her anxiety at the decision she'd made about her life, she felt at ease with them as they went about the business of starting their day. Her friend Ellen would have understood, she was sure of it, but she had decided to stay in the house until she got sorted with a place to rent. She felt safe here. Her feelings of shame at her situation had dissipated. She was angry now and that was good - that would keep her strong.

By nine o' clock on the dot she was through to her solicitor's office. They'd helped her with her property purchases and her business set-up and now she needed them to resolve her marriage. The receptionist said it was unlikely that she could give her an appointment that day. Orla insisted, telling the woman it was essential that she speak with Fiona, her solicitor, by the end of business.

The woman put her on hold, then came back.

"Fiona can fit you in for a ten minute appointment at four if it's urgent. She suggested I pencil you in for a full appointment later in the week, if that's any help?"

"Yes, yes, that's great; I'll see her at four."

The woman went on to arrange the later appointment as Orla scribbled the time in her diary. She thanked the woman and finished the call, switching off the phone.

She looked at her reflection in the small bedside mirror. Although her stomach was tied in knots, she had been assertive, stood her ground. She could face this, but not if she allowed Seamus to get to her.

She made a decision not to read his messages, answer his calls; she'd have to talk with him eventually, but not yet. She was still much too fragile, he might still get to her, persuade her to come back. She thought of Anne Marie's story and her high hopes for a better life before the miscarriage brought on by her husband.

She remembered the previous morning, and the blow to the side of her head, the blow that had lifted her from where she sat and spun her face down onto the floor. Orla knew she'd been lucky. She'd been in deep, deeper than she'd acknowledged to herself. She couldn't risk going back to him, not now, not ever. She was worth more.

Switching the phone on again, she hit the shop number. Jo answered cheerfully; obviously she'd had a good weekend. Orla spoke quietly, in a controlled manner, trying to maintain a composure she did not feel. She explained her plight to Jo, in half truths.

"Jo, Orla, eh I've a bit of a problem. Seamus and I had a bit of a row at the weekend, I'm staying with friends at the minute, I think it's likely Seamus may call into the shop. He doesn't know where I am, don't tell him I've been in touch, and do me a favour, could you ask your sister in law, eh Siobhan isn't it, if she could work my hours this week."

"Are ya okay, Orla, you sound a bit strange?"

Orla thought she'd been holding it together pretty well.

"I'm alright now, sorry to dump this on you, Jo, I know I've been a pain lately. I'll call later in the week. Oh, if the phone's off just leave a message if ya need me."

44

Jo sounded concerned but assured Orla she'd make sure the shop was covered in her absence.

For Deirdre and Geraldine, Monday morning arrived, wet, cold and bleak; fitting weather for the situation they found themselves in. They were all sitting around the kitchen table having breakfast.

Deirdre looked up at the clock, 9.24a.m. Her mother ate a full breakfast of scrambled eggs, bacon and toast. Deirdre noticed a slight shake in her hand as she lifted the small white cup to her lips, her eyes smiled at Deirdre over the rim. *God bless her, she's delighted to have a bit of company*, thought Deirdre.

She knew Geraldine had been doing her best, but she also had a husband and grandchildren to care for, as well as a house of her own to run. Deirdre now knew she'd been looking after two houses for almost a year. It was time to put a stop to that and share some of the responsibility.

Last night they'd agreed a plan to get her mother to the doctor. Geraldine administered her daily medication for blood pressure and arthritis. She would tell her mother she was running low on tablets, and then make the health centre appointment, calling the doctor to discuss their concerns beforehand.

"I think yer enjoyin' that, Mum."

"Aye yer sister makes a lovely scrambled egg and your tea was perfect Deirdre, ye can stay."

Deirdre laughed, topping her cup up.

"I can take a hint, Ma."

"Pass me up another slice o'that toast, too," Mary said as she raised the cup to her mouth.

The breakfast over, they worked together clearing up. It was still only 9.43 hopefully early enough to get an appointment in the health centre that day.

"I'll drop Ger home; I'll get some milk on the way back and pick that book up for ya Mum, the one you wanted from the library," she explained to her mother to cover for her absence.

No doubt, they'd have to wait until the morning surgery was over for the doctor to call them back. Her mother was sitting in her favourite chair, engrossed in a television programme about long lost relatives and unclaimed legacies.

"Mammy wouldn't miss this programme; she's convinced there's a stash of loot out there with her name on it, aren't ye mammy."

"It's very interestin' I like to see how they find the people, scattered all over the world some of them…"

Her eyes never left the screen as her daughters both bent to kiss her, waved their goodbyes and left the house.

"God love her, she's in a wee world of her own, but she's still sharp enough in some ways. At least she can still concentrate on a TV programme, read a book," Geraldine told Deirdre, tossing her overnight bag into the back seat.

"She seems contented enough," Deirdre said.

"She's in good form, because you're here. She loves the company, but she can have her moments. I get a lashin' of her tongue brave 'n' often."

It had always been the same over the years, since Deirdre moved to Belfast. Deirdre saw the best side of her mother because she was a visitor; Geraldine, a permanent fixture, was more likely to see her at her worst. Deirdre winced inwardly, she knew Ger hadn't meant to hurt her.

Geraldine took in the look on her sister's face.

"I'm sorry, Dee, that was thoughtless. You know I didn't mean anything by it, but her recent moods can be hard to take when you're bending over backwards to please everybody."

Deirdre's voice was gentle.

"Of course, I know ya didn't mean anything, but that'll be part of the process of the dementia Ger, mention it to the doctor. He'll maybe prescribe her with an anti-depressant if he thinks she needs one, it might help lift her mind."

They drove the rest of the journey in silence as the wipers swished the rain across the windscreen, both alone in their thoughts, knowing they were doing what had to be done for their mother but dreading the conversation with the doctor. They'd agreed Geraldine would speak to him, being the one who knew the situation best. Deirdre would stay in the house and listen as they talked on the telephone, to provide her sister with the moral support she'd need as she voiced their concerns to the GP, at last acknowledging what she had feared all this time. It would ease the burden somewhat for Geraldine, but Deirdre knew how hard Geraldine had tried to keep it from her. Telling it to a stranger, someone outside of the family, would seem like an act of betrayal to Geraldine. Deirdre knew her sister well enough to understand that. Loyal to extremes, Ger would feel her admission of her fears for her mother was an act of weakness - airing your dirty linen in public.

As a nurse, Deirdre understood the illness better, could look at it more objectively. But Geraldine had her own way of thinking, and all of the reassurances from Deirdre had done little to alleviate her feelings of guilt.

Geraldine shook off her coat and set her bag down on the hall table, breathing in and out slowly and deeply as she picked up the phone to make the call. Deirdre walked through to the kitchen sink and filled the kettle. She could hear Geraldine's voice from the hall.

"Ten past two, that'll be grand thanks. Eh, I was wonderin' would it be possible to have a word with Doctor Bradley this morning if it's not too much trouble, it's about my mother, something I don't want to discuss in her presence..."

Deirdre stood staring into the back garden as the rain lashed against the window pane focusing on a black cat that had leapt over the shared wall. It scuttled over the lawn and jumped the fence on the far side, disappearing out of view as it sought shelter from the downpour.

Her gaze rested on a back upstairs window of a neighbouring house. Bart Simpson hung suspended on an invisible sucker clinging to the glass at a jaunty angle, resplendent in bright yellow and blue. A boy's bedroom or maybe a girl's, Bart was impartial, wouldn't mind whose window he dangled from. Her mind came back to the phone call her sister was making. She hoped the doctor would be available to speak between appointments. Their mother's age would be a consideration, like children elderly people always got priority in health centres. Deirdre hoped the receptionist had enough wit to hear the stress in Geraldine's voice. It was all too apparent to Deirdre, but then she knew her sister like the back of her own hand. She poured two mugs of coffee, stirring them in turn for much longer than was necessary to dissolve the sparse amounts of sugar added.

Had Benny been in the kitchen with her he'd have said, 'Are ye tryin' to stir a hole inta the bottom o' that mug Deirdre?'

She'd only been here two days but she missed him desperately, needed his support and reassurance. Benny always had the ability to see things another way. Deirdre decided to call him as soon as Ger had spoken to the doctor. She would ask him to drive up later.

They had agreed to get together with their husbands this evening and have a family meeting to decide their mother's fate. She'd think of some excuse to leave her mother for an hour or two.

On the previous night she had written an email to Benny filling him in on the details of the incident with the pot of boiling potatoes, telling him that she had suggested to Geraldine that her mother live with them for a period of time each year, to help lighten the load. Benny would journey up and stay the night in Geraldine and Liam's. They couldn't talk in Mary's house, couldn't risk her overhearing them discussing their fears for her health and their plans for uprooting her from her home. As Geraldine had pointed out despite her forgetfulness their mother's mind was still sharp as a blade in so many ways. All options would have to be mulled over before presenting Mary with their decision for her future. It was the only way. She heard Geraldine end the call and looked up expectantly as her sister entered the kitchen.

"Today at ten past two. I explained to her I needed to talk to Dr Bradley first, she said she'll give him the message straight away. The surgery's over in ten minutes."

They drank their coffee, both nervous, interjecting in turn as they thought of points to bring to the doctor's attention.

"I'll tell him about the time she…"

"Don't forget to mention…"

The phone rang on the stroke of eleven o' clock and Geraldine rushed to answer it, spilling her coffee as she went. Deirdre wiped the mess and listened, half-holding her breath in case she missed anything in the act of inhaling and exhaling.

Sipping the now almost cool liquid she looked at the clock. Fourteen minutes had passed. She'd no doubt Geraldine had covered everything. Her sister's voice, audibly strained throughout the call, had almost broken as she told the doctor about her mother's fits of aggression, bouts of anger flaring up with no obvious reason, dissipating and fizzling out just as quickly as they had occurred. The mood swings a total block to her, Mary would smile or begin talking about a completely unrelated subject as her temperament returned to calm again.

Geraldine struggled to regain her composure as she related these episodes. Fearful she would sound selfish to the doctor. A middle aged woman more concerned with her own fragile feelings than getting on with caring for her ageing mother. Deirdre looked into the hall to where Ger was sitting on the seat attached to the telephone table nodding into the phone, hunched over so tensely Deirdre could practically feel her muscles straining, shoulders down, knees up, talking and continuously nodding into the phone, her hand across her mouth, trying not to cry, fearful of sobbing out loud if she allowed the tears to flow.

Deirdre walked quietly back into the kitchen the tears pricking her own eyes at the sight of her sister sitting hunched over the phone. Geraldine's body language was saying she was still trying to hide her secret, to keep it in. The doctor was obviously reassuring her as any doctor would. She was facing something so many people had to as their parents reached old age. The doctor would have heard stories like theirs over and over again during the course of his daily surgeries. He would understand the terrible burden Geraldine had been carrying. The feelings of guilt tinged with relief as she unloaded it to him. All the months of keeping her fears unspoken, all the months of hoping her mother would go back to normal if only she didn't voice her concerns, all the months of hope dissolved with every disclosure. And her heavy heart broke.

The call over they stood in the kitchen doorway holding each other both in tears for what seemed an eternity, neither spoke as the clock ticked away the minutes. They came back to reality with the noise of the rain lashing against the kitchen window as the wind changed.

Deirdre went upstairs to the bathroom as Geraldine reached for the kettle. It was out in the open - now they could move on. Deirdre splashed her face with cold water in the bathroom before calling Benny. She gave him an update from her email the night before. He didn't waste time talking he could hear the tension in her voice, could visualize the scene in Geraldine's house that morning. He told her he'd be there that afternoon.

She touched up her make-up before leaving to pick up the milk and the book from the library, knowing she couldn't look upset or her mother would become suspicious. Geraldine walked her down to her car.

"I'll call you around teatime, make some excuse for you to call round for an hour. Don't worry Mum'll be alright for an hour or so. We'll not risk talking in front of her when I pick yous up for the doctor's appointment. Ma always hears what she's not supposed to."

"She always did," Deirdre smiled and kissed her sister on the cheek. "You'll feel better now. Have a lie down for a while. See ya at half one."

The doctor who had been so understanding to Geraldine as she poured her heart to him was business-like and cheery as they sat in his office. There was no trace of over concern toward Mary as he took her blood pressure and wrote out the prescription. Dr Bradley had already told Geraldine during their earlier conversation that he would arrange for a hospital appointment to have her mother assessed. They would talk to their mother about that when the time came. Meanwhile plans for her immediate care would be discussed between them that night when the four of them gathered in Geraldine's.

Later that same Monday afternoon in Belfast city centre Orla had arrived for her meeting with her solicitor. Although still consumed with anger Orla's overwhelming feelings were of shame and embarrassment.

To be sitting in this office in this public building confiding the most intimate details of her private life was a humiliation beyond belief despite Fiona's professionalism. But it had to be done.

She advised Orla to have no contact with Seamus, to leave all of that to herself and his solicitor. Orla stressed to Fiona that she wanted to keep her business. Much as she would have loved to run home and leave Belfast behind she knew it would be the wrong move. It would deprive her of her dream. If her Art Gallery/Gift Shop failed due to the financial downturn Orla could cope with that but she had to believe she'd given it her best shot. Running away wasn't an option.

Fiona told her she'd prepare the documentation immediately for the necessary court orders Orla would need for her personal protection. Meanwhile, she should stay away from the shop and under no circumstances was she to return to the apartment alone.

The appointment over Orla drove back to the house with an overwhelming feeling of relief. She'd done it. And she was more than happy to pass the burden on to her solicitor but she was drained, completely exhausted. Her right eye had continued to twitch with nerves on and off since the previous afternoon, the lid fluttered sporadically again.

As she made her journey from the city centre she felt an immense wave of tiredness sweep over her, the events of the past twenty four hours beginning to take their toll. She would have an early night, try to wind down. The wheels were in motion and she had decisions to make but the biggest one was now made. She could stay behind closed doors for as long as she needed in the coming days. Allow her mind and body time to relax, to recover, and to recharge.

Chapter 6

MONDAY NIGHT FOUND DEIRDRE AND Benny in Geraldine and Liam's house. All of them gathered to discuss Mary's fate.

Geraldine handed Benny a beer and he nodded his thanks. He watched her leave the room and waited until she was out of earshot. He turned to Liam.

"You should've told us all this before now Liam! Why didn't you call me at least?"

"Ach, I wanted to Benny, I told Geraldine as much. Said you both deserved to know the truth after the episode with the cooker. But no she'd have none of it just kept on tryin' to hold it all together. Y' know what she's like, she'd've blown a fuse if I'd told yis."

"Well we know now, that's the main thing. Yous have done yer best now we'll have t'work out a way of sortin' this without takin' away Mary's dignity. God knows she's a proud woman."

Liam nodded. The two men drank their beer and made small talk, neither of them really caring who had won the match yesterday. With an unsaid mutual agreement the conversational exchanges puttered out and they lapsed into their own thoughts.

Benny remembered the day forty years ago when he had stood in the Devlins' kitchen as Deirdre and he had announced their intention to marry. Her mother had reached for her cigarettes. She lit one and paced the floor distractedly, announcing that she wouldn't hear tell of her daughter getting married. Mary's words from that long ago day still echoed in his ears.

"I don't think it's a good idea right now, not when you're in the middle of yer trainin' fer the nursing.' What's the rush?"

Then she reached the conclusion that Deirdre was pregnant. Benny had almost died of embarrassment, saying, "I know it's all a bit soon, we should'a left mentioning our plans 'til ye got used t'me."

Johnny, Deirdre's father, had stepped in.

"Ach fer God's sake Mary, make a drop o' tea and give the wee fella a chance to gather his thoughts."

Deirdre had given Benny a signal with her eyes that her father was with them. She'd assured him later in the day that she'd work on her mother, make her see that she could get married and continue with her nursing career. Benny wasn't so sure Mary would give her blessing. But he had left it in Deirdre's hands.

Of course, Deirdre had won her mother round and Mary Devlin and he had become firm friends over the years. Both straight talkers they always knew exactly where they stood with each other.

Deirdre and Geraldine entered the room with a couple of trays of sandwiches and Benny was brought back to the present as the food was placed on the central coffee table. The two sisters took their places alongside their husbands on the facing sofas. Four people, preparing to sketch out plans for an old woman's life, an old woman who connected them all, plans that would affect all of their lives, one way or another.

Chapter 7

CASSIE WAITED AT THE BUS stop at the top of her street to ride the journey to her first shift. The road was still half asleep, the early morning traffic sparse. Passers-by were few and far between. Just the odd dog walker and daybreak worker like herself.

Cassie sniffed the cold air. She loved that smell. It told her she was alive. Not that she had any doubt about that over the past few days. Since Friday the adrenalin had been pumping and pulsing through her veins at a rate she couldn't remember it doing in years.

Her time had come at last. And she was ready to embrace it, wholeheartedly.

She boarded the bus and sat at the front. The city centre was only a few minutes away at this time of the day. Her cheque would probably be on the hall mat when she pushed the front door open later that morning. She had posted the scratch card on Friday by registered post as advised by the helpline operator. It was probably delivered on Saturday morning and the cheque processed yesterday. She would arrive home mid-morning. No danger of Dean being awake until midday and Lara would be at the playgroup with Mia.

The bus stopped at the City Hall and she walked the short distance to the building she worked in. The streetlights still casting their shadows on the pavements as the windows of the city offices replaced them with their fluorescent slots. Ready for the day's business, Fred, the doorman, looked up from *The Sun* and gave her a grin.

"Mornin' Cassie, how's yer sex life?"

"Great, same as yours, Fred, see yer still readin' the quality press."

"Aye, sure I only luk at the pictures, don't care if I do go blind! Here, did ye hear this one?"

He proceeded to tell her yet another of his tasteless unfunny jokes.

Cassie laughed heartily. A real laugh, not the bored, "Ha, ha, ha, give m'head peace" sorta laugh she usually exchanged with Fred. He smirked delighted with himself.

"Isn't that a good'n'?"

She grinned at him as she stepped into the lift. Normally she could barely raise a smile at this time of the day for the oul eejit but she was still grinning as she reached her floor. Why not? She'd plenty to grin about.

As she swung the door open into the hallway of her house she saw the large white envelope. It was lying alongside two brown rectangular ones. She lifted them and walked toward the kitchen. Disregarding the brown ones she slit open the large white one and felt inside for the cheque. There it was. She checked the details: Mrs C. Gallagher.

Yes!

And the address was spot on. The amount: *£500,000!* It sang out to her in numerals and letters.

Running her fingers over them she double checked. All correct and it didn't say *'Bank of Mickey Mouse, Disneyland, California, USA'.* Her legs had turned to jelly as she sank to a seat at the kitchen table and said aloud, "Oh my God! How sweet is this?"

She placed the cheque carefully back inside the safety of the envelope fearful of rubbing the amounts off and read the letter.

'Dear Mrs Gallagher,
Congratulations you're a winner!!!...'

Her eyes scanned the words again. Just to be sure. It was true. She stood unsteadily feeling giddy with excitement and reached for the kettle. With shaking hands she made herself a pot of tea. Her heart was thumping as she digested the news. News she'd been hugging to herself for the last four days without a soul to share it with. It was too soon.

She sipped her tea as her brain went into overload. Droplets of steaming hot liquid trickled down the mug as she clasped her hands around it to control her own shaking.

Ring the bank! No, drink your tea first! You don't want to sound like a babbling idiot! Call someone, call anyone! Who? Shut up!

Cassie Gallagher was going to start her own business. She had thought of little else since Sunday morning. The image of the navy blue uniformed women lined up to clean the cinemas as the Saturday night revellers milled around the entertainment complex stayed with her. She did the earlies, they did the lates. How many women and men were employed out there in this huge industry? She had seen invoices on occasion lying on desks as she cleaned. Documentation submitted by the contract cleaning companies to the businesses for cleaning services. Services she and people like her carried out. Cassie had read them over and felt sick at the fee the companies were charged compared to the meagre hourly rate she earned. She and hundreds like her.

Well, she was going to have some of it. She was unsure whether she would aim for the commercial or domestic market. She still had to think it through; had been afraid to think about it too much in case it was all a hoax.

But this cheque was no hoax.

Cassie reached into her bag and pulled out the letter with the bank's phone number on it. She dialled the digits and waited. It rang four times then she was through,

"…you're speaking to David, how can I help?"

"Hello, I'd like an appointment with one of you relationship bankers, Shiralee North."

She gave him the branch details and her account number and waited. *Please God, let her not be off on leave…*

"Ten o'clock, Friday the 30th?"

It was a question. Cassie panicked. Jesus, was that next week? She couldn't wait that long. Her eyes rose to the calendar above the kitchen table. It was this Friday, relieved she uttered inwardly, *Thank you, God!* Then speaking into the phone, "Yes that'd be great… Cassie Gallagher."

She gave him her account details again but when he asked for the reason for the appointment she just said, "I need a bit of advice about my account."

She left it at that, made it appear she was probably looking for an overdraft. She had to see Shiralee's face as she read the cheque. Ten o'clock was an awkward time for her, too close to her early shift finish for comfort. But she wasn't going to turn it down, leave it until next week, she'd arrange to swap shifts with one of the other cleaners in her team, she was owed a few favours.

She made herself a sandwich and planned her day. She would go out and do some food shopping. Anything to get her out of the house. She was bursting at the seams with excitement. It was still early, plenty of time to shop before she'd to head out for her next shift.

Her feet took her to the park. It was quiet. The winter day was still with a slight frost in the air; she sat on a bench and searched her pockets for a cigarette, her brain moving into overload. She'd need a vehicle, maybe a van, maybe an estate car. It would have to be sign-written to look professional, to advertise her services. She'd need a website. She couldn't do it all alone though, she'd need help. She could employ a small team and bring in casual staff for bigger jobs as required; but a partner would be the ideal. Her daughter was the obvious one who came to mind. But not with the child, it would put Lara under too much pressure.

She thought of the endless applications Lara had made for work without success and here she was, her mother, thinking the same way. A woman with a young child, too many responsibilities, too much risk of time off for sickness, too many sleepless nights, and too many late arrivals for shifts. Of course she'd offer her work, but not a partnership; it was too soon. Lara was too young. Cassie had to be honest with herself, she knew her daughter simply didn't want or need the chance enough. It had to be a woman around her own age who had lived a bit, suffered the knocks and rolled with the punches but where would she find that? Her friends were either happy in their work, or stuck in the benefit system.

Much as she loved them, this chance was hers; she wouldn't be financing anyone else.

She thanked God she'd renewed her driving license. Although she hadn't driven in years she had no qualms about it, she was a good driver. They'd had a car in the early years of their marriage, but once the babies came along and Cassie had had to give up work, there hadn't been enough money coming in to maintain a vehicle. Gerry had been in and out of employment since she'd known him, always searching for a cushier number with more money. He'd been a bone idle Mammy's Boy.

On reflection she acknowledged that she had been as responsible as his mother for his laziness. Taking over where his mammy had left off by tending to his every need. It was only when both of the children arrived that Cassie had woken up to her situation.

She had three children to care for and that was one too many. Gerry had to go. Not the worst in the world he hadn't drank to excess and he'd never beaten her but money burned a hole in his pocket. If he had it he'd have bet two flies crawling up the wall.

Things had come to a head one Saturday when he had gambled money she'd needed for baby shoes and she'd turfed him out. A less gutless man would have come back home full of apologies but Gerry took the coward's way out, gratefully. She hadn't seen him since. She had started her night cleaning job in a local school soon after, her mother coming round to baby-sit the children while she worked. And to date that had been her life, struggling and penny pinching, robbing Peter to pay Paul.

She inhaled the cigarette, what was the expression: *'Carpe Diem?'* She remembered it from the movie, 'The Dead Poet's Society.' *Seize the Day.*

She intended to, with both hands.

Chapter 8

BY WEDNESDAY NIGHT CASSIE KNEW she'd have to tell someone or her head would explode. On impulse she decided to call up to see Gail telling Dean she'd be back in a few hours. He barely lifted his head from the movie he was watching and then her words registered.

"Two nights out in a week! Have you found a Toy Boy, Ma?"

She shouted back, "Aye I have, I'll be bringing him back an' all, so get that kitchen sorted!"

She stopped at the off licence to buy a bottle of wine and walked the short distance to her friend's house. It was starting to spit. The rain fell lightly on her face reviving her. She'd been staring into the fire, nodding off as her thoughts swam in her head, tired from the day's work and tense from keeping the secret. She could trust Gail. She wouldn't say a word to anyone until Cassie said she was all right with it.

She'd just pushed the doorbell when the voices rang out, the chimes of the bell unable to mask them.

"I'll pick Josh up, then I'm going fer a pint!"

"Yeah, you do that!"

Gail and Dave were having a row.

Loud angry voices followed by an internal door slamming.

Crap. Too late to reverse down the path now, she stood on the doorstep cringing with embarrassment clutching her bottle of wine as Dave threw the front door open. Expecting one of Josh's mates he yelled, "He's out!" as his eyes met hers. "Oh, Cassie, sorry! How ya doin,' c'mon in, Gail's in the lounge."

Cassie followed him up the hall making small talk. Even to her own ears she knew she was jabbering like the village idiot.

"Not a bad night, it's just starting to spit, that fine rain that soaks you through y'know, as Peter Kay would say…"

"Here's Cass, Gail." He gestured for her to enter the room. "I'm just goin' to pick Josh up, see ya later."

Dave bolted down the hall, face glowing like a beacon, out of sight. Gail gestured for her to sit down.

"I'm sure ya heard that, we were having a row…Oh Jesus, Cass, I've been made redundant!" Cassie was stunned, her own good news forgotten for an instant. "They told me on Friday but I didn't want to put a dampener on Danielle's night out so I didn't mention it. I couldn't have I was still reeling from the shock. I intended breaking it gently to Dave but I blurted it out as soon as he came through the door on Friday night. We hardly spoke all night. I was out Saturday night, Sunday he stayed in bed 'til lunchtime, then lay about reading the papers, had his dinner and went to the club. That night he rolled in drunk about nine and went to bed. We've hardly said a word to each other the past few nights apart from making small talk in front of the kids…"

Cassie's look said, *"Where are the kids,"* fearful they'd overhear.

"It's okay, Josh is at his mates, Dave's just gone to get him and the girls are at the youth club. I haven't told anyone, not even Jo. We just booked a bloody holiday to Florida."

"Here open this, things always look better through the bottom of a glass!" said Cassie offering the wine to Gail; she accepted it gratefully, leaving to grab two glasses from the kitchen. As Cassie sipped hers she watched Gail knock her glass back in two gulps.

"I wouldn't have minded but there was no sign of it. There're three of us going out of the five part timers and of course one of the ones being kept on is the biggest lick in the place - Arselicking Andrea!"

Cassie couldn't help laughing. Considering if tonight was the best time to share her news, she topped up Gail's glass. Gail laughed despite herself saying,

"It's true, ya know, things are never so bad, they can't get worse."

They heard Dave arrive back a short time later. Josh tumbled into the room to say he was home and Dave made a brief appearance looking shamefaced, all talk of going to the pub forgotten.

"We'll be in the other room playing the Wii. Have a good

60

night," he nodded at Cassie and threw Gail a look that said, "Sorry."

Gail grinned at his discomfort. The girls were back soon after, it being a school night. The house was relatively quiet by eleven as the girls listened to the radio in their room and Josh lay in bed reading. Dave didn't make a reappearance obviously deciding on an early night too.

The bottle of wine finished, Gail produced another from the kitchen.

"May as well, I don't work tomorrow. I made the lunches earlier so I can lie in 'til the girls get up. Josh is always last, he'd sleep in his school uniform to get an extra few minutes in bed."

As she poured the wine, she looked at Cassie as though seeing her for the first time that night.

"I just realized; everything okay with you? It's not like you to drink two nights in a week."

Although they shared a bottle occasionally through the week it was more likely to be a Friday night thing. The Saturday night out would usually have been the sum of their social contact for a few weeks.

Cassie cursed her own predictability. She couldn't contain herself. She replied quietly for fear of being overheard.

"I've won £500,000, Gail, on a scratch card, I got the cheque today!"

Gail leapt to her feet and half jumped, half dived onto the sofa to hug her friend.

"Good for you! I'm delighted for you! When did you buy it?"

"Shush, I haven't even told the kids yet, you're the first to know..."

Cassie related the story of her scratch card purchase with relish, enjoying every minute.

Gail may have had bad news herself but she couldn't have been happier for her friend.

"I'm so pleased for you, Cassie, you're overdue a lucky break."

They drank their wine companionably and Gail began to question Cassie, the words spilling out of her, "You'll clear the mortgage first, yeah?"

Like many people who buy lottery tickets on a regular basis Gail and Cassie had often shared their dreams of how they'd spend a 'jackpot win.' Clearing the mortgage had always been top of both of their lists.

"The kids will be delighted. You'll see them both right, won't ya? And you've been talkin' about puttin' on an extension for years, you'll be able to go for it now alright, maybe a conservatory, too. What about a holiday! God Cass, it's brilliant for ya, have you thought about investing a wee bit, too."

Gail knew Cassie wasn't stupid but she'd been broke for so long it would be understandable if she went over the top and spent the lot on luxuries for her family and herself.

"That's why I haven't told them. I've done nothing but think since the weekend. Yes, I am going to invest it. Invest it in me. I'm going to start a business Gail."

The wine had made her more assertive about her plans than she had even been on receiving the cheque. She'd no doubt; she was going to change her life.

Gail's eyes lit up at her friend's enthusiasm.

"Doing what?"

"What I know best, cleaning."

"In a recession though, Cassie, I don't want to rain on your parade but small businesses are folding every day."

"I know. I watch the news, too. I've an appointment in the bank Friday morning. I'll ask for advice on investin,' if the time's not right now, I can wait. I know we've drunk a fair amount of wine but put it like this, people always need cleaners…"

She related the image of the cleaners outside the cinema on Saturday night. It was doubtful Gail or any of the others had even noticed them. But then people didn't notice cleaners, they're just always there.

"Banks, offices, cinemas, pubs, clubs, gyms, schools, restaurants, private houses, they all need cleaners, recession or no recession."

Gail stared at her. She had never seen her friend so assertive, so fiery. Well not since school. Back then Cassie was always the girl most likely to take a chance. Take a chance on anything, while the rest of them watched from the wings. She'd almost forgotten that side of her as Cassie settled for her lot in life. Getting on with her day to day existence without moaning or whingeing, in a way seeming to be contented with her lot despite the hard hand fate had dealt her. Gail realised she didn't know the half of it and she was unlikely to ever hear it from Cassie.

"You go for it girl and if I can help in any way… I'm leavin' the bank but I've a couple of good mates there if you need extra advice after you've spoken with your own branch. You know where I am."

"Thanks, I appreciate that Gail. What are your plans now?"

Gail downed her glass, her face sombre.

"Haven't had time for plans. I'll get a bit of redundancy but I'll be looking for work. Some chance. I was watching breakfast TV this morning, there was this woman, 39 she was, our age; well presented, softly spoken, she'd been made redundant five months ago. They'd invited her on with this Life Coach to sit on the sofa and share her story, see if they could help her in her quest to find work. Five hundred CVs she'd sent out. Can you believe it? Five Hundred! She'd received three replies and no interviews to date. Yer woman the Life Coach says, 'Start by rewriting your CV and build on your achievements rather than focusing on your weaknesses. And remember not to include your date of birth on your application as it's illegal to age discriminate.' Like her list of jobs from she left school wasn't going to be a dead giveaway she was touching forty."

Gail sipped her wine and continued, "Yer woman goes on, 'That should help get you in the door for that all important interview. After that, it's up to you.' The presenter nods, looking none too convinced and asks, 'so what about dress code when you do get that all important interview?'"

Gail's mood was lightening as she got into the story,"Now, get this image. Life Coach is wearing Deirdre Barlow glasses, Aunt Sally make-up and a denim and floral print outfit that appears to be one of Raggedy Ann's cast-offs, set off by a pair of bright red leather, platform boots, with a voice like Kermit the Frog on helium. And she's advising this woman on how to present herself. I'm thinking, have they got the right one?

Maybe it's another Newsnight scenario, y'know when they grabbed yer big black fella from the reception area of the BBC, plonked him down in the studio and miked him up to talk about computer downloading; when he'd been sitting there minding his own business waiting to be interviewed for some manual job.

Anyway Life Coach says, looking pointedly at the job seeking woman, 'If you're over thirty five wear a simple outfit with long flowing scarves and loads of chunky jewellery. A big chunky necklace will take away from those deep age creases around the neck. Keep this in mind for the face too, big earrings will detract from laughter lines around the eyes and lips and it's best to wear gloves or keep your hands out of sight to avoid drawing attention to those telltale ageing signs the hands can't hide.'"

Cassie was starting to giggle.

"Oh my God..."

"Wait, there's more...I don't know who was cringing more, the poor woman or the embarrassed presenter, it was the blond one, y'know, with the spiky hair. The woman was sitting there losing the will to live so the presenter quips, to lighten the moment, deadpan-like, 'So if you've no gloves with you, sit on your hands?' And Life Coach Woman nods vigorously in agreement, smiling, delighted with herself. I swear to God." Then Gail added her face serious. "Cass, how do ya get to be a Life Coach?"

They both collapsed into bouts of convulsed giggles sliding off the sofa and onto the floor where they ended up banging heads and screaming with laughter like children, the tears blinding them.

When they'd recovered Cassie asked the question that had been on her mind since Gail broke her news.

"I'll be needing a partner, would you consider comin' in with me, givin' self-employment a go?"

Gail blinked, considering.

"I'm sure we could work together Cass, but maybe we should have this conversation tomorrow when we're both sober."

"Think about it. Remember no one else knows; I know you'd have to talk to Dave but play your cards close to your chest. I better ring a taxi; I've still to work tomorrow if you haven't."

They waited for the taxi saying nothing more about the business plan. But the spark was lit. Gail was thinking.

The taxi driver chatted easily on the way home saying fares were few and far between these nights. Money was tight and people weren't venturing out much even at weekends, he was working round the clock to make ends meet.

As she paid him and thanked him they wished each other luck and parted company. Cassie had almost told him of her win, the wine loosening her tongue. She hadn't though. But she felt better for sharing the news with Gail, it made it more real somehow.

She entered her kitchen and put the light on almost laughing out loud at the scene. The surfaces were free of the usual odds and ends that accumulated on a day to day basis after her weekend clean up, fresh smelling and spotless.

Dean had taken her at her word and tidied up for her bringing her 'Toy Boy' back. *God love him, what an eejit,* she thought. She put the kettle on and shoved off her coat. The house was warm and cosy. She opened the living room door, the fire was still glowing behind the guard. She'd bring her tea in and sit and watch the flames die out. Cassie could never leave a room with a fire to go to bed, it was a waste. It was one of her few luxuries in life, gazing into the fire late at night, relaxing and dreaming. She carried her tea in and sank onto her favourite chair. Kicking her shoes off, curling her toes, toasting them at the heat of the hearth.

There was plenty for her to dream about tonight. It was well past one when she made her way up the stairs to bed.

Chapter 9

AS CASSIE SAT READING HER paper and sipping her tea Thursday mid-morning the phone rang. She knew before she checked that it was Gail.

"Sobered up yet?" Gail asked.

"I've half a day's work done. S'pose yer still in yer bed?"

"Not at all, I've been up from the crack of dawn cleanin', gettin' into practice for our venture."

"You serious, Gail?"

"I am if you are."

"Oh I've never been more serious in my life, but I can't say much y'know."

She was aware of Dean's presence in the house, albeit his sleeping presence.

"I understand. You've the appointment with the bank tomorrow, yeah?"

"Yeah, ten o'clock, I'm all excited, but still can't believe it, y'know. Until it's firmly lodged, y'know."

Cassie was talking in code in case her son walked into the kitchen unexpectedly.

"Good luck with the appointment, text me after it and we'll arrange to get together to talk. I'll do my sums too, see exactly how much I'm getting for redundancy, I haven't really read the whole agreement in depth yet, I'm still reeling from the shock."

"We'll talk it over, work out the best way for us to work in partnership. It sounds good doesn't it, 'in partnership?'"

Cass was smiling into the phone like the cat that had got the cream.

Thursday, this was her fourth morning in the safe house. Orla looked out of her bedroom window over the now familiar rooftops. She scrutinised her reflection in her handheld mirror. Her lip was still swollen and the side of her face, although badly bruised, was beginning to yellow.

On Monday afternoon, as she'd rushed for her solicitors' appointment she had slapped a bit of make-up on, covering it as best she could, not really minding if Fiona saw her husband's handiwork. It was more important to get the divorce proceedings started. The meeting had helped. It had put a full stop to one part of her life and given her the lift she needed to plan her next move. Being behind the refuge doors since Sunday lunchtime had given her a safe place to live, a place to think and plan, but it was time to make contact with her life again, time to get out into the world again.

She worked on her make-up to disguise the discolouration. Now her pride wouldn't allow her to forget about her appearance. She didn't want people looking at her, elbowing each other as she passed, whispering, making assumptions. She was going to get her life back together and she needed to talk to Jo face to face. She had treated her badly recently, with all the last minute phone calls asking her to cover. She had let her down, expecting her to work on her study days. Orla knew she had to come clean with her, if she lost Jo at this point the business may well go down. She wanted to get back into working, putting her energy and enthusiasm into the shop as she had done in the beginning, before her domestic situation had deteriorated. She'd make the call now, she was ready.

She rang Jo and asked her to meet her for lunch, told her to put a sign on the door, close the shop for an hour. It was unlikely that Seamus would be anywhere in the vicinity but on the off chance that he was she arranged for them to meet in a restaurant she knew would be busy. Orla knew he'd never make a scene in public, his image meant too much to him for that, she'd be safe in Jo's company for an hour. Jo agreed, telling her Seamus had called into the shop on Monday as Orla had expected. He had asked Jo if Orla was due in that day, as though he didn't know the days that she worked. Jo had thought on her feet and told him as far as she remembered Orla was away at a trade show in Birmingham all week. Had he forgotten?

She said he'd looked a bit bemused but seemed to accept her explanation for Orla's absence.

"Did I say the right thing? I knew you didn't want to see him so I thought that was the best way to keep him out of the shop until you made up."

"You said exactly the right thing, Jo. See you at one."

She ended the call thanking her lucky stars that she'd found Jo. She'd make this business work, she knew it, with Jo's support she couldn't fail.

Meanwhile, Jo sat looking down the length of the shop at the boxes of items she'd been stocking the shelves with, her heart pounding. Was the shop closing or was Orla just cutting her overheads by letting her go? She could run the place herself, she had done before Jo's time.

Gail had called earlier with her bad news. Jo had been really sympathetic, knowing how much her friend needed her job but she needed hers too.

She busied herself rearranging stock and dusting already spotless display cabinets, singing along to the radio as she worked. She had to do something to get the time in.

It had been a strange couple of years since she'd left Kieran, after discovering his adultery. Living with her father in her old family home, renewing her friendship with Gail, her old school friend, getting this job on Gail's recommendation to her ex colleague, Orla, selling the house she and Kieran had shared for eight years (she had never really thought of it as a home), and then her Dad arranging for her to buy the old family home, he and Kate coming out about their newly formed relationship in the years after her mother's death, and their decision to sell up both their homes and buy a house in the country together, starting university to pursue her talent for painting, and most importantly - meeting Aiden.

Jo smiled when she thought of Aiden. She couldn't believe her luck after her unhappy marriage to Kieran. Aiden had been a frequent visitor to the shop, nipping in on his lunch break from the advertising agency down the road.

When he was the first person to buy one of her paintings from the gallery, she'd been ecstatic. Orla had viewed a sample of them on Gail's recommendation and agreed to carry a few "to see how they go." They'd gone and then some. Aiden had continued to call in to buy candles, "gifts for my mother." Eventually, on confirming she too was separated, he'd asked her out to dinner, confessing, "There are only so many candles one woman can burn…"

Two women had entered the shop. She recognised them as customers. They were browsing round the back shelves lifting expensive pieces to admire. She didn't mind that, they spent plenty and freely. Jo had made the mistake of confiding in them that she was going through a divorce. One was the recently divorced Dolores, an Ivanna Trump lookalike, with an *I'll-tell-ya-better-than-that* attitude. She proudly boasted she had just divorced her third husband and had taken him to the cleaners, and was now looking out for her fourth 'victim.'

Her friend Maxine (call me *Maxie)* was a shorter, slightly orangier version of Dolores, with a loud, infectious dirty laugh. A self-confessed Merry Widow, who was having a ball spending her deceased husband's hard earned dosh.

Jo watched them totter around the shop in their high heels, for all the world like two overgrown kids let loose in a toy shop. Dolores waved and Jo smiled her acknowledgment.

At twelve fifty she closed up and made her way down the road to meet her boss.

The restaurant was busy with office workers and lunchtime shoppers. Orla picked a small booth toward the back to sit in. It was far enough away from the window for her to remain unseen from the street and private enough for them to talk undisturbed. Jo arrived at one 'o clock exactly. Orla waved to her and Jo made her way across the room to sit at the table with her.

Jo searched Orla's face for signs of her impending dismissal, signs that would confirm her fears were justified.

"Sorry to bother you like this Jo, my personal life shouldn't be your concern but I feel I owe you an explanation for my behaviour of late."

Jo was relieved; it wasn't about the business after all. But she noted the tension on Orla's face and all thoughts of her own position were forgotten. Although the corner where they were seated was dark Jo was almost sure her face was bruised under the carefully applied make-up and her lip appeared to be swollen but she couldn't be sure, such was the angle she held herself at. Orla looked distraught. This was no lover's tiff.

"I told you Seamus and I had a row – well, it was a bit more than that. He hit me, not for the first time, but certainly for the last time. I left him on Sunday morning. I'm not staying with friends as I told you; I'm staying in a safe house, a refuge."

Orla's voice was low but she sounded strong despite the quietness of her tone. Jo understood she was loathe to be overheard by other diners.

Jo reached across and touched her arm gently.

"Oh, Orla, I'm so sorry, is there anything I can do to help? Do you want to stay with me for a while until you get yourself sorted?"

Orla shook her head.

"Thanks for the offer, Jo, but no. You've your child to think of and I don't want to be bringing trouble to your door, it's kind of you to offer...I was going to contact an old friend on Monday but after the first night I knew I was safe. I knew I was fine. The workers are supportive and the other women there have all been through bad experiences, it helps in a strange way. It's kept me focused hearing their stories. You realise how easy it is to fool yourself, believe he really is sorry, he really won't do it again. They've all been there, too. I know it must sound weird, but I really am fine there for now. I went to see my solicitor on Monday and all of the wheels are in motion for the divorce already. And you needn't fret - the shop's in my name."

"It's that *final?*"

"It's that final, Jo. I almost waited too long."

She couldn't bear to tell Jo the whole saga; it was enough to have related it to Anne Marie on Sunday night and then again to her solicitor on Monday. She'd had to come clean to ensure Jo's future support but she had her pride. Much as she liked Jo, she was her employee and she didn't wish to embarrass herself anymore than was absolutely necessary.

"Does he know yet?"

"Well, he will now. The letter went out on Monday evening but I haven't spoken to him yet, my solicitor advised me against it. She should hear from his legal representatives by next week she reckons."

They broke off to read the menus the waitress handed them, ordering as she waited, neither of them particularly hungry.

"How long can you stay where you are?"

"As long as it takes. I have the advantage of money, thank God. I've started looking for a place to rent already. Unfortunately to no avail. There's plenty on the market if you want an apartment in Belfast but I want to be out of town, as far away in the other direction from him as is humanly possible. It doesn't have to be an apartment, a house would be fine, but it must be out of town. I couldn't bear to live close to him. I'd be too frightened. To be honest it would be easier to go back home to Dublin. But I can't consider it. That would prove he's won."

Jo's look must have said she was concerned that Orla might be swayed and return to Dublin, sell the business and start over at home. Orla was quick to allay her fears.

"Don't worry Jo, I intend being back to work as soon as this clears up." She indicated to her face. "And I don't mind travelling, I'm used to it. I've driven to Dublin and back many a day before I met Seamus. Once I find the right place for me to live, the business will keep me going, give me something to get out of bed for again. I'd soon get into the way of commuting if I find the right accommodation, but y'know…finding it is going to be the problem."

Their lunch arrived and they ate in silence. Jo was relieved for herself but her heart went out to Orla. How often had she envied her? Thinking she was a young woman who had it all. Orla paid for the meals and they prepared to leave the restaurant, Orla assuring Jo she would be back to work as soon as possible. Jo rushed back to open the shop while Orla made her way across town for a dental appointment.

Back in her car, Orla checked out her appearance in her handbag mirror. The bruising was still visible under her make-up. Another layer may have camouflaged it entirely but she didn't feel the need to hide it completely. In a perverse way she had wanted Jo to witness it. Building up the layers of make-up simply built up the cloak of lies she'd been sheltering under for too many months. Coming out in the open with the effects of her beating would prepare her to face Seamus, when the time came. She shivered at the prospect of coming face to face with her husband. The more people who had seen the effects of his handiwork, the less likely she would be to go back to him, if he put her under pressure.

The dentist was next. She could have waited for an appointment until next week when her face was bruise free. The tooth although chipped was not very painful, nor affecting her ability to eat but she had to do it this way. As she slid onto the big white leather dental chair she registered the look on her dentist's face.

He didn't speak but his expression asked the question, "What's happened to you then?"

She replied to his unasked question, her words quiet but forceful.

"My husband did it. I've been to see my solicitor, I'm divorcing him."

The elderly man looked slightly embarrassed then he pulled himself together, smiling at her honesty.

"Good for you, dear!"

He proceeded to repair the tooth taking care not to hurt her split lip but apart from that it was just another appointment. Perhaps Orla should have felt self-conscious, ashamed. That's how she normally would have felt about visible signs of her husband's violence. But she didn't. Acknowledging it had empowered her.

It was only the start, she knew she had a long road ahead before she would be back to her old confident, fun loving self again but it was a start and that was enough. For now.

That Thursday morning in Derry, Geraldine was helping her mother on with her coat, preparing to take her out shopping for new shoes. Or that was the excuse, anyway. They had all agreed on Monday night that she would go to Belfast with Deirdre on Friday and stay for three or four months, leave things loose for the time being. It would have created more confusion to tell Mary of this plan too soon. That conversation was for later. Deirdre would get on with packing and cleaning the house, while Geraldine kept her occupied.

"Enjoy yourselves, don't spend too much money!" Deirdre waved them off.

Relieved to be able to get on with the tasks in hand Deirdre rummaged through the wardrobes and emptied drawers and cupboards. Packing everything she thought her mother would need for a long stay with her. The cases ready, she loaded them into the car boot for the next day's journey and got down to cleaning the house. She thanked God that her brothers were so attentive. If Geraldine looked after her mother physically, they maintained the house, making sure it was in good order and sound repair. Painting it inside and out as needed. The house was old, their parents had lived there all of their married life and they had all been reared in it, so it needed constant work, although the double glazing and central heating they'd installed years ago made it comfortable and damp free.

Now the question was: how would they keep it from falling into bad repair if it was unlived in? Of course, they couldn't think of selling it, not yet, but Liam had suggested letting it.

Geraldine and Liam's son Declan worked in the university in Coleraine and said there was always a demand for good family homes from the lecturers contracted on a yearly basis. Deirdre and Geraldine were unsure. They didn't know how their mother would take the news that her house was being rented by strangers. Benny and Liam were more practical about it saying they'd cross that bridge when they came to it. Geraldine doubted there would be much demand for an old country house like their family home but Liam was adamant it could be let, backed up by Benny who said it was close enough to the big town and the motorway to Belfast to be desirable.

Deirdre felt riddled with guilt as she went through her mother's house, feeling like she was ransacking it as she came upon boxes of documents and old photos in the cupboards. Tidying up and securing personal effects as though her mother was already dead. She knew as Geraldine did there was no alternative; their mother's days of living alone in this house were over.

This was to be Deirdre's last night before leaving to go back home to Benny and Belfast. She was to prepare a meal for the three of them, her mother, Geraldine and herself. Then they'd broach the subject of her going back with Deirdre for a visit. She was dreading it. Benny had suggested there was no need to tell Mary how long she was staying. If her mum was as far gone as they all feared, time durations would have little meaning to her, long explanations would be unnecessary and may even lead to more confusion for her. Benny said that for now everyone should take it one day at a time and wait for the results of the hospital assessments before making any permanent decisions.

The tasks completed Deirdre looked around trying to see the house through a stranger's eyes. Would anyone want to live in it? Of course, they'd remove all of the personal belongings and steam clean carpets and furniture, it was a lovely house to her of course, the first place she'd called home.

A lump formed in her throat as she thought of telling their mother she'd never live in it again. Benny was right; they couldn't tell her in that way. It would be too much. Maybe the tests would prove her ailment was treatable and she would be able to move back after the break with them. Deirdre knew she was clutching at straws but she also knew they had to tread very gently; her mother's heart was in their hands.

She busied herself preparing dinner, making her special recipe chicken casserole. She'd serve it with champ, her mother's favourite, followed by apple pie and ice cream. God the guilt, she felt like she was setting her own mother up. Geraldine had called their brothers and explained the situation as Deirdre and she saw it. In turn they'd discussed it with their wives, all agreeing it was for the best that their sisters took their mother home. Part of Deirdre thought, *they would wouldn't they*...But she knew she was being unreasonable, who else should care for Mary but her own daughters?

On Monday night as they'd thrashed the plans out Benny had been insistent that Geraldine and she shouldn't be expected to do it all without help. He'd suggested they employ a nurse part time and then when the time came for Geraldine to take over she should do likewise, he'd foot the bill. Liam had interrupted saying he wouldn't hear tell of it, they would pay their own way.

It had progressed to a full blown argument, then Geraldine had told them both to shut up, saying if money was the problem she had put every penny Benny and Deirdre sent for their mother into an account for her old age. They had enough money in the bank to employ a team of nurses. Benny had backtracked, seeing the effect all of the discussion was having on Geraldine. But they all agreed that nurses would be brought in to help. Deirdre looked at the clock - almost four fifteen. Geraldine had said they'd be back by five.

She pulled her apron off and went through to the bedroom, the room that had been Geraldine's and hers for so long, all the way through childhood and their teenage years. Deirdre pushed the memories from her mind, grabbing a dress from a hanger, she made for the shower. She lathered her hair, scrubbing all sentimental thoughts from her head and rubbed her skin vigorously with a sponge. She knew Geraldine would be an emotional wreck, tonight would have to be down to her.

Talking to herself out loud she coaxed, "Keep it together Deirdre, it's for the best. For the best for us all."

Chapter 10

THEY FINISHED DINNER AND DEIRDRE could wait no longer, she'd say her piece before dessert - another mouthful would stick in her throat.

"Mum, I've really enjoyed being home with you this week, it's been lovely."

Her mother, still eating, nodded her acknowledgment. Deirdre looked over to where Geraldine sat head down, shuffling the remainder of the meal around her plate.

Deirdre swallowed hard.

"Benny and I were wondering if you'd like to come back with me, stay with us for a while."

"How would I get home?" Mary looked slightly bemused.

"No Mum, I mean stay for a few weeks, a few months even. Would you like that?"

Her mother mumbled words Deirdre could barely hear. Geraldine interjected.

"No Mammy, you are not a burden to us, Deirdre just thought it would be a change for you, what d'ye think?"

"Since Benny retired he's all this time on his hands but I hardly ever see him, it would be company for me and with the wedding coming up I could do with a shopping partner."

Deirdre realised she'd said too much, confused her.

"Who's gettin' married?"

Geraldine was impatient with her.

"Aiden and Jo. Mammy, y'know that."

"Oh."

Deirdre tried to steer the conversation back.

"It must get lonely for you in this big old house since Daddy died…I know you've Ger just along the road but the days must be long for ye…"

Mary looked up, her eyes brimming with tears, "I'd love it. D'ye not mind, Geraldine?"

Geraldine's nose was twitching. She was struggling to contain her own tears.

"I think it'd be great for ye, all those big new shopping centres, you'd be in yer element. Then when ye come back up you can stay with us for a while, no need for you to be on yer own at all."

"What about me house, yer not gonnie sell me house?"

Mary was agitated. Geraldine jumped in, fearful they'd lost her.

"No Mammy we wouldn't hear tell of it, it's just to get ye through the winter."

Benny and Liam had urged them not to give her any long-term plans and add to her confusion, they'd simply get her as far as Belfast and take it from there.

"So, is it a yes, Mum? Benny's running round the house with a feather duster at this very minute!"

"I like Benny. Does he dust? Yer father didn't dust, said it was women's work, hadn't time to run a farm and dust. So Benny's gettin' married?"

Geraldine jumped in, the tension getting to her.

"Aiden!"

"Aye, that's who I meant, I just forget sometimes. I'll go," their mother nodded, pleased, like a child preparing for a Sunday school trip.

Deirdre heaved a sigh of relief as she left the table to prepare dessert. They ate in silence and then Mary said, "Have ye anymore ice cream? This pie's very dry. Is it shop bought?"

The sisters grinned at each other as Deirdre rose to lift her mother's dish. Same old Mary, never afraid to say exactly what she thought, no matter who it offended.

Benny wasn't dusting the house. At that precise moment he was sitting in Aiden's apartment eating Chinese food with his family.

Throughout the week he'd been keeping them up-to-date with their mother and Geraldine's plans for their granny, now Aiden had gathered them all in his apartment for dinner, Kelly, Rosie, Benny and himself. Rosie said, "Dad's right about the nurse, isn't he? Mum's just got her independence - it would be too much for her to care for granny every day."

"Yeah I know, she's really enjoying the volunteering, it would be a shame for her to have to give it up. I mean, what would she do with herself for the rest of the year?" Kelly asked.

Benny thought there always seemed to be something for Deirdre to do. It seemed with her grandchildren - the older they got, the more attention they needed. If it wasn't a dress to be made for a school formal, it was a free driving lesson. But they loved it, Benny and Deirdre, so he kept his thoughts to himself.

Rosie added, "And she's gone to all those training courses, it would be a shame to waste all that."

They reached across the table, piling the food straight from the foil containers onto their plates. Deirdre would've had a fit.

Benny spoke, "Don't worry, I'll make sure she rings the nursing agency first thing on Monday when your granny's not within hearing distance…"

They all stopped and looked at him, then burst into laughter. When was Mary Devlin ever not within hearing distance?

"…I know, I know, but really if I have to I'll call in and see the woman myself. Her agency's just down the Lisburn Road, your mother nursed with her years ago in the early days in the Royal, Lorraine, I think her name is…"

"Make sure you do, Dad." Aiden looked serious. "Mum's not getting any younger herself."

"I know son, don't worry. It's the only way. Yer granny was probably starting to lose her memory even while granda was alive but they kept each other goin'…"

He tailed off, thinking of his own mother and father both in their eighties, riddled with pains but coping. He had called in with them on Tuesday on his way home from his trip to Geraldine and Liam's, they'd asked after Mary Devlin when he'd explained the reason for his weekday visit, his mother saying, "God help her, all on her own in that big house."

He dreaded to think what would become of his mother or father if either of them died but he'd seven brothers, they'd deal with it as they had to when the time came. A time Benny dreaded, but that was for the future. Now they had to agree on Mary's care.

It would change their lives, but they'd manage, he was sure of it. She may even venture to Portugal with them in the summer. After all the years of coaxing, Johnny, never a man for travelling, had always declined their offers of holidays in the sun and Mary had had no desire to go without him.

Benny ate his spicy chicken staring out the window over Belfast. The night was damp and misty, the lights of the city shone out in the darkness, the roads still busy with traffic, this being late night shopping. The Big Wheel dwarfed the dome of the City Hall, even in this weather some loopers were daft enough to be up in the swinging capsules, eager to see the sights of the once trouble torn city. He'd taken his teenage granddaughters Clare and Hannah up in the wheel when they were out Christmas shopping together, the girls were unimpressed. It was their home town, why would they be?

Clare remarked, "It's okay but there's not much to see, only a load of streets and a bunch of buildings in the midst of Cave Hill and Black Mountain."

Benny who had loved it, smiled at their blasé attitude.

"What were ye expectin' to see... the Sydney Opera, the Statue of Liberty... it's Belfast for God's sake. Open yer eyes, take a good look around you, it's yer home town!"

The girls laughingly interjected, saying in unison, "We know, we know... You'll appreciate it someday, when you're sitting in some far off place, many miles from home..."

He'd given them pretend clips on the ear, knowing all the talking on his part wouldn't make them see it differently; they'd have to leave it first to miss it.

His city, his adopted home. Mary would be fine with them. She'd have to be. There was no way Benny was leaving this place. Not now. His eyes came back to the room where his children talked animatedly as they ate, discussing their mother. Concern for their granny and her had gathered them here tonight. He was lucky. He loved them all, retirement had given him time, time he'd never had as they were growing up. Not that they'd been neglected, their mother had reared them as she worked part time. He'd provided well for them all.

This apartment they sat in was his, lived in by Aiden while he waited for his divorce to be finalised. Benny was delighted his son was remarrying, delighted he'd found Jo. How could he separate himself from this town, from his family and their offspring? Deirdre hadn't suggested it, she knew it wasn't an option, not for her, either. They'd weather this storm as they'd weathered all the others, together, with their family around them.

Aiden walked them to the residents and visitors parking area within the multi storey complex, the girls headed off at the same time while Benny and Aiden stood talking at Benny's car, their voices reverberating around the enclosed space.

"So how's Mum bearing up after a week with Aunt Ger?"

"They're thick as thieves, you know yerself what they're like when they get their heads together to concoct a plan."

Aiden nodded at his father. They both knew, without mentioning it directly, that Benny was referring to the time at the beginning of Benny and Deirdre's retirement when Deirdre and he had set off for their first stay in their new holiday home in Portugal; Benny unaware that Deirdre had been recalled after a routine mammogram. They'd gone back and forth from Portugal to Ireland over the subsequent months, Deirdre working the trips around her follow up appointments, every one of which she attended with her sister, unknown to Benny or any of the rest of their family.

Deirdre and Geraldine had covered the hospital visits by making up excursions to the beauty salon, a new spa, lunch dates, or just plain old-fashioned shopping trips. Benny had merely assumed she was making the most of her retirement after a lifetime of nursing. Deirdre had only told him about the scare after she had received the final all clear. Of course the news had come as a shock to Benny and he'd spent many hours since reflecting on the state his life would be in if his wife's diagnosis had been different. Aiden's voice interrupted his thoughts, "You'll let me know how it goes Dad."

"Of course. I'll give you a call in the morning, let you know how the land lies…"

Aiden interrupted, "No, call me tonight as soon as you hear from mum, I'm headin' up to Jo's now, so I'll be up and about until around midnight anyway."

"Okay I'll call ya later, take it easy son. Give my love to Jo."

Benny stepped into his car and Aiden headed toward his own. Both alone in their thoughts as they drove out of the complex into Ormeau Avenue, the streets late night shopping busy as usual, despite the recession.

79

Meanwhile in Derry, the ice cream finished, Mary pushed her dish away from her although it still held a large portion of pie. Deirdre made a mental note to herself not to buy supermarket pie.

"Would you like tea, Mammy?" Geraldine asked.

Mary nodded, preoccupied.

"I'll need to pack, won't I?"

"Don't worry, Mum, Geraldine and I can take care of all that later when you're safely tucked up in bed."

They daren't let their mother know her cases were packed and in the boot of Deirdre's car. All of this had to be her decision, or at least seem that way. They had to allow her to hold onto the little independence she still had, keep hold of her dignity, otherwise she really would feel she was a burden to them.

"What night is it? Do I watch 'Millionaire' t'night?"

"No Mammy, that was last night, this is Thursday, will I put a DVD on for you, one of yer films?" Geraldine replied.

Mary nodded, still not convinced it wasn't her night for 'Millionaire'. Deirdre rummaged through the pile of movies and held out a romantic comedy.

"Doris Day and Rock Hudson…"

"Aye, one o'them one's, I like a good romance…"

She sat at the hearth contentedly watching her movie, in another world as her daughters washed the dishes. Both thinking this may be her last night in her own home. Neither said a word, they just got on with the tidying up as their mother chuckled at the onscreen antics. Both exhausted after the stress of the day the sisters agreed on an early night after their mother was settled. Deirdre had a long journey ahead of her the next day.

As she lay in bed staring out of the window at the stars Deirdre was aware of the tears rolling down her face, tears she'd kept at bay all day, as she cleared her mother's belongings, packing her bags for a journey that would leave the remnants of her old life behind; this window, this view, all part of Deirdre and her early years. She'd be back, of course, but not in the same circumstances, maybe not to stay, not to sleep in this old familiar room again.

She blew her nose, chastising herself, she had to stop this nostalgia, concentrate on the future. She couldn't let her mother see she'd been crying or all of their deception would have been in vain. Mary would know she was being taken out of her home, probably for the last time, know her daughters had plotted to get her to leave, never to return. Mary Devlin wouldn't be told what to do. She was a strong woman despite her ailing mind.

Deirdre lay watching the shadows flicker across the ceiling, praying for the strength and guidance to do the best by this fragile old woman. Across the fields in her sister's house the light burned late into the night as Geraldine sat by the fireside, doing the same, praying for strength and guidance.

Late that Thursday evening as Jo sat watching television with Aiden, his phone rang. She gathered from the exchange that it was his Dad. Jo turned the volume of the TV down and left him to talk in private.

In the kitchen she filled the kettle and made toast for supper. Her son was fast asleep in bed, no doubt dreaming about the coming weekend and his day out with his Dad, Kieran had custody visits every other weekend. She took her time making the tea, Aiden had been tense all night waiting to hear from Benny on the outcome of Deirdre's suggestion to her mother. By the time she returned to the living room with the tray of tea and toast Aiden was watching the late news, the call finished.

"Well, how'd it go with yer Mum?"

"Dad got an email from her a while ago, Gran's agreed to come home with her but she took Dad's advice and made out it's only a temporary arrangement otherwise she'd never have gotten her out of the house. They're talking about maybe six months here and six months with Aunt Geraldine. Whatever way it goes she can't live in that house alone anymore, Dad and Liam have advised them to consider renting it out short term. Declan says he'll put the feelers out in the university. Poor Mum, she must be exhausted."

Jo squeezed his hand reassuringly.

"Well, at least yer granny has agreed to come back with her, that'll be a relief for all of you."

Aiden nodded, folding a slice of toast and eating it in three bites.

"The house is so old it'll be riddled with damp if it's not lived in through the winter, then they'll have no chance of letting it to anybody."

Jo listened to his concerns as she drank her tea, a thought

bubble forming in her head. She would sleep on it, then consider it fully in the morning. It was only an idea, she'd weigh it up, consider it carefully before voicing it.

Aiden left for home around midnight and Jo went to bed soon after, mulling the idea over as she lay staring at the ceiling. Could she possibly have the solution to Orla's problem? She had started the day with the call from Gail about her imminent redundancy, then at lunchtime Orla's news had stunned her.

Sleep didn't come easily that night, when it did it was restless and disturbed.

Chapter 11

BY FRIDAY MORNING CASSIE COULD barely contain herself.
Although she had swopped shifts, she'd still been up at her usual time
to prepare for her appointment with Shiralee North.

She'd a lovely tailored suit and high heeled shoes she'd
bought for Mia's christening, the wardrobe had worn them since, but
today was a day for presentation. Her lifestyle didn't much call for
dressing up, now that lifestyle was about change and with it Cassie's
image.

She took time with her appearance, styling her hair carefully
and applying more make-up than the minimum amount she usually
wore for work. For a special occasion like this she had to look the part.
She donned the killer heels, prepared to put up with the pain in her legs
for this momentous day.

Only two more shifts to go this week, she could stick the
discomfort. She'd thought of little else since she'd received the cheque.
Bag in hand, she left the house, but not before slipping her fingers
inside to ensure the cheque was still there.

Cassie felt nervous as she waited in the bank. In the reception
area the red fabric of the seats scratched the back of her knees and
calves through the light Lycra mesh of her tights. She looked at the
clock. Ten exactly. She hoped Shiralee wasn't going to play head
games, put her in her place in the pecking order by making her wait.

A door opened opposite and Shiralee approached, meeting her
halfway, indicating for Cassie to come through. In the office Cassie
wasted no time in producing the cheque. She'd gone over the moment
a hundred times in her head since she'd received it. She'd slide her
hand deftly into her bag and sweep the life changing piece of paper
onto the desk with a flourish. And she did.

Shiralee's eyes did, indeed, almost pop out of her head and her jaw did drop to her skinny little chest but Cassie hadn't been prepared for the genuine pleasure in her eyes as they made contact with her own, waiting for the explanation.

"A scratch card, after I was in here last Friday…" she stopped to see if Shiralee remembered her.

"Yes, I remember, I was just about to go to lunch when I spoke with you…"

"Well, I bought a paper and a scratch card as I waited for my bus home and hey presto! I thought my eyes were deceiving me…"

Cassie continued to relate the phone call. How the woman had confirmed that she did indeed appear to be a winner.

"Well done, Mrs Gallagher! That'll be a shopping trip and a half, eh?"

"That's what I want to talk to you about. I need a bit of advice, as you probably know I'm a cleaner…" The bank official nodded. "Well I'm thinking of starting up my own business, making this chance work for me, I mean I have a mortgage and family, it would be easy to go through it, but I haven't told them anything about this. Not yet. I mean, after clearing the mortgage and booking a few foreign holidays, seeing my kids right…How many months would it last?"

Cassie looked at Shiralee to see if there were signs of condescension in her face, an eejit like her starting a business. But her look was interested, if somewhat intrigued. She was probably going over the conversation they'd had last week - Cassie's inability to pay her heating oil direct debit on time.

"First things first, Mrs Gallagher, I'll need to advise you how best to invest this amount short term. If you're planning on using it to start a business then I would have to advise you to see one of our Business Advisers as that area is outside of my remit, I can make an appointment for you now if you like." She scanned the appointment book. "Next Wednesday around twelve suit?"

Cassie nodded. "Yes, that'd be great, thanks."

Noticing that despite her carefully applied make-up, Shiralee's eyes were edged with deep lines, Cassie softened toward this woman who was around her own age, maybe she'd her own troubles, even a Gerry Gallagher of her own at home.

Shiralee took the cheque and lodged it for Cassie. Opening up the appropriate account for the meantime, she gave her advice on the best accounts to open for her family. She rang the Business Advisor to confirm the interview for the following week and found he'd had a cancellation for his ten thirty appointment that morning.

"I know it's short notice but if you like you could have a quick chat about your idea in general terms now, then come back in next week on Wednesday to cover things in more depth, what do you think?"

Cassie agreed. "Why not? It'll give me a chance to find out what's involved in the start up. I know it looks like money's no object now but I still have to be careful to use it wisely. It's taken a while for fate to shine favourably on me."

The meeting over, Shiralee North handed all the documentation across the desk to Cassie and stood, she extended her hand; her handshake was firm and warm.

"Good Luck, Mrs Gallagher, maybe some of your luck will rub off on me and my lottery numbers'll come up tomorrow night, then I'll not have to come back into this place on Monday morning."

They exchanged a conspiratorial grin and Shiralee left the room. Soon after the Business Advisor entered the office and introduced himself. "Mrs Gallagher - Paddy McHenry."

Cassie was shy at first, self-conscious, sure this young man was thinking, *Well she doesn't seem the type to set up a business, but I'll have to humour her for a few minutes.*

On the contrary he was open and enthusiastic about her plans, scant as they were. He told her what she'd need to have thought about for their meeting next week: business premises, budget for vehicle, modes of advertising, insurance and the catchment area she planned to operate in. Terms that were alien to her now but ones that would become second nature as her plans progressed toward her goal. He scribbled down ideas as they arose in the course of their conversation and at the end of their short meeting handed her the large sheet of paper.

"Mull that over with your future partner and tell me how you see your ideas progressing. Perhaps your partner would like to accompany you on Wednesday? Feel free to bring her along."

By the end of the meeting Cassie no longer felt like she was hallucinating. This was real, she was wealthy, and she was in a position to get wealthier still. Paddy McHenry showed her out, smiling, saying he looked forward to their next meeting.

Cassie walked down the length of the bank toward the doors,

recalling how heavy her heart had felt the last time she'd exited this building. Was it really only a week ago? She'd had Shiralee wrong, or perhaps the lucky break had simply given Cassie a generosity of spirit she herself hadn't possessed before.

Her step was light as she walked through the morning shoppers. Shiralee had said the cheque would be cleared by the end of this week and there was no way it wasn't genuine; Cassie would be able to give in her notice any time.

Of course, she didn't have to work her notice, she could simply have said, "Take this job and shove it!" She had so often dreamed of doing that but now that she could, she knew she wouldn't. It wasn't her way. She would do the right thing, not leave anyone in the lurch. But she'd use the time to plan her business venture, talk to Gail and get the wheels in motion. If she planned it right they'd be up and running by the time she'd finished her last shift.

Unable to contain her excitement she took out her phone as she entered a nearby coffee shop. She texted Gail with her news and they agreed to meet later. Gail said she would call in on her way to the supermarket; they'd be free to talk as Dean would be out for the night with his mates.

That same Friday morning found Orla sitting on the bed in her room in the refuge poring through the property section of the Belfast Telegraph, the Thursday evening edition. She had already been through it from front to back the previous night. She was examining it again carefully just in case she had missed something in the packed pages of new apartments and turn key developments.

As a builder Seamus knew just about every new site in the country, certainly in Belfast. Orla wouldn't feel safe renting any of the properties listed. Maybe she would have to widen her search, try the internet for rural estate agents.

It was still early, not yet ten, she would head out to one of the internet cafes. Unsure of the area, she would have to check out the nearest one with the staff on duty in the house.

Sarah, the woman on duty, drew a detailed map for her, highlighting the roads around the house and two internet cafes within a short distance. The only computer in the house was in the office and although the staff wouldn't have minded her using it, she felt it would be an intrusion on their workspace.

She made her way out into the day, the air cold and crisp, with a hint of rain on the way. But it was winter. She pulled her coat around her as she crossed the car park to her car.

The café was only minutes away. Inside, she ordered coffee and logged on, fumbling in her bag for a list of agents she'd made from Yellow Pages. Twenty minutes later, the coffee finished, she closed the computer down. Her search had been fruitless. Maybe it was the wrong time of year for rental properties, most of the students would be sorted with accommodation by now but surely people's circumstances changed all the time. There had to be something out there that would suit her. She could put the word out that she was looking for a place but with whom? She'd already acknowledged to herself that most of her friends and acquaintances were Seamus's so that wasn't a route she could take. Even if they did know her version of the events leading to the break up, their loyalty would remain with him. Apart from Jo and her old friends from the bank, she couldn't think of anyone she could turn to for help.

Orla left the café and walked to her car, head down to cope with the elements, despondent. *What now?*

In Derry that Friday morning Deirdre was up with first light preparing for the journey back. Geraldine arrived shortly after eight, looking like she also had slept little.

They kept busy with the tasks in hand, listening to the early morning news on the radio, discussing the weather, anything to pass the time. Geraldine got their mother dressed and ready for the journey, making sure she had cash for the trip. Liking to be prepared for all eventualities, Mary wouldn't leave the house without cash in her purse. Although unspoken, her favourite phrase came to mind, *Y'never know.*

She hadn't said it this morning, she hadn't said much at all. Assuming she remembered where she was going, they went about getting her organised to leave. It would have been too heartbreaking for all of them to go over the whole scenario again.

In Belfast, Benny was keeping himself occupied, listening to the same early morning radio programme delivering him the same news as he tidied, in the kitchen, in the living room, all around the house. Vacuuming, dusting, opening windows and drinking endless cups of coffee as he waited for the online shopping delivery. It was to be there before ten.

He had ordered flowers for Deirdre and her mother. To welcome Deirdre home and to welcome Mary to her new home, her home for now, at least.

He reached for the Yellow Pages and turned to Nursing Agencies, his eyes ran over the entries. He found two on the Lisburn Road. He would check with Deirdre later to be sure which one was her friend's and make a note of the number.

If Deirdre hadn't done it by Monday he would contact the woman himself. He wouldn't allow her to attempt this on her own, Geraldine had been doing that for too long and anyone could see she was at breaking point.

Poor Liam, he should have asked for help. Benny wasn't prepared to see Deirdre run herself into the ground, her mother's health was important but so was his wife's. As the radio droned on in the background unnoticed he waited and drank his coffee.

The girls arrived as he was unpacking the shopping. Kelly who taught part-time had Fridays off and Rosie was on a job share. They had insisted on coming today to greet their granny and show their support to their mother.

"It's very good of you girls, yer mother will appreciate it, but for God's sake don't give yer granny any inkling that this was preplanned or she'll hit the roof. Remember to say Mum texted you with the news last night."

Kelly hugged him, saying, "Don't worry, Dad, we know."

Rosie turned from the cupboard where she was packing food into shelves.

"Did you order anything we could make lunch for all of us with or should we go down the road and pick up a few things?"

"I did a full shop, I'm not completely useless without your mother y' know."

Kelly placed the flowers in water and grinned at him.

"We know, flowers 'n' all, sure yer the perfect man, Dad."

They worked together to clear the bags of groceries from the floor, then the girls prepared lunch for their mother's return. Benny felt nervous. He thought of last Friday morning when he'd been in the gym, as usual, looking forward to the weekend, before he'd got Deirdre's call.

What a difference a week made.

Jo had been unable to motivate herself to do anything that Friday morning apart from sit at the counter in the gallery staring out the shop window at the passers-by on the Lisburn Road.

She sat sipping her coffee pondering the possibility of Orla renting Aiden's granny's house. She didn't want to seem callous, asking about her employer renting the property, when the poor old woman had barely closed her front door for the last time. It may not even work out for her with Deirdre and Benny but if that were the case she still wouldn't be allowed to live alone again. It would be down to Deirdre's sister Geraldine to care for her. Either way they'd have to let the property. Aiden had said last night, *"...the house is so old it'll be riddled with damp if it's not lived in through the winter..."* Although Orla said she didn't mind travelling and the house was close to Coleraine and the motorway to Belfast, the old farmhouse in Derry may be a bit too far for her even to consider.

Her phone rang breaking into her thoughts; it was Aiden.

"Jo, how's it goin'?"

"Slow, I've only had one or two customers across the door since I opened up."

"That good eh? I'm havin' a similar sorta day myself, cheer up it's nearly the weekend. I'll call round to Mum and Dad's tonight on my way up to your house. The girls are there now, they said they'd call over and make some lunch, have a bit of a welcome party for Mum and Granny's arrival. I won't stay long, just want to see how she's settling in and how Mum is after a week with Aunt Ger."

Jo laughed, she'd heard plenty of stories about Deirdre and Geraldine and their sibling rows to get his drift.

"Could ya spare ten minutes to call in here sometime today?"

"Sure, I'm in the office at the minute, I'll head up now. What is it?"

"Just something that's come up. I need to check it out with you."

He assumed it was something to do with their wedding arrangements.

"See ya in five minutes."

Aiden pushed the door into the shop and the doorbell rang out signalling his arrival. Jo looked up from her magazine. She was still trying to get ideas for their dresses for the wedding. Little Sarah would be easy enough but it was harder to find just the right thing for Gail and herself.

"I see we're really having a productive day."

"I'm on my break! I'm glad you're not my boss."

He put his hands out bear-like and made a sweep for her, saying, "No, I'm yer loverman!"

"Shut up, I've to work here."

He turned round, and made a show of acknowledging a shop full of pretend customers. "Sorry, I didn't see all these customers."

"Sit down a minute…"

"Bossy Boots - Jo, if it's about the photos, I told you not to worry about the expense. My Dad's insisting on paying the photographer. He's always gone on about the fact that Mum and he only had four Polaroids to show for their wedding day…"

He sat down beside her at the counter on a stool provided for customers.

"It's not about the wedding, it's about yer Granny's house. I know she's only just left it, I don't want ya to think I'm being unfeeling. You know what I told you yesterday about Orla?"

He nodded.

"Well, it's proving difficult for her to find a place to rent. She doesn't want to be in town because he'll know where she is, y'know with him being a builder he knows all of the new developments that she'd be likely to consider. It may be a long shot but she said she wouldn't mind travelling if the place was right for her. It doesn't have to be an apartment, she'd consider a house…"

"Yeah, but they live in Hillsborough. She's not going to move to Derry, is she? Yer not serious, Jo?"

"Well from the way she was talking yesterday she wants to be at the other end of the country from Seamus and when I asked her where she'd consider living, her exact words were, *"…as far away in the other direction from him as is humanly possible…it must be out of town…"* and ye can't get much further away from Hillsborough than Derry. She would be prepared to travel if the place is right for her, that's what she said. I'm only telling you in case Declan puts the word out in the university and somebody snaps it up."

"Are ya sure she's really divorcing him though, Jo. I mean I know you said she was upset but I thought it may be a bit of the dramatics. Will she really go through with it d'ye think?"

"She'll go through with it, I've no doubt. You didn't see the bruises on her face and I didn't have to either. She arranged to meet me because she wanted me to see her face, to bring it out into the open. If she wasn't serious about leaving him she wouldn't have done that, Aiden."

Aiden nodded, he didn't know Orla well but he was prepared to take Jo's word for it.

"Okay, as you say, it's early days yet. Gran's just arriving but I'll suss things out and make sure nobody else gets the chance of the house if you think it may be worth asking Orla. I'll play it by ear. If it looks like things are workin' out for Granny with Mum and Dad, then I'll talk to Dad. Leave it with me."

He bent to kiss her.

"See ya later, remember it'll probably be about nine."

"Give my love to yer Mum, I'll see ya later."

Meanwhile Orla was shopping for food to see her though the weekend. She couldn't help remembering her shopping spree last Friday when she'd been shopping for the special meal for Seamus. Was that really only a week ago?

She was tired and anxious due to the lack of progress in finding somewhere to live but she knew she had made the right decision. For the time being she had peace of mind and a safe place to stay. The feeling this week was much more preferable to the knots of anxiety tightening up her stomach and the creepy nervy feeling that crawled along the back of her neck almost constantly. She hadn't realised how badly affected she was on a daily basis until these past few days. She didn't know what the future held, but she knew what it didn't hold. That was more important.

Orla thought of the other women staying in the house, all with their own stories. She'd found out Maggie, who'd offered to shop for her last Sunday on her arrival, had been in an abusive marriage for almost fifty years, she was sixty-nine years old. One day she had gone to the shops as usual and on her return had found the house empty. Her husband had gone out and, of course, he hadn't left her a note. What he had left was her entire collection of books.

She was a great reader, she told them, Maeve Binchy, Danielle Steel, Barbara Taylor Bradford, Catherine Cookson, Josephine Cox...She liked to read about other women, found solace in their stories, their strength. All of them lined up on either side of the small staircase, in piles of three or four on each step from the bottom to the very top. Not a step was missed.

The scene before her was the last straw. She had quickly packed a bag and left, leaving her library behind her.

The tears rolled down Maggie's face as she shared her story and silence fell upon the kitchen. One of the younger women spoke first.

"I don't get it, why did ye leave him over that, a pile of books, if he'd been beatin' ye fer years?"

Maggie explained, "The books were my world, my way of escaping him, his moods and his rages. His elaborate display of them on the staircase was his way of telling me he resented my time spent with them, it took my attention from him and allowed me to escape him, for a time. The display said he hated me more than any beatin' ever did. I knew right there and then I'd run out of time. I had to leave before he killed me."

Orla had been upset for the woman as they all were, her mouth so dry she could barely part her lips but she'd felt privileged to be there in that kitchen with those women as they shared their secrets and gained strength from each others' comfort.

Maggie blew her nose and someone rose to put the kettle on. The mood was broken. Minutes later they were laughing together, tears rolling down there faces for a different reason.

It was an emotional rollercoaster but it was one she had to ride to get her feet firmly back on the ground again. And she would, she had no doubt, she would. It would be a bumpy ride with many fits and starts along the way but she would land on her feet. She had to.

Deirdre's car pulled into the driveway at exactly 12.10p.m. His daughters stood back to allow him access and Benny rushed out to greet his wife and mother-in-law.

Benny's heart went out to Mary as he watched Deirdre help her out of the car onto the driveway. As they had kept his presence from her, Benny hadn't seen Mary on his visit during the week and he noted she looked thinner in the few weeks since his last visit. Although a tall woman, she looked small and vulnerable. He strode forward, arms out to greet her in a bear hug, careful not to squeeze her fragile bones too hard.

"How's m'oul sparrin' partner?"

Mary gave him a playful slap.

"Still able fer you, Benny Brannigan!"

The spirit of the woman, though dimmed, fought to sparkle in her eyes through the slight hint of tears. Benny kissed her gently in welcome as Mary's granddaughters appeared at the front door and ushered her into the warmth of their parents' home.

As he turned to greet his wife the words of a song he'd heard on the radio that morning flitted through his mind... *"This is the end of the beginning, not the beginning of the end..."*

By mid-afternoon Deirdre stood with her mother looking out of the window, waving, as Benny saw their daughters out to their respective cars. Kelly drove off first and Rosie followed. As the latter vehicle revved up, Benny's hand did a pat-a-pat on the roof and Rosie drove out of the driveway. Deirdre wondered to herself, *why do men do that?*

Benny stood watching the two cars disappear down the road and then walked back up the path, into the house.

"It's good to see them, eh, Mary, aren't they lookin' great? Sure yer lookin' great yerself!"

Mary laughed at his palaver.

"And I feel great, amn't I well looked after by yous all. That was a lovely lunch they prepared fer me, God love them."

Deirdre guided her to a big chair by the fireside.

"Sit down, Mum, and take the weight off yer feet, you must be tired after that long journey, I know I am."

"Both of you sit down and put yer feet up fer an hour before dinner, sure yer on the go from early mornin'," Benny said.

He was sure Deirdre had been up from the crack of dawn. He could suggest she go up and lie down for a while but he knew she wouldn't consider it on her mother's first day with them, not while her mum was up and about. Deirdre had told him on the phone that Mary thought she was a burden to her daughters. She would be very aware of her mother's feelings, be very careful not to give her any reason to believe her fears had any foundation.

Benny set a large pouffe at his mother-in-law's feet and gently lifted her legs onto it. Deirdre put the radio on to Classic FM and watched as her mother's eyes closed almost immediately. Within minutes she was fast asleep by the hearth.

"Coffee?" Benny asked.

"Yeah, I'll have a cappuccino and a slice of that nice cake Kelly made. It was good of them to do that, wasn't it? Any word from Aiden?"

"Yeah, he's calling in tonight on his way to Jo's, around seven he said, and it's his week to have Sarah, so he said he'll bring her round to see us tomorrow. Why don't ya go up and lie down after yer coffee. I'll keep an eye on your Mum, you can't look after her if yer exhausted yerself," he remarked gently.

Deirdre nodded and said, "I think I will."

Benny left the room and went into the kitchen to make the coffee, while Deirdre sat by the fireside, watching her mother sleep. Fifteen minutes later she was fast asleep herself. Still fully clothed, she had kicked her shoes off, sank onto her own bed and pulled the duvet around her, the worries of the week over, she was home.

As his mother-in-law slept in the armchair, and his wife slept upstairs on their bed, Benny sat flicking through a television magazine, the hall phone rang out shrilly, breaking the winter afternoon stillness. He threw the magazine across the sofa, and almost leapt over it, to get to the ringing phone before it disturbed Mary. He grabbed it on the third ring with an abrupt, "Yes?"

"Benny, is it a bad time?"

It was Ann, Deirdre's colleague from the age charity she worked for voluntarily two days a week.

"To be honest, it is a bit. Deirdre's just home from Derry, she's having a nap and her mother's fast asleep, I don't want to disturb them…"

"Sorry, Benny, she emailed me yesterday; I just thought I'd give her a call before I leave the office. No worries, tell her I'll catch up with her on Monday."

Ann knew the situation with her mother, she didn't hang about talking.

Benny replaced the receiver thinking, *Jesus, only a few hours and I'm turning the radio down to an almost indiscernible level, and jumping at the ring of the phone, for fear of disturbing Mary. What a change this is going to be to our lives.*

He re-entered the room and saw the frail, old woman sleeping; her arms folded across her chest, at peace in their care and he knew, despite the upheaval for Deirdre and himself, it was the only way. At least they had Geraldine and Liam to share her care.

They had agreed to a three month stint for the first period. May would normally see them spending time in Portugal, and Geraldine and Liam had insisted they would take over then as they themselves always holidayed at home.

It would work out okay. At least they had the summer together to look forward to. Benny looked up as he heard Deirdre enter the room.

"Phone wake you?"

"Yeah, it's okay I got an hour anyway."

"It was Ann, said you'd emailed her, she'll call ya Monday."

"It'll be about the St. Valentine's Tea Dance, I've to organise the transport to the hotel in Newcastle, as newly appointed Travel Co-Coordinator...I'll do this one anyway then I'll see..."

Benny's voice was low.

"You'll see nothing. You've made the commitment and you enjoy it, so we'll get the nurse organised on Monday. That reminds me which agency is it? I looked it up, but there're two on the Lisburn Road..."

"It's 'Helping Hands' Lorraine Donaldson...but we may not..."

Benny put his hand up to stop her, looking to the seat where his mother-in-law sat.

"Now's not the time, Deirdre, we'll talk later. What do you want to do for dinner? We could go out if ye want."

"Sure ya said Aiden's calling, and I think Mum would be too tired to go out after he leaves, it'd be too late. She's had a big day with the girls making that lovely lunch and everything..."

She saw his face drop, and knew he was thinking, *Too late to go out at eight o'clock on a Friday night...*

He gathered himself, knowing she'd read his thoughts, thinking of the food delivery that morning.

"What about a nice piece of fillet steak, baked potato and some salad, and a nice bottle of red. Yer ma likes a nice drop o'wine, eh?"

He tried to make it sound like a party, but Deirdre knew that like her, Benny was terrified. In one way for what the future held for her mother, but in another way, selfishly, for what it held for the two of them.

Chapter 12

GAIL ARRIVED AT THE FRONT door, shortly after Dean, Cassie's son, left for his night out. Cassie was buzzing after talking to the business advisor earlier that day.

She laid the sheet of paper out, showing Gail the ideas they'd discussed. Premises, estimated amount they'd need to spend on a vehicle, insurance, advertising budget, website design, the rough percentage to set aside for tax.

"Jeez, it's scary isn't it, Cass?"

"Only if you think about it all at once, we'll break it down, for next week, talk it over with Paddy."

"Oh, Paddy already is it? What's he like? I know the name, Paddy McHenry, but I can't put a face to him."

"Young, mid, maybe late twenties, friendly, but very professional, not your usual number cruncher type, lively looking, y'know, like he'd grasp the chance to run a business himself if he'd the money to spare. As I said, he wants you to come in next week too."

Gail looked over the list.

"I know a few accountants who bank in the branch. Maybe when we tell Jo, Aiden would give us a bit of advice on advertising and marketing that would help; I haven't a clue about all that."

Cassie offered her tea or coffee.

"I'll not, thanks, I need to get my skates on or I'll be shoppin' in the 24 hour. I'm usually organised by this time of the week, but it's hardly been a normal one, my head's all over the place," Gail said.

"We'll have a quick brainstorming session, I've thought of a name for our business already," Cassie paused, "'Nitty Gritty Grime Busters', I've Googled it 'n' all, there's only one company called that on record, and it's in America. What d'ya think, see what ideas we can come up with for the corporate image, y'know the sign on the side of the van and all that."

Gail nodded, dubious. "Okay…"

"Right, say the first thing that comes into yer head when I say, 'Nitty Gritty Grime Busters.'"

Gail grinned and replied, "Cagney and Lacey…remember, from years ago."

She was referring to an American detective show from the nineteen eighties, re-runs of which appeared from time to time on one of the satellite channels.

Cassie nodded, looking bewildered.

"Not getting' it. You on drugs or somethin'?"

Gail explained, "It's a play on words, Grime Busters/ Crime Busters - get it?"

"Right, go on."

Cassie didn't look convinced.

"Two women on broom sticks, Cagney and Lacey's faces superimposed on them, flying through the sky, one in front of the other."

Cassie was warming to it.

"Go on."

"Their right hands gripping the broomsticks, with maybe a bucket dangling from each of their right arms, a chamois leather hanging over the bucket edges…" Gail was on a roll, "…and their left arms, extended into the sky, projecting a miracle duster each, you know the ones on expandable handles, Luke Skywalker light sabre style, with the logo underneath reading, 'Fighting the Filth!'" Gail went on, "and if we decide to advertise on TV or radio their theme music playing out, Da Da Da   Da Da Da…"

Cassie joined in, "Da Da Da   Da Da Da…" Then stopped, despondent, saying, "We're crap at this!"

Gail was dejected.

"*You're* crap at it! That was 'Hill Street Blues' you were hummin'!"

Cassie threw a folded up newspaper at her and Gail ducked, laughing, as her aim missed.

"We'll talk to Jo, Aiden might be able to help. I rang her yesterday, told her about my redundancy, of course I didn't mention what we'd talked about, you hadn't even put your cheque in the bank yet."

Cassie looked pensive.

"An advertising agency's going to be expensive, but maybe if we talk to Aiden first maybe he'd help us out, point us in the right direction."

Gail laughed saying, "After that session, y'have to admit, we need all the help we can get."

"What about Dave, how did he take the idea?"

Gail looked down at her feet.

"Well, I didn't exactly say what it was."

"What exactly did ye say?"

"Oh, Cass, it's been really stressful, I wanted to tell him before I called ya yesterday morning, but I couldn't take another row this week, I mean we don't usually row much at all, y'know that. But, well, it's been a bit of an odd week. I just said that you may be able to put something my way; that was all. He was getting ready to leave for work, so he assumed it was a job in the building society you clean, a cashiering job..."

"Ach, Gail..."

"I know, I know! I will tell him tonight I'd every intention of it. Look, I'll rush on, get a bottle of wine to butter him up, then give him a massage..."

"Stop! Too much information!"

Cassie had her fingers to her ears.

"Eejit! I'll call you tomorrow night promise. And I'll talk to Jo tomorrow, we're meeting for lunch then shopping. She still hasn't found a dress, but its early days. I just hope she doesn't pick a big pink meringue for me."

"Sure you'd look lovely."

Cass left her to her car.

"Aye right. Have a good night, Cass, when are ya tellin' the kids?"

"Tomorrow, can't keep it any longer, not when Dave and Jo'll know about it. I don't want to keep it any longer anyway. I'll be able to open the accounts for them next week, so I may as well put a smile on their faces, eh?"

Gail hugged her.

"It's great news, Cass, great for you, but it's come at exactly the right time for me as well. I better head to this place before they close the doors."

Gail drove out of the street and Cassie walked back up her

front path and closed her front door. She was looking forward to the evening alone when she could think through how she was going to break her news to her family, prepare herself for the looks on her children's faces tomorrow, when at last her secret could be shared.

The road was still busy as Gail made her way home from the shops. Not normal Friday night busy, but steady. Today was pay day for a lot of people, and as she passed the coffee shops and restaurants, there seemed to be a steady flow of people entering and leaving. Perhaps, people like her last week, people who had received life changing news, drowning their sorrows, spending the redundancy. Or she thought wryly, maybe just well off bastards, who the recession hasn't touched, doing the usual Friday night thing, oblivious to the effect this bloody economic downturn was having on normal people's lives.

She was delighted for Cassie, and hoped against hope that Dave wouldn't put a dampener on their plans.

The house looked lovely from the outside. She always loved her house as she approached it in the winter, lamps glowing in the downstairs rooms, the fire flickering in the living room, the inevitable computer screen casting its light in the other front room, where her daughters sat, listening to music, watching movies, talking, laughing and planning the lives that lay ahead for them, far, far away from this dull, boring place. Just as Jo and Cass and she had done. Sure things would be different for them, better for them, sure the road ahead would be littered with chances and opportunities at every juncture, every crossroads. It would just be up to them, to decide which one to take. Sure, that they wouldn't settle for the lives their parents lead, how could they?

An image of Cass and herself came to her, as she pulled into her driveway, the two of them at fifteen or sixteen, in Cassie's bedroom preparing for a night out in a disco at the local hotel. It was Christmas. She remembered the lights from the trees lit the road, as they headed toward the town. On foot, too poor to afford a taxi, Cassie in a black taffeta dress, gypsy style, dark red hair in loose, full curls, cascading around her shoulders and Gail in a green satiny outfit with a Ra Ra style skirt, hair big, blond and bold, sprayed to look glam, but not to move. Both slim, sexy and salubrious. Laughing, always laughing.

They were invincible, ready for anything life threw at them. Although it seemed like yesterday, it also seemed like very long ago, in a place, far away. A place only memory could reach.

Gail got out of the car, and waved at Dave sitting in the front room. He came into the driveway to help her unpack the car. It was almost ten. "That took a while, I thought you'd run away with a Kiltie."

"I was snoggin' yer man behind the bacon counter, Gorgeous George."

"Oh that's alright then, did he give ye extra rashers?"

The shopping packed away, they returned to the front room. Gail poured two glasses of wine and handed one to Dave, she sat down in the chair opposite him.

"Can you turn the music down a bit? I want to talk to you."

The girls were still at the computer in the other room, and earlier in the evening she'd dropped Josh off for a sleepover with a mate. Gail knew she had to tell Dave of her plans tonight.

"I don't like the sound of this. Last week you tell me you're losing yer job, what is it this week, oh I know, yer leavin' me for Gorgeous George from the bacon counter."

"I can't help myself, Dave, it's the lure of all those thickly sliced rashers."

He drank from his wine glass and waited.

"Remember yesterday morning, I told you Cassie may be able to put something my way? Well it's not a job exactly, more a business proposition, a partnership to be precise."

"With who?"

"With Cass. Okay, I'll start at the beginning. Remember she called up on Wednesday with a bottle of wine?"

He looked sheepish, recalling the row they'd been having as he opened the front door.

"Of course, I remember."

"Well, after I finished moanin' to her about my redundancy, I realised she must have a reason for calling with wine, y'know, because we'd all been out together on the Saturday night before. So I asked her if everything was alright and her eyes lit up, and she says, 'I've won £500,000 on a scratch card!'"

"Jesus! Good for Cass! Where'd she buy it?"

Gail had Dave's full attention.

"I dunno, somewhere in the town, that's not the point. Isn't it brilliant? Anyway, she told me it had happened the previous Friday and she'd got the cheque an' all and she was going into her bank to get some advice on the best way to invest it short term 'cos she's thinkin' of startin' her own cleaning business. She has seventeen years' experience of workin' as a cleaner, and she said since she'd had it confirmed that she'd won such a big amount she knew it was her big chance. Knew the money could change her life completely if she made it work for her. She knows the kind of money the companies she works for charge the client, so why shouldn't she set up and get a share of it, make a living that way? I know it sounds like a fortune, but it's not really, not in this day and age. She's right, Dave, if she starts spending, it'll go quickly and she'll be back to square one, but if she sets up in business, it will change her life. She said she knew she needed a partner and she had thought of me, but she didn't think I'd give up the security of my job in the bank. Well, when she heard I'd been made redundant, she asked me to go in with her. What d'ya think, Dave?"

"I think it's brilliant for Cass, what sort of money are ya talkin' about fer a partnership? And she may have experience, but what do you know about cleanin' or runnin' a business, Gail?"

"Sorry?"

"Ach, don't be like that, Gail. I know you know how to clean a house, but there's more to it than that. For a start those people have to use those big machines, the floor polishers, that's gonna be a fortune on liability insurance alone."

"We've all that to learn, I'm not exactly thick."

"I'm not saying yer thick, Gail...it's out of the blue that's all. What's the initial outlay gonna to be?"

"Cassie has an appointment in the bank next week, with a business adviser and she'll go over all that with him. She wants me to go in to see him with her. It's a chance, Dave, before we go through the redundancy money. God knows, there'll be little chance of me getting another job in the present climate."

They were silent for a few minutes. Gail kept quiet to give Dave time to digest the idea. His music played quietly in the background, The Ramones. Gail struggled to recognise the song. *Not music to be listened to at low volume,* she thought. She didn't want to increase it, though, almost frightened to breathe too loud, in case she broke the mood. Dave liked Cassie and she felt sure he would agree to the plan. She waited for his response.

"Who's this boy she's gonna see in the bank, do ya know him?"

"Just by name, but he has a good reputation and Cass had a short meeting with him today, she said he seemed sound. He suggested I came in with her next week, after we've got our plans worked out more thoroughly."

"So you've already said yes to Cass, before you discussed it with me?" he said, looking at her, his eyes dancing with mischief.

"No, no, God no. She just mentioned to him, that she may have a friend interested in a partnership, that's all. She knew I'd still to talk to you," she lied.

"I'm not sayin' yes or no at the minute, but get yer heads together, work out the practicalities, then go in and see this fella, by all means. Let's see how much money's needed before you make the commitment, okay? Five hundred grand, eh? Fair play to Cass, I think I'll buy a few tomorra."

Gail knew that was as good as a yes from her husband. She wouldn't push him further tonight. She bent to kiss him, as she reached for the bottle of wine.

"What's that for?"

"Just love ya, that's all."

She moved away from him to turn the music up and they settled down on the sofa, just a normal Friday night, but Gail's heart was soaring. She was really going to do it. She and Cassie were going to start a business.

Dave's voice broke into her thoughts, "Gail…"

"Yeah?"

"Remember, next time yer talkin' to Cass…"

"Yeah?"

"Ask her where she bought it!"

Aiden arrived at his parents' house just after seven; Deirdre hugged her son close and whispered, "It's good to see ya love, c'mon in."

She ushered him into the living room, her mother looked up expectantly.

"Look who's here to see ye mum," she announced.

He rushed across the room and hugged his grandmother.

"How ya doin', Granny? Are they lookin after ya well?"

"The best, son, the best. Yer lukin' well, I believe yer gettin' married?"

Benny and Deirdre exchanged a look. At least she'd remembered that.

"I am indeed, I believe yer goin' to stay fer awhile to help Mum shop fer an outfit fer the wedding, God knows she needs help when she gets started, are ye fit to carry bags, Granny?"

She laughed and hugged him back.

"I'll stay 'til they get sick o'me, then I'll go back home. Everybody likes their own place, isn't that right, son?"

"Ah you'll be fine here fer a while, sure you've no good shops out there in the sticks. It'll pass the winter for you. I'll bring Sarah round to see you tomorrow."

Her mother nodded, but Deirdre knew by the look on her face, the distance in her eyes, that Mary Devlin had no recollection of who Sarah was. Her own great granddaughter whom she loved dearly, who had visited her at least half a dozen times a year since she was born. Aiden, also sensing her confusion, changed the subject.

"So who do you think's goin' to win the match tomorrow?"

Mary looked puzzled.

"Match, I don't know…"

"The rugby, Granny, ye'll have to get used to it if yer staying here, yer man's a fanatic…" he said, indicating his father.

"Don't you listen to him, Mum, we'll hit the town… get you some nice new things for yer room, eh what d'ye say?"

"I like the shops…"

Benny interrupted, "C'mon into the kitchen, Aiden, the coffee's ready, you can help me serve."

The two men faced each other over the breakfast bar, talking in whispers as Benny poured the coffee.

"She looks well, but I can see already she's gone downhill since the New Year. How's Mum?"

"Tired. I'll get a chance to talk to her later, she still thinks hiring a nurse is an option we can do without. But I told you, if need be I'll see to it myself. I've the agency name now, so that's it. Yer granny only thinks she's goin' back to her house. How could we let her live alone again? It's just not goin' to happen. She's too far gone, but yer mother needs to keep her own interests for the sake of her sanity, we have to start as we mean to go on."

Aiden had been thinking over Jo's idea all afternoon. He knew his Dad was right, this arrangement would remain in place for the rest of his granny's days, she was too far gone to cope alone. If she couldn't even remember her great granddaughter whom she loved, how could she remember to lock her front door at night?

"I know it's early days, but have you had any more thoughts on renting the house?"

"As I told ye, Declan's goin' to put the feelers out in the university, see if anybody's interested. Meanwhile Geraldine will make arrangements to have the carpets and suite steam cleaned. As yer mother said, thank God her brothers have been attentive to the house. It's well presented despite its age, we'll place it with an agent as soon as Ger's got it spruced up with the steam clean. If it's kept dry there should be no bother letting it, the trouble will start if it's allowed to lie unoccupied though the remainder of the winter. Geraldine and Liam will keep an eye on things of course, but they've their own lives to get on with, God knows they've carried enough on their own up until now."

Benny arranged biscuits from the packet onto the plate and said, "C'mon, we need to be careful what we say, we don't want her overhearin', you carry the pot in."

Aiden sat in his parents' living room drinking tea and eating biscuits. They chatted for over an hour and in that time he knew his Dad was right, his granny was far gone. If they had decided to place the house with an agent he needed to talk to him about Orla's predicament sooner rather than later. As it neared eight Benny rose to carry the tray in and make a start on the meal.

"I'll head on and let you folks get yer dinner."

Aiden rose with him to carry the coffee pot back to the kitchen.

"No rush, son, I just want to get it prepared, I'm sure yer Granny's gettin' hungry."

"Don't be changin' yer routine on my account," said Mary, but they knew she was ready for her dinner, she ate by the clock, they'd learned Geraldine normally delivered her meals by six.

The two of them left the living room and entered the kitchen.

"We haven't eaten yet either, I better head on. Dad, about the house, Jo had an idea earlier, but it'll keep 'til later, I'll give you a call around ten thirty. If ya can't talk just say yer watching a programme ya don't want to miss, okay?"

Benny, Deirdre and her mother sat around the dining room table eating in companionable silence, all of them hungry after the long day and too tired to make more than small talk after the events of the week. By nine thirty Mary's eyes were closing, but she was too polite to say she wanted to go to bed.

Benny nudged Deirdre who was close to nodding off herself and she picked it up.

"Want to go up to bed, Mum? It's been a long day."

Mary was grateful for the opportunity. Benny stood to kiss her goodnight, feeling her frail old bones through the fabric of her cardigan. As she hugged him tightly back he had no doubt they had done the right thing in bringing her to live with them.

Deirdre stayed with her until she was safely settled in the bed.

"This is a great big house, love, I'll be losing myself in the mornin' tryin' to find my way down the stairs."

Although Deirdre knew she was joking she reassured her, "Benny and me are just across the landing, just call out if you need anything, don't be attempting those stairs on yer own, the intercom's on beside the bed so we can hear you, just call out if you need us."

She didn't want to tell her mother the intercom was actually a baby listener, they had kept it on hand from when the grand children were small. Deirdre kissed her mother's cheek gently, and left her to rest.

Chapter 13

WHEN HIS PHONE RANG AT ten thirty Benny had almost forgotten the earlier exchange with Aiden.

"Aiden!"

He spoke to his son and then turned to Deirdre, "I'll take it in the other room."

He left Deirdre to watch the end of the movie and made his way out to take the call. As Aiden told him about Orla and her need for a place to stay, Benny listened, nodding into the phone.

"I know yer probably thinking as I did, it's more likely to be a bit of a row that's got out of hand, but Jo knows her well, she's convinced it's serious. Look there's no point in me telling you second hand I'll put Jo on…"

"Hi, Benny. I just found out about Orla's situation yesterday, she took me out for lunch and explained, remember how I'd been saying last week she seemed to have lost interest in the business, ringing in with excuses and expecting me to work my days off this past while back, well she said she felt she owed me an explanation. Apparently Seamus her husband has been knockin' her about for some time now. She'd been tryin' to hide it by staying out of the way, not turnin' up to work, lying low until her bruises disappeared. Well I'll tell ya, Benny, they were there for all to see yesterday. All one side of her face and a swollen lip as well. It all came to a head on Sunday. She's staying in a safe house at the minute. I offered her a room with me, but she wouldn't accept on account of Corey. She wasn't hysterical or anything, on the contrary she was calm. She's already been to a solicitor, says she'll be back in work as soon as her face heals up. Her solicitor has applied for protection orders for her, should he decide to look for her in the shop again. He called on Monday, but I lied for her, told him she was in England at a trade show. When Aiden mentioned about you all considerin' renting his granny's house last night I thought of Orla, but I didn't want to say anything then. I know how Deirdre must be feeling and it seems callous to jump in talkin' about renting her mother's house out when she's only just left it, but…"

Jo barely stopped for breath. Benny could tell she was upset about this young woman she worked for. Of course, Benny had met her now and again in the shop, he didn't really know her though. If appearances were anything to go by Orla looked like a young woman who had it all, immaculately groomed, designer clothes and the obligatory sports car. But he had lived long enough to know you couldn't judge by appearances, he was prepared to accept that what Jo said was true.

"Derry, though, I mean don't they have one of those studio apartments out Hillsborough direction, is she prepared to travel or is she thinking of selling the business and headin' back to Dublin, d'ye think?"

"Absolutely not, Benny. That was my first reaction, too, I put it to her and she says she'd be willing to travel if she gets the right place, but she wants to be as far away from her husband as possible."

"I trust yer instincts, love. God help the girl, I'll talk to Deirdre and see what she thinks. I'll tell Aiden tomorrow when he calls round with Sarah."

"Thanks, Benny, I appreciate that. Make sure to tell Deirdre I'll understand if you haven't decided on letting yet, it must've been an awful hard week for her and Geraldine. I'll see you both on Sunday anyway. Here's Aiden."

His son finished off the conversation. "So there ya go, I'll leave it with you to talk to Mum and see what she thinks, g'night, Dad. See you tomorrow."

Benny shook his head as he ended the call and walked back in to talk to Deirdre. She'd already reached for the remote to turn the volume down. It wasn't like Aiden to call when he'd just seen them.

"Everything alright?"

"Fine with Aiden and Jo, but it seems that young girl Orla who runs the gallery has been beaten up by her husband…"

Deirdre jumped in saying, "Oh my God, is she alright?"

"Yes, she is now, it happened on Sunday apparently…"

Benny could see Deirdre was trying to work out why Aiden had called at this late hour to tell them someone else's week old bad news. "She needs a place to live, she took Jo out for lunch yesterday to explain, it seems it's been going on for some time…"

"That explains why she kept takin' time off from the shop…" Deirdre said.

"Yeah, she wants to keep the business on, but she's had enough, apparently she's started divorce proceedings. At the minute she's staying in one of those women's refuges. Jo offered her a room with her, but she turned it down, said she couldn't think of it with wee Corey in the house, s'pose she's afraid of yer man comin' lookin' fer her…bringing trouble to Jo's door…anyway when Aiden told Jo last night that yer mother had agreed to come back with you and yis were considering puttin' the house up for rent, well …Jo didn't say anything at the time, but she thought the girl needs a place to stay, she doesn't want to be anywhere near her husband, doesn't mind travelling…it might be worth asking."

Deirdre looked surprised.

"She's probably still in shock, that wee girl with her designer clothes and flash car wouldn't live in an old tumbling down farmhouse in Derry."

"Well, Jo seems to think she'd be glad of it. I suppose she just wanted to ask before we place it with an agent, if you don't think it's a good idea she'll understand."

Deirdre considered it.

"It would help her and it would help us, keep the house dry and lived in while we see how the land lies…but it's a bit of a distance to travel, Benny."

"She's not in Belfast every day and I suppose in that motor she drives, she'd be in Belfast from Derry in about four minutes flat, allowing for traffic!"

"Ah right enough, it is a flying machine. Poor Orla, you can never judge the book by the cover…I've to ring Geraldine around eleven. She said if Mum wasn't asleep by then she'd wait for the call anyway. She'll not settle if she doesn't hear from me. It'll do no harm to ask her what she thinks of the idea."

Benny hugged her, and they sat down on the sofa together and held hands.

"You've had a rough week, we've done the right thing y'know. It's goin' to be hard I know that, you could see the look on yer mother's face when Aiden mentioned Sarah, she didn't remember her own great granddaughter…Geraldine's been keepin' a lot from us, but she's also been hiding the truth from herself, you can tell that by things you observed yerself throughout the week. Jo picked it up at New Year, she said as much to Aiden."

"Did she, what did she say?"

"He was telling me last Friday night when we met for coffee, when they'd gone up at New Year to see yer mother with Corey. It seems Aiden phoned Geraldine beforehand so that she'd know to expect them at a certain time, but when they arrived yer mother picked up the phone and told Geraldine, 'Deirdre and Benny are here with young Aiden…'"

"Jesus…"

"I know. Geraldine put her right and she made a quick recovery saying she knew well enough who they were and she was just a bit mixed up. Jo noticed it at Christmas as well, but she put it down to the fact that the house was packed, it would have been easy enough for any of us to get confused. It seems she talked to Kate about her fears, Kate's mother-in-law lived for many years with dementia and she advised Jo to mention it to Aiden. She did and he agreed to talk to you about it, but God help him he couldn't bring himself to do it."

Benny sniffed back the tears, and looked down at Deirdre who was crying outright for the first time that week, allowing the sobs to release the pain, that had been building up in her chest, to free the lump that had been gagging her throat, at last. The tension of the week had taken its toll, but knowing that a stranger had seen what she'd missed herself, broke her heart.

"I'll say to you what I said to Aiden love, don't beat yerself up, it's the people closest who are the last to see the signs. D'ye think I'm not askin' myself how I managed not to see them? Jo couldn't bring herself to say anything to you in case she'd got it wrong."

They sat and held each other in the dying glow of the firelight. Benny stroked Deirdre's hair as she cried herself out, clinging to each other in the knowledge that they had entered uncharted waters. That all of them had. As her sobs died down they had sat in silence watching the flames flicker in the hearth until they almost faded.

An hour had passed without them noticing, then Benny had risen and placed a log on the still hot mass of coal, bringing it back to life and Deirdre back to reality. Deirdre sipped the glass of red wine, she felt released after the bout of tears. She still had to phone her sister.

It was just after eleven thirty. She walked to the kitchen and splashed water on her face, drying it with a paper towel, while Benny poured another glass of wine for her. Just to be sure she went up the stairs to check on her mother. She couldn't risk this conversation being overheard. Benny had put music on low, to relax her no doubt. She hit the button and dialled Geraldine's number. The phone was answered almost before it rang.

"It's me, Geraldine. Sorry it's later than we agreed. It's been a long night. Everything's okay, Mum's in bed sleeping like a baby. How are you?"

She took another sip of wine as her sister spoke, "I'm fine," she lied, "I just couldn't rest 'til I heard from you, that's all."

"The girls were here today, they'd laid on a special lunch for her and Benny gave her flowers, then Aiden arrived around seven, he stayed for an hour, and we'd dinner shortly after eight. The poor oul crater was exhausted, she was in bed by half nine. Why I didn't ring earlier…Aiden rang around half ten, it seems Jo had been thinking about a friend of hers renting the house if we decided on it. She only found out yesterday, Orla the girl who runs the gallery, was beaten up by her husband the other day. She's left him, needs a place to stay and Jo thought it might be a possibility that Mum's house would suit her."

It still felt strange for Deirdre to refer to her old home as *Mum's*; she'd hardly come to terms with the fact that her father was dead, a year on.

"I know it's very soon, she said she didn't want to sound callous, but if we are, well…"

"Dear, dear, that's awful for the poor girl, of course Jo's concerned for her. What do you think?"

They discussed the possibility of letting their mother's house, a possibility they'd discussed already this week. But this time there was a potential tenant, a scenario they had not been prepared for, not so soon. After a few minutes Deirdre could hear the tiredness in Geraldine's voice, a tiredness she'd been trying to keep at bay all day herself. They agreed to talk it over the next afternoon, after Deirdre had returned from her visit to the shopping centre with her mother. Geraldine wished her luck with it.

She thought that strange. *How much luck could a trip to the shops need?* She was to find out.

111

Chapter 14

CASSIE HAD BEEN AWAKE FROM before six. She lay listening to the radio as she did every Saturday morning, her head was spinning since she had lodged the cheque yesterday.

Shiralee had told her she would have to bring her son and daughter in to open the bank accounts for them. Only a few more hours and she'd be able to share her good fortune with them. As she thought of their reaction she couldn't stop a grin from spreading all over her face.

The early morning D.J. played the next track introducing it with the words, "Here's a song to get yer feet tapping at this time of the day, Mental As Anything, 'Live it Up' …"

As the opening bars of the song rang out, Cassie lay in bed wiggling her feet in time to the rhythm, had it not been for waking her son she would have leapt out of bed and danced around the room! Yes! It was time for her to live it up, at last! She was a bit concerned that Gail hadn't actually spoken to Dave yet, but she trusted her. Gail knew her husband well, she would pick her moment. Dave and Cassie had always gotten on well so hopefully he'd go along with Gail's instinct and be prepared to take a chance on their venture.

She showered and gave the bathroom a quick clean, but this morning, she was only going through the motions, until Lara arrived at one with Mia. Cass had agreed to keep Mia overnight, to allow her daughter to have a night out. Lara would be able to hit the town with a heart and a half tonight, when she heard what was coming her way. And as for Dean, he always said money didn't matter to him, at eighteen he was the 'King of Cool', but she would be prepared to bet his face would light up with the news as well, when he heard it.

Her heart went out to him, he'd sent off three more job applications yesterday. Maybe there would be some course he'd want to do, that she could support him through, when he had time to take in her change of circumstances.

She had decided to give in her notice on Monday; she was looking forward to it. The idea of the four weeks of working for someone else didn't bother her now. If her plans worked out it would be the last time she ever worked for anyone, but herself.

She heard Dean get out of bed and walk across the landing around eleven, she busied herself ironing, watching some eejit on TV cooking scallops and some unidentifiable green mush in a pan of hot oil, all topped up with fresh cream. He whooshed it around with a spatula until the cream merged completely with the green mush, resulting in a paler, but no less unappetizing-looking concoction. Then he piled it onto a scallop shell, fired a couple of slices of garlic bread and two tiny cherry tomatoes onto the side, proclaiming it, "Beautiful!"

"Aye," muttered Cass "Yer word's enough!"

"Mornin', Ma, I see yer still talkin' to yer imaginary friend!"

"Mornin', son, I'm just watching this eejit servin' up a dog's dinner. Watch yer man's face..."

The obligatory 'soap star' had been wheeled in to stand by Chef Man's elbow and sample his delights.

"Well, wha'd'ya think, Chris?"

They both watched as the actor called Chris tucked in greedily. The expression on his face saying he'd just burnt the gob of himself as the roasting hot liquid did its work on his tongue, rendering him speechless, his face turning puce. They laughed out loud at the onscreen antics as Chef Man rushed to pour Chris Soap Star a glass of water, saying, "Apologies, mate, I may have heated that just a touch too much!"

"State o'ye!" cried Dean, who was loving it.

Cass watched her son's glee filled face as she ironed, and thought he didn't laugh often enough.

The time dragged until one, when at last she heard Lara push the buggy into the hall.

Cassie served the quiche and chips she had been preparing as Lara took Mia's overnight bag up the stairs, calling out, "I've put her fleecy jammys in as well as her new silky ones, she likes the silky ones, but it might be a bit cold yet for them..."

Cassie went through the motions of general chit chat until they were all seated to eat. Lara and Dean got stuck in to the meal, while she played with hers, and helped Mia sort out her knife and fork. They ate hungrily, apart from Cass, she was too excited. The plates almost cleared, she could hold back no longer.

"I've some news for ye," her son and daughter both looked up alarmed, "it's alright, I mean good news. I've won £500,000!"

Lara literally spluttered her mouthful of tea across the table. Cassie grinned, ripping off a piece of kitchen roll and handing it to her daughter. Dean was also grinning like a Cheshire cat, he spoke first, saying "Good fer you, Ma, does that mean you've given up your cleaning jobs?"

"Not yet, I'm handing in my notice on Monday, I only got the cheque yesterday. I was afraid to say anything until I took it to the bank in case it was 'The Bank of Mickey Mouse', but there's no doubt it's the real thing. I've taken advice on investing it, and I'll be opening bank accounts for both of you later in the week, when it clears."

Lara had recovered herself.

"Was it the lottery, Ma?"

Cassie told them the full story of the scratch card the previous Friday.

"You've kept that to yerself fer a week?"

Lara was beyond excited, her eyes were on stalks. Mia had no idea why everyone looked so happy, but she was walking round the table clapping madly anyway.

"Well, I had to tell someone, I went up to Gail's on Wednesday night and we'd a few glasses of vino to celebrate!"

Dean remembered his 'Toy Boy' comment.

"So that's what ye were at. Yer a mystery woman, Ma, and there's me thinkin' I was gettin' a new Daddy."

Lara looked intrigued as Cassie shook her head, saying, "Never mind, I'll explain later…anyway what I'm planning on doin' is starting up a business, a cleanin' business. I've asked Gail to go in with me." She noted their concerned expressions. "Don't worry yer mother's not daft, it'll be her own money she's investing. Gail's a mate, but I've waited too long fer this chance, to be financing anybody apart from my own family. By coincidence, Gail was told she was being made redundant last Friday, so it's an ill wind. I'll be needing a partner and she'll be out of a job, so we're goin' to give it a go, if her husband's in agreement, she was going to tell him about the plan last night."

Dean was delighted.

"God, Ma, yer a dark horse, my mother, a business tycoon!"

"Easy on, tycoon might be takin' it a bit far, but we'll make a good livin' out of it, I'm sure of it."

"Is it the right time though, I don't want to be a pessimist, but what about the recession?" Lara came in.

"If it's not the right time, we'll hold off. I've thought of all that. People always need cleaners. We're going in to see a business adviser, in the bank, next week, I already had a short talk with him yesterday….so wha'd'ya think?"

Dean rose from his seat and kissed her.

"I think it's been a long time comin', good luck t'ye, Ma!"

Lara came to her senses, and also left her seat, to kiss her mother.

"What am I thinkin', askin' you twenty questions when you've had such great news. Of course, I'm delighted fer ya, Ma, Gail's sound, you and her will make a strong team, you go for it!"

"So you're both available to accompany me to the bank with signatures?"

Lara beamed.

"Try stoppin' us."

Corey was sitting watching television, his bag at his feet packed, Jo checked the time, just on ten, the doorbell rang and Corey jumped to his feet and ran down the hall. Jo followed, opening the door to her ex-husband.

Kieran was wearing his Brad Pitt smile.

"Dad!"

"Jo, lookin' well."

His son hurled himself at his father's legs.

"Hey Buddy Boy, ready for the road?"

He put his hand out and casually messed his son's hair.

Jo handed Kieran the overnight bag, with a tight smile.

"See you tomorrow at one, have a good time, Towser."

She hugged her son and waved as he piled into his Dad's beloved motor and disappeared down the street.

Ten minutes later she was outside Gail's house, her friend saw her arrive and signalled that she was ready to leave.

Two minutes later she was seated in the car.

"Where is it today?"

"I thought we'd try Ballymena again."

They had already exhausted Belfast city centre, and every surrounding town, in the quest for the perfect dresses over the past few months.

"So what's the plan? Are we going to completely redo the entire route?"

"Don't be so cynical, we'll find them today, I've a good feeling. But I am beginning to think Aiden was right, it would've been cheaper for the two of us to head to London for a weekend to shop, the amount of fuel it's taken to travel the ground we've covered. Lunch first yeah?"

"Yeah, we'll need sustenance."

The traffic was Saturday afternoon slow as they headed toward the Westlink and the motorway. Gail was bursting with her news, and as they entered the motorway she blurted it out, "Guess what?" She didn't wait for the response. "Cass won half a million on a scratch card!"

Jo turned to look at her, incredulous.

"Eyes on the road please, true bill, she's got the cheque an' all."

"YOU ARE JOKING! Jesus. Good for her. If anybody deserves it Cass does, she must be ecstatic."

"She's delighted alright, but she's keeping her feet on the ground, she's going to start up a business. She's a bit scared about taking the leap by herself though, reckons she needs a partner, so she's asked me!"

Jo turned to look at her again.

"Are ya serious?"

"I knew I should have kept this until we'd stopped drivin'!"

"Sorry, it's a bit of a shock after the mood you were in on Thursday morning when you called me. Brilliant, that's what I call great timing."

Jo decided to keep her news about Orla until they'd arrived, Gail was in such good spirits she couldn't bring her down yet with the sad news of her old colleague's circumstances. Alone in their thoughts until they reached the town centre, they followed the lanes of the motorway. Jo found a place in a central car park and brought the engine to a stop, turning to Gail. She'd have to tell her now, she didn't want to discuss the girl's fate in a public place. Orla hadn't asked her not to tell Gail so she wasn't betraying a confidence. If anything she seemed to want to make her situation known, to bring it out in the open at last.

"I'd a call from Orla last Monday, she couldn't make it in this week; she asked me to get Siobhan to cover."

"Not again; what's she playin' at?"

"She took me out to lunch on Thursday to explain. Apparently Seamus has been knockin' her about. Her face was a mass of bruises all along one side, she'd tried to cover it with make-up, but it was still visible. It seems it's been goin' on for some time and it all came to a head on Sunday. She's been staying in a women's refuge since then. It's over, she's divorcing him."

"Christ! I never liked the bloke, but I wouldn't have put him down as a wife beater. I met him at a few of the bank's Christmas dos. If anything, I'd have thought he was a bit of a womaniser, y'know all over you like a rash after a couple of vodkas, but not that. Poor Orla, all on her own up here, her whole family's in Dublin. What's she going to do?"

"She's not goin' home. She says that way he'd win. She wants to make a go of the business. She's comin' back in as soon as her face has healed. Her solicitor has put the wheels in motion for personal protection orders, from what I can gather that means he's banned from coming into the shop or anywhere near it."

"Yeah, I've read about those; he'd be arrested if he breached the order. Jesus, I wasn't expectin' to hear that. To be honest, I feel a bit guilty, I used to envy Orla. She seemed to have the Life of Riley."

"Yer not the only one. I used to look at her breezing in wearing her gladrags as I was sitting totting up my bank statement, making sure I'd enough left to get through the month, and I'd think, *It's well for you, you've no worries about anything apart from which new line to bring in, what's goin' to make ya the most profit.*"

"My mother used to say, if everybody's troubles were lined up side by side, you'd run to pick up your own."

"Ain't that the truth. She didn't ask me not to tell you so it's not like I'm betraying her confidence, but I wouldn't mention it in work, Gail."

"God, no. Some of them in there hated Orla for escaping the

nine to five they were trapped in themselves. No way. They'd be sympathetic, but secretly gleeful. No, I wouldn't give them the pleasure. I thought she'd've trusted me enough to call me for help though, instead of going to strangers."

"It was the way it happened, because it was Sunday morning she didn't feel she could land in on us with our families around us, she mentioned some girl Ellen from the bank, she'd considered calling her on Monday, but by that time she felt at ease in the refuge, safe."

"Yeah, Ellen would have put her up no bother. I'll not say anything though, I'll leave it to Orla who she tells."

"So, sorry to put a dampener on the day, but you had to know. Anyway I may be able to help her out. Remember I told you about Aiden's granny coming to stay with Deirdre and Benny? It seems she's worse than they feared."

She related the story Aiden had told her about the burnt pot and how Geraldine had been cooking for her for the past year.

"When I heard they were planning on letting the house I immediately thought of Orla, I'd just had lunch with her that day. It may seem a long way to travel, but I thought I'd ask, so Benny's going to put it to Deirdre. I'll see them tomorrow for lunch and find out if it's a possibility."

"Well, ye never know, it's a long way to us, but Orla used to go up and down to Dublin to visit her sister most weekends from what I remember, before Romeo came on the scene. The distance never seemed to bother her."

"Anyway, let's have lunch and hit these shops, there's serious shopping to be done."

"Oh, just before we do. Cass wanted me to ask if Aiden could give us some advice on advertising and marketing the business. We've an appointment with a business adviser in the bank on Wednesday. We want to have some sort of figures together, y'know, make it appear that we're not complete eejits. If he could give us some direction, and an idea how much it would be to go through his agency."

"Sure, I'll ask him tonight."

"Thanks, Jo."

They exited the car park and headed for a restaurant they liked for a quick lunch. Their conversation now devoted to Jo's favourite subject, the wedding, stopping along the way to window shop. It was shaping up to be a long afternoon.

118

That Saturday morning, Deirdre had set out to shop with her mother. They reached Forestside shortly after ten and Deirdre made a direct line for Marks and Spencer's.

As they rummaged through the rails, Deirdre had been stunned by how long it took her mother to walk around the store. She found herself stopping constantly to allow her mother to keep up. Although aware that trips to the shops had become less frequent for her mother since her Dad's death, she hadn't realised walking was such a chore. Geraldine did most of her shopping, but Deirdre had assumed it was out of choice, that it suited both of them that way and Geraldine had given her no reason to think differently.

After spending the best part of an hour and a half in one shop, Deirdre decided on an early lunch, steering her mother toward the nearest self-service café. The food on display consisted mostly of sandwiches and muffins. She lifted a tray for both of them.

"What d'ya fancy, Mum?"

Her mother had looked slightly bemused. Deirdre read out the types of fillings in the sandwiches, "Chicken and salad, tuna and salad, or what about a nice cheese and ham, Mum?"

Her mother smiled and tried to mouth the words after Deirdre, failing in the attempt, Deirdre thought, *Sweet Jesus she doesn't know what a chicken salad sandwich is...*

Deirdre made the choice for both of them, and they made their way across to window seats. She unwrapped her mother's sandwich and placed it on a plate in front of her.

As she watched Mary eat it with obvious enjoyment, she knew she'd made the right choice. They observed the passers-by through the huge window as they sat drinking their coffee. Deirdre felt lost for words.

"Did ye ever think ye'd see that many cars in the town?" Mary asked, as she looked out over the large car park, she must have thought she was on one of her long ago weekly shopping trips to Derry or Coleraine.

"It's not Derry, Mum, this is Belfast, remember?"

"Aye, I know."

She realised her mother said these words a lot of the time, now. She thought of their regular visits to her old home. In recent months she had noticed her mother ask questions she already knew the answers to, like, "Still workin' away, Benny?" He'd answer, "Sure, I retired a while ago, Mary." She would come back at him, "Ach aye, sure I know that." And to her, "How are things in the Royal these days, love?" And the reply, "Mummy, I left the Royal ages ago, remember?" To which she would respond, "Aye so ye did, I know that."

All of these incidents, and more, unrelated and disconnected, due to the days in-between, on the weekly visits seemed unremarkable. If her mum forgot the odd thing it was no big deal, she was getting older. The awful truth was, her mother didn't know much at all anymore.

Deirdre patted her hand, asking, "Fancy a wee bun?"

Her mother nodded and Deirdre beat a hasty retreat to the counter, out of her sight, she couldn't bear her Mum to see the pity, she knew must be written in her eyes. They would head home. This was enough for one day, for Deirdre anyway.

Back home in Stranmillis, Deirdre settled Mary into the seat by the fire, in the room where Benny sat watching the sport, she smiled back at him as he asked her if she had enjoyed her morning out, while Deirdre unpacked her bags in the bedroom. Benny followed her up and told her Geraldine had called.

"She knew you'd be out with yer mum so she didn't want to call the mobile, she said they've talked it over and both she and Liam are fine with that, if we are."

Deirdre nodded.

"God it's all movin' so quickly, okay we'll tell Aiden to give Jo a call or I'll maybe get a chance to call her."

"Leave it to Aiden, I'll go on down and sit with yer mum."

On her return to the room Deirdre asked Benny what he wanted for lunch, keen to go into the kitchen to get her thoughts together.

"What do you fancy, Mary?" Benny asked.

Deirdre couldn't go through that again so soon.

"It's okay we've eaten, you and Mum sit and relax and I'll make you something. Tuna and salad baguette?"

Deirdre didn't wait for his answer.

Benny nodded, despite the fact Deirdre was walking toward the kitchen. He usually liked to make his own eating choices, but Deirdre seemed edgy, ill at ease. It was only natural considering the decision they had all just made, but she hadn't been in good form on her return from the shops.

He chatted easily to his mother in law, all the while wondering what had upset Deirdre so on their trip out.

"What about Aiden and Sarah?" Benny called out to Deirdre, as she clattered around in the kitchen.

"Sure, he said last night they're not staying for lunch, he's taking her out. I'll make yours in the meantime."

Aiden arrived shortly after with his daughter. The child was delighted to see her great grandmother and ran to greet her. Mary smiled at the child, but the confusion was apparent on her face, as Sarah moved on to greet her grandparents. She was full of chat about school and her new cat, so it was unlikely that she had noticed that her great grandmother didn't remember her.

Aware of Aiden's reticence to explain his grandmother's condition to the child, Deirdre took her upstairs to view the present she had for her, and then ushered her into the kitchen for a drink. Aiden and his father chatted to the old lady, while Deirdre kept Sarah distracted. Already Benny was aware that this charade at normality was going to be much easier for him to play out than Deirdre, but then Mary wasn't his mother. For that very reason, he would find the part more comfortable to slip into.

He still didn't know what had upset Deirdre, when he had asked quietly in the other room, she had simply replied, "Ach, just something and nothing."

He had left it at that, knowing she would tell him later.

Aiden didn't hang about, sensing his mother's tension. He left to take his daughter to lunch at her favourite burger bar around one forty five. Deirdre saw him to the door.

"Geraldine rang, that situation we talked about, it's fine by them too. Give Jo a call and tell her it's okay to make arrangements. Tell her to call me on the mobile."

She said the words almost in a whisper, fearful of being overheard by her mother, who could always sense a conspiracy a mile away. But that was in the old days Deirdre reminded herself, they couldn't be too careful though, it still wasn't clear how much her mother could still grasp. Although confused, she was contented. It would wreck the whole plan if Mary rumbled that her house was about to be let, only a matter of hours, after she'd pulled the door behind her to "visit" her daughter and son-in-law.

Benny looked at the clock. It was shaping up to be a long afternoon. His wife needed to spend a bit of time out of the house, she'd been with her mother constantly now for over a week and the cracks were beginning to show. He knew the call from Geraldine wouldn't help her state of mind.

"Why don't you ring Janet, or one of yer other mates? Go fer a swim or a sauna. Mary and me can hold the fort on our own, can't we Mary?"

"Certainly."

Mary said that word a lot, too, Deirdre noticed. It was a one size fits all sort of word, she thought.

"I might do that. Are you sure you don't mind, Mum?"

The old lady nodded and smiled at Benny as he replied for her, "Of course, she doesn't mind, we'll watch the racin' do a few wee bets while yer away. Eh, Mary?"

She always reacted to Benny's patter.

"Yer a rogue, Benny Brannigan."

She screwed her hand into a fist and threw him a pretend punch.

"What's all this about? Ye gonnie tell me ye've given up the gamblin'..."

Deirdre smiled to herself, as she left the room to phone her friend, still listening to Benny and her mother banter each other, aware of how thick his accent became again when he was around her mother, or his own ones. Janet was up for a swim so Deirdre prepared to take her leave gladly. She was grateful for the time to rest her head.

The past week had been full on, walking on eggshells, trying not to offend Geraldine on one hand and on the other watching every word in case she gave the game away, and her mother realised exactly what they were plotting between them, realised her independence was gone for good.

Janet was at a loose end and was delighted at the prospect of a swim. Deirdre packed her things and slung them into the boot, grateful of the chance of respite for a few hours.

In Ballymena, their lunch finished, Jo and Gail rushed to the bridal shop. As they entered the shop Jo was surprised to hear the assistant call her name. Gail wasn't. She was sure they were known by name in every bridal shop in the land by now, such was the intensity of Jo's search for 'the dress.'

"Jo, I only just set the phone down, I left a message for you on your home number, but I had a feeling you'd be up this way today. I believe I have the very dress for you! The bad news is it's not in your size, but the good news is I have it on order in an eight, and I knew you'd want to see it anyway."

The assistant rushed to the rails and produced a sheath dress in oyster silk, dramatically holding it aloft for Jo's inspection.

Jo stepped forward and scrutinised its every detail, the bodice and main flow of the dress were covered in the tiniest embroidered shapes that told a fairy tale.

"I think you're right, it's perfect."

Turning to Gail for reassurance, she nodded back at her friend, it was exactly what Jo had been searching for. The assistant was delighted with herself.

"And for, Gail, isn't it?"

"Yes." Gail smiled.

"This…"

She rushed to the rails again and produced a simpler version of the wedding dress in the palest of greens. It was beautiful. But if she was honest, by now Gail would have agreed to wear a marquee in brushed nylon neon, such was her despair at the fruitlessness of their quest she was beginning to believe the dresses in Jo's head simply didn't exist.

"We should have your size, Gail. Do you want to try it?"

At last that was it. Jo paid a deposit on Gail's dress, not prepared to leave the shop with it and tempt fate. Still afraid that her dress in the correct size would not arrive, she held back from paying for her own before she'd tried it on. The assistant assured her it would be delivered within a few weeks, although there was talk of a French hauliers' strike, which may delay it slightly.

"Sure you've months yet, I was checking your dates in the contacts book. The eleventh of July isn't it? Don't worry Jo, that's the dress for you. I knew it as soon as I unpacked it. I'll call you the minute it arrives."

Jo gave the woman her mobile number as well and they left the shop elated.

"Didn't I tell ya I'd a feelin' about today? Oh, Gail, aren't they gorgeous? Understated but magnificent!"

"Just like us!"

They hugged each other like children at a birthday party.

"Right! Coffee and a huge piece of chocolate cake, I'll count the calories again on Monday."

As they ate their cake Jo's phone rang, Gail teased her, "That'll be yer woman, the dress has arrived!"

It was Aiden. He'd just left his parents' house. His mum had spoken to Geraldine late last night and they'd all slept on the possibility of offering the house to Orla. Geraldine had called today and agreed to her seeing it, with a view to rental.

"Mum wants you to give her a call, make arrangements for Orla to see it."

"That's brilliant, Aiden. I'll call her now, and guess what... I've found the dress!"

She went on to describe the dress in intricate detail, Gail was sure if Aiden was anything like Dave he'd nodded off after the words... "I've found the dress..."

Gail could hear he sounded delighted for her, though, not half as delighted as I am, thought Gail.

"Well, this is turning out to be quite a day, Deirdre and her sister have agreed to Orla viewing the house. I've to give her a quick call to make arrangements."

Gail nodded and continued to tuck into her cake, as Jo talked to her future mother- in- law.

"Geraldine's okay with it, Deirdre? I know it's all very soon, but I just have a hunch it'll be right for Orla. Can you talk at the minute?"

"Yes, I'm in the car. Benny suggested I go out for a while, have a break. So I'm going to meet a friend to go fer a swim. I've just had a trip to the shops with Mum, I took her to Forestside, thought it would ease her in gently rather than going into the town. Dear God, Benny's right I will need a nurse to help out for the sake of my own sanity. Poor Ger, no wonder she's a bundle of nerves. Anyway enough of me, I'll see you tomorrow. You're still okay for lunch both of you?"

"Yeah, of course we are."

"So, about the house; Geraldine's going to arrange to have it cleaned by professionals on Monday, y'know, the carpets and all that.

It would present better, but having said that, you know the girl's situation, if she's sitting in a refuge feeling depressed, you might feel you want to ring her now and let her see it as soon as possible. Even if it doesn't suit it might lift her mind. If she's interested we thought it would be better if you take her up, Jo. She's young and it may not suit, but it's our family home and she'll not feel free to turn her nose up to us, if she doesn't like it, what d'ye think?"

"If you're sure I'll call her now, I can take her up to see it when it suits."

"You go ahead, Jo, I'll see you tomorrow. Any luck today?"

"Yeah, I found it, not in my size though, but it's on order. I'll fill ya in on all the details tomorrow."

"Great, I'll look forward to it, love."

Jo related the conversation to Gail.

"Great, give her a call, see what she thinks."

Orla answered almost immediately.

"Orla, it's Jo, I've heard of a place to rent that might be of interest to you…"

Orla sounded cautious at first then excited. The location didn't seem to bother her.

"When can I see it, Jo?"

"Tonight if you want, I'm in Ballymena now, but I'll pick you up around seven if that suits…"

Orla didn't hesitate. Jo rang Aiden and told him to make his own arrangements for himself and Sarah.

"Yer sure you don't want me to drive her up? You've had a long day."

"No, I wouldn't embarrass her like that, Aiden, she hardly knows you. I'll grab something to eat when I get in, you look after Sarah and I'll see ya later. It'll mess up Saturday night, but she sounded so grateful I couldn't not offer to take her tonight."

"No worries see y'later," said Aiden before ending the call.

Gail finished her coffee as Jo attacked her cake.

"Quite a day all round, let me know how it goes, eh?"

The swim cleared Deirdre's head, and as she chatted with her friend in the café afterwards, Deirdre realised she had talked or thought about little else for a week, but her mother's condition.

125

Janet asked after Mary, but took the hint when Deirdre steered the conversation away from her problems. They spent an hour or more talking about nothing much. Janet had recently come through a divorce and heavy conversation was to be avoided at all costs, she'd had more than her fair share of that in recent months. It was exactly what Deirdre needed, a complete afternoon of relaxation and laughter with one of her closest friends.

They parted with a warm embrace, grateful for the chance to wind down in each other's company. The road back home didn't look half as grim. Benny had suggested Chinese takeaway for dinner, her mother loved Chicken Chow Mein. They would have a good night watching television together and tomorrow Aiden and Jo would be with them for dinner.

As she pulled into her own driveway Deirdre said aloud, "Count your blessings, Deirdre."

As Jo and Gail were setting out on their search for the dress, Orla was sitting quietly, in the refuge house. The day was cold and crisp, Orla looked out of her bedroom window and considered going out. She had done all of the shopping she needed to do yesterday and she didn't feel up to going into any of the shopping centres, as she usually would on a Saturday afternoon, but the quietness of the house was driving her crazy.

All of the children had been taken out by the workers for a trip somewhere. A treat for them, and much needed respite for their mothers. But for her, the absence of noise in the house just highlighted her feelings of sadness. Some of the mothers had taken the opportunity to have a day out themselves, shopping or visiting.

A few of the others were watching TV, a movie about some huge drooling dog and Anne Marie had gone to visit her family. She tried to read a book she'd bought yesterday, but her mind wouldn't allow her to take the words in. She had found herself re-reading page after page before throwing it to one side.

The strength she had mustered up by Thursday for her lunch with Jo and her dental appointment was beginning to ebb. Last night, she had allowed herself to take one of Seamus's calls, after forgetting to switch the phone off. When his name had appeared on the screen she had decided now was as good a time as any to talk with him. She had answered casually waiting for his reaction.

"What's the craic with this protection order lark, do ye think I'm some sort of mad man?"

"Yeah that's exactly what I think."

He changed his tack.

"C'mon, Orla. You know I love ya, it's just the oul drink, I'll keep it in check, c'mon home and stop this nonsense."

"I used to kid myself it was the drink, Seamus. You weren't drunk last Sunday morning.'"

"Right, have it your way, get yer stuff outta here by the end of the week, I'm sellin' up and goin' out to our Paddy in Australia, I've been considering it fer a while!"

"Oh, were ya thinking of telling me, Seamus? There's a recession there too ya know."

"I'm fuckin' tellin' ye now! Yeah, there may well be a bloody recession there too, but I'll be broke in the sunshine! Have your things outta here by next Friday or I'll bin them!"

"Fine. I will."

She had ended the call there, her hands shaking, as she set the phone down.

She'd gone downstairs and spoken to Carmel about going back to the apartment to get her belongings and she had advised her not to go alone, to arrange for a worker on duty to accompany her. Carmel checked the staff rota for the coming week and they'd made arrangements. While she felt brave enough, she had called Seamus back and confirmed she would be there next Wednesday morning with a friend, he had replied, "Suit yer friggin' self," and hung up.

The contact with him had drained her strength, left her feeling jittery and nervous, but it had confirmed, if she needed it confirmed, that she had made the right decision in leaving him.

She had slept badly and awoken that Saturday morning in a foul mood, a mood that so far had coloured the day. Her phone lay on her bedside table; she had left it on, confident that she was unlikely to hear from Seamus until she'd cleared the apartment of her presence. The ringing of it shattered the silence and she grabbed it, grateful for any diversion.

It was Jo. Orla thought at first Jo was telling her about a house in Belfast, when it became clear that it was out of town she was sitting bolt upright on the bed, as Jo explained the situation.

Chapter 15

ORLA AND JO HAD AGREED that Jo would pick her up in the car park of the safe house at seven that night. The hours dragged for Orla after she took the call, she made a quick meal for herself and showered again to pass the time. By six forty five she was outside the house pacing, hardly noticing the sharpness of the winter's night.

The headlights of Jo's car lit up the driveway and Orla rushed forward, delighted to see her, looking forward with anticipation to the house viewing.

Jo had the radio on.

"Do ya mind?"

"No, not at all. The house has been so quiet today, it's like a morgue. I was glad of your call, it's very good of you giving up your Saturday night fer me, Jo."

"I just hope I can help…"

She explained the situation with Aiden's grandmother, "Geraldine, Aiden's aunt, lives over across a nearby field and there are other neighbouring farms in the immediate vicinity, so it's not exactly isolated. And, of course, if you like it and agree to take it, Geraldine and her husband, Liam, would keep an eye out fer ya."

"I was reared in the country, so I'm no stranger to fields. My sister lives in a big old farmhouse in the Wicklow Mountains."

"I didn't realise that, Orla. I'd've had you down to be a townie through and through."

"No, I'm still a country girl at heart. I spoke with Seamus last night, he's in a right lather about the protection orders, on his dignity, asked me if I thought he was a madman. The audacity of him."

"You're not plannin' on meetin' up with him?"

"No way, I'm goin' up to clear my things out next week."

Jo did a double take.

"Not alone?"

Orla shook her head.

"No, one of the workers is going with me for support."

"Good."

"He told me he's goin' to Australia, sounded like he was just waiting for an excuse to bale out."

"Really?"

"Yeah, really. Can ye believe his cheek?"

"I shouldn't say it, but you really are better off out of it."

"Oh, I've no doubt about it, Jo. I just can't believe it took me so long to see it, that's all. I've been a fool, but it's over now. I wouldn't care if I never set eyes on him again."

They travelled the rest of the journey in relative silence, probably both anticipating Orla's reaction to the old house.

"Here we are."

Jo entered the laneway to the big old house, and they stepped out of the car, into the night. A frost was forming on the ground, and above them the huge expanse of sky twinkled with stars. They made their way to the front door, Jo held her breath as she opened it, afraid Orla wouldn't like it. She ushered her into the hallway and switched on the lights. Jo led her from room to room, rooms that still smelled of Mary's perfume, her presence strong, almost visible by the fireside in the old comfy chair, the smell of soot still evident, emanating from the hearth, which had so recently housed a fire. Jo had no doubt, she was the best person to show Orla round; Deirdre or Geraldine couldn't have coped with it.

As she turned to her for a reaction, she was surprised to see that Orla's eyes were brimming with tears. Orla shook her head, gathering herself to speak, "It's just like my sister's house. I love it."

She thought of the little picture frame with the prayer, sure her sister was with her, helping her, even though they hadn't spoken since she left Seamus almost a week ago. The house was exactly what she needed right now.

"I'll take it, Jo. And thanks, you've no idea what this means to me."

Jo held out her hand and squeezed Orla's arm gently.

"I think I do, Orla. I think I do."

They closed the front door and paused for a moment in the driveway as Orla took in her surroundings. The floodlit driveway, the lighting activated by their presence, up on the hill a neighbouring farm and across to their left Geraldine and Liam's house. The night was still and peaceful as Orla surveyed her soon to be new home.

Jo spoke, as they made their way to the car.

"That light up there is Deirdre's sister's place. They know we're coming up, said we were welcome to call. Now that you've decided to take it, we should probably go up and say hello. I know you'll want privacy, but as you can see it's not the sort of place you can do without neighbours. They won't intrude, but everyone looks out for each other up here."

Jo waited for Orla's response. In the floodlight she could see that Orla's make-up had camouflaged any sign of the bruising to her face.

Although Geraldine and Liam knew Orla wanted the house due to the situation with her abusive husband, Jo understood that she wouldn't have wanted to flaunt obvious signs of her beating to strangers.

"Yeah, we should, I'll have to meet them sooner or later. They won't have gone to any trouble I hope."

"No, of course not."

Jo knew Geraldine well enough to know she'd have sandwiches and cake prepared, but hopefully Ger would make it appear spontaneous. She needn't have worried. Geraldine and Liam, who minutes earlier had been sitting in their front room peering at them through binoculars as they stood in Mary's driveway, were discretion itself.

On the ring of the bell they counted ten before rushing to pull the door open, pretending to have been engrossed in a TV programme. Resounding from one of the outhouses, the barks of the family dogs, Jo picked up their spin, saying, "Don't switch it off on our account, we're just passing."

"Not at all, c'mon in, sit yerselves down."

Geraldine made her way to the kitchen and switched on the already boiled kettle, taking her time to make the tea, and uncover the trays of waiting sandwiches and cake, as Jo and Orla sat in the front room with Liam, chatting about the weather.

After a reasonable time lapse, Geraldine carried in the tea and trays of food. To take away from any embarrassment Orla may have at her predicament, Geraldine focused on Jo, "I was talkin' to Dee and I believe ye found 'the dress'!"

"Yes, it's hard to take in after all this time, but yes, I just have to hope they can get it in my size now."

The conversation seemed surreal to Jo, and considering Orla's situation, she decided to take the bull by the horns, "Orla loves the house. Don't ya, Orla?"

"Yes, it's lovely, really cosy and comfortable and just far enough out of town to be ideal for my present circumstances. If you're in agreement I'd love to rent it for a while."

Jo was relieved that Orla had referred to her situation. It dispelled any awkwardness that Geraldine and her husband may be feeling.

"We'd be delighted to have you, Orla. Now ye realise it's not ready yet. I've arranged to have the carpets and furniture steam cleaned on Monday, so it'll be a few days, but yes certainly it's yours from next week if you want it. I'm sure Jo has explained about Mum, she's not fit to be left alone, not anymore. I've been fooling myself until my sister's visit last week. Whichever way it goes with her care, she won't be returning to the house. It's been a hard fact to face, but now that we've talked it over, we know regardless of the findings when we have her assessed in hospital, the day will come when we'll have to tell her she won't be returning home. It's not that we're deceiving her in anyway, there's just only so much information she can process at the one time."

Geraldine began to fill up, but sniffed and carried on, "Anyway, Orla, that's not your concern, we'll exchange numbers and organise all the details over the next few days, if that suits."

Orla reached for a piece of paper from her bag and wrote her own numbers down for Geraldine and handed the paper and pen over for her to do the same.

Liam, usually a man of few words spoke up, "We understand you're coming up here for peace and quiet, we won't interfere with your privacy, but rest assured there's not much goes on up here that we don't know about. Our son Declan lives in the farm directly beside Mary's and the Dohertys are only a mile or two in the other direction, you'll be safe, girl. Make no mistake about that."

Orla liked his direct manner, "Thanks, Liam, I appreciate that."

"We'll discuss all the ins and outs with ya later, but ye saw the lights in the driveway and we had a camera installed for Mary and Johnny a lot of years ago, you'll be as safe as houses as they say."

The tea finished, Jo and Orla thanked them and rose to leave.

"Aiden has Sarah tonight, I don't want her to think I'm totally neglecting her. We'll talk to you during the week, Geraldine, Orla can keep me informed. Thanks again for the tea."

At the front door Geraldine and Liam shook hands with Orla as they confirmed the verbal agreement that sealed the fate of Mary's house. At the sound of their voices the barks from the dogs rang out again.

"Quiet you lot!" On Liam's words the dogs were rendered silent. "One of them's Mary's, if you want company."

"Liam! The girl works - she's no time fer a dog!"

"No, I'd love it. I haven't had an animal in years."

"C'mon and we'll introduce ye then."

They led the way to the outhouse, where the three sheep dogs lay together staring at them, the six gentle brown eyes staring out of the darkness, knowing not to disobey Liam's authority.

"That's Ant and Dec, I know, blame the grand kids. And this one's Mary's, Snapper."

Orla must have looked concerned.

"Don't worry he wouldn't bite ye, he's a tyre biter, thus the name. There's not a car enters these lanes that Snapper doesn't have a go at. He's the bane of the postman's life!"

In the car, Orla's mood was markedly lighter than it had been in weeks.

"I can't believe my luck, what strange timing. It must be hard for them though, when the old woman has been living there until so recently."

"In a way, it might make it easier for them. It would have broken Deirdre and Geraldine's hearts to see their old home become run down and unlived in. As she said, they both realise their mother's condition won't lend itself to solitary living anymore. It's been a hard fact for them to face, but now that they have, it seems to be for the best all round," Jo assured her.

In the farmhouse disappearing behind them, Geraldine and Liam sat silently drinking more tea. Liam looked at his wife tenderly as he reached out for her hand and squeezed it.

Geraldine squeezed his back, in response, gently nodding, incapable of words.

There were no words.

Jo broke into Orla's thoughts, as they headed out of the winding laneway.

"Oh, I should tell you, Liam mentioned their son in the neighbouring farm... his wife Molly died two years ago. She was only thirty eight, it was an awful time for all of them, as you can imagine. Declan was left with two teenage sons. They're seventeen and eighteen now, one of them's at the university, the other still at school." Jo, a great believer in fate, just thought she'd clarify the situation. "Anyway, they'll all look out for ya, Orla, I've no doubt about that, but they won't swamp you. They're not that kind."

"Thanks again for thinking of me, Jo. I'll call you on Tuesday after I've talked with Geraldine."

They travelled the narrow roads to the motorway and the rest of the journey back in silence. Jo turned the radio up, grateful for the light hearted Saturday night banter and music.

She drove into the car park of the safe house and dropped Orla off. As she turned the car, she noticed the spring in her friend's step as she entered the refuge and she was glad she'd spoken up.

It looked like Orla was sorted. Jo firmly believed that when a crossroads in life is reached, the hand of fate is ever present, there to guide us toward the road that is best for us. Only sometimes fate itself needs a nudge in the right direction.

The house was perfect for Orla. She thought of Declan, alone with his two boys in the neighbouring farm, and she was sure she'd done the right thing. She'd just have to wait and see.

Orla entered the house with a much lighter heart than she'd left. Going up to her room to collect her thoughts first, thinking she couldn't tell Anne Marie, not yet. Her friend had been out all day at her sister's. She would be back now, though.

Orla decided to leave it a few days before mentioning her good luck to her, remembering that Anne Marie was approaching her ninth week in the house.

Thinking of the conversations they had had, it was hard to believe they hadn't even known each other a week, the constant texting that got them through the long nights, from the polite, tentative, "R U OK?" "Yes thanx" of last Sunday night, to the, "Wot u doin'?" "Sleepin u eejit!" last night.

Their friendship had sustained Orla through the week and she felt sure it was strong enough to last. She didn't want to blow it by announcing, "I'm outta here!"

She feared that's how it would sound to Anne Marie, who got up each morning and waited for the postman, hoping that today he would bring her the news she had waited so long for.

No, she'd wait, who knew maybe the news her friend had longed for was just around the corner.

She looked into the front room where the women were watching television, and waved. Anne Marie caught her gaze and followed her into the kitchen.

"Coffee, please."

"It's manners to wait 'til yer offered."

Anne Marie grinned and asked, "Good night?" but her manner told Orla she was only being polite.

"Just a few coffees with a friend, what about you, how'd your day go?"

"Ye'll never believe it! Patricia, my sister, was closin' her blinds last night when she saw one of the neighbours doin' a moonlight!" Orla's face must have been a question mark. "Leavin' a place in a hurry after dark, a moonlight flit! It's what they do when they've debt or some other reason to leg it in a hurry. Anyway, Patsy watched them load the van and sail out of the street without a backward glance. First thing this mornin' she was down in the advice centre askin' fer the local representative, he's goin' to ring the Housing Executive first thing on Monday to see if there's any chance I can get it! He's not askin' if I can jump the queue, I've got the status. They just told me there was nothin' suitable in the area. Now we know there is. Isn't that brilliant?"

"Oh, Anne Marie, it is."

They hugged each other tightly both bursting at the seams with their turn of luck.

Orla considered telling her news, too, but decided it would keep until Monday, when hopefully Anne Marie and she would both be celebrating. For tonight, she was content to be happy for her friend, and hug her own secret to herself.

In the big sitting room, the movie had ended, to be replaced by a repeat of last night's chat show.

"Oh not that sycophantic toad!" someone complained.

"Oh get you, she's swallied a dictionary and it's comin' up in pages!"

"Toad's not that big a word, Charlene."

Charlene threw a cushion at her and threatened, "Watch yerself or I'll creep down in the night and eat all yer nice yoghurt, Lucy!"

"Will you two shut up, yer doin' my head in," Sue, one of the workers cut in, good naturedly.

Anne Marie marched forward to the shelf beside the TV.

"Right, let's have a nosey, there's bound to be something here we can watch."

She rifled through the selection of DVD's.

"Are y'jokin'… *Beaches, Sophie's Choice, Terms of Endearment, Ghost*…we'll pass the razor blades round now, will we? Ah, now yer talkin'…a bit o' Feelgood!"

She held the DVD case out with both hands for them all to see with the words, "Nobody puts Baby in the corner!"

They cheered at her interpretation of Johnny Castle's sexy American accent.

"Isn't it awful sad about him havin' cancer?"

"Jesus, Jane, you'd be quare craic at a wake!" Anne Marie turned on her.

Jane always seemed to have the knack of seeing two negatives for every positive. Of all the women in the house, Anne Marie would miss her the least.

"I'm only sayin' it's sad, that's all," Jane defended herself.

"I think we'd all agree on that, now can we put it on and enjoy it, please?"

The voices rang out from the other women, "Go ahead Anne Marie, let's have a perv at Patrick's Pecs!"

They all passed the rest of the night happy in each other's company, hanging onto the last remnants of Saturday night, as yet another Sunday loomed; Sunday the longest day of the week.

By the time the first five minutes of it had passed, Orla was snuggled under the cosy duvet, her head awash with her plans and dreams for the future; her future without Seamus.

Jo was right she was better off without him, she'd no doubt now. The idea of him, telling her he'd been thinking of starting a new life in Australia, had she ever featured in that life-plan? Maybe it was just bravado, his way of saying he'd gotten used to the idea of life without her, who knew?

As she snuggled down and waited for sleep she thought, *Who cares? I've the chance to make it alone now. I'll get through Sunday knowing Monday will herald the next phase, my chance of a fresh start. No more paper bags under the sink, no more nights with pseudo friends, it's my time to surround myself with real people, real friends who see me, not a useful appendage, a designer accessory, to be dangled and discarded on a whim.*

She drifted off to sleep, dreaming of green fields, blue skies and wide open spaces. She hadn't slept so soundly in years.

As her home in Derry was being viewed by a stranger, Mary sat contentedly in Deirdre and Benny's front room; the three of them sitting around the fire, watching Saturday night television after eating their Chinese meal.

Her mum began to fade as the programme neared an end; they watched her head nod, as she struggled to keep her eyes on the TV screen.

"You've had a busy week, Mum. It's alright to say you want to go to bed, we won't be offended."

"I know ye won't, love. Yer both very good to me, but just say when ye want to take me home. I don't want to overstay m'welcome."

Benny, noting the guilty look on Deirdre's face, jumped in.

"Sure ye've only just arrived, are ye fed up with us already, Mary Devlin?"

"No, I am not indeed, Benny Brannigan," she said, giving him a playful slap.

"What's with all this abuse? I'm black and blue and yer only here ten minutes," then seriously, "now you listen here, missus, yer here to stay fer as long as ye like, relax and enjoy being looked after by yer big daughter. Sure, what else would she be doin'?"

"I love her," Mary said, as she looked proudly up at Deirdre.

Deirdre's eyes filled up with tears, and she swung round before her mother noticed. She left the room to prepare her mother's bed.

Benny knew she was feeling bad about the decision they had all made about her mother's house without her knowledge, but what other way could they go about it considering the state of her mind.

136

And there was the nurse to be organised on Monday.

How the hell were they going to broach that one?

He put that thought to the back of his mind, remembering what Liam and he had said to Deirdre and Geraldine, "Take it one day at a time, it's the only way."

And it was. He knew that, only too well.

Geraldine rang shortly afterwards.

"Yes, it's okay. I can talk."

How many times had he heard those words since yesterday afternoon? Benny gathered from the conversation he was overhearing that Orla had decided to take the house.

He went into the kitchen and rang Aiden from the mobile as Deirdre talked with her sister.

"Geraldine's on with yer mother at the minute, it looks like that girl Orla has decided to take it. Jo's headin' back home now."

Aiden greeted the news with mixed emotions as all of them no doubt had.

"How's Mum taken it?"

"She's still talkin' to Geraldine. Let's put it like this son, I don't think she's any more tears left after last night. It's been a hell of week for the two of them. Something happened today when she was out with yer Granny. I haven't gotten it out of her yet, but she was fit to be tied when she got back here at lunchtime...I encouraged her to ring one of her mates after you left, so she went out for a swim. The few hours out seemed to lift her, that's why the nurse is essential..."

"Absolutely, I'm with you all the way on that Dad..."

The ringing of the phone broke into their conversation.

"Hang on a second, Dad, that's the landline..."

"Go ahead, son..."

Benny waited as Aiden picked up the call and he couldn't help overhearing the exchange or Aiden's side of it anyway.

"No, she's not here at the minute, she'll be back in an hour. Shall I get her to call you?"

"No, I wouldn't call her on her mobile, she's driving."

"No, I don't think that's any of your business."

"Why am I here? It's my fiancées house you asshole!"

Benny was getting the drift, it had to be Kieran. No one riled Aiden like Jo's ex-husband.

"What track? No, I can't say if that would be alright with Jo.

137

She'll call you back when she gets in, bye!"

The call ended curtly. Benny could almost see the steam coming from his son's ears as he picked up on their call.

"Jesus, what an asshole that boy is! Bloody Kieran. How the hell Jo stuck him for eight years is more than I know."

And in the background, Sarah's voice calling from the other room, "Language Dad, remember what Mum said!"

She was delighted with herself. Apparently, she'd returned to her mother after one of her recent stays with Aiden spouting some rather colourful phrases.

His ex-wife had been on the phone in a heartbeat, berating him for his bad parenting.

Aiden yelled back at her, "Don't be so cocky madam or I'll tell yer mother ye weren't in bed by nine!"

Benny was chuckling away to himself, glad of the diversion.

"So what's loverboy want now?"

Benny had had the pleasure of being Kieran Hughes boss a few years back, before he and Jo parted company.

"Wants to know if it's okay to take Corey to the track tomorrow afternoon instead of bringing him home for one!"

"What track's that?" Benny asked.

"I don't bloody know and I don't bloody care! He does this to her all the time, I wouldn't mind if it was for his son's benefit, but it's really all about him scoring points, trying to make himself seem so impulsive, living on the edge, bloody moron..."

"Dad!"

"Get to bed, Sarah!"

"Ye better watch yerself, if Sarah goes back 'bloodying' all over the show t'er mother, she'll have yer guts fer garters!"

"I know. He just winds me up like a spring. I mean he must have known about this when he picked the wee fella up this mornin', said some mate of his got him V.I.P tickets, V.I.P. my arse!"

"Dad!"

Benny laughed out loud.

"You better go and see to that child before she bursts with indignation! I'll see you tomorrow and calm down a bit before Jo gets in."

"Forget about him. Sorry, Dad, ya were saying about Mum? You really reckon she's okay with the house thing, then? I know it's all very sudden."

"Seems to be, in a way it's probably for the best. It would have broken Geraldine's heart going in and out of an empty house, checking for burst pipes and God knows what. They're still talkin' I can hear her voice, no it's strange the way things work out sometimes. I'm sure that's the last thing Jo thought was goin' on in Orla's life."

"Yeah, it was a shock to her alright. She'd a call from Gail early on Thursday morning, it seems she's being made redundant."

"Ah that's too bad, sign of the times we're livin' in."

"So, when Orla rang shortly afterwards and asked Jo to meet her for lunch she put two and two together and got five, assumed Orla was either letting her go or closing up completely."

"Well, I suppose that was a natural enough conclusion to reach, considering the way the girl has been runnin' the business recently. At least Jo's still got her job."

"It's been a strange turn of events, but if Orla can find peace of mind there it's better than the house lying empty. Poor Mum and Aunt Ger, look I'll let ya go, try to enjoy the rest of yer night. Give my love to Mum, g'night, Dad."

"You too, son, g'night.

Benny sat in the kitchen looking out the window at the lights of the city, Deirdre and Geraldine were still engrossed in conversation. He poured himself a generous glass of wine and went into the other room to top up Deirdre's and she smiled her thanks at him.

He was relieved to see her eyes were tear free. Maybe this was the best thing that could have happened after all. He was glad Jo had taken the decision to ask about the house for her friend.

In the kitchen, he switched on the radio and listened to the music in the darkness, sipping his wine. He let the bluesy voice wash over him. He knew all of the words to the song, but couldn't remember its title.

It took him back to a time and a place long, long ago - the old shabby bed-sit, in Lawrence Street, where he had lived, when he had first come up to the city from Derry to work.

It was one of the many songs that drifted up to him, in the long, lonely night times through Sammy Stevenson's ceiling, infiltrating the floor boards, long after Benny had turned off his big wooden radio and waited for sleep; the nights before he had met Deirdre.

Not for the first time over the years, he wondered if his old friend Sammy, was living or dead, wondered if he ever knew, he had a beautiful daughter called Jo, a daughter, who was about to become Benny's daughter-in-law.

Not for the first time in months, he pondered the truth in the old adage, that 'Fact is Stranger than Fiction.'

Part Two

Spring in the Air

'Spring fever, they say that
it can go to your head...'
Orleans

Chapter 16

CASSIE AND GAIL WERE SITTING in Aiden's office going over the final plans for their corporate identity, a term that they were both capable of using now without collapsing into fits of schoolgirl giggles.

Over a month had passed since they had first spoken to Aiden about their advertising and marketing needs for the business. They'd had a brief meeting with him in Jo's house, on the Monday night before their meeting with Paddy McHenry, and he had given them a few tips to get them started, saying he would get back to them with a cost for the initial outlay they would need to plan for.

Today, they were checking out the end result of the whole package. Aiden had emailed them the web design ideas and now, at last, they could see the finished product, including glossy brochures and company stationery.

"Call-A-Cleaner," Aiden announced, handing them each a pamphlet. "The name says it all. Simple and direct, the colours are bold, fresh and clean, what more do you need. Convinced?"

Cassie and Gail nodded their approval. When they had first spoken with him Cassie had told him of her idea for the business name: 'Nitty Gritty Grime Busters.'

Aiden had managed not to laugh, but only just. Gail had explained briefly about their 'brainstorming' session and Cass had added, "That's why we're here, we really haven't a clue."

He had let them down easy.

"Why would you? It's not something you've ever had to think about before now…I'll be honest, I see where yer coming from, but it's a bit well….how can I put it, you know all those hairdressing salons with names that are a play on words? They were probably named in the eighties, but the owners still hang on to the signs, obviously still thinking they're okay, like say…The Best Little Hair House in Town."

Cass replied, "Well, I must admit I haven't seen that one."
Cassie and Gail both giggled.

"Trust me, I have. Really. Y'know what I'm saying, it must have seemed like a good idea at the time, but you look at it now and think, No, don't ya?"

They got it. When he came back to them days later with a price, they had agreed without hesitation. Some things were better left to the professionals. Now a month on, they are ready to start up in just two weeks.

"So, you decided on a van, yeah?"

"Yeah, it's being sign painted this week, we were just waiting to agree the colour shades."

"That's great, the ball's rollin' then. You should be up and running within a few weeks. I take it you went for the unit in the business park?"

"We did, they're central and the rent's reasonable, time enough looking for something bigger if we grow," Gail confirmed.

"When we grow," corrected Cass.

"Sorry, partner."

"There's no reason why you shouldn't, you've done yer homework. Remember to give that guy Tony O'Connor a call as soon as you get sorted. He's loads of rentals on the market at the minute, and they all have to be cleaned each time they change hands."

Aiden had spoken to one of his clients, O'Connor, and had passed on his number to them. He had agreed to discuss terms when they were up and running.

"Thanks for everything, Aiden. We'd've been lost without you."

"Well, that's what they pay me for. Anything else comes to mind don't hesitate to give me a call, good luck with the launch, Monday the 23rd, isn't it? Enjoy yourselves tomorrow night, go easy on the cocktails."

"We've no intention of it, that's why we're allowing two weeks in between before the start up, to recover from the hangover!" Cassie laughed.

"Ah well, sure it'll get Jo into practice for the hen night. These lunatics I work with are trying to convince me to have the stag do in Prague, make a weekend of it. Mind you they're all younger than me, I doubt I'd stick the pace, I'd probably have to spend most of it in bed. I think I'll go with a few pints and a curry down the town."

"Yeah, you better, you get Prague, we get Barcelona!" Gail came back at him.

"Don't be putting ideas in Jo's head, she's bad enough after a night on the tiles here. Have a good night and all the best for the 23rd, if I don't see ya before."

"Thanks, Aiden, see ya," both women chorused.

They walked out onto the street. It was just gone three o'clock. Gail was heading back up home and Cassie was going to the supermarket to shop. Gail's phone rang as they were saying their goodbyes, it was Jo.

"I don't believe it! Thank God fer that, I was beginning to have visions of you still sitting by the phone on the 11th of July. The mornin'? Fine yes, no bother, around ten. Yeah, we've just left Aiden. Your ears should be burning, we were talkin' about ya…"

Jo's response to this was lost to Cassie.

"… ach we were just sayin' yer a terrible woman fer the drink!"

Cassie could hear Jo's cries of outrage from where she stood as Gail held the phone away from her ear.

"Ya nearly deafened me there! No, of course I'd didn't agree, it was Aiden and Cass who were sayin' it."

There was another angry outburst from Jo. Gail calmed her down.

"I'm only windin' you up, no it was nothin' really. See ya in the mornin'."

"Did you hear that? I thought she was havin' a canary."

Cass grinned and said, "I take it 'the dress' is in, at last."

"Yeah, I don't know about Jo, I was beginning to panic. It seems that hauliers' strike was affecting deliveries from France for weeks, but at least it's here now. We're goin' to get it tomorrow."

"That'll be a load off her mind. Have a good day. I'll see yis tomorrow night, about eight."

They parted ways both looking forward to their night out, it had been a long time coming. Cassie had flatly refused to celebrate her win until everything was in place for the business. Now it was all organised, even the phones and computers were connected. The countdown was on until the big day, Monday the 23rd of March. The road was Friday afternoon busy, as the two friends set out to travel their separate ways.

Cassie was happy with her lot in life. She had left her jobs last Friday. Since then the realisation of the turn of events she had experienced finally kicked in, she really was about to start her own business. The feelings of excitement were still mingled with fear, What if they didn't get enough contracts? What if they couldn't find the right staff? What if Gail and she couldn't work together? What if it was all a complete failure?

In her heart of hearts, Cassie knew it would work out fine. But it was still hard to really believe it had all happened, after her years of struggle. It had worked out well for Dean too. He had decided to go to university; he'd be applying for a place in Media Studies. She had been delighted, of course he had never mentioned it before, as they both knew university wasn't an option, but the money had changed that. Cassie had agreed to support him through his time there.

Then wonder of wonders - he'd been offered a part-time job in one of the computer gaming shops in the town. She had thought it ironic that he couldn't get a job when she really needed him to be earning, now he'd been offered one, when money wasn't a problem. It was good for him though. Both the job and the prospect of university had lightened his personality.

She thought back to how she had watched him sink into the depths of despair after leaving school, his normally fun loving, outgoing personality had been disintegrating before her eyes, and she had felt powerless to do a thing about it. He still sat up half the night, but had no bother getting himself up and out to his job on time. She was proud of him and grateful every day that her change of fortune would enable her to give him the chance he deserved.

Lara was a different story. Initially Dean's talk of university had inspired her also to think about going back into education when Mia started school in September. Cassie had been elated and offered to help her financially while she studied also, but the feeling was short-lived.

A few days later, when Cass asked her had she given it any more thought she had replied, "Yeah, I've decided it's not right for me at the minute. Jake thinks Mia's first year in school would be a bad time for me to consider a college course."

Cassie had to bite her lip. She thought, *Jake, when did he come back into the picture?*

Cass couldn't stand him, was absolutely convinced that he had heard about the money, probably from Lara herself, and decided it would be a good idea to get back with her. Cass knew she had to be careful, if she said as much Lara would defend him, be more inclined to stay with him. She hoped and prayed her daughter would see sense and dump him, but she couldn't make the decision for her.

Lara's news was the one cloud on her horizon and she couldn't help worrying about her. Dean had been livid when his mother shared her concerns with him, but he too knew his sister's stubbornness would kick in, and she would be likely to make more of the relationship if they voiced their opinions. He had agreed saying nothing was the best way, Lara wasn't stupid, but she was lonely and that made Jake a more attractive prospect than he would have been otherwise.

Dean was sure the affair would fizzle out as it had done before. She had put it on the back burner, trusting her son's instincts and kept her thoughts to herself.

Gail, too, had finished her job on the previous Friday. She had refused her boss Jerry's offer of a night out with the other victims of the decision and the remaining branch staff. When the final day rolled round she couldn't wait to get out of the place once and for all.

Dave had come round to the business idea after Cassie and she had the appointment with the business advisor, agreeing to Gail investing in the venture, with her redundancy money and some of their savings. He saw Cassie's reasoning; no matter what the economic climate, people always need cleaners. It had to be worth the gamble.

The past week had been particularly odd for Gail. Now, that she had time on her hands to think, she was getting cold feet. She was so used to working within the constraints of a large organisation, she seriously wondered if she had the necessary entrepreneurial skills to be self-employed.

Of course, she knew she couldn't voice her concerns to Dave after doing such a good job of convincing him of the viability of their plan, but she had to talk to someone. She called up to Jo's on one of her days off, and told her of her reservations. Jo listened and said all the right things, as she aired her fears. Once talked through Gail knew Jo was right, she and Cass could make a go of it.

As Jo said, "Sure the two of you have been practically joined at the hip since the first day of primary school. You know each other

146

well, you know each other's strengths and weaknesses, that's so important in any business partnership. It can't fail."

Jo had no idea where she had gathered all this business acumen, but she must have said it with enough authority. Gail left convinced of their success and was now looking forward to a great night out to celebrate their venture.

Life was sweet.

Chapter 17

SATURDAY MORNING JO WAS UP at the crack of dawn, she was so excited about her wedding dress she had barely slept. After all the waiting it was finally here. By nine thirty she was ready to leave, she had to fritter away the extra minutes as Gail was only five minutes down the road. On the stroke of ten she was outside her door. Gail waved out the front window and Jo watched her gather up her coat and bag to leave.

Gail reached for the seatbelt and quipped, "You're the early bird, keen as mustard eh? God help us when the day finally dawns, you'll be standing at the front door with the dress on from daybreak."

Gail's mood was light, she was delighted for her friend, but couldn't resist teasing her.

"Just so long as I don't receive a letter at twenty minutes to nine, or I'll be hobbling around the house in my one shoe, stopping all the clocks."

"What?" Gail was lost.

"Y'know, like poor jilted Miss Havisham."

"Nah, no way, that'd never be you, sure she left her wedding cake to rot."

"Aye yer right, being devastated for a lost suitor's one thing, but leavin' a whole wedding cake to rot…that's just takin' it too far! Seriously though, I'm startin' to count it in days now rather than weeks. I'll be on the Quiet Life tablets washed down with gallons of Sanatogen. What about you, the nerves settled down a bit?"

"I'm fine now. I just had too much time on my hands this week. I mean I was absolutely sure I'd made the right decision while I'd still to go into work, then I got the jitters, but after leaving Aiden's office yesterday it seemed more real somehow, y'know all the parts in place, just waiting for the final countdown. Cass is beside herself, wait 'til ya see the cut of her tonight she'll be dancin' on the tables."

"Good for her, I'm lookin' forward to it, too."

The journey seemed long, but that was probably down to their feelings of anticipation. At last, Ballymena was in sight. Jo found a space easily and parked quickly.

"Here we go!"

The bell on the shop door dinged their arrival and the assistant greeted them like old friends, "Jo! Gail! Lovely to see you. Apologies for the delay, but as I said it was out of our hands, let's get you organised."

She ushered Jo toward the fitting room and produced the dress in her size. Gail waited in the shop while the assistant fussed over Jo. Minutes later she heard Jo's voice calling her into the changing area. Jo pulled back the curtain, her face crumpling with disappointment.

"Look, the zip won't budge! I can't believe this, I never go above a size eight!"

Jo was close to tears and Gail was lost for words, the assistant stepped in.

"Look, Jo, it's alright, it comes in a ten too. Give it until next week, it's probably just fluid retention, you'll have lost a few pounds by then. If not, try the ten and we can have it altered if need be. I'll keep them both over until next Saturday."

Jo agreed, still upset. Gail suggested they go for coffee. They made their way from the bridal shop to the nearby coffee shop. Jo had managed to contain the tears, but her face was the picture of misery.

At the counter, she flatly refused to have anything to eat, just a black coffee, Gail had a cappuccino, but knew she better forego the chocolate muffin she had been looking forward to.

"It probably is fluid, Jo, sure yer like a stick, and it's not as though you've been overeating."

"Oh, I don't know. It's such a disappointment after all the weeks of waiting, maybe it is fluid."

"That'll be it. Is your period due?"

"I don't know, they've been a bit erratic at times. When I first separated from Kieran I didn't have one for months, but the doctor said it was the stress, that could be it I suppose."

"When did you last have one, though?"

"I don't know, I can't think. Maybe it's the menopause. Kate told me one time Mum was early, in her thirties I think. Maybe I should get one of those hormone tests done, I am forty."

"If you haven't had a period in a while maybe you should get a hormone test done; the one with the blue lines."

"What?"

"When did you last have a period? Think."

Jo sipped her coffee.

"It was probably five or six weeks ago."

"And you stopped using contraception when the divorce was finalized, didn't you?"

Jo had told Gail months before that Aiden would love another child, she wouldn't mind, but she didn't think it was likely at her age. They had both decided to forget about contraception and leave it for nature to take its course.

"Yes, but I don't even know if it is that long. I've been so busy, with the wedding and everything. Hang on, I've my diary here, I'll try to work it out."

Jo pored through the pages and checked out signs that would indicate when she had last had a period. She was going to start keeping track of them from this month, because her sister-in-law had suggested she may want to think about going back on the pill, if her period looked like it may be due around the time of the wedding.

"That's it, the second week in January, I remember because I was going swimming with Sarah and Corey."

"So that's…"

"Eight weeks! Jesus, I can't believe it's been that long."

"Well, maybe it is the menopause, but let's go for the more obvious conclusion. Drink that up and we'll head over to Boots."

Jo looked like she'd been hit around the head with a cricket bat.

"Okay."

Gail asked the assistant at the pharmacy counter for the pregnancy test, Jo seemed to have lost the power of speech as she handed her friend a twenty pound note and watched her pay for it.

"Right there's a hotel round the corner, we'll go to the toilets in there."

"Do you not have to wait until first thing in the morning?"

"Not with these modern ones, they can practically tell you you're pregnant before the sperm start swimming."

"Really?"

"Yeah, really. I heard the girls in work talkin' about them."

The rest rooms in the hotel were empty, and as Gail hoped each cubicle was spacious. She unwrapped the packaging and handed the test to Jo. Jo looked like a caricature of herself, her eyes were dancing in her head and her face was flushed with beads of sweat forming on her upper lip.

"You remember what to do, I take it?" Gail asked.

Jo looked at the test.

"Yes. Right, I'll do it now will I?"

Gail nodded, giving her a reassuring smile, as Jo closed the toilet door. She waited. Jo appeared moments later with the wand in her hand. She wiped it on a paper towel and set it on the side of the sink, before washing her hands. Gail held her phone to time it, but they didn't need to wait for the time indicated on the box. The test worked as they watched, two blue lines, at first one more faded than the other, but soon they were the same shade, two deep sky blue lines.

Jo was pregnant.

"Congratulaions, you're goin' to be a mummy again, kid!"

Jo burst into tears as Gail reached out to hug her best friend, saying, "Aiden'll be over the moon."

Still speechless Jo clung to Gail and wept. Eventually she spoke.

"I can't wait to tell him. My God, what a shock this is goin' to be, he'll be expecting to hear me enthusing about a weddin' dress. Oh my God, what am I goin' to do now about the dress, how big will I be by July?"

"Good, you've found yer voice again. First things first, get to the doctor on Monday and check out yer dates, everything else will fall into place from there. Oh this is great news, Jo, I'm delighted for you."

"We're goin' out tonight, Christ, lucky I found out today."

She thought of the cocktails they had planned on downing that night.

"Thanks, Gail. Jesus, I'm an awful eejit. It never even crossed my mind...I don't even care about the dress. I'm goin' to have a baby! God the dress, Kate will want to see it, what'll I tell her?"

Kate and Andy were coming up to babysit Corey while Jo had her night out.

"Aren't you going to tell them?"

"Not yet, I'll not see Aiden until tomorrow at lunch time, I can't have everyone knowing before he does. I'll tell Cass, of course, I know she won't say anything to anyone else."

"Tell Kate the dress is being altered, it's a perfect fit, but just a touch too long. That'll get you off the hook for the time being, then you can decide when to tell them, after you've told Aiden tomorrow."

"Yeah, I'll do that."

"Are you sure ya still want to go out tonight? We won't mind if you want to see Aiden instead, given the circumstances."

"No, I'll go, it would only raise Kate and Dad's suspicions if I opt out of the night out, I can wait to tell him tomorrow. I'll not stay out late though, I am tired, but at least now I know why. What am I goin' to do about the dress?"

"Stop worrying for a start, relax. Things will fall into place when you've time to get used to the idea of being pregnant."

Gail put her arm around Jo and gave her shoulder a reassuring squeeze.

Back in Belfast that Saturday afternoon Orla was standing at the front of the City Hall waiting for Anne Marie. It had been four weeks since they had left the refuge. By coincidence they both found accommodation in the same week, at the start of February.

And what a week that had been. Anne Marie had received a phone call from the local councillor she had contacted with her sister, telling her the wheels were in motion for her to get the flat she wanted.

She heard the news she had waited for from the Housing Executive on Wednesday. Wasting no time, she moved in that weekend. Orla had left the refuge on the Friday and Anne Marie on the Saturday. On the Thursday night they had sat at the kitchen table drinking tea together. Orla had asked the question that had been hanging between them since they had both got confirmation of their places.

"We'll keep in touch, won't we?"

Anne Marie looked cynical.

"Oh sure we will, like you keep in touch with the people ya meet on holiday, the woman you swap holiday reads with, sip margaritas with by the poolside every day, have the odd meal in the evening with her and her husband. You promise to keep in touch. Get home, ya both email each other the holiday photos, send the odd text, but that fizzles out. Then at Christmas you receive a card saying, 'Happy Christmas, love from Natalie and Nathan xxxx' And you think, Who? That sorta keep in touch?"

Anne Marie's tone was caustic.

"You're such a cynic," Orla said.

They sipped their tea, both reaching out for the plate of chocolate Hob Nobs at the same time, their knuckles bumping over the plate. Orla knew that like her Anne Marie was thinking back to that Sunday night, Orla's first night there, when they had bared their souls to each other. The intensity of their friendship would be difficult to maintain when they both returned to the 'real world'. Perhaps they would be unwilling to see each other, not wanting the reminder of this traumatic time cluttering up their new lives. Orla honestly didn't know how she would feel about seeing Anne Marie outside of these walls. But she was willing to try to maintain their relationship if her friend was.

They both looked up from their mugs and met each other's eyes saying in unison.

"We'll wait and see yeah?"

They smiled at each other.

"Great minds eh?"

Orla was pleased they had agreed to think it over. Time would tell if it was possible to for them to stay in touch.

They had; the nightly texting still sustained them, and at least once a week one of them picked up the phone to speak to the other. Today for the first time they were meeting for lunch. Orla pushed her way through the shoppers as she saw Anne Marie approach; she looked well. Orla felt strangely shy meeting up with her in such a public place, but after a couple of minutes they were chatting and laughing as they hurried out of the cold to a nearby restaurant.

It was going to be fine.

Chapter 18

THAT EVENING, JO AND GAIL were waiting in the taxi outside Cass's house watching as she came strutting down the driveway in her new dress and killer heels, looking ten years younger than she had looked before her win.

"Doesn't she look brilliant?" said Gail.

"Gorgeous, Cass was always a stunner when we were young, this money has given her a new lease of life. It's great to see her enjoying herself."

Cass piled into the back of the taxi beside them.

"Well, did ye get it?"

"No, there was a slight hitch."

Jo was loving this, she watched the expression on Cass's face change from excited anticipation to incomprehension.

"It wasn't there? After yer woman phonin' you?"

"Oh put her out of her misery, tell her."

Cassie looked to Jo for an explanation.

"What?"

"Y'see the dress wouldn't fit and we got talkin' and Gail suggested I do a test in case it wasn't just fluid retention and it turned out it wasn't and that's why the zip wouldn't go up!"

"Test?"

"Pregnancy test, I'm pregnant!"

The taxi driver's head jerked back with a bounce as Cassie cried out, "Pregnant? Are ya jokin'?"

Orla reached home in Derry around six. Snapper the dog greeted her with a wagging tail and a series of barks. He was her constant companion.

She was grateful to Liam for suggesting she take him. Snapper stayed in one of the outhouses during the day when she worked, and early in the evenings she felt safe as he scampered around the yard, but last thing at night she called him in. He slept in the kitchen off the main hall. Orla felt at ease with him in the house through the night time hours, no intruder would ever make it past Snapper.

She was only through the front door when her phone vibrated indicating a text, "Hey girl we did it! Luks like we really can b m8s, tlk soon, luv Anne Marie xx"

Orla was happy the day had gone so well, she had no doubt now, they were friends and it would remain that way, she returned the message, "Enjyd the day, luk 4wrd 2 nxt tme, luv Orla xxx"

She switched the television on for company as she cooked her dinner. Flicking through the listings she opted for a natural history programme, the Scottish presenter, the bloke with the long dark hair, wittered on in the background, as she grilled a salmon fillet and steamed some vegetables for herself. She had become used to solitary living easily, and always made a point of cooking a meal, no matter how late her return home. She thought of the old house as home now.

It hadn't taken long for her to adapt to her new environment, having Geraldine and Liam and their family close by helped, of course. Jo had been right they didn't intrude, but it was nice to see the lights burning in the windows at night, comforting to know help was only a phone call away, if she needed it.

She ate her meal at the kitchen table thinking over the events of the day. She was pleased things were working out for Anne Marie who was working again, in a local supermarket. She told Orla she had been a Team Leader in another of their branches before she had left Seamus, but she couldn't cope with returning to work after losing the baby, so she had resigned. Now she was working on the checkouts, and given her previous experience, they had said she was welcome to apply for a position of Team Leader, if it arose. Life seemed to be treating her well.

Orla was washing the plates she had used when she heard the dog bark at an approaching car, then the doorbell rang. It was probably Geraldine checking everything was alright. She rushed to the door drying her hands, the dog's barks still ringing out. It couldn't be Geraldine after all, she only had to look at Snapper and he froze. Flinging the door open, she almost fainted when she saw Seamus. He pushed forward past her up the hall, the dog in hot pursuit.

155

"Can you calm that thing down before it eats me!"

She followed him in, leaving the front door open. Orla allowed the dog to pursue him up the hall, telling it firmly to sit, when it was well within the walls of the house. How could she have been so stupid? She had forgotten to switch the camera back on after she returned home. She hadn't even thought of checking out who the caller was, such was her feeling of security here. It had never even occurred to her that it could be Seamus.

Her legs shook as she watched him sit down.

"I didn't invite you in and I didn't ask you to sit down."

Her voice sounded defiant, strong, the dog was standing alongside her, she knew it would tear him apart if he made a move toward her.

"Cut out the melodramatics, Orla, I just wanted to talk to ya."

"You're breaking the protection order. I could call the police now and have you arrested. How dare you come here. How did you find me? Have you been following me?"

"No, I haven't, I'm a busy man. I had you followed."

"You had a private detective follow me?"

"Just a bloke I know, does a bit of investigatin' for people like me who've been badly treated by their spouses."

"Are you serious?"

"Are you not goin' to offer me a cup of tea after me coming all this way t'see ye?

Their exchange was interrupted by the sound of feet pounding up the hall, the dog barked furiously and ran toward the door. She swung round to see Declan standing in the doorway with a shot gun raised ready to fire, his father at his shoulder.

"Yer trespassing on this land! What's yer business?"

Seamus's face had turned the colour of freshly worked putty.

"Don't shoot! I'll go quietly."

Orla almost laughed. She felt like she was in a film, *the damsel in distress.*

"Ring the police, Da!" Declan ordered.

"No, please, don't. I can explain."

"It better be good, fella."

"This is my wife. I just wanted to speak to her."

"Oh yer the wife beater, yer not lookin' so brave now big fella, what's yer business?"

Seamus turned to Orla.

"I wanted to ask ye, if you'd forget all this divorce business and come to Australia with me?"

Orla, reassured by the presence of Liam and Declan, was perfectly calm now, in control.

"Not a chance, Seamus. And Declan's right you are trespassing. I didn't invite you in."

Liam took up the gauntlet, saying, "Right that's it, I'm calling the police."

"No, don't please," Seamus pleaded as he made to rise to his feet, all the while his eyes never left the gun. "Don't involve the police. I've applied for immigration to Australia, they'd never let me through the airport with a police record. Please, I'll go quietly."

"You should've thought of that before you came up here harassing this young woman. We'll not involve the police tonight, but Orla will be expectin' to hear from your solicitor this week, confirming your intention to leave the country. If she doesn't get the letter by the end of the week I'll see that she presses charges!" Liam roared.

The two men stood aside, clearing a pathway to the door, indicating it was time Seamus took his leave.

Seamus was on his feet, and out the door heading for his car in an instant. Orla had never seen him move so quickly. All the while Declan followed behind him, the gun pointed in his direction, Snapper growled after him, baring his teeth ready to hurl himself at the intruder should he make a false move. Orla told him to stay, more worried that the dog may end up under the wheels of Seamus's motor as he made his getaway, than any damage the dog may do to Seamus.

Seamus jumped into the vehicle and revved the engine, the wheels spinning a trail of dust into the air in his haste to leave. Like a bat out of hell he was gone from the farmyard and out onto the road. The car sped away into the distance as Orla and her neighbours watched.

Overwhelmed by what could have happened, hysteria swept over her and she passed out.

Rapidly passing the shot gun to his father, Declan put his arms out to save her, deftly he swept her up and carried her to the sofa. Liam rang Geraldine and told her briefly what had happened.

She had no doubt about who the intruder must be. All the while she had been sitting at the front window watching through the

157

binoculars. Declan had been visiting his parents when they had noticed the strange car outside Mary's house. Putting two and two together they had surmised it was Orla's husband and Declan had grabbed the shot gun and jumped into the jeep, his father in tow, shouting back to his mother, "Don't worry about ringing the police, we can handle this boy!"

Geraldine had no doubt they could. She ran to pick up the binoculars and watched the unfolding drama. She said afterwards she would have paid money to see the look on Seamus's face when Declan had stormed in with gun cocked.

She climbed into her car and made the short journey across to the house, thankful that they had been there for the poor girl. Orla had come round by now and Geraldine rushed to the kitchen to boil the kettle.

"Make it strong, Ger, with plenty of sugar, she's had a terrible shock." Liam called out.

"Don't worry, Orla, he'll not be troubling you again, I guarantee it. Women beaters are always cowards, did ye see his face when he saw the gun he was damn nearly crying, I think he might've wet himself! All over the seats of his lovely motor too!" Declan said.

Maybe it was relief, or maybe it was nervous tension, but the four of them laughed until they cried at the memory of Seamus jumping into the car and flying out onto the laneway, like the hounds of hell were chasing him. They drank the welcome tea, all of them quiet now, the reality of the evening's events sinking in. Geraldine realised Orla really was crying now. She moved to sit beside her.

"Yer alright, love, there'll be no more bother out of him, Declan's right he'll not pass this way again."

"I know, but I'm so stupid, I should've had the camera on. What was I thinkin' of letting him in?"

"You've had a shock, Orla, now I'm goin' to sleep on that sofa tonight, I wouldn't dream of leavin' ye in this state. I'll give the boys a call, they'll be fine on their own, you won't. You need company tonight," Declan insisted.

Orla didn't protest, she was glad of the offer. She knew they were right, Seamus was a coward, he wouldn't be back. But what if they hadn't seen him arrive? She couldn't stop shaking, couldn't believe he really thought she would ever consider taking him back, never mind going to Australia with him.

Geraldine and Liam left shortly after nine and Declan rang his sons to explain what had happened, telling them he was planning on staying the night in the house to ensure Orla was safe.

Orla went upstairs to fetch a couple of pillows and a spare duvet for him. She was grateful he had offered to stay. She had been so at ease here, so at peace, she had let her guard slip and it could have cost her dearly. It wouldn't happen again. She would double check her security every day from now on. She was exhausted. Declan assured her he would be fine on the sofa as she made her way up to bed. Orla felt completely safe with him, with these people she had only recently come to know. They were like family to her. She closed her eyes and slept a troubled sleep. The demons had made a return with her husband's visit.

Chapter 19

THAT SUNDAY MORNING FOUND CASS pottering about the house in her silk pyjamas and fluffy bed socks, drinking glasses of fresh orange juice waiting for her hangover to clear.

It had been worth it though they'd had a great night celebrating her big win and their future business venture. And, of course, Jo's surprise news, but only three of them knew about that.

Cassie still couldn't take it in, another child at forty, as her fortieth approached she knew the prospect of rearing another child would fill her with dread. Cass loved her grandchild, but one of her own would be another kettle of fish entirely. Jo was delighted, though. Why wouldn't she be? She was half way through her university course and she was getting married to Aiden.

Still, Cass thought, she would rather be doing what she was doing. She downed yet another glass of orange she remembered why she didn't drink spirits. What was it her Dad used to say...? "Merry, Merry Nights make Sad, Sad Mornings..."

Orla awoke that Sunday morning to the smell of bacon frying. Making her way to the kitchen, she found Declan standing at the cooker.

"I hope ye don't mind, I had a rummage through yer fridge, thought you could use a hearty breakfast. I know I could. How'd you sleep?"

"Like a baby, I must have conked out as soon as my head hit the pillow, I'm sure you didn't have a comfortable night."

She had lied. She didn't want Declan to feel his vigil had been wasted. It wasn't about him. It was about the memories in her head.

"Not at all, I was fine. Molly always said I could sleep on the proverbial clothes line."

"Molly was your wife?"

"Yeah, she'll be dead two years next month, God rest her."

"Shall I do the coffees?"

"Well, it is your kitchen. Yeah, that'd be great. This is nearly ready to go, hope yer hungry."

"I am."

They sat eating together like old friends. Orla had taken to this craggy faced man who had come to her aid, she felt comfortable with him, protected. He smiled across the table at her.

"I'm sure you think I've a right cheek, scavengin' through your fridge, helpin' myself."

"Not at all, I'm delighted, I can't remember the last time a man made me breakfast."

"That's another thing..." Declan started.

"It must be odd..." Orla began.

"Sorry, you go first." Declan said.

"Oh, I was just thinking it must be odd for you all, having me here in your family home."

"To be honest, I think it's the best thing that could have happened, certainly for my mother anyway. She couldn't have watched this place go empty, run down with damp and decay. No we're glad to have you, Orla. Believe me."

"Thanks, what were you going to say?"

"Just that, eh, I may have spoken out of turn last night, calling yer husband a wife beater. I couldn't help myself. I saw red when I watched him push past you up the hall..."

"No, you didn't. May as well tell it like it is. He is a wife beater and a coward. I'm very grateful you and your father intervened. Thanks again."

Declan nodded his acknowledgment, "Happy to help."

They continued to eat in companionable silence.

She wondered about his wife, but didn't want to intrude by asking too many questions, thinking it must be hard for him with teenage sons still at home. She wouldn't ask the questions now; there would be other times. She felt sure of it.

Jo looked at the clock, eleven thirty three, Aiden was due around twelve, her Dad and Kate had stayed the night and were now upstairs getting organised for the journey home to Islandmagee.

She hadn't been late back last night having made her excuses to the girls early on. Cassie had calmed down eventually, apologising for her outburst in the taxi, throwing her arms around her in congratulations. They had agreed Jo wouldn't share the news with the other friends joining them, Helena and Naomi. It was early days. Aiden still didn't know, and she had barely had time to digest the news herself.

Throughout the night she made a show of complaining about her imaginary cold, finally making her excuses to go home to bed around eleven thirty.

On her arrival back Kate and Andy were surprised to see her so soon. She had given them the same story, feeling slightly guilty about the lie. She knew she had to tell Aiden the news before anyone else now. It was bad enough that Gail and Cass knew and he didn't, but they had planned the night out for so long. She knew Cassie in particular would give her a hard time about abstaining from alcohol if she didn't know the reason.

The Saturday celebration had been in the pipeline for weeks, and despite being the only sober one in the party, Jo had enjoyed the night, thrilled to share in her friends' jubilance. She would call Kate and her Dad as soon as she had told Aiden. Deirdre and Benny would probably be at Rosie's for dinner today. Aiden and she could call round this evening with the news. Corey was over in his friend's house across the street. She hoped he would still be there for a while, to give her a chance to talk to Aiden in peace.

She had no doubt he would be pleased, but if her calculations were right she would be around twenty four or twenty five weeks by the wedding.

She groaned inwardly. *Six months pregnant.* He would think he was marrying Nellie the Elephant.

Kate's voice broke into her thoughts.

"That's us ready for the road. We'll wait and say hello to Aiden then we're off. What about coming down to us next weekend, say Saturday, for dinner?"

"Yeah, I'm sure that would be fine. I'll call ya through the week, Kate."

Andy appeared at the kitchen door.

"You look after that cold, m'girl. You don't want to be laid up. March is a deceivin' oul month. I've seen it snow many a March. Have you plenty of Lem Sips and cough medicine, if not we can get ya some before we leave?"

She felt guilty at her Dad's concern. Even though she was forty Andy still mollycoddled her like a child; she loved him for it. Her Dad was her rock through everything. She would never have gotten through her divorce without him. Jo would have loved to have told them there and then, but she would ring them as soon as possible. She hated lying to them; they were both so good to her.

She was squirming inside as she told another lie.

"I've loads, really. Ah here's the man himself."

Aiden came bounding up the path. *At last*, Jo thought. *I'd never make a liar.*

Corey seeing Aiden's car came bouncing over the road to see him. Aiden and her Dad chatted easily for a few minutes, and then Kate turned to Corey.

"Right, big fella, we're off now." Kate looked at Jo. "See ya next week?"

Corey sprang over to hug Kate and his granda.

"Yeah, I'll talk to ya later, Kate. Thanks fer everything."

She turned to her Dad and hugged him, whispering, "Safe home."

"Take care, love, talk to ya later."

They saw them out and Corey headed back over to his mates.

"Well, good night then?" Aiden asked. "Are ya sufferin' or did you behave yourself, what was that about the dress havin' to be altered?"

She had sent him a brief text last night. She couldn't let it go unmentioned overnight or he would have wondered what was going on after all the weeks of waiting.

"Well, actually it didn't fit."

He looked at her critically. Jo was of a very slight build, never having put much weight on, not since he had known her anyway.

"It's probably just an odd size, don't worry what the label says, get them to order it in for you in the next size up. I know it must be a disappointment to you after all these weeks, but sure a few more won't matter if it's the dress you've set yer heart on."

She couldn't drag it out with tales of zips that wouldn't meet and pregnancy tests. The concern for her in his eyes melted her heart.

"Aiden, I'm pregnant."

"What? When did ya find out? Jesus!" He put his arms round her and held her tightly to him. "That's brilliant, Jo. I'm delighted. You're sure?"

She nodded, the tears flowing, her throat was so tight she couldn't speak.

"What's wrong, are you not pleased, too?"

She found her voice.

"Of course, I am. It's just such a shock, that's all. I thought it might be the menopause, y'know. The assistant and Gail thought it may be fluid retention. Gail made me go to Boots right away and buy a pregnancy test; it never even occurred to me. Gail was thrilled to bits for me. I can't believe I'm so stupid, I didn't even realise I was so late until Gail asked me to think about it. What about the wedding though? If I'm counting right, I'll be about six months, what kind of wedding dress can you wear to disguise that?"

Aiden grinned from ear to ear, as Jo blathered on, not knowing whether to laugh or cry. He grabbed her by both shoulders and made her sit down.

"Right, first things first. Lunch. You're in no state to cook and neither am I. The three of us will go out somewhere plush and celebrate with a big nosh, you can relax and get used to the idea. I take it you haven't seen a doctor yet?"

"No, I'll make an appointment in the morning. We can celebrate, but Corey doesn't know yet; it's a bit soon."

"Okay, but see the doctor first, then we'll think about the wedding. Sure if all else fails, we can use some of the old sailing material from the boat to make you a dress."

She grinned back at him.

"I won't be that bad. I hardly showed at all with Corey before six months. But the dress is out. It was a beautiful elegant simple, straight, sheath. There's no way you'd conceal a bump in that."

"So, you'll find another dress. Whichever way, we're getting' married on the 11th of July and shortly after we're havin' a baby. It's great news, Jo. Don't worry, it'll be fine."

Over in Benny and Deirdre's, Deirdre was getting her mother organised for Sunday lunch in Rosie's.

She sat her down on the bed and rubbed her back with the big soft towel, thinking that look of contentment wouldn't have been on Mary's face, had she known about the scene that had unfolded in her house the previous night. Geraldine had phoned late and talked for nearly an hour, of course the incident had shaken her. She said poor Orla was in bits, but their Declan had stayed the night to put her mind at ease. *God help the wee girl. Even at that distance the bastard had found her,* Deirdre thought.

She came back to her mother. Mary was talking and Deirdre hadn't heard a word.

"Sorry, wha'd ya say, Mum?"

Mary repeated the sentence and they chatted as Deirdre finished drying her back.

"There ya go, Mum, all dry. Now let's get you dressed."

Geraldine had told Deirdre the previous night that the notification for their mother's hospital appointment had arrived that Saturday morning. They didn't talk much about it due to the events of the early evening, both of them knowing they were only going through the motions. They would take their mother along for the tests and listen to the doctor explain the results to them, nod in the right places at the words, which would only be confirming what they already knew.

Deirdre and her mum had fallen into a routine by now, her mother still had her moments, but all in all the arrangement was working out. Deirdre had gone to see her old friend Lorraine on the Monday after her mother came to stay, that first week in February and they had been able to send three nurses for interview that week.

She had decided on a cheerful, chubby woman called Ellie, a woman in her mid-forties, with years of experience in nursing the elderly and glowing references from past employers. Deirdre who had taken to her from the start was sold; she knew her mother would relate better to the older woman than a younger girl. Before making the decision Benny and she had sat down with Mary and explained the situation.

Deirdre told her, "I've still got a job, Mum, even though I'm not a nurse anymore. I work with some of the older people in the community, helping them organise days out and things, it's only a few days a week, but…"

Her mother had replied, looking bewildered, "Everybody has to look after their work."

165

Benny had shook his head behind his mother-in-law's back, indicating Deirdre was saying too much. He had told her to explain only the bare minimum of information, otherwise the shutters went down on the old woman's eyes and you knew you'd lost her.

He took over the explanation.

"What it is, Mary, we need somebody here to take care of you when Deirdre's out. To do things for you I can't do, like take you to the toilet or whatever. Deirdre's found a lovely woman, a nurse she wants you to meet. We want you to tell us if you like her or not, after she leaves y'know, alright?"

"If I didn't like her I wouldn't say it in front of her. I wouldn't be ignorant to anybody."

"Good woman, Mary. She's coming round today."

And that had been that bridge crossed.

Deirdre had glanced at her husband, grateful for his support. Benny had a knack of knowing when to bring conversations to their natural conclusion whereas Geraldine and she were prone to long and involved explanations for the simplest scenarios, doubtless a nod to the guilt overwhelming the two sisters.

They'd broached the subject of her staying with Geraldine and Liam for the summer months. Mary accepted this without much question, as they explained to her that she was too weak to live alone and that her house was being looked after by a friend of the family. This explanation seemed to satisfy her. They knew convoluted tales of Jo's friend would only add to her confusion, so they kept it simple and explained, she would be staying with Geraldine and Liam "…for a while…" when she returned to Derry.

When the subject arose, she would nod her agreement, saying, "So long as Geraldine's keeping an eye on m'house. Some people would rob ye blind." Or: "I hope she doesn't think it's hers now that she's got her feet under the table."

Her old spark still there. And that would be it forgotten again. Until the next time. Every now and then she would ask, "Have I still got my house?"

And so, the explanations would begin again.

The debilitation of her mother's mind broke Deirdre's heart. Sometimes they had glimpses of her old lucidity, making it seem she understood and remembered everything perfectly, but the next instant she couldn't remember how to put her arm into the sleeve of her cardigan. They knew in their hearts it would get worse before it got better and that Deirdre was one of the lucky ones she knew not everyone could afford hired help.

Her mother and Ellie had taken to each other at the first meeting and now, over a month on, the arrangement was working well for all of them. The time spent with Ellie seemed to stimulate her mother, giving her a rest from Deirdre, and the time spent working, gave Deirdre the outside company she needed to return to her mother afresh.

Today, Mary was looking forward to going to her granddaughter Rosie's house for Sunday lunch. The girls had been great, taking their granny out the odd day and having them over for meals or coming to them as usual on Sundays, it all helped.

Now, with her mother firmly ensconced in her chair by the fire, Deirdre was flicking through some notes in her file in preparation for the next day. Each month, the charity she worked for and the local community centres got together to organise an event. Last month it had been the St. Valentine's Day Tea Dance; this month it was a St. Patrick's Night Concert and Dance.

As travel coordinator she worked with the community representatives, organising the transport and ensuring they had sufficient buses laid on to transport people to and from the venues for all the centres involved, but as she found when she started the voluntary work, that was only the half of it. Nine times out of ten someone was off sick or on holiday and the volunteer workers had to double up on jobs.

Ann, her colleague, had contacted her about delivering the concert tickets to the various community centres this week, on top of her usual workload. So she was sorting through the centres listed to plan her route for the morning, rather than leave it until they got home that night. By two o' clock she was organised and looking forward to the day out, Rosie was expecting them at three.

Chapter 20

BY LATE SUNDAY AFTERNOON ORLA was sitting curled up on the sofa talking to Anne Marie on the phone. Declan had left immediately after breakfast and she had spent the day washing and cleaning, generally keeping busy. Geraldine rang shortly after two to ask her over for a cup of tea, she declined the offer.

"Thanks very much for asking, but I really am busy. I've a lot of washing to catch up with, what with the all rain this week, I've fallen behind. I'm fine, but I do appreciate your concern, Geraldine."

It would have been too easy to accept the offer. Fall into the way of calling into Geraldine's for company, allowing Declan to check up on her every night, it would become a pattern and Seamus would have won, whilst she would have lost her peace of mind. She knew she had been stupid, become complacent, too comfortable in her surroundings in this lovely part of the country and it had almost cost her dearly. Orla knew in her heart of hearts she would never be that stupid again. The camera would be on no matter what, the doors and windows would remain firmly locked, until she was absolutely sure that she was no longer in danger from Seamus.

Strangely enough, she believed the threat from Declan had done the trick; she doubted he would ever bother her again. But she wasn't prepared to leave her personal safety to chance. Now, almost twenty four hours on from her husband's visit, she was on the phone to her friend, telling her about the previous night's drama.

"Oh God, I'd've loved to have seen his face when Declan came stormin' in with the shotgun. I'm sure he nearly shit himself."

"Damn nearly. He was a gibberin' wreck by the time Declan and his father allowed him to get out the front door and into his car; you literally couldn't see him for dust as he spun out onto the laneway."

"Good. Good for Declan! Is he your hero now?"

168

"Well I certainly appreciated him staying the night. I wasn't worth tuppence afterwards. I keeled over at one point and then I was just so tired, I suppose it was the shock."

"So Declan slept on the sofa did he?" she could almost see the leer on Anne Marie's face.

"Isn't that what I said?"

"Just checking, but he is nice this, Declan?"

"Yeah, not in an obvious sort of way though. He's sorta craggy lookin', y'know what I mean?"

"Like who?"

"Like, oh I don't know, maybe a young Michael Parkinson."

Anne Marie started to hum the 'Parky' theme music, "Da Do Da Da Do Da Do...Da Do Da Da Do Da Do ..."

"Very funny."

"You like him, I can tell."

"Of course, I like him, you'd like him too if he saved your bacon. Ach no, he's just a really genuine person, down to earth, honest, funny."

"Craggy good looks and he's a widower. What more could a girl ask?" Anne Marie was enjoying winding Orla up.

"Will you stop, I'm not even divorced yet! Anyway what're ya at, did you start your painting?"

"Yep, the colour's lovely on, but now that I've started I'm going to have to do the rest of the rooms. They really are cryin' out for a makeover. Maybe you could send Declan up to give me a hand?"

"Find yer own hero! Anyway, I'll let ya get back to work, I'll talk to ya later in the week, have a good night."

"You too. Talk to ya soon, Orla."

"Bye, Anne Marie."

It was almost nine when Deirdre, Benny and Mary arrived back. Aiden called Benny just as they pulled into their street.

"Yeah, that's right we were at yer sister's. We'd a good day, what are yis up to yerselves?"

Deirdre, who was driving could hear him say to his father, "We were thinking of callin' round."

"Of course ye can call round. Come when it suits ya. We'll look forward to it."

By now they had fallen into a night-time routine, Mary was ready for bed most nights by nine thirty or ten, so they got her upstairs regardless of the company as she got agitated if she didn't get enough sleep.

"That was Aiden they're calling round for an hour, but they won't be staying long, the babysitter's staying with Corey for a while because he's got school in the morning. They'd be lost without that wee girl, she's great with him."

Deirdre nodded, wondering what was bringing them round at this time on a Sunday night, she replied, distractedly, "Yeah, she is."

By nine thirty five, her mother was safely tucked up in bed, happy, but exhausted after her day out. Deirdre kissed her goodnight and closed the bedroom door. As she descended the stairs she saw the headlights of Aiden's car reflected in the hall mirror.

She opened the front door and greeted Aiden and Jo, directing them toward the front room with a flick of her hand.

"Go on in, yer granny's in bed. She's worn out from all the company. She'd a good day, though. So how are you both?"

Benny stood as they entered, saying, "Good to see ya. How's tricks?"

"Great. You had a good day then?"

Benny answered Aiden, as Deirdre observed. Something was up; maybe the dress hadn't arrived.

"So, did you get your dress, Jo?" Deirdre asked.

Jo and Aiden exchanged a look. Jo spoke, "No, there's a bit of a change of plan."

"What, they didn't get it for ya after keeping you waitin' all this time?"

"They had it, but I won't be buyin' it." Jo paused, "I'm pregnant."

Benny was on his feet rushing to hug Jo.

"Brilliant!"

Deirdre and Aiden nearly fell over each other and Benny and he bumped noses in the excitement as they embraced.

"Well done you two, I knew there's was something in the air when you were calling round at this time on a Sunday; that's great news!"

"Well the dress is going to be a problem, I'll have to look for an alternative now. Going by my reckoning I'll be about six months by the wedding date, so a straight sheath won't really do the trick."

"I offered to make her one out of the material from the sail on the boat, but she won't hear tell of it."

"You would," Benny came back at him. "C'mon into the kitchen 'til I get ye a beer, this is a cause for celebration. Jo, what'll you have?"

"Just a soft drink, thanks Benny."

"Deirdre?"

"I'll have a glass of wine. Go on you two get the drinks, Jo and I have serious women's talkin' to do."

As the men left the room Deirdre turned to Jo.

"That's great news, love, but a bit of a shock for you, all the same."

"You're telling me, I didn't even realise I was late, with working and trying to catch up on my course work in the evenings the days have just flown by. Turns out I'm probably about six weeks gone we reckon. If it hadn't been for Gail, I'd have been on a diet for the next week. The shop assistant thought it could be fluid retention, so I immediately thought I should get a hormone test done. She's keeping the dress over for me until next Saturday and a size ten as well, but now that I know I'm pregnant there's no way I could carry it off. I'll have to rethink the style I'm after. Would ya listen t'me, I'm talkin' like a washin' machine. I'm just so ...excited."

"Of course y'are, I know it's a disappointment when you'd found the dress you'd set your heart on, but don't worry there'll be other dresses. Have you told Corey yet? And your Dad and Kate?"

"Corey doesn't know yet. I want to keep it quiet until I get over the three month stage, but I had to tell Dad and Kate. They were babysitting for me last night, y'know, for the night out with the girls. Of course, I couldn't drink and I was so tired, I think it must have been the shock. I'd to leave early. I fobbed Dad and Kate off tellin' them I'd a cold. Since Aiden didn't know I couldn't tell them. As they were leaving today I just wanted to blurt it out, but I called them this evening, they're delighted for us. Kate had suspected something was up of course. Y'know what she's like, she knows me inside out, said I was much too subdued for a girl who'd just bought her wedding dress."

"Yes, I must admit I suspected something when Aiden rang. You don't normally visit on a Sunday night. Anyway, I'm so pleased for both of you. Are you goin' to see your doctor this week then?"

"Yeah, but y'know Aiden, he already knows the due date he reckons."

"Oh yes. Maybe as his mother I shouldn't be asking this, but it was a memorable night then?"

Jo laughed and replied, "Remember the Friday in January you went up home to see your mum? That's a stupid question of course y'do. Aiden had coffee with Benny to see how things were, y'know they were both worried about what you'd find when you arrived after getting the call from Geraldine that morning. Well, Benny offered to take Corey out for tea and to the bowling to give us a chance of a night out. We jumped at it, it had been a bad week all round for everybody with all the doom and gloom about the economy. We went to the cinema then on for dinner. I think we can safely say we forgot our troubles and got happy. Aiden's sure that was the night, so by his reckoning the baby's due on the 16th of October. We'll see."

"He's probably right."

She smiled at her future daughter-in-law, who was blushing slightly at her shared confidence.

She didn't tell Jo that Benny had been exactly the same with the conception times of their children - that was possibly too much information for her. But she was sure if Aiden thought he knew, he knew.

Benny and Aiden returned to the room with the drinks.

"Here's to both of you and your good news; may it all work out happily for all of you."

They drank the toast and the men sat down to join them, it had been quite a weekend. Deirdre kept the news from home to herself knowing it would worry Jo to hear Orla's husband had tracked her down. She would find out soon enough.

For now, Deirdre was happy to sit with her son and future daughter-in-law and celebrate their great news, observing Aiden, his eyes dancing as he talked animatedly, she was overjoyed for both of them.

172

Chapter 21

THAT NEXT MONDAY MORNING EARLY, Orla was in the shop processing an order when Jo arrived.

"Hey how's you? Ya just can't stay away from the place."

"You busy?"

"Just putting this order through; nothing that cannot wait. Is something wrong?"

Jo looked down the shop, "There's no one in?"

"No, it's been quiet. Oh you'll never believe this - we've sold the glass sculpture! Thank God for rich Daddies, a sun bronzed medallion man bought it for his daughter's fortieth! You look worried, what is it?"

"I need to talk to you."

Jo walked round behind the counter and stood beside Orla where she sat at the computer.

"You've been up front with me, now I have to be up front with you. I'm pregnant, Orla."

"What? That's great news, Jo. Why do you look so worried, yer happy about it aren't you?"

"God yes, it's just a bit of a shock that's all."

"Here sit down."

Orla got up and gave Jo her seat as she herself slid onto one of the big stools beside the high counter.

"I just wanted you to know as soon as possible. I'm not telling everyone until I pass the three month stage, but I wanted you to know now. Of course, I don't want to leave or anything. I love my job, but obviously I'll need time off when the baby's born...I, oh God, I can't think straight. I've to look for another wedding dress, after all the waiting. I've been to the doctors; first thing this morning. My date's the 16th of October, so I'll be like a beached whale on my big day."

"Oh calm down." Orla smiled at her worried expression, "I'll make us a cup of coffee, nice 'n' strong, eh?"

Jo sat and waited, forgetting she should avoid strong coffee now. Although she was saying the word "pregnant" the reality of being pregnant hadn't really sank in. She gazed out the window, feeling happy and sad and confused all at once. All these years to get around to doing a degree and she had to get pregnant halfway through.

Orla appeared with the mugs of coffee on a tray with a plate of biscuits.

"It's great news, Jo. Everything will work out fine. We'll get something sorted out for yer maternity leave, don't worry. It's just a lot fer ya to deal with at once, I understand that, but you've got Aiden, he must be like a dog with two tails."

Jo grinned, "He is."

"This'll take yer mind off your own problems; guess who came looking for me on Saturday night?"

Jo knew immediately who she meant.

"Oh no, ya didn't let him in, Orla?"

"I'd the door opened before I realised who had knocked, and he was up the hall in a flash, with Snapper at his heels, thank God."

"What about the camera?"

"I forgot to switch it on. I'd been out. Don't worry, I know it was careless of me. I won't be that stupid again."

"So, what happened?"

Orla related the story as Jo sat listening open mouthed, interjecting occasionally, "Jesus, he's lucky Declan didn't shoot him. He'd be very thick about outsiders comin' onto the farm."

She continued with her tale, concluding, "So that was that. I honestly don't think he'll be back, but I'll take no more chances I can tell ya!"

"Thank God Geraldine and Liam were about. I told ya they'd look out for you. Declan must have been visiting his mum and Dad."

Jo knew there was no way Geraldine wouldn't have been on the phone to Deirdre on Saturday night telling her this news, she would have told her last night if it hadn't been for their news about the baby.

"Yeah he was. I owe him big-time. He mentioned his wife, Molly wasn't it?"

"Yeah, she was lovely by all accounts, only thirty eight when she died. I never met her; I'd only just met Aiden when she died. It was quick from what I can gather, diagnosed in January and dead by April."

"Cancer?"

"Yeah, breast cancer. It's terrible for him. I don't think he's come to terms with it yet. They were together from school, each of them only fourteen when they started going out, Deirdre told me. And the poor boys, they were still so young to lose their mother."

"He stayed the night." Jo's head jerked up from her biscuit. "On the sofa, I mean. You're as bad as Anne Marie. It was a comfort I can tell ya, but I don't want to impose on his good nature. He offered to call in to check up on me each night, until it becomes a bit lighter in the evenings, but I said no. It wouldn't be right to expect that of him."

Jo's eyes twinkled.

"Maybe, he'd like to."

"Now you're at it. I'm still married."

"Not for long, not for long."

Jo smiled at Orla's embarrassment, thinking she would have to keep an eye on things in the country. This was just what Orla needed.

Orla changed the subject; she was back to being all business.

"Now about you; its early days, but what about Siobhan? Do you think she'd want to cover for you, or would it be too long a stint for her?"

"I can only ask. I'll give her a ring and see how the land lies, but I'll leave it a week or too if you don't mind, I'm still getting used to the idea of having another baby, I'll let you know. Thanks for the coffee, Orla. I feel better now. Seriously, don't take any more chances, don't open the door unless you're sure who's in front of it."

"I won't, promise, see you tomorrow."

Kieran checked out his reflection in the men's room mirror, ruffling and rearranging his already perfectly sculpted 'bed head'. He searched through the pockets of his jacket for the pack of breath mints, shook out two and placed them on his tongue; giving his image another quick glance in the full length mirror, he nodded to himself. "Go for it, Kieran, today's the day!"

It was approaching nine thirty on Monday 9th March and Kieran was on his way to a staff meeting. Juliet had called an impromptu meeting when she arrived in, quite a few of the sales team were panicking. Eve was sure the axe was going to fall on her today, she had failed to make target three months in a row.

Kieran, with the others, gathered around the water cooler was sympathetic, reassuring her with platitudes. In reality, he couldn't understand why she was still there. In his opinion, she was a waste of space. Juliet had been back and forth to London office for blocks of days at a time over the last lot of weeks, so she probably just wanted to give them a pep talk. He wasn't overly concerned that the meeting had been called on a Monday morning, outside of her normal routine; she was catching up that was all.

Her absences over the previous weeks had made it almost impossible for Kieran to get a chance to speak with her alone. He had decided to put his plan of action into play today, he would make an excuse to wait behind and when they were alone he would ask her out. He joined the others as they thronged down the corridor to the conference room. No one spoke now. They were all alone in their thoughts.

Juliet strode in, her P.A. by her side. They made their way to the two remaining chairs in the centre of the circle at the top of the table. She remained standing, gripping the back of the chair with both hands as she spoke, "I'll make this brief. There's no easy way to break this news to all of you. The branch is closing. The business will be transferred to Singapore. I myself will be relocating to the London office, but I'm sorry to tell you, for yourselves relocation will not be an option. Lisa has a letter for each of you outlining the terms of your severance. Lisa, please."

She turned to her P.A. who rose to her feet and handed the letters out in silence, no one spoke as they took their letters in turn.

"Sorry it had to be this way, thanks for your time."

She turned on her heel and walked out, Lisa followed behind her.

The first thought in Kieran's mind was the concert he had just forked out for, two tickets for Springsteen in Dublin, with accommodation.

The next, was of the commission payment due to him for last month. His figures had been through the roof. He thought, *The bastards! I better see the money!*

The communal thought must have been of the monies due to them, apart from Eve who was sobbing into a large tissue. She hadn't seen a bonus in months.

The rest of them looked to the envelope in their hand, and the sound of ripping paper ensued, as they each checked out their terms of redundancy.

Someone spoke, "Well I was expectin' a bit of a bollockin', but I wasn't expectin' this."

Another voice joined in, "None of us were. Fuckin' Singapore, what's all that about?"

Kieran thought he couldn't be arsed doing a post mortem, they were history that was it. He stood and pushed his chair out of the way and left the room.

Back at his desk he began clearing out the drawers throwing bits of rubbish into the bin, he thought of Juliet's words.

I myself will be relocating to London office, but I'm sorry to tell you, for yourselves relocation will not be an option.

He looked around him at the devastated faces. Relocation? He thought about it, not for the rest of these losers certainly, but for him surely it was a possibility. His figures were consistently high, throughout the duration of the time he had been there, that was bound to be an incentive for them to send him to the London office.

He would choose his moment, talk to Juliet. She couldn't overlook him, not after all the hard work he had put in to building his area up. She couldn't.

Kieran was still mulling the idea over in his head, but it was hard to think straight with Eve boo-hooing in the background. She had now exhausted all of her colleagues and was systematically going through the contacts on her phone it seemed, stabbing at it after each finished conversation. Not that they appeared to be actual conversations, from what Kieran could hear, they were a series of 'poor me' monologues directed at anybody who would listen.

He had had enough; he went into the men's room to pee. At the mirror he scrutinised his face. What would be the best tack? To go in all guns blazing and demand to be relocated, telling her it was obvious he was such an asset to the company they couldn't possibly do without him or to finally ask her out. Appeal to her feminine charms, take her out, wine her and dine her, and put his proposal to her after sex. Make her realise now that they had finally got it together, it would be a shame to throw it all away, going to London, leaving him behind.

Yeah, he would go for the second option. Sex would help his case, he had no doubt. He would strike while the iron was hot. No time like the present. Reaching for the breath mints again he sucked on them, stopping at the full length mirror to check out his stance. Breeze in, one hand in trouser pocket, casual, confident, cheeky grin, how could she refuse? He grinned at himself as he pulled the door toward him and marched down the corridor toward Juliet's office.

The door to the outer office was open, he sailed in smiling his smile at Lisa.

"Hey, Lisa, Juliet got a moment?"

I'll check, what's it about?"

He said conspiratorially, "Personal."

Lisa rose and went in, seconds later she returned.

"She can see you for a few minutes. She has a meeting in ten."

"It won't take that long, thanks, Lisa."

"Yes, Kieran, what can I do for you?" She didn't offer him a seat so he stood smiling at her, striking up the casual pose.

"I was wondering if you'd like to have dinner with me."

"Sorry?"

"In light of today's news, I thought I better ask you out while I have my chance."

"Out. Why?"

"Well because it's obvious there's an attraction between us, we're both divorced, young and free and single."

Her face was tense.

"Have you lost your mind, Mr Hughes? Your marital status is of no interest to me whatsoever. Just for the record I may be divorced, but I live with my long-time partner, a beautiful woman called Jane. Yes, Mr Hughes, not that it's any of your business, but I am a lesbian. I think this exchange is over, goodbye."

Kieran was stunned, he looked at her. She was tall, slim and blond, dressed in an expensively cut pale blue linen dress with a string of pearls round her neck and matching earrings, a vision of womanly femininity. She couldn't possibly be a lesbian.

As though reading his thoughts, she came back at him.

"I keep my Doctor Marten's for Saturday nights. Please close the door on your way out thank you."

Her head dropped and she returned to her computer screen. Kieran walked out past Lisa still unable to believe what he had just heard. He could have sworn Lisa giggled to herself as he passed. What was he going to do now?

As he walked back to the office and toward his own desk, Eve was still sobbing into the phone. She was getting on his nerves big-time. He grabbed his own tissue box and fired it across the office at her. It landed bang in the middle of Eve's desk. She looked up like a startled deer, as he snarled,

"Dry yer eyes!"

Grabbing his bag he threw it over his shoulder and made his way to the lifts. He would have to do the employment agencies again, now was as good a time as any. As he stood in the lift going down, he still couldn't believe he had gotten Juliet so wrong. What about all the secret signs? Frig! Women! He'd never figure them out.

Out on the street he walked toward the Cathedral Quarter to eat his packed lunch. The day was dry and bright, the pigeons flew around his head as he ate, he swatted his displeasure.

The passers-by swarmed past, chittering into his thoughts. Christ, was there no peace to be got? The sandwich eaten, he rolled the wrapper up and tossed it in the general direction of the litter bin; his aim missed. He swigged his water down and got to his feet, heading in the direction of High Street. He'd had a few successes with one of the agencies there; he would start with that one.

Rummaging through his inside pocket for the business card he checked out the name. Suzanne, that was her, he would go and see Suzanne.

Kieran bounded up the stairs two at a time, stopping to allow two girls to pass as they walked down toward him. They smiled their thanks, as they edged alongside him in the narrow space, he murmured, "How's it goin', girls?"

They responded, smiles widening.

Women liked him, he had charm, now it was time to use it again on Suzanne.

As he swung the door open he could see her behind the receptionist, in the main office. She nodded acknowledging him, "Hello… looking around again… Kevin isn't it?"

"Kieran, yes, afraid so."

"I'll not be a moment… Kieran… just finishing a CV."

A few minutes passed then she indicated for him to take a seat opposite her.

He explained the morning's events.

"That's awful... what a shock for a Monday morning. Things are getting worse every week... this recession is really taking its toll." She remembered her role. "But never mind... there's plenty out there for experienced executives like yourself, Kevin..."

Suzanne was starting to annoy him now; she had one of those whiney sing-songy voices. And she was a 'cake bake.' *Where do ya go to buy make-up in that shade of orange?* he asked himself.

"Kieran!" he interjected, forcefully.

"Sorry... I'm having a bad day... bit of a hangover... I was out on the razz last night... didn't get home 'til four... I think I must be getting too old for it." Her mouth dropped in an unbecoming grimace and then she laughed at her own unfunny comment. "Now, Kieran ...let's get yer...details up..."

She sounded like one of those call centre operators, the ones that you get when you ring up to complain to your phone company. Singing every word at you, the tone reaching a crescendo at the end of each sentence, as they ask you your mother's maiden name and your inside leg measurement. When all you want to do, is find out why you have been charged seven hundred quid for a call to the Maldives, you have never actually made.

Her fingers flickered over the keys.

"Here we go... Now what was your last position?"

He wanted to get up and walk out, but he was desperate. Jo would go bloody ballistic if he couldn't meet the maintenance payments. Yer woman Suzanne was lovely looking though, only about twenty four or five. Maybe he should ask her out, see if she could help him fall into something quickly before he had to face the prospect of signing on again. Anything was worth a try. He answered her questions helpfully as she updated his CV trying to press the mute button on her tone of voice. She was here to help him so he may as well let her do her job.

She completed the CV with a big cheesy grin, a grin that said, "How smart am I?"

Suzanne then proceeded to scan the screen for suitable vacancies.

"Here's one...merchandising for a leading U.K. based company...no that's no good, only eight hours a week...Ah here we go... insurance sales... commission only...no?"

Kieran was toying with the idea of asking her out. Could he stick her through a whole night? Why not, there was nothing else happening. Maybe they could each wear their iPods', zoom each other out, he thought. As the episode came to an end without any possibilities of immediate interviews he decided, *What t'hell, go for it!*

"Thanks, Suzanne, I've no doubt you'll find something great for me before I've even cleared my desk. I was wondering eh, I hope you don't think I'm out of order, would you like to go out for a meal tomorrow night?"

Suzanne considered, looking him up and down. She usually preferred her boyfriends to be in well paid, secure, occupations. He had potential though, loads of experience, and he was well presented. But he was a bit old, "pushin' forty from the wrong end" as they referred to men like him in the business. He definitely was good looking in a sexy obvious way though, but then nothing wrong with that, she chuckled inwardly to herself.

This was her last summer of freedom before her long-term boyfriend returned from university in Bristol. They had been together from sixth year and before Ian left for England they had made a pact that they could both see other people. *Sow our wild oats for a few years.* Then on his return he'd find a suitable position for himself and they would get engaged and marry the following year. It was all planned. Ian would settle into a secure position within the legal profession, and she would find herself a place in society and settle down to married life. Both sets of parents approved of their match, the merging of two old Ulster/Scots families, everyone was happy. So what was the harm? It was her last few months.

"I'd love to." She glanced down at her screen to check his name, "Kieran, that would be lovely."

Kieran thought, *Yeah, Loveleeeeee!*

He left her with one of his special smiles. They loved that. He bounded down the stairs into the street, thinking of where he would take her to eat. He couldn't afford anything flash, but he knew Miss Suzanne wouldn't settle for a 'Happy Meal'. Kieran knew he would have to think about this one. It might be worth speculating a few bob if she could open doors for him.

Meanwhile, he had to consider when to tell Jo. He dreaded it, but he would have to tell her sooner rather than later. These company relocations and redundancies were all over the news at present.

As he turned the corner toward the building he worked in, he half expected to see a local TV news crew outside, filming yer man Delargy, as he reported yet more jobs losses for the province. Kieran knew he would have to tell Jo before the news got out, or she would go mad. She'd go mad either way. Jo was hard to stick most of the time, and even harder to stick now, since she'd picked up with her fancy boyfriend, Aiden. Blokes like him made Kieran sick. Born with a silver spoon in his mouth, his rich Daddy was an ex banker who probably owned the advertising agency he worked in. By coincidence Brannigan senior was the banker who had fired Kieran from his last position. Kieran had no love for the name Brannigan, neither the banker father, nor the boyfriend son. Kieran couldn't bring himself to even think the word fiancé. Stupid bitch betrothed at her age. Aiden was welcome to her and her house full of paints and canvasses.

He sighed, as he entered the doors into the foyer. This was the last thing he'd been expecting to deal with today. Maybe he should consider moving to London anyway. He entered the office and strode toward his desk, thinking that it was unusually quiet. One of his colleagues spoke.

"Eve had to go home; she was very upset."

Good. There is a God.

But, on realising all eyes were on him, he stopped and spread his hands out from his body. His stance asked the question, *What?*

Chapter 22

BY MONDAY MORNING, CASSIE WAS back to normal, buzzing and ready to go. Now that everything was in place she had no idea how she was going to get through the two weeks until they could move into their business unit. They even had their staff sorted. Gail and she had interviewed a couple of dozen applicants for the cleaning posts in a city hotel. They had chosen a small team of permanent workers from them with a bigger backup pool of casual workers, to be called upon as and when required. She just hoped they weren't being too optimistic.

They had placed a few newspaper adverts to promote the launch of the business, but couldn't start the advertising proper until they were up and running and ready to man the office. The website looked excellent, simple, but striking. Aiden had no doubt the enquiries would flood in from it, but as yet they had no jobs on for the waiting staff. Cassie felt they needed to do something now to drum up business. Maybe it wasn't too soon to contact Tony O'Connor.

She rang Gail.

"I was thinking of ringin' yer man O'Connor today, put the feelers out see if he's any jobs coming up that would get us started. After all, it's only two weeks today 'til we're in business. Oh, I love sayin' that!"

"I know it's great, isn't it? I was walking past the bank today on my way to the shops and I looked at the place as I passed and thought, Thanks, Jerry you did me a favour. I'd never've had the nerve to consider leavin' if they hadn't gotten rid of me. Yeah you go ahead, ring him. Let me know how it goes. Good luck."

Cass reached out to put the kettle on. *After this cup of coffee* she thought, *I have to psyche myself up.*

She sipped the coffee as she turned the business card over in her hand. For the umpteenth time that morning she checked her list of things to do that day.

This morning, she had a few loose ends to tie up, and she had to pick up the stationery after lunch. Gail had to do a final check, with the company fitting the unit, to ensure the blinds had been installed that morning. She looked at the card again, now do it. She dialled the number and waited.

"Tony O'Connor Property Rentals," sang out the telephonist.

"Hello, I'd like to speak to Mr O'Connor, please."

"May I ask who's calling?" she trilled.

"Cassie Gallagher."

"And the nature of your call, please?"

"Eh," she replied, standing up from her stool to give herself more confidence. Where had she read that? "Contract cleaning, I'm a director of 'Call-a-Cleaner.'"

"Hold on, please."

She had wanted to say Aiden had given her his number, but the girl was too quick. Maybe just as well; she would have started to babble.

She gathered her composure as the girl's voice came back to her.

"Mr O'Connor on the line for you."

"Tony O'Connor."

"Hello, Mr O'Connor: Cassie Gallagher here. I was given your contact details by Aiden Brannigan…"

"Yes, 'Call-a-Cleaner.' He mentioned you to me. I've your business card here; you're just setting up, isn't that right?"

"Yes, on the 23rd of the month. I thought I'd give you a call to introduce myself. Maybe we could arrange to meet up and discuss terms, before the launch."

She sounded in control, but her legs were shaking. She couldn't sit down, though. She waited for his reply as she strode up the length of the kitchen.

"Sorry, I'm checking my diary; this week's out, I'm afraid I'm in Dublin from tomorrow…"

She was relieved, was about to say, *"Thanks anyway, sorry to bother you,"* and hang up.

She felt like a child making a prank call, she wanted to put the phone down and go into the other room and watch Philip and Fern, back to her real life where she had no business calling up men she didn't know…Jesus, he was talking again. "I've half an hour this afternoon; may be short notice for you though, around four?"

"Four would be fine. Where?" she replied in a confident casual tone, far removed from the way she was feeling.

"Do you know the new apartment blocks …?"

He gave her an address over the east of the city. She had heard of it, quickly wrote the details down and read them back to him.

"That's it, four o'clock, see you."

Oh Christ, she couldn't get out of it now.

"Thanks, I'll bring my business partner, bye."

"Look forward to it, bye."

She grabbed the stool and sat down. She had done it, their first business meeting. Her fingers reached for the phone and she fumbled at it searching for Gail's number.

"We've got a meeting with him today at four o'clock."

"Today? Christ, the state o'me, I'm up to me oxters in flour…seriously, *TODAY?*"

Gail had been baking muffins Nigella style, wallowing in her newfound status, enjoying playing Superwoman, Goddess in the kitchen and future Business Director extraordinaire, but she wanted to daydream about it for a while yet, make a few more preparatory phone calls, before getting into the zone for real.

"Afraid so. He's in Dublin all week. He said he'd fit us in around four for half an hour. So forget the 'Domestic Goddess' bit girl, we're on. It's time to don 'the suit!'"

They had both shopped together and bought a couple of business suits each, with matching power statement accessories and the obligatory killer heels. They'd had a laugh trying them on for themselves and their families. Now, it was for serious.

"Okay, I'll finish up and get myself sorted. What time?"

"I'll pick you up about a quarter past three, it's a bit early, but allowing for traffic at that time. Calm down, we'll be fine. Lucky we got the hair done on Saturday. See ya then."

Gail strode up and down her front room, practicing her walk in the high heels, checking out the time. It was just gone three. She tried a few more attempts, then lifted the jacket from the hanger and carefully put it on.

As she scrutinised her reflection in the hall mirror, she decided she looked the part, there was no doubt about that, and surely that was half the battle.

She caught the image of the van through the window in the hall door. Dave had organised the new van and signage for them, picking it up on Saturday morning. They had assured him there was no hurry, but he had insisted saying it was better with them, than sitting in some dealership yard. It felt strange to be using it for the business so soon, but she was ready.

Earlier, as she showered and dressed for their first meeting together, Gail had struggled to contain her nerves. But as she thought back to that Friday morning in January, and the devastation she had felt when her manager had called her into his office and informed her she was being made redundant, she found the control she needed to get through this first challenge. They were strong Cassie and she; they would make a success of this business together. She knew how lucky she was to be given this chance for herself and her family. She wasn't about to squander it by giving in to nerves. Taking a deep breath, Gail held her head up and strode down the path to meet her friend. They were in business.

They arrived much too early, as they knew they would. It was better that way the extra time gave them a space to collect their thoughts.

Cassie had all the prices in her folder, and the boxes of leaflets in the back of the vehicle, outlaying their services and charges.

"What did he sound like?" Gail queried.

"Business like, a bit brusque, but friendly enough."

They checked out the accommodation around them.

"Pricey area, suppose they let to a lot of professional types round here."

"Yeah, it's not really a family area anymore, but then where is? It's hard to believe there's really a market for all this accommodation in Belfast isn't it?" Cass remarked.

"Changed times, thank God. Buildings like these would've had the bejaysus blown out of them when we were growin' up. But then, that's the very reason no one would have spent the money putting them up in the first place. Look at the Europa Hotel, how many times did they try to flatten that over the years, I lost count round about attempt twenty three…"

They sat surveying their surroundings reflecting on the changing face of the city.

"Riverside living; who'd've thought it? In those days you'd have needed to wear a gas mask passin' the Lagan, the honk would've knocked ya out, remember, in the summer?"

Gail nodded her agreement, saying, "I wonder what he looks like. We don't even know who we're waiting for."

"Probably small, fat and baldy. And he'll be driving a Porsche," said Cass.

"Is that what he told you he drives?"

"No, but sure that's what they always drive. Probably a red one, oul fellas with loads o'money always do. A big fat gut and a big fat wallet," Cass replied her voice loaded with sarcasm.

Gail was about to say, "How do you know he's old?" Her words were halted by the sight of a car swinging into the car park at speed. "Oh, here we go! Wrong about the car."

They watched as a slick, shiny black convertible pulled up beside them, glancing over at the driver as he stepped out into the car park. Tall, blond and tanned, he smiled at them, a smile that showed a row of white even teeth in a full generous month. A movie star smile. Gail watched as Cass stepped out of the van to meet him, and thought, Wrong about the car, and oh so wrong about the man.

"Tony O'Connor, good to meet ya."

He walked round to greet them, his hand outstretched, his eyes did a quick once over on Cass, almost indiscernible, but Gail saw it. His gaze falling back onto her face in time for her greeting, "Good to meet you, Tony, I'm Cassie, we spoke earlier and this is my partner Gail Burroughs."

Gail extended her hand and met his smile saying, "How are ya, not a bad day?"

"Nippy enough still, let's get inside. I'll show you round, sorry it's such a rush, but as I said I'm away all week and I was keen to meet you, Aiden told me all about your venture. You'll be in at the deep end, I'm telling ya, in the present climate. I can't keep up to the demand for rentals."

They stepped into the lift and he explained about the properties he rented in the city, and surrounding areas.

"We get a lot of business people, professionals of all sorts. It's transitory, people who are here today gone tomorrow, so I use a lot of

187

contract cleaners. Usually the same two companies, but I'm willing to give you a go if the terms are right, here we are."

He stepped out of the lift and walked toward a door opposite, putting a key in the lock.

"Have a look, go ahead."

He stood back to allow them to enter. The room was sparsely, but elegantly furnished with two matching brown sofas and a glass coffee table, the floor was covered in a white carpet, the décor all beiges and creams. He led them out onto the balcony which overlooked the river, the view was stunning.

"It's lovely. I can see why you've no bother renting these." Cass observed.

"The carpets are beautiful, but white must be a problem. Do you have much bother with spillages?" Gail asked.

"Not too bad. In the main, I think a lot of these people only use the apartments for sleeping in. There's never much evidence of cooking in the kitchens, and most of the electrical appliances are still in showroom condition."

"Are they all three and four storey?" Cass queried.

"Around here, yes, I've a few fives and multi stories too, but the riverside ones are all three and four. I'll show you the gardens." He closed the big patio windows and locked up. "Obviously these clients don't have time to garden, that's all included in the rent."

They went back down to the ground in the lift and through more glass doors to the small, well-kept gardens. Mostly heathers and alpines set in areas of loose stone landscaping. He spread his outstretched hand toward the pathway.

"I take it you do pathways and windows?"

Gail was about to say no, but Cassie got in first, "Oh yes of course, we offer a full service."

"Great, well, I'm sure we can do business then."

Gail tried to catch her eye to give her a 'What the hell are you playing at?' look, but Cass refused to glance in her direction to receive it.

He indicated a greenish patch on the path before them.

"The build-up of moss on these paths can be a bugger, a compensation seekers dream! For the windows on the multi-storeys, I use a company of high rise window cleaners, but with the smaller complexes I prefer to leave it all to the contract cleaners, keeps it all in the one box as it were. Can you give me a leaflet and a price list, sorry to be so abrupt, but I'm running behind time. When ya get to know me you'll realise that's always the way with me, always lookin' for twenty six hours outta every day."

As they reached the car park Cassie walked ahead to the van to get the leaflets. Gail was almost sure he was checking out Cass's legs, but she couldn't be sure and right now she was too annoyed to care. Cass handed him the paperwork.

"Thanks for coming down at such short notice. I'll be in touch."

He shook both of their hands, and again, Gail thought his gaze lingered slightly longer on Cass than was professionally necessary. With a wave he was gone, revving out of the car park onto the road.

"Well, that went well." Cass looked pleased.

"Windows and paths? Have I missed something? Are ya mad or drunk?" Gail shrieked.

"Stop panicking. He's goin' to give us business, what did you expect me to say?"

"I expected you to tell the truth. 'No sorry, we don't offer those services.'"

"Don't be daft, it's no big deal. We've two weeks yet; we just need to buy some telescopic cleaners for the windows and a couple of power washers." Cass's tone was casual.

Gail interjected, "And advertise for people who can operate them, and get in touch with the insurance company for a quote for the extra coverage! What if he gives us a job to try us out and we can't find anyone to operate telescopic window mops and power washers, what then?"

"We will, trust me. I've a feeling about this. Mr Tony O'Connor could be the making of this business. We've been aiming too low, just thinking of basic office cleaning. No, this is where the money is and we're goin' to get our share of it. Believe me, all we need is self-belief, really, Gail, we're on the road now. Have faith. We'll place the ads right away, we'll find the right people. I know it."

Gail looked out the window as they travelled back home still a bit huffed, neither of them saying much. Cass was right; it had gone well. Tony O'Connor had loads of properties. They had checked him out on the internet when Aiden gave them his details. They couldn't afford to look this particular gift horse in the mouth because they were ill equipped or over cautious.

Gail knew Cass was right to think on her feet. She turned to her friend, her face serious as she drove.

"I don't like surprises, that's all. Promise me you won't pull a move like that again. You are right; we have to take the chance. He could put a lot of business our way."

"I'm sorry. I know my mouth runs away with me sometimes, we'll discuss all decisions from now on, okay. But I am right." She grinned at her. "He was a bit of alright too wasn't he, neither fat nor baldy, eh?"

"Yeah, and he fancied you!"

"He did not! Did he?" Cass replied, turning to glance at her to see if she was serious. Gail's face said she was. Cass grinned again, delighted with herself.

That same Monday had found Deirdre travelling around Lisburn, Saintfield and the surrounding districts, delivering the St Patrick's Night concert tickets.

While she did the deliveries she double checked the transport quotas to kill two birds with one stone. She had worked through half of her list by one, only one more to do in this area then she could move on to the second part of the list. Most of the recipients were fine about the lateness, although she did notice the odd dirty look. But a few of them complained outright to her that the tickets were a week late.

"How are we supposed to sell them now with only a week to go?"

The final straw was the next call as one oul bugger remarked, "If you can't deliver on time we'd be better off doing our own, the way we used to!"

Deirdre had had enough. She was hungry and tired, volunteering was usually rewarding and stimulating, but on days like this, she seriously questioned why she bothered. She couldn't help but think, people like him should jump off a cliff when they turned sixty, put the rest of us out of their misery. Then she remembered her own age and thought, *Not long to go now. Maybe Benny and me should make a pact to jump off Cave Hill together. Nah, we've too much to live for.*

She bit her tongue and replied, "Apologies again for the delay, but as I explained when I phoned, it couldn't be helped, the woman looking after the printing has 'flu."

She turned on her heel and walked out. He was still ranting as she walked out onto the street.

Dunmurry community centre was next on her list, then she could stop for lunch. She pulled up in the car park checking the name on her contact list, Mrs Joan Gibson. As she entered the front doors she turned to the reception window, a woman inside pulled the glass open, asking, "Can I help you?"

"Yes, I'm Deirdre from Activity Age. I'm looking for Joan Gibson."

"Joan's not in today; maybe somebody else can help. What's it about?"

"I've the tickets here for the St Patrick's Night do and I need to check your transport needs for the night."

"Sammy'll be able to help you with that. I'll give him a shout. C'mon ahead."

Deirdre pushed her way into the main hall through the big double doors, while the receptionist entered through the office door, calling out, "Sammy, it's the woman about the do next week, the tickets and that. What's yer name again?"

"Deirdre."

The old man called Sammy picked up a file and shuffled over to Deirdre.

"Deirdre, this is Sammy. He should be able to sort ye out."

The woman returned to the office.

"How ya doin' love, I'll take that box off ye. Do ya need me to sign anything?"

"How are ya? Yes, if you could just sign here," she indicated the line on her sheet, "that's lovely. Now, I need to confirm your numbers for the buses."

"Joan left all that with me." He opened the file and handed Deirdre the relevant paperwork. "There ye go, job's a good'n,' Deirdre."

"Thanks very much, Sammy."

Deirdre wasn't about to start explaining about the lateness again, she was out of there. She smiled her thanks at the old man and turned to leave. As she walked away from him, he called after her, "Sorry, I didn't get yer surname."

"Brannigan, Deirdre Brannigan."

She turned to walk on.

It was an impulse, but he had to ask, "How's the Benny Boy?"

She spun around. "You know Benny?"

"I think I do indeed, and I know you too, Deirdre. How are things in the Royal these days?"

She looked at him and glanced down at the signature on the sheet of paper.

'S.Stevenson.'

"Sammy Stevenson!"

"The very one!"

She saw him now, really looked at him.

"My God, after all these years."

She rushed toward him and he held his arms out.

"It's a small world," Sammy uttered.

Deirdre was speechless as she hugged their old friend. Benny was never going to believe this. He still had the cheeky, lopsided grin and 'the devil looking out of his eyes'.

"It's a shock alright. I thought about yous many a time over the years, Deirdre, wondered how yis were getting' on."

"Benny tried to find you so many times, all we knew was you'd moved out Lisburn direction…"

"Dunmurry, I'm just up Riverside Row, been there since the day I left Belfast just gone thirty six years."

"Jesus, we never even thought of here. He even asked in the shops in Sandy Row, where he knew you shopped…"

"Ach, I never went back down much after I moved, too many memories. Have ye time fer a drop o'tea?"

"Of course, I have, Sammy. My God this is unbelievable."

For Deirdre it really was unbelievable. After the initial few years of Benny's efforts to contact Sammy, Deirdre had discouraged him. Sammy had been a chronic alcoholic at one time and it was her belief that the likelihood was he had gone back on the drink, was possibly dead. Otherwise, why wouldn't he have contacted them? He had their address and phone number.

"C'mon ahead."

She followed Sammy toward the small kitchen area at the back.

"Sit yourself down. It's quiet now after the exercise class.

192

There'll be nobody about here until after two when the yoga starts. Tell me all your news."

"Well, we're grandparents now, both retired, but not that long ago. We're living on the Old Stranmillis. We were in the wee house on the Stranmillis Road until the three kids were born, then they outgrew it. We moved up the road and we've been there ever since, thirty years. What about you, Sammy? You're lookin' awful well after all these years."

"Aye, ye wouldn't have put money on me surviving to this age, eh? I wouldn't have put money on me surviving to this age," he laughed.

Deirdre felt guilty, he was right, she'd been sure he was long dead, said as much to Benny any time his name was mentioned.

"It was the that voice got me. I recognised it right away. Then I looked at yer eyes and I knew, still sparklin' full of mischief. You haven't changed a bit, Deirdre."

"Neither have you, you're still a sweet talker."

"Oh, I wish! Ida, my girlfriend, no *partner*, isn't that it nowadays, she says I could charm the birds out of the trees. Life's been good to me, Deirdre. I got a second chance. My daughters and me made it up after their mother died. They helped me get the wee place out here and we got to know each other all over again. I've grandchildren and great grandchildren, too. I spend my days putterin' about, and helping out in here when they need me. Keeps me outta the pubs. No seriously, I haven't had a drink in over forty years, wouldn't risk it. It nearly cost me my life. Have a biscuit."

"No I couldn't eat a bite, I'm too excited. I can't wait to tell Benny, will you give me your phone number, so that he can call you?"

"Of course I will, love, but he may not want to be bothered, there's been a lot of water under the bridge since then."

"Believe me, Sammy, it'll be no bother, he'll be delighted. He still talks about ya 'til this day."

Sammy wrote the number down and Deirdre gave him theirs, she looked at the clock it was almost two.

"I better go and let you get on with yer work. I've still all these tickets to get out. I'll get Benny to call you, he's never gonna believe this!"

They both rose and embraced, she searched his face.

"You knew where we lived, Sammy, why did you lose touch?"

193

"Ah it's one of those long stories, love. You get the Benny Boy to call me. I'll look forward to it."

"I will, I promise, Sammy, bye for now."

She rushed around doing the deliveries over the rest of the afternoon hours, like a woman possessed. Yesterday, Aiden and Jo's news; now this.

Benny was going to be ecstatic. She couldn't wait to see his face.

Chapter 23

DEIRDRE WANTED TO WAIT UNTIL later in the evening when her mother was in bed to tell Benny about Sammy. Mary could be easily upset, if she thought Deirdre wasn't giving her the attention she needed.

They chatted about the wedding over dinner, but they had decided not to tell her mother until closer to the time about the baby. It would be too long-term for her to comprehend; better to wait until nearer the due date.

Her mum liked some of the Monday night programmes; they viewed them together sitting round the fire. Deirdre was miles away. She watched the clock until her mother showed signs of dozing off. This was the pattern. Mary didn't like to leave the fire until sleep overtook her, no matter how tired she was.

Finally, her mother showed signs of tiredness, and Deirdre got her up the stairs and settled.

Back downstairs, she poured two glasses of wine and returned to the front room offering Benny one. He reached out for it, saying, "Wine on a Monday night - we still celebrating? Why not, it was great news, eh?" He was referring to Aiden and Jo's news about the baby.

"It certainly was, but I've got another surprise for you."

"Don't tell me, you're pregnant too!"

"Cheeky. No, this might shock you as much as that though. I met an old friend of ours today."

Benny looked bemused.

"Oh aye, who would that be?"

"Sammy Stevenson!"

The blood drained from Benny's face.

"No!"

"Yes! Alive and well and volunteering in the Dunmurry Community Centre. He's been livin' in Dunmurry since the day and hour he left the bed-sit."

"Dunmurry…we thought Lisburn, Jesus, it's only a village, how hard would he have been to find? Christ, I'm astonished. You're right, I needed this drink." He drank it back and left to bring the bottle in. "How? Tell me it all…"

Deirdre noted the shake in Benny's hand as he held the glass. This news really had knocked him for six. He too had been convinced that his old friend was long dead.

Hours later, Benny was sitting alone gazing into the fire. The wine had been replaced by a glass of whiskey. They had talked for hours about Sammy, asking each other all the unanswered questions. Deirdre had told Benny of his response when she had asked him why he hadn't kept in touch.

"It's one of those long stories."

Thirty six years had passed since they had last seen each other, losing touch shortly after Deirdre and he had moved into the wee house on the Stranmillis Road.

Their old neighbour, Minnie, from the big house in Lawrence Street had died in the January of 1973, and they had searched her address book for a new address for Sammy Stevenson. Under his name, they had found only the number 8; it was possible she had been writing the details down, when she'd had the heart attack that killed her. Sammy had a sister who lived in the area, but they had no idea where. They had attended the funeral, with only some nephew of Minnie's representing her family.

Over the following months, Benny had searched for Sammy, to no avail, checking with the surrounding shopkeepers in Botanic Avenue and Sandy Row. It was a small close knit community, and Sammy had frequented most of the local shops, he was sure someone would know where he had gone. Sure Sammy would have called in with one of them at some point. He was a talker and was well known by all of them.

The nearest Benny got to an address, was a bit of scant information from a butcher in Sandy Row, "Out Lisburn direction, he went out that way to his daughters."

And that was it, but he already knew that. Lisburn was a big place, even then, and trying to find him without an address would have been like looking for a needle in a haystack. Benny thought it was ironic, when he considered how easy it was to get information on people nowadays, but it was a different time, information wasn't that readily available and with the onset of 'the troubles' people scattered from the city and lost touch, whole communities broke up as the paramilitaries took hold of their areas.

Benny had worked in Belfast throughout that time, just getting through the daily bomb scares was an achievement in itself, and often they weren't just scares. By comparison to Deirdre, he'd had it easy. She had worked as a nurse in the Royal Victoria Hospital through those horrendous years, right in the thick of it.

Life had been hard for everybody, but they had just gotten on with it, year after year. And as each New Year dawned, they'd met it with hope believing they'd seen the worst of it, that 'the troubles' wouldn't last another year. Believing the politicians wouldn't let it. If anybody had told any of them it would last thirty years, they would have laughed out loud in sheer disbelief.

Their parents had pleaded with Deirdre and Benny over the years to leave Belfast, come back home and settle with their own people. But they were young and optimistic, they stayed.

Benny got his first promotion that January in 1973, chief cashier, he was young and ambitious, busy living his life with a growing family. Occasionally, he would discuss Sammy with Deirdre, he had been hurt that Sammy hadn't contacted them, feeling the friendship they'd had over his first three years in the city was strong, despite the twenty year age difference, sure it would have survived a house move. Sammy had their phone number, had been in their house, and Benny wondered why he hadn't bothered to call them when he had gotten settled in his new home.

They'd had a Christmas card from him that first year in the house, Kelly Anne's first Christmas, 1972. He'd put a note in telling Benny he had landed a new job out Lisburn direction and one of his daughters had been informed by the Housing Executive that he was going to be offered a new bungalow in the area, the tone was positive and upbeat.

Then, he and Deirdre had called in to see him with a Christmas present, the weekend before Christmas. Sammy had been in great form, looking forward to the holiday season with his family. He had a new job and he was looking forward to the New Year and the prospect of moving out of the bed-sit.

As time passed, and weeks became months, Deirdre was convinced that Sammy, a recovering alcoholic, had gone back on the drink, was possibly even dead, if he had gone at it as he used to, in his wildest days.

Deirdre had never known about the affair Sammy had confided in him about, Benny felt it would be breaking a confidence. The affair had wrecked Sammy's marriage, and damn nearly wrecked his life. He told Benny the woman had gone back to her husband and he had found himself living in the lonely bed-sit in the university area. When Aiden had met Jo, his parents had been pleased for him, his life had been a lonely existence after his marriage failed.

They became engaged in early December 2007, and Deirdre had invited all the family round to celebrate their good news, just before Christmas. Jo's father, Andy, and his partner, Kate had been invited, it was to be the first time they had met Benny and Deirdre and the rest of their family.

As the conversation unfolded, Benny was picking up on similarities to a long ago story he had heard from his old neighbour Sammy. That day, Benny had made the astonishing discovery that Jo's Dad, Andy, was Sammy's old love, Liz's, husband. Liz had died some years before. Kate, Andy's partner and Liz's lifelong friend, was the same Kate who had been a nurse all those years ago, the Kate, who had nursed Sammy through a life threatening beating. He had told Benny years before, that he couldn't believe his eyes, when he had come round in the Belfast City Hospital and seen Liz's best friend, Kate, looking down on him. A friend, who had known of their affair and kept the secret. Kate had been his lifeline. She had been the one who had finally convinced him to seek help for his addiction.

The coincidence was unbelievable, but Benny knew it was true. Jo had always reminded him of someone, that day it all fell into place. He recalled a conversation he'd had with Sammy, after he had been going out with Deirdre about six months.

Benny had confided that he wanted to ask her to marry him, but didn't have the money to buy her a decent engagement ring, Sammy had said, "Ask her, Benny. Girls like Deirdre don't come along every ten minutes. If she's the one, don't wait, life gets in the way…trust me, you know when it's the right one, but for some of us, she turns up too late."

He had proceeded to tell him of his love for Liz Jordan, and how they had spilt up after a few months, because she was married with two young sons. But Sammy had confided they had met up again years later, before Christmas 1967. Both of them were out at separate Christmas functions at a city hotel, and one thing had led to another and she had gone back home with him. They had made love, for the last time. He knew it was a final goodbye, he vowed never to contact her again, to leave her in peace with her husband and sons, but he had been grateful they'd had the chance to be together again, due to the strange twist of fate that had found them both in the same hotel that Christmas.

That day of the party, Christmas a year ago, as everyone talked and laughed in this living room, the final piece of the jigsaw clicked into place. There was a moment when he caught Kate's eye, and he knew for certain, she also knew Jo wasn't Andy's daughter. She had kept Liz and Sam's affair a secret, and she had also kept Jo's parentage a secret. Benny had had to make an excuse to get out of the house, to get his head around the information his brain was trying to process, all at once. He had driven to the garage to buy ice they didn't need. The journey out gave him the time he needed to collect his thoughts. Not only was Andy, Liz's husband and Kate her best friend, Jo, Liz's daughter, was also his old friend Sammy's daughter, it was written all over her face, her familiar smile, shape of the eyes and her love of art. Sammy had a talent for art; he had painted watercolours. Benny remembered his words as he had admired his striking paintings, "Ach, it's just a hobby, something to keep me occupied..."

From the first day Aiden had brought Jo to meet them, Benny had taken to her, she reminded him of someone, he could never quite put his finger on it though. On that day of the Christmas gathering Benny had no doubt who she reminded him of. He did the mental arithmetic, recalling that first visit to the villa in Portugal, when Aiden had brought her out for her birthday. At seven years older than Aiden, she was then thirty nine. Her birthday was in August; she had related the story of her surprise birth four weeks early. Her mother had been in the chemist shop she worked in when her waters broke. He remembered her words, "Four weeks early, my mother said that was the last time I was ever early for anything."

Benny still couldn't believe Sammy was alive and well, and living just a few miles up the road from them. He did a quick mental calculation, Sammy would be eighty two now.

Benny wondered if he knew Liz was dead, wondered if he knew he had a daughter to Liz. He knew one thing for sure, enough time had been wasted, he would phone him tomorrow and arrange to meet up with him.

They had a lot of catching up to do.

Chapter 24

CASS SPENT MOST OF TUESDAY morning scanning the internet for suppliers of telescopic window cleaning equipment and power washers.

She found what she wanted at the right price, but knew she had better check with Gail before ordering them. She had really annoyed Gail yesterday, telling Tony O'Connor they offered services they didn't. Cassie knew she had been right. Sometimes in life you have to think on your feet, but Gail wouldn't take kindly to her making decisions without her again. She would have to tread carefully.

She reached for her phone and hit Gail's number. After their brief conversation about the equipment, Cassie broached the subject of advertising for cleaning staff qualified to use power washers and window cleaning equipment, the insurance company had stipulated unqualified users would not be covered by them. They decided to use the same local papers they had gotten the good response from when looking for the cleaning team as it would be a bit late to advertise in the weekend supplements.

"I'll go ahead and place the ads then. D'ye still love me?"

"Just about, ya headcase. Any word from Tony O yet?"

"God, I wasn't expecting to hear from him that soon. If I do, we might have to don the overalls and do the jobs ourselves."

"Well, if there's any window cleanin' or power washin' required, you're doin' it!"

"Nah, I won't need to. We'll get the operators with these ads, I know it. I'll place them now and we'll be interviewing by the weekend, trust me?"

"I used to. Go ahead, ring them in and we'll see. I better go, I'm baking those muffins I didn't get to make yesterday, I can smell them, better grab them before they burn black."

"Away ye go, Delia."

"No, not Delia, I see myself as more of a Nigella in the kitchen. I'll save one for you, see ya tomorrow."

"Save me two."

"I will. This'll have to be my last pig out, then I'll be on the diet for serious from next week, otherwise I'll never get into this bridesmaids dress in July."

"Yer not a bridesmaid, I keep telling ya, yer a Matron of Honour."

"No, I don't want to be that, that sounds like a big busty oul doll with bingo wings."

"What's happening with the dresses anyway, are you goin' back up this weekend?"

"Yeah, Jo's goin' to ring the shop and tell them her news, explain that particular dress is out now, then we'll head up on Saturday and see what she can find. Considering she's goin' to be six months gone she says it'll have to be a layered effect, but sure she's so slight of herself she'll probably not put on much weight, she didn't with Corey."

"What about yours, though, are you keeping the one she paid the deposit on?"

"That's up to Jo, depends how it looks with whatever she decides on, but it's a simple enough style, I think it would look alright with most types of wedding dress. After all the waiting it's hard to believe we've to start all over again, but I suppose considering her news it's a small price to pay."

"Yeah, says you, so long as you're not in for the full tour of the province again."

"I know. I was starting to have nightmares about bridal shops. Oh no not another one! Please don't make me try on any more dresses! Anyway, I'm away to check this oven before the bloody house burns down, bye!"

"Bye."

Gail removed the tray of muffins from the oven and put another batch in, then made herself a mug of cappuccino and cut a whack of the carrot cake she had baked earlier in the morning. She sat on the sofa with her feet up, watching television with her mid-morning treat, enjoying this short period of full-time domesticity, before their business start-up in just over a week.

She was licking the crumbs of her fingers when the phone

rang again. Reaching for a tissue she wiped the sticky goo off her hands before answering. It was Cass.

"Me again, yer never goin' to believe this."

"What is it?"

"I've only had a call from Tony O'Connor's office, he's given us our first job."

"Jesus, we haven't even opened up yet," shrieked Gail, sputtering her mouthful of coffee.

"Calm down, he knows that. It's for week beginning the 23rd of March, a brand new apartment complex in the city centre, the builders are still putting the finishing touches to it. He wants us to give it a thorough goin' over before the carpets are fitted and furniture is delivered on the 30th."

"Sounds like a big job. How will we know how many cleaners we'll need?"

"The woman in his office, Marlene, said she had full plans of the complex ready for us to pick up at our convenience. She said Tony had stressed that we're just starting up, and we'll need to see the size of the site to work out the labour force we'll need. I said we'd collect them today, we don't want him to think we're not on the ball. Are you okay with that?"

"Of course, we should, but I've Josh's prize-giving this afternoon, I can't disappoint him, I missed it last year because of work. Can you pick them up, Cass?"

"Of course I can, if you're okay with that. Isn't it brilliant, we've at least one job for our first week in business. I told ya I'd a feeling about him. This'll be the start of many, I know it."

"Let's hope we can carry it off."

"We'll carry it off alright. We'll muck in ourselves to keep an eye on progress; it's the only way to get a true estimate of the workforce we need."

"I'll come round tonight and we'll sort out who we need to phone for the first day start and…"

A loud beeping noise resounded through Cass's phone. She asked Gail, "What's that noise?"

But no reply came back. Gail had dropped the phone on the sound of her smoke alarm, and leapt from her sofa to investigate the kitchen.

Flurries of black smoke were wafting from the oven, filling

the kitchen with eye watering clouds of fog-like smoke. She grabbed the oven glove and pulled the door open, inside her tray of beautiful chocolate brownies were burnt to cinders, she dumped them into the sink, running to grab a towel to flick the smoke from the area of the smoke alarm to stop it beeping, at the same time opening the back door to let air in.

Remembering Cassie, she made her way back to the living room and the discarded phone lying on the sofa. Cassie, realising the unfolding scene, could be heard shouting from it, "Are you okay...Gail...Gail?..."

Gail picked it up, "My bloody muffins, I forgot about them. T'hell with this Domestic Goddess crap, go and get those plans, I'll see ya tonight."

Kieran was ticked off about the whole Eve thing. He had been given the cold shoulder since his return to the office yesterday lunchtime. She still hadn't weighed back into work today and he was being treated like a leper. Like he cared, with everything else he had on his plate that day.

He still hadn't told Jo. He had Corey his son that weekend, so he was thinking over if he should just throw it in casually on Saturday as he called to pick him up, "Oh, by the way, I've been made redundant."

Or, should he ring her specifically to tell her that? Either way, he was fucked. She would go mental if she didn't get the maintenance payments. Then there was Suzanne; he was to take her out tonight and money was already tight. But he couldn't let her see he was broke even before he was made redundant or he would be dropped like a hot potato, he knew her type.

'No mon, no fun.'

He hadn't realised his bank account was quite so low until he had checked his online balance that morning. There was nothing else for it; he'd have to tap his ma. He would buy her a bunch of flowers and a couple of cream buns, call in for half an hour at lunchtime and plead his case. He would think of something to tell her he needed the money for. The news of his pay off could wait for another day.

If things took off with Suzanne, he may not get to the stage of being out of work at all. Right now Suzanne was his only hope, he had to impress her, or he was really up shit creek without a paddle.

His mobile rang, it was Jo.

"I just heard the news that your company's pulling out. Relocating to Singapore, all but one member of management will be made redundant. I take it you were going to tell me."

"Of course I was, Jo, I just found out myself today."

"That's funny, the guy on the radio said all staff had been informed first thing yesterday morning."

"Well, they hinted at it, y'know…"

Jesus, why had he bothered answering the call, he was going to get the full on Christmas Lectures now.

"Make sure you get something arranged and quickly. Your son isn't going to suffer for this, no matter what it means for you."

He was about to tell her he had already a few interviews lined up, when she hung up. Kieran looked at the clock, just gone twelve. He would go to lunch now, see if his ma could help him out of a hole until Suzanne came up with something.

Kieran drove back to the office from his brief visit to his mother's. He'd had a quick cup of tea and a sandwich, then he had broached the subject of the loan. He explained about Suzanne, how he was a bit short and really wanted to impress her. He hadn't mentioned the imminent redundancy or the fact that he was only bothering to spend a bit of money on Suzanne because he believed she could help him. He sold it to his mother like he had just met the love of his life, and wouldn't you know, it had to be when he was broke and he couldn't bear the thought of missing his chance of happiness over a simple thing like money.

Of course, his mother fell for it. Firmly believing, her son had been unlucky in his choice of wife. All he really needed was a good woman, the right kind of woman and he would settle down and become the perfect husband. How could she refuse him?

He managed to get out after forty minutes. He knew she liked to see him, knew that she didn't see him often enough, she just wanted to talk, but he had to get back to work, and she did go on. Kieran had a lot on his mind right now. He kissed her lightly on the cheek and promised he would pay her back as soon as he could.

Once inside the car, he counted what she had lent him. More than enough to take Suzanne out for a great meal in one of the new city centre hotels. They were pricey, but it would be worth it if she got him a job. His mood lightened as he headed back to work.

He might even enjoy the night with her. *Loveleeeeee*, he thought.

On that same Tuesday, by ten in the morning Benny was alone in the house. Deirdre had taken her mother shopping, so he knew they would be away for some time. He decided to take the bull by the horns and make the call now.

He took the piece of paper with the phone number on it from his wallet. It was a mobile number, he didn't know Sammy's routine, didn't know if he went to the community centre every day, or if he would find him at home. He didn't care; he had to make the call now.

He dialled the number. Sammy answered on the third ring, "Hello."

The familiar voice sounded in Benny's ear, it was older of course, but he would have known it anywhere.

"Sammy, Benny, it's been a long time mate, how are ya?"

"Benny Boy, I'm the best, the very best. How are you, son?"

"Couldn't be better, Sammy, I couldn't believe I was hearing right when Deirdre said she'd run into ya. It's been a lifetime."

"Fit and well she's lookin' boy. It was the accent that got me first, then I had a good look at her face, she hasn't changed a bit, you've looked after her well, boy."

"You sound exactly the same. She said ye were lookin' well too. Any chance of us meetin' up, we've a lot of catching up to do, mate."

"I'd love to, Benny. Any time that suits you, just say the word."

"What about today, or do you work in the community centre most days?"

"No, I just give them a hand when they need it a few days a week. I'm in the house today putterin' about, why don't you call up and we can have a good yarn."

"I'd love to. Where exactly are you?"

Sammy gave him directions to the estate he lived in and Benny wrote them down carefully, he couldn't afford any hitches now they had finally made contact. He ended the call, telling him he would see him in an hour or so. He didn't want to arrive at Sammy's door with his two arms the one length after all these years. He would go and do a bit of shopping, take him some food and a present of some sort. Benny grabbed his jacket and car keys. The adrenalin was rushing through his body; he couldn't wait to see Sammy face to face.

In the supermarket he bought, bread, cheese and ham, some cake and biscuits, then looked through the CD's for something suitable to give him. Sammy had always loved music, everything from swing, to blues, from country to rock, he had always amazed Benny with his musical knowledge. They had spent many a happy hour in that wee bed-sit listening to Sam's choices from the record library, and then when he found something he really liked, he would buy it.

Benny found a collection by John Lee Hooker and The Best of Ella Fitzgerald; they would be sure to please him. Benny doubted his love for music had waned over the years, if he was the same Sammy he remembered. The shopping piled into the back seat, Benny got into the car again, and drove up the Lisburn road toward Dunmurry. Although only a short distance from Belfast to Dunmurry, the road was always busy throughout the day. He settled his nerves by listening to the radio. Gerry Anderson was on Radio Ulster, bantering some eejit who had phoned in saying, "I'm lukin' to buy a part for an oul relic of a tractor, cud ye put the word out fer me, Gerry."

The caller was loathe to part with too much money. That would do; he liked Gerry, whose relaxed style would calm him down for the meeting with his old mate. He felt like he was going on a first date. He still couldn't believe they were really going to meet up after all these years.

The estate was easy to find. It was small and well-kept with a large green area in the centre of the main square. He quickly saw the sign reading Riverside Row. This was it, he had arrived. He parked the car opposite the row of well-presented bungalows and walked toward them. Number eight. He found it easily and put his finger out to ring the bell. He didn't get time to. The door swung open and there stood Sammy, an old man, but still unmistakably Sammy. The lines on his face were deeper and the hair was whiter, though just as thick and wavy and he eyes still twinkled, the life shining out of them. His hand was outstretched in greeting. Benny grabbed it, then threw his other arm around him. They embraced standing swaying on the doorstep, both momentarily incapable of words such was the depth of feeling between them. Sammy spoke first, "C'mon on in outta the cold, sit yerself down. We've a lot of catching up to do, Benny Boy."

Benny entered the small tidy living room and handed the bags to Sammy.

"Just a few bits and pieces I thought you could use, didn't want to eat ya outta house and home. I got you a couple of CDs, too. I take it you still listen to music."

He grinned at the sight of the expensive music centre Sammy pointed to.

"Ya better believe it, I've come a long way from the oul Dansette, d'ye remember?"

Benny sat on the seat Sammy indicated.

"How could I forget, Johnny Cash, Hank Williams, Louis Armstrong, Frank Sinatra, The Ink Spots, Cream, Moody Blues… I've still never met anybody else with such a wide musical taste. Remember, I used to try to out do ya with my finds, but yours were always the best…"

"Aye, I'd experience on my side, you were only a learner! Jesus, boy, you haven't changed a bit. I'll get us a pot of tea on the go, then we can get down to reminiscing in earnest, c'mon inta the kitchen while I rattle the teapot. God love Deirdre, she looked like she'd seen a ghost yesterday, you should've seen her face."

They sat drinking the tea and eating the cake and biscuits Benny had brought.

"Let's get one thing outta the way first, I can tell by yer face yer worried about something. If it's Liz, I know. I saw the death notice in the paper. I can tell ya, Benny, it was a shock, of course I hadn't seen her in years, but the oul feelings come to the surface even at that. It was sad. She'd probably only about retired then, too. God rest her. But this isn't a day fer sadness, by God the oul bank treated ya well, Benny, I kept up to date with yer progress ya know."

Benny was astounded.

"How?"

"The business section of the 'Belfast Telegraph,' of course. I saw yer picture on yer various promotions, the odd charity event. I knew ye were doing well and I was delighted fer ya, son. I'd say yer glad now ya didn't jump on the train fer home that first Friday ye arrived in the big smoke. And ye've family; Deirdre was telling me all about them. Yous have done well, the two of you."

Benny had to tell him about Jo, but he didn't know how he

was going to get around to it, "Aye we've done well, what about yerself, Sammy, the family all well?"

"Aye the best, grandchildren and great grandchildren and they're all good to me, who'd o' thought it, eh? God bless Leila, it was her death bed wishes that brought all this about. She forgave me everything and she made sure the girls had done the same before she'd allow her eyes to close fer the last time. She was a good woman, too bloody good fer me in them days and that's the honest truth. Now, I've a wee woman called Ida who looks after me. I'd marry her in the mornin', but her attitude is, 'If it's not broke, don't fix it.'"

"Good fer you. Yeah Deirdre told me you'd a partner. I'm pleased fer ya, mate, life's been good."

Sammy poured them both more tea. Benny decided to say what he needed to say, he just hoped to God the shock didn't give Sammy a heart attack. His old friend glanced at his face as he set the teapot down.

"There's something else botherin' you, Benny. I can tell by yer face, what is it?"

He might have known Sammy would guess he had something else on his mind; he could always read him like a book.

"What I have to say will come as a bit of a shock to ya…"

"I haven't reached this stage in life without a few shocks. Go ahead, Benny, spit it out."

Benny braced himself, "Did you know Liz had a daughter after you last saw her?"

"Well, I wouldn't have, but I saw the girl's name in the death notice, so I knew then."

"The thing is, Sammy, I know her, I know her well. Her name's Jo and she's engaged to be married to my son, Aiden."

Sammy was speechless for a moment, then he asked, "How d'ye know she's definitely Liz's daughter?"

He told him the whole story, about the Christmas gathering with Kate and Andy. How Andy and she were now living together since they were both alone, how he had built the whole picture up and realised who Jo was.

"She even lives in the same house. Her old family home in Locksley Park, Finaghy. Andy, her Dad," explained Benny almost flinching as he said the words, "sold it to her a few years ago. She was going through her divorce and he made sure she got it at the right price.

I've no doubt. Andy Jordan, retired wedding limousine driver, Kate McGeown retired nurse, Liz's old friend. Jo Hughes, nee Jordan, is Liz's daughter. She was born in 1968 Sammy. August to be precise. She was a month early, due in September."

He related Jo's story of her birth, as told to her by her mother.

The penny had dropped. Sammy looked directly at Benny, "You're sure?"

"Sure as I've ever been about anything in my life, Sammy."

"My God, yer right, this is one hell of a shock, I can't believe it."

"It's not just the dates, Sammy, she looks like you. See for yourself..."

Benny reached for his jacket and produced a photograph from his inside pocket. He handed it to Sammy. The picture was of Jo, alone on the day she'd gotten engaged to Aiden - the wide, slightly crooked smile, the straight even teeth, the twinkling eyes. Sammy couldn't fail to see the likeness.

"Jesus, she's more like me than Donna and Diane. I can't get over this."

The old man's eyes had filled with tears.

"I had to tell you, Sammy, I just couldn't keep this to myself. You deserve to know. Kate knows, I'm sure of, but she's kept it all these years. She's not likely to talk now, there's only the two of us. I never mentioned anything you told me to Deirdre, it didn't seem right. I would've felt like I was betraying you even talking to Deirdre about Liz."

Sammy looked directly at Benny, trying to comprehend his words, "Kate McGeown, God bless her, she wouldn't say a word, I can rest assured she wouldn't. Jesus. You're telling me, your son is about to marry my daughter."

Sam shook his head in disbelief, looking directly at Benny as he spoke, "Ye couldn't make it up, Benny Boy, ye couldn't make it up."

"I know, I know. And you, turning up now after all these years, it's fate, Sammy. You'll have to meet her. Will you think about it?"

"Andy's her father by all accounts, Benny, I couldn't just sail in now and start wrecking lives after all these years..."

"No one needs to know. I like Andy, I wouldn't dream of

telling Jo, but you should allow yourself to meet her. As far as anyone else is concerned, you're simply an old friend. I'll invite you to one of the family gatherings before the wedding. My family have all heard about you over the years, about how you were my first human contact in the early days in Belfast, before I met Deirdre. They'd love to meet you…"

"I don't know, Benny, I'll have to think about it, I just don't know."

Cassie changed into her business suit and paid special attention to her make-up. She had just washed her hair and styled it before she received the call from Tony O'Connor's office. Once again she checked out her appearance in the bathroom mirror; yes, she was ready to go.

She drove toward the city centre. Marlene had given her an address at the Laganside. The whole area was a mass of large apartment and office blocks. She stopped to read a site map inside the entrance and located the building she was looking for. It was huge. On entering the premises the sight before her took her breath away all shining glass and chrome, perfectly lit with what seemed like millions of tiny spotlights. She almost sank into the carpet it was so thick and luxurious.

She walked to the lift and pressed the button for the seventh floor, where Marlene told her she was located. The office was all open plan taking up most of the floor area. She told the receptionist she was there to collect plans and sat down in the waiting area, as the girl rang through to Marlene. Seconds later she appeared with the documents in hand.

"Hi, how are ya? I'm Marlene. Here are the plans. You can collect the keys Friday week, that'll save you havin' to waste time calling in here on the following Monday morning. All the information you need is in there, good luck."

"Thanks, I'll call in on Friday week then, cheerio."

And that was it they had landed their first job.

Cassie couldn't wait to open the envelope, but she didn't want to sit in the van poring over the plans, so she rushed back home and laid them out on the kitchen table.

She counted the number of apartments. Some single, some double and did a quick calculation on the number of hours it would take to clean it to specification. They had a whole week to do it in, so it should be possible to cover it with the permanent staff they had hired without calling in the casual workers. Being a new complex, the grounds would have been maintained to standard, so they wouldn't need power washers, but all of the windows were included in the job and they would need to be done thoroughly due to dust from the construction debris, lucky they had advertised. She just had to hope now, they had found some experienced window cleaners, or she would be doing them herself. And there were a lot of them, apart from the bedroom and kitchen windows the balconies all had floor to ceiling patio windows. *That's an awful lot of elbow grease,* thought Cass.

"Hey, Ma, what's ya at?"

Dean had just got up to get ready for his afternoon shift. She looked up from the paperwork, "We've landed our first job; yer man with the property rentals business I told ya we met yesterday, his office rang me this mornin' offering it. It's a brand new complex in the town, never been rented. We've to get it ready for the carpets and furniture delivery. We've a week to do it in."

"Will ye be able to manage it in a week?"

"Put it like this, son, if Gail and me have to get down and our hands and knees and scrub it out ourselves, we'll manage it. We'll be fine. She's coming round tonight to look at these," she indicated to the plans, "then we'll calculate how many workers we need over how many hours. Easy peasy, lemon squeezy."

"Good for you. I'll not be home 'til late I'm goin' to the cinema after work."

"Make sure ya get something decent to eat well, what time will ya be back?"

"Probably about eleven, I'm on the earlies tomorra. Did Lara ring ya?

"No, why?"

"She texted me last night. She'd a row with Jake, told him to get out and not come back."

"I haven't heard from her."

"Well, look, don't say I told ya. I think she's comin' to her senses, but she knows we don't like him and she doesn't want to lose face."

"I've never said I didn't like him."

"I know ya haven't, but she knows you well enough to work it out. I have though. I told her he's takin' her for a right soft touch. She didn't like it, but she knows I'm right. Don't say anything anyway. Okay, see ya later, enjoy your business meetin' with Gail."

"You'll not be laughin' when I'm rakin' in the dosh."

He kissed on the cheek and left for work. Cass was delighted to see him with a spring in his step. The news of her daughter lightened her load considerably. She prayed to God Lara would come to her senses, as Dean believed she had.

Time would tell, but for now Cass would say nothing when she called, leave it up to Lara to tell her if she had finally dumped Jake, once and for all.

Chapter 25

GAIL ARRIVED AT CASSIE'S SHORTLY after seven that evening.

"Well how'd it go, did ya manage not to cry?"

"Of course I didn't. I was doin' fine until he spotted me from the stage as he was being presented and he gave me one of his big grins. I went to pieces, then I was dabbing my eyes like a mad thing to make sure it wasn't obvious I'd been crying. He'd never have forgiven me, makin' a show of him in front of his mates. So what was Tony O'Connor's office like, nice?"

"Nice wouldn't cover it. Wall to wall glass, sumptuous, knee high carpets and the whole place was lit up like a film set, I'll tellin' you that boy's worth a few bob. Here are the plans," she pointed toward the kitchen table, "it's big, but I reckon we'll get away with the permanent team. It's over a period of a week, so it should work out okay, just depends on how much builders' dust is in evidence. What do ya think?"

"God, it is big, Cass, if we're going to be landing jobs like this we will need a supervisor to oversee the jobs…"

"Of course, we will, but let's get the first one out of the way for now and see what comes our way from there."

They had agreed Cass would supervise this first job and Gail would man the office, then they would change roles, so that they both got the feel of the whole business, but this was much bigger than Gail had anticipated. If she was honest it was much bigger than Cass had anticipated also, but at least she had experience of working in a hands on environment, if she started to show signs of panic Gail would lose her nerve.

The newspaper would be out tomorrow, they would get their extra staff sorted and take it from there. Cass was sure Tony O'Connor would be watching them very closely, she wasn't about to let him see the cracks in their organisation.

Her coolness seemed to have rubbed off on Gail.

"So, since I'm going to Ballymena with Jo on Saturday, we'll try to organise the interviews for Friday, yeah? And any overflow can be seen on Monday. Do ya want me to book the interview room in the hotel again, the same place as last time? That was fairly central and they all seemed to find it easily enough."

"Yeah, if you can get it, go ahead and book it."

Gail was still staring at the plans spread across the kitchen table, she looked daunted, but she was trying to be calm. Cass spoke, trying to sound positive, "This'll make us or break us with Tony O'Connor we both know that; I'm sure we can do it."

"Yes I am too, I'm looking forward to it, it'll be a challenge."

Gail didn't feel as confident as she sounded, but she knew they'd had a lucky break, Aiden had done them a big favour giving them the introduction to his client, she was sure they wouldn't let him down, but she was terrified.

Chapter 26

ORLA WAS ON HER WAY out to work on Wednesday morning, when she spotted Declan down the lane in front of her. He indicated to pull in, and she did the same, knowing he must want to speak to her.

"You're the early bird. I don't normally see you goin' out at this time of the day."

"No, I've a room to set up this morning. There's a training day on."

Declan worked as a lab technician in the university.

"I just wanted to catch you, to ask you something."

He had called her on Sunday night to ensure everything was alright, making sure she had his number in case of emergencies, but she hadn't seen him since Sunday morning.

"Yes?"

"Next week, on Tuesday there's a night on in the local pub, bit of a diddly dee y'know, fer St.Patrick's, I was wondering if you'd like to go with me."

She was surprised, but not unpleasantly, she thought to herself, *Why not?*

"Yeah, that'd be great, I'd love to."

"It's only a local, nothing fancy, but it's usually a good night, bit o' craic y'know. Give you a chance to meet the neighbours."

"I'd enjoy that, thanks. I won't keep you if you're on yer way to work. Call me later and we'll make arrangements, yeah?"

They drove on, going their separate ways. The invitation had lifted Orla's mood; she really liked Declan. There was something about him, despite his sadness.

He had a sense of humour that shone through, a resilience that gave him strength over and above his physical build, and he had the deepest blue eyes.

Stop it Orla, you're starting to get carried away, it's only a night out at the local, he said as much, "Give you a chance to meet the neighbours."

She listened to the news on the radio as she drove, her thoughts wandering to her own problems. The news from Jo had been a surprise, great for Jo and Aiden, although she guessed it was quite a shock to Jo. She had confided to her once that Aiden would love another child, so they had stopped using contraception, but she doubted it was going to happen now that she had turned forty. She'd said with the job, plus her course work for her art degree and the plans for the wedding she had more than enough to contend with.

Orla had discovered Jo's artwork through Gail. Gail and she had been colleagues in the bank. Gail had told her she had this friend who was going through a divorce and she had been helping her clear out her house to redecorate, when she had discovered a room full of paintings.

"I mean, we went right through school together, were best friends. I knew Jo was always good at art, she would have gone to Art College but she was planning on getting married. Then we all left school most of us got jobs, or went on to college. Jo didn't get married after all, but she travelled for a while, so Art College was forgotten about. I didn't realise she was still painting. We still saw each once a year or so as you do, but it's only since she separated from her husband that we've become close again. I couldn't believe my eyes when I saw the bedroom full of canvases. You might be interested in having a look. I told her I'd mention it to you."

Orla had said, "Yeah, why not?"

Assuming Gail was over enthusing about her friend's talent, Orla had rummaged through the collection of paintings. Immediately seeing Jo's potential, she had taken a few to sell, to see how they went. They had sold quickly and Orla knew she had found a genuine talent. Shortly after she had offered Jo the part-time job as the gallery was becoming too much for her to run on her own full-time with all the other commitments keeping the business afloat entailed.

The small Art Gallery/Gift Shop had long been her dream, and she had to give it her full attention, if it were to be a success. The shop was situated on one of the most expensive retail sites in Belfast, so she had to constantly diversify to keep her customers interested, and keep the money rolling in.

Jo had stepped into the breach while she had been busy. *Busy, busy, busy,* she thought to herself. So busy she couldn't see she had married a violent control freak.

At first, Jo had worked when she needed her, so long as it fitted round her young son's arrangements, making flower arrangements and small dried flower gifts at home, to be sold in the shop, as well as some of her paintings. When she had broken the news to Orla that she intended applying for an Open University course she had been pleased for her, saying, "I was hoping you might come to that decision, Jo, but I didn't want to suggest it in case you took it as a criticism of your work."

Orla knew Jo would be even more of an asset to the business after completing her course, so she agreed to be flexible with her, agreeing to work in with Jo's plans until she qualified. Although Orla had gone to Art College herself, she merely had an appreciation of art, Jo had real talent.

As she pulled off the Westlink and headed toward the Lisburn Road, Orla thought it was typical of life, Jo had just started to get it all together, when she had found herself pregnant. But then she thought of her own situation, she had started to get it all together too, the only fly in the ointment had been her crazed husband.

Orla knew she had been the envy of many of the women she worked with when she had left her job in the bank to follow her dream, knew many of them saw her as a stuck up bitch playing at being one of them, when really she had a wealthy husband in the wings, who was prepared to pander to her every whim. He may have helped her set the business up, no doubt she couldn't have done it without Seamus's support, but she had earned every penny she made by putting up with his violent flare ups.

She silently thanked God she had insisted that the shop be in her name, determined she would pay him back every penny when she made a success of the business. Had she known all along in some secret part of herself that she had made a big mistake? She would pay him back, she had instructed her solicitor to ensure his financial input to the gallery was deducted from the sale of the apartment. It had been bought from their joint incomes, but she would take a lesser amount on the sale of it, preferring peace of mind to monetary gain.

As for his business interests, they were his, and she wanted nothing from them as long as she got what was legally hers. And she had peace of mind now, no doubt about that. She loved the house she was living in, the fresh air and the space were all contributory factors to that peace of mind.

Her sister Aine and her husband Rory were due to visit this Sunday with their children and she was looking forward to it, thankful it hadn't been planned for last weekend when Seamus had made his appearance. She couldn't have coped with putting on a brave face to her sister. Declan and his parents were strangers and so easier to fool, although they had taken her in like one of their own, they didn't know her like family. No, her sister would have had her out of there, and back to Dublin in a heartbeat.

As she had thought, Aine had suspected Seamus was violent seeing past his 'Mr Nice Guy' façade. She had told her as much when Orla confided in her on the phone weeks ago. She said she hadn't been sure though, so she had kept her suspicions to herself, not even sharing them with Rory.

Her mother and father were still in the dark about her situation, she had been down to visit a few times since their break up, but they thought nothing of the fact that Seamus wasn't with her, she often visited her parents alone while Seamus was in Dublin, on business. It would be hard for them to take. They both thought of their daughters as being successful, in different ways, but most importantly they had made good marriages. The icing on the cake now for them would be for Orla to announce she was pregnant. Having a successful business was one thing, but really in their eyes she knew, they thought it was time she settled like her sister and reared a family.

Although Aine ran a successful business also, they didn't see that in the same way. Her alternative therapy practice was just a pastime, something to keep her occupied, when the kids were at school. Aine had been sworn to secrecy. Of course, Orla would have to tell them, but in her own time, when everything was finalised and they couldn't sway her in any way. Of course had they known the truth about their charismatic son-in-law they wouldn't have had their daughter within a hundred miles of him. They saw Seamus as a respectable, hardworking business man, who was held in high esteem within the construction industry, her admissions of his domestic violence would come as a complete shock to them. They were the type of decent, unworldly people who judged the book by the cover. It would be hard for them to believe the fault didn't lie with Orla.

She would deal with them in her own time. Her solicitor had warned her about the attitudes of family and friends, how people outside of a shared home were ill equipped to judge, or give advice, on matters of violence behind closed doors. She said that Orla must follow her own heart, taking help and support where she needed it most, initially, in the form of the refuge and its workers, and now in the legal advice and support she provided her with. So far, that had proved to be right.

She parked the car and walked toward her business. With every day that passed she felt stronger; this place was her world. She opened the door and flicked on the lights, ready for another day.

On the way in that morning Kieran had stopped to buy Eve a box of chocolates, not that he gave a damn about her, but the silent treatment from the rest of them in the office was starting to get to him. He had overheard someone say on his way out last night that she was due in again today, and he thought, *Please! Do me a favour, a day and a half off work for hurt feelings? Bloody typical woman.*

Nevertheless, he had bought the chocolates anyway; if nothing else they might keep her from whingeing.

As he entered the office he saw her sitting at her position, like a frightened mouse. On his way across to his desk he stopped to give her the gift wrapped box. She looked up at him, nearly jumping out of her skin, "Oh!"

"Good Morning, Eve, just wanted to give ya these, a peace offering for being a thoughtless pig; can you forgive me? I suppose we were all a bit wound up after the bad news, no hard feelings, eh?"

As her eyes started to fill up again, he reversed from her and made his way to his own desk, thinking, *No more please, I'll have to strangle her.*

He was saved from any further conversation with her as Lisa approached and asked Eve to follow her to Juliet's office. Kieran overheard and sincerely hoped they were going to let her go today. She was depressing him by her mere presence already.

He settled down to check out a mortgage completion for a client, his mind wandering to last night and Suzanne. The meal had cost him an arm and a leg, and the conversation had been less than scintillating. More than once, he had zoomed out picturing himself spread out on his sofa with a beer in hand, watching the football. He felt like he had sprinkled magic dust and brought Barbie's wee sister to life. At one point she'd asked him, "What are you doing for St. Patrick's Day, Kevin?" - quickly correcting herself – "Kieran?"

He had told her, honestly, he hadn't thought about it, she had replied, "We're going down to Dublin a crowd of us, we're planning an all-day pub crawl, then we're going to a friend of a friend's house for a party. You should come with us. I'm taking Wednesday off, what do ya think? I suppose you'd have to be back for work though."

He was glad of the out: "That's it, I have to be back in the office, wouldn't look good on the CV if I didn't turn up to work the notice eh? Otherwise I'd love to."

"That's a shame. We always have a blast on Paddy's Day. Last year, a whole team of us headed up to the Holylands for the craic, just to observe, y'know we weren't actually planning on joining in the rioting or anything." She stopped to giggle. "God, that would've been gas. No, we just went up to have a look. My brother was at Queens and he was saying it was brilliant the year before, but the bloody PSNI wouldn't let us anywhere near it, spoilsports."

Kieran looked at her, incredulous, hoping she couldn't read his mind, her head really was full of banging doors; he tried to get his money's worth.

"Talking of CV's, any luck in matching me up with any of your clients?"

Apart from the monetary outlay, he wasn't sure he could handle another night like this.

"God yes, what am I thinking of, I found the very position for you..." She looked to her empty glass, shaking it gently in the air, "Ah no, we're out of Champagne..."

Kieran flicked his fingers at the waiter, quickly ordering another bottle. He flinched at the price; the first one had nearly cleared him out, but he thought, *Needs must.*

Suzanne gave him a big smile.

"Lovely."

She continued to smile at him saying nothing.

Loveleeee, he thought.

He asked, "So, what is it, what's this position?"

She explained, giving him all the details, telling him she had submitted his CV by email to them for that position, together with three others that morning.

"Told you I'd do my best for you."

He gave her a big smile in return, "Good girl."

He thought, *But I hope you don't think I'm your boyfriend now.*

The waiter poured the Champagne into their glasses, placing the bottle in the ice bucket.

Suzanne sipped hers, fluttering her eyelashes over her glass at him, thinking, *Good, he's still got money then. Nice meal, nice Champagne, only a few more months 'til I'm engaged, no time to lose. what did her Aunt Susie always say... "So many men, so little time!" that was it!*

She chuckled at her own thoughts.

"What?"

"Nothing, I'm just having fun, that's all."

And, so had he, later. It had almost been worth the expense. But she had better come up with some interviews for him soon, he was skint again.

Chapter 27

IT ALL SEEMED LIKE A dream after all these years. So it was hardly surprising that Benny woke up from the dream where he had met up with Sammy again, forgetting it had actually happened for the first waking moments that morning.

He looked at the clock 7.00a.m. Another hour until the alarm was due to go off. Deirdre worked in the Activity Age office Wednesdays; she was still fast asleep.

He lay staring into space for a few minutes. It was no good, sleep had left him. He pulled the duvet back gently, so as not to disturb Deirdre and swung his feet onto the floor. He would make a pot of tea, try to get his head together.

Benny hadn't slept well. He kept seeing Sammy's face, as the realisation of the words he was telling him dawned on him. He had to speak to him again, make sure he was alright. He hadn't told him Jo was also pregnant; that could wait. Sammy had had more than enough to take in for one day. The reminiscing had stopped there and then, as Sammy digested the news that he had a third daughter he had never known about. There were still endless questions Benny wanted to ask him, but they'd had to wait.

As he pulled on his robe, Deirdre's voice reached him. "What's wrong, can't you sleep?"

"Nah, I'll go down and make some tea, you go back to sleep, you've nearly an hour 'til the alarm."

Deirdre understood he wanted to be alone to think. It was great that Sammy was alive and well, but Benny had been exhausted after their meeting yesterday. It must have been like turning the clock back nearly forty years, good in many ways, but also strange and surreal. She had felt that way herself on Monday as she had sat sipping tea with their old friend, as though she was in a time warp. And of course, it would seem much more so to Benny, the two men had been so close through those early years.

"If you're okay I'll grab another quick nap. I've a lot to do today, see ya in a wee while."

She rolled over and went back to sleep.

In the kitchen Benny flicked open the blinds. It was almost fully light as he peered out the window. In the garden, the first signs of spring were in evidence. The snowdrops and crocuses were already out, with a few daffodils peeking through, the day held a promise of sunshine as Benny filled the kettle.

Only Wednesday, he thought, and already two surprises. Aiden and Jo's news had thrilled him to bits. He knew how much Aiden loved his daughter Sarah, and how much it had affected him when Frances and he had split, and he'd had to become a part-time Dad. Jo and he were made for each other; it was great news.

In the kitchen on Sunday night, he'd told his Dad he was so pleased, but he had thought it was quite a shock to Jo. If anything she had suspected she was going through the menopause. Benny had reassured him that Jo would be fine when she had time to get used to the idea, saying she'd had quite a lot on her plate this past while back going through her divorce and moving house, working, completing her art work to deadlines and planning the wedding, now this. She was bound to be reeling a bit, he had no doubt they would be fine. Then the news of Sammy on Monday, it had been quite a week so far. Sammy had told him he would be in all day today, if he wanted to give him a call.

Benny poured his tea and decided he would. He looked at the clock it was 7.25a.m. Ellie started work around nine thirty, and Deirdre left for work at the same time. He usually left the house, went down to the gym for an hour, did a bit of shopping, anything to get out of the house and leave Ellie in peace to look after Mary. She liked Ellie to read to her or they would watch television together. Now that the weather was getting more spring-like they would be able to get out into the garden and enjoy it. He was glad he had insisted on Deirdre hiring a nurse to relieve her. Ellie had been a godsend. Mary liked her, and they seemed to have struck up a genuine friendship. It made Deirdre's time with her mother more enjoyable too, neither of them having time to get stressed out or agitated with each other.

He would shower quickly and head down to the gym, then call

224

Sammy from there; give him time to get up and about. He would drive up to see him mid-morning. They had still a lot to talk about. He turned as Deirdre entered the kitchen, saying, "Sorry, did I disturb ya rattling about?"

"No, just couldn't settle. I keep thinking of Jo and her wedding dress, it's a shame after all the weeks of waiting, but she'll find something else. It's a bit of a disappointment for her that's all, but it's a small price to pay for a baby. Gail'll not be long in helping her get sorted. Aiden was practically bursting with pride wasn't he? Imagine we're going to be grandparents again."

He kissed her gently on the head.

"You don't look old enough to be a granny at all, Mrs Brannigan. Cup o' tea?"

She nodded.

"Thanks, I feel it this morning I can tell ya, bloody aches and pains. It's been a long winter, all that rain how could you feel well, it's great to see the sun strugglin' through. Roll on summer and the warm sea in Portugal. I put it to Geraldine, about coming out with Mum for a few weeks. She said, *'I'll think it over, but you know how Mum feels about travelling.'*"

Over the years, Deirdre and Benny had tried to convince her mum and Dad to go on holiday with them, way before they had bought the villa in Portugal, but they had always declined. Her mother and father's ideal holiday destination was Donegal. They had a week in the same guest house every year and never had the desire to travel further afield. Johnny liked to fish all day, whilst Mary liked to sit on the beach with a book and read and people watch, then go back to a good plain meal in the evening. But now that their father was dead, Deirdre was sure her mother would enjoy a week or two in the sun if she was with all of them.

"To be honest, I think it's more likely to be Liam who's the stumbling block, he's just yer typical man from the sticks, *Garlic bread? The filthy pigs.*"

Benny laughed at her take-off of one of their favourite comedy routines.

"Aye yer probably right. Liam's idea of exotica is puttin' both Tomato Ketchup and HP Sauce on his fry."

"If she worked on Liam I'm sure Mum would enjoy it. Anyway we'll see. I better jump into the shower or I'll be late."

"Don't be jumpin', Mrs Brannigan, remember yer nearly sixty!"

She flicked him with the drying cloth.

"Not as near to it as you are, Mr Brannigan."

He grinned at her as she left the kitchen and bounded up the stairs like a young thing.

Talking to Sammy had brought it all back, meeting Deirdre on a wet Saturday in the rain, in the record library in Knight's in Botanic Avenue. He had seen her before with a couple of other girls, but that day she had been alone as he had been. He had stood at the counter watching her, as she flicked through the records making her choices, willing the shop assistant to take as long as possible processing his LP selection from the library, but she was still at the back of the shop as he left. And then, he had stood outside in the pouring rain looking into the shop window waiting for her to come out, determined not to miss his chance of talking to her alone.

She had tripped down the step, almost dropping her LPs. Benny had swung his free arm out and stopped her, steadying her and her records, his arm round her waist. She had straightened herself up looking straight at him, he had asked, "Are you okay?" She had replied, "Yeah thanks," while looking straight into his eyes.

Benny had become flustered and looked at the records peeking out from under her arm; he had stuttered out, "I just brought that back."

Her eyes were laughing at him, mischievously, as she said, "Well aren't you the lad?"

He had recovered his composure enough to ask her if she would like to go for coffee. She had accepted and that had been it. They were in love. They had been a long time married when she'd confessed to him that she'd staged the trip down the step of the shop to get his attention.

It was a cliché, but when he thought back to that day it really did seem like yesterday. They had both been eighteen, eager, full of life and hope, ready to conquer the world.

Benny washed the mugs out and dried them before showering, leaving the house as soon as Ellie arrived.

By eleven, he had finished in the gym and was sitting in the café sipping from a bottle of water. He dialled Sammy's number and it was answered right away, as though he had been expecting the call. Benny asked if it would be okay to call up, "C'mon ahead, Benny, and don't be bringing anything with you, there's no need. Just bring yerself, I'll be glad t'see ye."

Twenty minutes later, Benny was sitting opposite him.

"I dreamt about ya last night, dreamt we'd met up again, then I woke up and realised it was true."

Sammy replied, "Aye, I know what you mean. I kept drifting off to sleep, then I'd think about what you told me and I'd be wide awake again. It's hard to take in. You like her then I take it?"

"It's the weirdest thing, Sammy, I took to her right away. I mean she's lovely, there's no reason why anybody wouldn't take to her, but it was more than that. I felt I knew her. That first trip out to Portugal, when Aiden brought her out for her birthday, Deirdre said to me, 'You've really taken to her haven't you?' And I'd said. 'I just think she's right for him that's all.You like her too.' But I knew Deirdre was naturally wary, after the time he'd been through with his first wife, she'd said, 'I'm just worried about him getting hurt, getting involved too soon…' Frances, his wife, had just announced one day out of the blue, 'I don't want to be married anymore, I need to find myself.' And that was it. T'hell with him, t'hell with the effect divorce would have on their child. With Jo the resemblance thing took me to last Christmas to work out, as I told you. Every time I saw her I'd almost been able to put my finger on it, then it would be gone, like a butterfly on the breeze, as they say. But, once the penny dropped, I got it. It was your face I'd been seeing every time I looked at her. Sammy, I know it's a lot to take in, there's no rush, let me know in your own time if you'd like to meet her."

"Benny, of course, I'd like to meet her, I just don't want to put the cat among the pigeons, that's all. Gimme time son, I'll think about it."

Benny decided to let it lie for now, "We tried to contact you when Minnie died, you must believe that."

"I wondered at the time why ye hadn't to be honest. She had my address, it was the last thing I said t'er as I left the house that day, 'make sure ye write the address down, 8 Riverside Row, Dunmurry.' She'd nodded assurin' me she would."

"Ach, Sammy, we searched through her address book in the bed-sit, she had your name written in it alright, but underneath it, where the address should have been she'd only put the number 8. We thought at the time it was possible she was writing it when she'd taken the heart attack, God rest her."

"Jesus that's so sad, the poor oul crater."

"You said yesterday you knew. We'd so much catching up to do; I didn't get asking you how."

"I'd just moved in here a short time, I was busy getting sorted out, ye know how it is. My daughter, Diane, had ordered the daily papers for me, y'know fer delivery. Well they'd been comin' in every day, and after a week or two, I realised they were piling up and I hadn't had the chance to read any yet. So I sat down one night, put my feet up and started browsing through them, to see if there was anything worth reading in them before clearin' them out. And there it was, Minnie's name, in the death notices. I hoped I was wrong and it was somebody with the same name, but no it was her alright. I looked at the date, of course it was way too late. The funeral was over. I couldn't understand why you and Deirdre hadn't got in touch."

"Well, we tried believe me, I even asked in the shops in Botanic and Sandy Row. Was sure somebody was bound to have seen you, heard where you were going, but all I heard was, 'Out Lisburn direction...' that was all that kept coming up again and again. I even rang the company you had worked for, but they said the same thing, they'd sent your details onto the tax office and that was all they knew. If Dunmurry had been mentioned we might have had a chance of finding you."

Sammy explained, "Ye see, Diane had originally lived in Lisburn, like Donna, but shortly after Leila died she'd moved because of her husband's job. Dunmurry was handier. And she'd managed to get me this, being close to where she lived. Donna moved here eventually too."

"If only we'd known, we'd have tracked ya down sooner."

"Anyway that's water under the bridge. I'm more to blame myself." He looked a bit shamefaced as he confessed, "In the pile of newspapers, there was a photo of you on yer first promotion, chief cashier I think it was..."

"That's right."

"I was delighted for you, son, I lifted the phone to ring you there and then, but then I thought maybe not."

"Why?"

"Ach I don't know. I suppose I thought you mightn't want to know me, you didn't need an oul fella like me hanging onto yer coat tails…"

"Sammy, surely ya knew me better than that…"

"I know, I should've, but when you hadn't contacted me about Minnie's funeral I didn't know what to think. I thought maybe I'd be better just to wait. I did intend ringing eventually, but y'know how it is. Weeks became months, and it just never happened. The more time that passed, well I felt I'd left it too long."

They looked at each other in silence, all those years lost due to a misunderstanding.

"Well, as you say, Sammy, it's water under the bridge. But don't ever think we didn't want to hear from ya. Deirdre got sick listening to me goin' on about it at times. There were even times in later years, when I'd drop her off in the town to shop with kids and I'd take a dander round Botanic Avenue and Sandy Row and scan the faces, on the off chance that I might bump into you."

"Did ye, son?"

"I did."

Sammy was emotional. To think he had been stupid enough to believe Benny would be above wanting to know him. Benny could see the old man was close to tears.

"Well here we are now. Did ya listen to those CDs yet?"

"As soon as you were out the door; ye picked them well. Ye want t'see the collection I have now. The grandchildren taught me how to download from the internet. Did I tell ye I went on a computer course after I turned seventy?"

Benny was impressed, but not surprised. Sammy was bursting at the seams with life for a man of his age. They talked for hours, catching up on each other's lives again. After the bombshell he had dropped yesterday, Benny was mollified. Sammy was alright, but he would have to give him time to adjust to the information he had given him.

Sammy would meet Jo. He was sure of it, but in his own time.

Chapter 28

JO HAD BEEN FURIOUS TO find Kieran was going to be out of work again, not that she blamed him for losing his job; there were plenty of people in the same boat right now, but it was so typical of him to let her find out from the radio report. Surely he had realised the media would carry it. And then the cheek of him, trying to make her believe he had only just found out himself.

Deceit and denial – the main ingredients of their relationship throughout their years together.

Jo's thoughts returned to the phone call, that phone call. The final nail in the coffin of their dead, rapidly decaying marriage.

September 2006: Kieran had been preparing for a sales conference in the Waterfront Hall. Many of the big guns from Head Office in London would be attending. They had stipulated in the local office they wanted everyone to remain together and stay in the same hotel to get to know each other informally. When Jo had asked for the name and number of the hotel where he would be staying for the two nights he got all defensive and said, "What are you asking me that for, you can get me on the mobile?"

Jo had said, "Well' it's just in case of an emergency, you'll hardly have your phone switched on during dinner. We have a child now y' know. I may need to contact you."

Kieran blew up, calling her an over possessive bitch who should have enough self esteem to let him go to a business conference for a few days without having a nervous breakdown if she didn't know what he was up to every second. And with that, he threw a brochure for the Ramada Hotel at Shaw's Bridge onto the hall table and went to bed. He left early the next morning and they still hadn't spoken.

When she got in that evening there was a delivery of flowers from him to apologise. Jo took the brochure from her bag and rang the hotel to thank him. It was just coming up to six, so she reckoned he would be just back into the room to shower before dinner. Not knowing the room number she rang reception and was put straight through.

"Hello," answered a woman's voice.

"Who's that?" Jo had asked.

"Oh my God!" the woman had uttered as she slammed the phone down. There was no going back – her marriage was over.

Later that night she had sent Kieran a message telling him she was taking their son to her Dad's home in Belfast for two weeks. Stipulating that on her return she wanted all signs of Kieran gone from their house, the locks would be changed and the house put on the market.

The next morning, Jo had sat at the computer in their home in Bangor composing a letter to the C.E.O. of Friendly Finance. The words tumbled onto the page as the anger in her released the pent up emotion she had been consumed with since the previous night. When it was finished, she read it over one more time before printing it and placing it carefully into an envelope and sending it guaranteed next day delivery.

Jo packed two cases with everything Corey and she would need for their stay and filled a small grip with bank statements, marriage and birth certificates, any documentation she may need to have at hand and hurled them into the boot. By lunchtime she was on the road out of Bangor and back to Belfast, the road back to her Dad and home.

Jo shook her head to clear the memories. She rarely thought of Kieran and herself as a couple anymore; nowadays his presence in her life was merely to accommodate their son, nothing more.

But he had obligations to the child and it was her role in life to make sure he kept his promises. She was immune to his lies, his scheming; he could deliver when he chose to and Jo insisted that he did. No exceptions and no variations. It worked. Mostly.

She had intended ringing the bridal shop yesterday, but the conversation with her ex-husband had put her off her rhythm. She had forgotten. She would have to call them today, since they'd had the decency to hold the dress over for her for a full week in two sizes.

She couldn't remember the assistant's name, but when she had given her own name to the woman she was speaking to on the phone, she knew immediately who'd dealt with her initially. When she was put through she announced herself. *Harriet - that was it.*

"Hello, Harriet speaking, how can I help you?"

Jo explained her predicament; Harriet was unfazed.

"Well, if you want to change your mind, we can certainly find you layers or folds in abundance, but really nowadays there's no need. A lot of ladies like to show their bump off, rather than try to disguise it. You could still wear the same design, granted in a larger size and with a few nips and tucks, you'd look wonderful, but I'll leave it with you, Jo. We'll keep both these dresses for you until Saturday, then we'll look at your options. And congratulations!"

Jo could just see herself in the beautiful slimline sheath with her six month baby bump. She knew a lot of women liked to flaunt it with clingy Lycra being the order of the day in maternity wear. She hated that look in general, but for a wedding dress, she just couldn't see herself carrying that off. It wasn't as though she was sweet sixteen, there was really no big deal in her being pregnant, but she would prefer not to advertise it on her wedding day.

They would go up and have a look around on Saturday, and she would try not to be too disappointed that she would have to give up on her dream dress.

Chapter 29

THAT WEDNESDAY ON HER ARRIVAL home, Orla opened the door to the house and saw the letters lying on the mat. Two bills and one from the solicitor; she ignored the bills ripping open the one from the solicitor. It was good news.

The apartment had sold. At well over the reduced price they had agreed a couple of weeks ago. The purchaser had loved it, insisting on early completion for the two thousand over their asking price. Orla thought, even in today's market, there are still people out there with money, prepared to spend it on property; she was over the moon. And as she read the letter through, her face broke into an even wider smile.

Seamus wanted her solicitor to inform her, that it was his intention to travel to Australia to his brother to pursue his application for immigration. On finalisation of their divorce and the dissolving of his business interests, he would be leaving Ireland for a new life in Australia.

She couldn't believe it. He was really going to go through with it; wait until she told Declan. Rushing into the kitchen she reached into the fridge and poured herself a large glass of wine, thinking of her fear as he had rushed into this house only nights ago. Declan had put the fear of God into him and she had no doubt Declan was right, he wouldn't be back. She placed the letter firmly inside her bag and proceeded to cook her dinner.

A couple of hours later she had settled down to watch a movie when the phone rang.

"Well, any news?"

It was Anne Marie.

"Yeah, I got a letter from my solicitor today, the apartment's been sold and Seamus really is going to Australia. Can ya believe it? I know I can't."

"Oh my God, isn't that brilliant? Declan really did put the

wind up him then, that's great news."

"Don't I know it. I've almost downed a bottle of wine, so it's as well Jo's in the shop tomorrow. Declan asked me out for a drink on St. Patrick's Night. What about you anything strange?"

Orla's tone was so casual Anne Marie almost missed the last bit for a minute.

"Nothing as exciting as you, but I got my room finished and I've started on project two." Anne Marie went quiet, "Did you just say Declan asked you out?"

"It's no big deal, more of a community thing down here. Bit of a diddly dee, as he put it, for St. Patrick's Night, but I am pleased; he's nice."

"I think I'll crack open a bottle of wine, too. Maybe if I drink to your good luck, my ship'll come in, too."

"Your ship has come in, sure you love your wee place, you couldn't be happier, working away with yer paint brush."

"Yer right y'know, I love it, it's small, but it's all mine. And my sister's just across the road. All I need now is to get that promotion and I'm sorted."

They chatted on happily for over an hour, unaware that Declan was trying to get through. When Anne Marie hung up, Orla checked her messages and returned his call.

"Hi it's Orla, got yer message, how are ya?"

"Orla, glad you called, I just wanted to talk to ye about next week. I didn't have much time this mornin'."

After they had made their arrangements, she told him about the solicitor's letter and he was nearly as pleased as she was herself.

"He must've took me at my word. That's great news, Orla, you'll be glad to have it all over ye."

After they had talked some more she realised she had better warn him about her visitors on Sunday. Aine's husband was big, not unlike Seamus from a distance. She didn't want Declan charging down with the shotgun putting the frighteners on him. Her sister, and quiet peace loving, Rory, would run to the hills, their children gripped firmly by the hands. Although Orla had made her life up here years ago, Aine was still convinced that the North was awash with paramilitaries hiding out in every nook and cranny. Orla loved to bait her about it.

"Do you not read the newspapers down there, did ya not know we're living in a "bright brand new day" up here now?"

She repeated the words on every politician's lips after the securing of the 'Good Friday Agreement' in the late nineties.

Declan's voice brought her back, "It's lucky ye told me, I'll keep the gun out of the way, they'd think you'd landed yerself with 'The Clampetts.' I'll let you get to bed, Orla, take care and sleep well. I'll talk to you Monday night, if not before, enjoy your visit from yer family."

"Thanks, Declan, have a good weekend yourself, see ya, g'night."

She placed the phone on its cradle, smiling from ear to ear, thinking, *Could you be any more pleased with yourself, Orla?*

Later, as Benny and Deirdre lay talking in bed that night, he told her of his conversation with Sammy earlier, everything was now clear to her too.

"I knew Sammy would've been at Minnie's funeral if he'd known. Imagine him thinking we just hadn't bothered telling him. I suppose you can understand why he didn't get in touch after that. He must have seen your photo in the paper, on the way up the corporate ladder, and thought to himself they'll not want to know me now. That's sad, Benny, and he was still keeping up to date with your progress throughout the years."

They lay in silence for a time alone in their thoughts.

Then it came up that Deirdre had been speaking to Aiden earlier. She had mentioned how she had bumped into Sammy, and told him that Benny and he had been reunited. Of course, he had heard of Sammy Stevenson often over the years.

"He couldn't believe the coincidence. He said he'd love to meet him. He's going to ring the girls and tell them. He thinks we should organise for all of us to go out for a meal to celebrate."

"Oh I don't know, Deirdre. It might be a bit much for Sammy to be launched into a full family gathering so soon."

Benny was panicking. He had agreed to let Sammy come round to the idea of meeting Jo in his own time. Next, she would be suggesting they invite him to the wedding.

"Why would it? It's not like he's shy and retiring, Sammy would love to meet them all I'm sure of it. He said as much to me on Monday."

Benny thought, *Yeah, but that was before I dropped my bombshell.*

"Anyway, Aiden said he'd call you tomorrow to get the arrangements under way."

"Good." Benny replied, his heart heavy, "Now I'm goin' to get some sleep, g'night."

"G'night."

Deirdre stroked his cheek as he turned to kiss her.

He lay beside her, his eyes closed waiting for sleep, but his head refused to shut down. He pondered how he was going to deal with this one. Of course, the family would want to meet Sammy, the stranger who had fed Benny the homemade broth, on his lonesome arrival in the big smoke, *"eighteen, eager and naïve..."* They had heard that story so often over the years, it had become a family joke, exaggerated to legendary proportions by Benny himself, *"...nothing to my name, but a battered suitcase and a pocketful of dreams..."*

The week's events had exhausted him, finally tiredness overcame his frazzled thoughts, and he drifted into a long, dreamless sleep.

Chapter 30

"OK WE'L COM UP SAT and sty, tlk ltr luv Aine xx." The text from her sister was in response to a message Orla had sent late last night.

She was pleased. It was going to make the visit more relaxed. Aine and Rory wouldn't have to worry about driving the whole way up from Wicklow and back the same day, and their children would have a chance to rest without the prospect of a journey home again, that same night.

The children - that brought her back to reality. She would have to get a few extra duvets for them. There was a bed and bedding for Aine and Rory, the kids could share the other room with the big double bed and fight over who lay on the bed or the floor, so long as they had a duvet each.

She replied to the message, telling Aine she would call her later to make arrangements. It was Thursday morning, one of Jo's days in the gallery. Orla would have all day to shop.

By nine thirty, she was on the road to Coleraine. Stopping at the shopping centre for food, presents and the bedding she needed. As she was leaving the centre she turned, feeling someone's eyes on her. It was Declan.

"Orla, I've been trying to catch you up, by God you women when yer shoppin' you take no prisoners, straight in fer the kill."

He looked at the trolley jam-packed with groceries and duvets.

"I'm gettin' organised for the weekend. My sister and her family are coming up on Saturday now to stay 'til Sunday and I'm just makin' sure the kids won't be fighting over the duvets."

"Doesn't matter what you do they'll find something to fight over, kids always do. Do ye fancy a coffee?"

"I'd love one, but aren't you supposed to be in work, are ya skivin'?"

"No, I've a day off, they'd owed me some time. Is this one of Jo's days on?"

"Yeah I've all day to shop without feeling guilty. Then tomorrow it's back to the grindstone."

"I'll give you a hand to pack the car first, eh?"

"Thanks that'd be great."

They walked across the car park toward Orla's car. Declan indicated for her to stand to the one side while he packed her boot. It quickly filled with the purchases.

"It's not really a shopping car. Throw one of those duvets in the front. It's totally impractical, I know. I bought it for myself to celebrate my first year in business, a totally selfish indulgence. But sure, why not? We'll be a long time dead. Oh Christ, that was a thoughtless thing to say, Declan, I'm sorry."

"Don't be sorry at all, Orla, the world doesn't stop turning when someone close to you dies. You may expect it to, but you realise very quickly it doesn't."

They walked back toward the shopping centre.

"I remember the day after Molly's funeral, being out here in the town shopping, my mother had offered, but I'd insisted on doing routine things again immediately. I had to for the sake of the kids. If I went down it would affect them. So I shopped because that's what we'd normally have been doing on that day of the week. I remember passing people, chatting, laughing, pushing babies in prams, listening to music in their cars, talking on phones, having rows, all the day to day stuff, and I wanted to shout at them, 'Stop, my wife's just died!' but I didn't. I just got on with it, blended in with crowd 'doing normal.' That's all you can do. As soon you realise the world's not going to stop turning, you start moving on. Will this do?" Declan waved his hand at a nearby coffee shop.

"Yes, of course, this'll be fine."

"What'll you have?"

"Just a latte, please."

"I'm having a slice of that gateau. Go ahead, it'll do ya good."

"Oh alright then, I will."

"Don't ever worry about upsetting me over my wife's death, Orla. I've come to terms with it now. As I say, I had to for the sake of the kids. They're both well up now, one at university, one finishing upper sixth year, life goes on. So, how do you feel about your husband

238

movin' to Australia, or is that none of my business?"

"No, not at all, I don't mind talking about it. I spent too long over the past few years not talking, living a lie, now that it's out, it's a relief. Only my parents don't know yet, but I'll talk to them in my own time. If you'd told me a few months ago, I'd be living up here alone, and Seamus would be planning a new life without me in Australia, I dare say I'd've been devastated, but not now. I met a woman in the refuge house; did you know I was in a refuge for a short while? Declan nodded. "Anne Marie her name is; she was the turning point for me. She told me her terrible story. It shocked me to the core, but it got me talking, really looking at my life, made me realise I was living a lie every day, walking on eggshells in case I upset him. It was like livin' with the bloody sleeping giant, covering up bruises, putting on my party face to entertain his friends, then quivering in fear when they left. In constant turmoil, waitin' for his mood to turn, day in, day out. I'm glad the apartment has sold and I'll be so relieved when he finally leaves for Australia. I've no love left for him. He beat that out of me. Anyway here I am. Anne Marie and I are keeping in touch and I couldn't be happier about where I'm living, I'm so grateful that Jo thought of me."

Declan's eyes shone at her as she spoke.

She thought he said, "So am I." But she couldn't be sure.

He lifted his coffee and drank deeply as she watched him. He really was a nice man.

Meanwhile in Belfast, Benny had left the house early on the pretext of filling the car up with fuel. He needed fuel, but he needed to talk to Sammy more.

On the way down the road he stopped to make the call.

"Sammy mate, listen, sorry to call you so early, yer probably thinkin' not a word for bloody years, now he's on the phone every day. But what it is, Deirdre was saying last night she was speaking to Aiden, y'know, my son, and of course she told him the news about meetin' up with you. It seems he's calling me today to arrange a family meal where we can all get together. He's calling his sisters and getting back to me today with the arrangements. He wants me to invite you and Ida to meet them all."

There was silence on the other end of the line.

Eventually Sammy spoke, "I suppose we knew this was goin' to happen. When I met up with Deirdre on Monday she said the family would love to meet me, and of course I said I would be all for it. God help her, she doesn't know what's at stake."

"Well, that's it. I tried to put her off by saying it might be a bit soon to throw you into a full on family gathering and her exact words were, 'Why not, it's not like Sammy's shy and retiring.'"

"No, no one could ever accuse me of being that. We've got ourselves a predicament here, Benny. The biggest problem would be if I'd to come face to face with Kate. She's a good woman, Benny, you must know that. I couldn't bring grief like that to her. She was a good friend to Liz and she was a good friend to me too when I was laid up in hospital all those years ago."

"I remember you told me, Sammy. Look if I can manage to arrange this with Aiden without inviting Kate and, obviously, without inviting Andy, will you accept?"

"I can't really see how I can't. Deirdre wouldn't understand. I don't want to hurt her feelings, she was so happy when we we're talkin' on Monday. Then when she asked me why I hadn't kept in touch with yous, God help her she was damn nearly in tears."

"Well, that's all sorted, don't be worrying about all that now. I told her it was a misunderstanding and she sees it as we do, an awful waste of years. But no matter, it's the present we're concerned with. Like I told you, Sammy, I promise you, she doesn't know a thing, and I certainly won't be telling her. So without Kate present the secret is between you and me. I know my son, Aiden, won't let this go until he meets you. He's like a dog with a bone when he gets an idea in his head."

Sammy chuckled on the other end of the phone, "Like father, like son, eh Benny?"

"'fraid so. Can we go along with Aiden's plans then?"

"Yes, Benny. It'll be difficult, but to be honest I've thought of nothing else since you told me. I'd love to meet Jo."

"I know, Sammy, I promise I'll make it as easy for you as I can make it. I'll call ya later after I've talked to Aiden, alright?"

"Dead on, son. Talk to ya later."

Back in the house Deirdre was making breakfast.

"Where did you run off to?"

"I needed fuel, thought I may as well do it now. It's not a bad day, still a bit crisp though."

"What can ya expect, sure it's only March. Mum do you want a wee bit of bacon with your scrambled egg?"

Mary nodded, laughing at Benny.

"I've no bother shiftin' a good breakfast. Sets ye up fer the day; hate that yoghurt. Geraldine likes that, I don't. It's like eatin' sour milk."

"Yoghurt's good for you, Mum, full of vitamins, helps strengthen your immune system."

"What does?"

And she was gone again, into a world of her own. This was the pattern of these exchanges. Deirdre became frustrated and as usual tried to explain too much, exacerbating the issue. Benny found it easier to go along with Mary. Benny chatted to her while Deirdre cooked the breakfast. Sometimes when he talked with her, Mary understood every word. She would come back at him with a caustic comment and he would see the spark was still there. At other times her eyes would dim and he knew he wasn't making contact, although she nodded and murmured the odd, "I know," or "Is that right?"

But she was only going through the motions. Apart from that, she was contented in her environment and today she was looking forward to a day out. Deirdre was going to take her to the nearby park, then on for lunch.

"So you two are leaving me on my own again, yis have a quare time of it I'm tellin' ya, swannin' about in the sunshine."

"What are you at today?"

"I might do a wee bit in the garden. I'll see when I've had my second cup of coffee."

"Hasn't he a great life, Mum?"

They continued to chat as they ate. Benny's mind was elsewhere, he was sure Aiden would call him that morning; he didn't hang about when he was hatching a plan.

Sure enough, only ten minutes after Deirdre and her mother left the house Aiden called.

"Dad, how's it goin'?"

"The best, son, how are things with you?"

"Good. I was talking to Mum yesterday, she was telling me about meeting up with Sammy. Isn't that amazing after all these years, ya must be glad, I'm sure you'd given up on ever seeing him again?"

"I couldn't believe it when yer mother told me on Monday night. I must've downed the best part of a bottle of wine myself, followed by a few whiskeys, it was such a shock. It's great news. Did she tell ya I'd been up to see him?"

Benny knew she had, he was stalling for time.

"Yes, I was telling Jo about it too. And then I rang Kelly and Rosie."

"What did Rosie say?"

"*Oh, so he's not an imaginary friend after all*. Said we'll all have to meet up with him. What do ya think, Dad?"

"Certainly, son, I'm sure he'd love to meet yis all."

"What about St.Patrick's Night, we could all go out for a meal?"

"That wouldn't suit Sammy. Sure yer mother has been arranging that Activity Age do for St. Patrick's Night; that's how she met him, delivering the tickets to the community centre."

Maybe he could get this onto the back burner yet. Benny was hopeful, but of course Aiden wasn't that easily put off.

"Well, during the day then, most of us are off. I'm sure Orla could change days with Jo. We could go out for lunch all of us. Corey won't be a problem because Kate and Andy are taking him out for the day with it being a holiday. Wha'd'ya say?"

Benny gave in to the inevitable.

"That sounds great, son, I'll give Sammy a call and ask him. Where were ya thinkin of, bearing in mind now that Sammy and Ida will be going out that evening?"

"The girls and I were thinking it would be good to go somewhere round Botanic, then the two of you could retrace yer steps if you wanted to, take a trip down memory lane. There're a few good hotels and restaurants round that way. Would that suit? I'll pick Sammy and Ida up, and leave them home in good time for their night out."

"That's sounds good, son, I'll give him a call and I'll get back to you. What about Jo; everything alright?

"She's fine, Dad, everything's fine. I'll talk to ya later."

Benny dialled Sammy's number. "I just heard from Aiden. He's suggested lunch on St. Patrick's Day, he did suggest dinner, but I reminded him about your night out, so if it suits he'll pick both you and Ida up and run yis home."

"Yer right, Benny, he doesn't let the grass grow under his feet. That's fine, Benny, I'll look forward to it. Who all's goin' to be there?"

"Well, first and foremost, you can rest assured Kate and Andy won't be. They had already arranged to take Corey, Jo's son, out for the day, it being a holiday. So it's going to be the immediate family and spouses, Mary, Deirdre's mother, you and Ida and Deirdre and me."

"You go ahead and arrange with yer son, Benny, I'll talk to Ida. We'll fall in with whatever plans are made."

"Thanks, Sammy, I'll call you as soon as Aiden confirms the details."

Aiden's phone was on fire. He rang Jo first, and then his sisters. He had the restaurant booked for the eleven of them, within an hour of talking to Benny.

Chapter 31

THAT THURSDAY EVENING, AIDEN SAT talking with Jo in her house.

"God, it's unbelievable, after all these years. Mum was convinced the old man was long dead. When she saw him the other day she said she felt like she'd seen a ghost. It'll be great for us all to meet him and he has a partner, Ida. The girls are looking forward to it. I know it doesn't mean the same to you, Jo, but we all grew up with stories of those early days, especially from Dad. I could never imagine my Dad young. I suppose nobody can, but as you get older yourself and you have a child, children."

He grinned at her.

"It doesn't seem so unlikely that your parents were young once, y'know what I mean. It'll be interesting to meet this man who was such a good friend of my father's when he was only eighteen. Dad met Mum shortly after he arrived in Belfast, and the two of them continued to live in that wee bed-sit for the first few years of their married life, a bed-sit, can you imagine it? They're just about big enough for one person to turn round in. When they got married they literally had themselves and a handful of guests, Sammy was one of them. Maybe we should invite Sammy and Ida to the wedding. What do ya think? I'm sure Mum and Dad would love that."

"Yes, if you want. Two more people will hardly make much difference to the plans. I'm looking forward to having lunch with this Sammy, with all his tales of your father as a young buck. I do understand what you mean. Take Kate, she and Mum met up when they were both in their early twenties, the boys were young, Kate and Mum used to wear all the latest fashions, go out dancing with a crowd of nurses from Kate's work. I could never imagine them young, y'know to me they were just Kate and Mum. So I see where yer comin' from. You're right, it was only after I had Corey that I could even imagine my mother as a young girl. Your mum rang me on Tuesday to see how I was feeling and she told me she felt like she'd seen a ghost when the old man called her back to ask after your Dad. Talking of plans, now that I've gotten over the shock of last Saturday, my head's gone into overload again with wedding arrangements. Presuming I can find a dress on Saturday and we do get married on the 11th of July..."

Aiden interrupted.

"No, we *are* getting married on the 11th of July, if I've to make that dress myself."

"Okay well... I've been thinking..."

Aiden interrupted again, pressing a cushion around his head, to cover his ears, shouting,

"Oh no. I hate it when women start sentences like that!"

She pulled the cushion off his head.

"Stop, it's nothing dramatic, well not really. Y'know how yer Dad is insisting on paying for this photographer to film the wedding from morning 'til night, well I'm really happy that we've been lucky enough to book Belfast Castle for the reception and the grounds are beautiful for photographs...

"I'm sensing a *but* here..."

"What I was thinking was, why not have some photographs taken in the city, for instance in Thanksgiving Square beside the river. I'd love to have 'The Angel of Thanksgiving' in some of the shots just around sunset. It would look great all lit up with those blue lights, us standing in front of it, the river flowing alongside, it would be really different..."

"Yeah, it would look like 'Nuala with the Hula' was a bridesmaid..."

"*Nuala with the Hula*... Gail calls her 'The Doll on the Ball,' anyway. Don't call her names; she's the 'The Angel of Thanksgiving' and she's there for a reason, so that people like us don't forget what this city has survived... in the past forty years.

"I know we were lucky Aiden, we grew up in different parts of the city, your background was certainly more privileged than mine, but neither of us really experienced 'the troubles' firsthand. We may have worked through the odd bomb scare as we got older, but our parents must have gone through hell as we were all growing up, insisting on going wherever we pleased, convinced we were invincible, that nothing could touch us.

"I remember Gail and me, when we were in our teens, Mum would stand at the front door watching us walk down the street as we headed out for the night, she'd call out, 'Be careful now, watch yerselves.' We'd look back at her and laugh, come back at her with some smart comment, you know we didn't have a care in the world, but there must have been nights when she sat with her heart in her mouth waiting for me to come home…"

To Aiden's dismay he realised Jo was crying.

"What is it?" he asked, putting his arm around her as she reached for a tissue.

"I don't know; maybe it's my hormones. I just think back to those years, not only me, the boys too. Your mum must have felt the same, sitting listening to every news bulletin, hoping we'd arrive home in one piece. Now, we all take peace for granted. It's not perfect now by any means, but this place has come such a long way. Can you imagine watching Sarah or Corey go out knowing there was even a slight chance of an explosion or a shooting in the town that night? I know it sounds odd, but it would sort of be a tribute to my mum, to acknowledge the Thanksgiving area of the city, that's all."

Aiden hugged her close.

"Well, if it means that much to you, of course we'll do it."

Chapter 32

BENNY'S HEART SANK AS AIDEN said the words he was dreading.

"Jo and I were talking, Dad, and we thought it might be nice if Sammy and Ida could come to the wedding. We thought we'd invite them on Tuesday. What do you think?"

"Sure you've everything organised, son, Sammy wouldn't want to put you to any trouble."

Of course, Aiden said it would be no trouble at all. Benny said, "Why not?"

He rang Sammy immediately. It was Friday morning, Sammy was in the community centre. Benny could tell by the noise in the background. He got straight to the point.

Sammy replied, "Let's look to the obvious solution, Benny, maybe I can't make it. What's the date?"

"11th of July."

"Problem solved, Benny. Ida and I will be in Canada for the whole month of July, visiting her granddaughter."

"God bless her, that's a relief for both of us. Let them ask you, then look crestfallen as you have to decline. Right mate, I'll let ya go, I should've phoned ya last night, I've been awake half the night worrying, talk to you soon, bye, Sammy."

Friday morning found Gail and Cassie getting organised for a full day of interviewing. By 8a.m. Wednesday morning, both of them had taken calls in response to their advertisement in the local papers, and for the next couple of hours their phones rang constantly. That was to be the pattern for the next two days. The sheer volume of calls took the two of them by surprise.

They'd had a good response to their adverts for cleaners in the previous weeks, but this one for experienced window cleaners and power washer operatives was much better than they had anticipated. The fact that they were offering over minimum wage was probably a factor. Unfortunately, many of the applicants had little or no experience, or were so completely over qualified it was obvious they had been made redundant and were clutching at straws. It was up to them to find the balance from the huge pool of applicants.

They spent a long two days doing initial interviews on the phone to eliminate unsuitable candidates, then arranged the interviews over the coming Friday and Monday, deciding to work the recruitment procedure as before. They would select a small permanent crew, then put the others on a casual call back list, to be contacted as and when the work required.

Now they were both in Cass's house, preparing to leave for the interviews. Once again, reading through the leaflets they had picked up from the local government department of economy.

"God I feel like I'm back in school again, my heads meltin' with all this legislation," said Gail.

"I know, it's an awful lot to take in, but we only have to employ one person without a national insurance number or a work permit and we're in for a huge fine. We really need to know this stuff inside out."

"I think we know it fairly thoroughly by now, but just to be on the safe side we should get together again after the interviews and go through it all again before reaching our final decisions. Say, Tuesday night, wha'd'ya think?"

"Yeah, I feel okay about most of it, but we're better to be one hundred percent before makin' the final selections. Oh, there's Lara and Mia."

The front door was open. They heard Lara and her child make their way up the hall. Cass called out, "We're in the front room."

Lara entered with Mia by the hand. The little girl ran to greet her granny.

"Easy, Mia, Granny's going to work, she's got her nice clothes on, don't mess them up."

"She's alright, sure she's not a messy girl, are ya sweetheart?"

Cass kissed her and swung her round, before setting her back on her feet. Her daughter kissed her mother and said, "You both look lovely, all ready for the interviews then?"

"Aye, we scrub up well, don't we, Gail?"

Gail smiled at Lara and her child.

"Where are you two off to at this early hour?"

"Playgroup, it starts at nine. I just wanted to have a quick word with Mum."

"What is it, love?"

Gail made to leave the room.

"I'll just put the kettle on."

"Don't bother on my account, Gail, we just had breakfast. It's okay, it's nothing personal. I was wondering if you'd be free to mind Mia on Saturday night, that's all."

She turned to her mother.

"Yeah, that should be okay. I'll hardly be out boogying again this weekend. I'm still gettin' over last Saturday night."

"Yer sure? It's just that it's Cary's birthday and Nikki rang me about goin' out to a club."

"That's fine, love, give me a ring tonight. Sure you can drop Missy off at lunchtime tomorrow, if you want."

Mia giggled; she knew 'Missy' meant her.

"Thanks, Mum. I better get on or we'll be late. Have a good day interviewing. Go easy on them now, remember you both used to be workers yerselves once!"

"Get outta here!"

"See ya girls," called Gail.

Cass kissed her daughter and grandchild and saw them to the door.

"We better be headin' too," Cass said.

In the van, Cass drove as Gail had another quick look at their interview schedule for the day.

"First one's at ten, so that gives us time for coffee when we arrive. Lara's looking well. That's good news she's planning a night out with her mates. D'ya think that means she really has finished with Jake?"

"I don't know, Gail, Dean seems to think it's definitely off, but she hasn't said a word to me. I'd hate to see her ending up with that wee toe-rag. It's so bloody blatant, he only came sniffin' back round her because he heard about the money. I'd hate to think my good fortune was goin' to fund his lifestyle, lazy wee shit, he's hardly worked a day from he left school. I got rid of Gerry Gallagher. I don't want her living with a younger version of him."

"Lara's not stupid, Cass, she'll see through him."

"That's what Dean says. I mean, I understand that she's lonely, but she was lonely for two and a half years when he walked out on her, and anyway I know she's not going through the money I gave her."

"Did ya ask her?"

Cass turned and gave her friend a sheepish look.

"Oh, Cass, you haven't been snooping on her?"

"I have. Don't look at me like that. I'm not proud of it. I was with her when she opened the account, I remembered her password. I feel bad about lookin' into her bank account, but she's my daughter and I gave her that money to improve life for her and the child, I had to know she wasn't handing it to him. Don't be pretending you wouldn't do it too, when it's yer child's welfare at stake. You use whatever means are at yer disposal. Anyway, I feel bad enough about it, I won't do it again. But I had to see she wasn't withdrawing big amounts at a time to finance Jake and the lifestyle he'd like to be accustomed to, I know now she isn't. I just have to hope she really has thrown him out for good this time."

"I think she has. Sure he never liked her going out with her mates. It's a good sign that she's makin' arrangements for the weekend. You're doin' the right thing not askin' her. Leave it to Dean, he'll keep you informed. How's Dean, is he still enjoyin' the job?"

"Loves it, it's given him a new lease of life and he's really lookin' forward to university. Let's hope he gets in. Apparently they're expecting a big upsurge in the applications for university places this year because of the recession. Thank God he got good grades."

"Don't talk about grades. I've all that ahead of me. The girls had been doin' well with the course work until these boyfriends appeared on the scene."

"Aye, that's when the trouble starts. If only they were more like us, sure we were never out the door when we were at school; we sat in studying every night, didn't we?"

"We did, aye. I remember it well."

"Here we are. Good, the traffic wasn't too bad, plenty of time for coffee to get us revved up."

They drove into the hotel car park, and walked to the

restaurant looking forward to the much needed sustenance. It was set to be a long day.

Kieran had an interview for one of the positions Suzanne had put him forward for and the time was set for lunchtime. He felt pleased that his monetary outlay had not been in vain.

Suzanne had invited him to a friend's house party that Friday night. He had been going to decline, using his early start on Saturday morning to pick up his son as an excuse. But the prospect of the interview cheered him, and he didn't want to get on the wrong side of her when she was trying so hard to get him sorted with a position before the end of the month. He had accepted the party invite and as the interview time approached, he was feeling good about it. At least the prospect of a job offer would keep his spirits up over the weekend, and he would be able to tell Jo, in all honesty, he had a chance of another job coming up.

The interview was with a finance company in the city centre; it went well, although he was disappointed to find it was commission only. Afterwards his hopes were high, he had sold himself well and knew if he knuckled down and put the hours in, he would make good money from it. It wasn't ideal, of course, but it would see him through for a while. He had no doubt they would offer him the position, but he would have to stick with Suzanne for a while yet, until she could land him a sales position with a salary commensurate with his experience.

By late afternoon, Suzanne took the call telling her they were interested in giving Kieran Hughes a three month trial run. She rang Kieran straight away. He was happy, it would keep his ex-wife off his back, and Suzanne was happy, she'd made a decent commission on the placement and she was in for a night of grateful sex.

Money and sex; what could be better?

Chapter 33

DAVE WAS WAITING WITH A chilled bottle of wine when Gail arrived home that Friday night.

"Hard day at the interview panel, dear?" he asked, smiling at her as he handed her a glass of wine.

She took her jacket off and kicked off her high heels, gratefully accepting the drink.

"Thanks, it was a long, long day. We saw some good people. We'll definitely get a few decent workers from today, but we've more to see on Monday. Where are the kids?"

"Josh is upstairs watching TV and the girls are on their way up from the town; I just rang them. So it went well then?"

"Great, I'm glad we decided to offer over the minimum wage. Cass knows too well what it is to work for a pittance. She reckons we'll get our money back in staff loyalty by just that small gesture. You feel sorry for people though. Some of them have been out of work for months, even years. And a couple of recent arrivals from one of the Eastern European countries had no paperwork at all. They said they'd drop it in when we're there on Monday. Doubt we'll see them again. They appeared to have good experience, too, but we need to see the paperwork. We'll have to be so careful about documentation; it could cost us dearly if we slip up. It's lucky that fella Paddy from the bank advised us where to get the information on employment legislation; it's a minefield. What are we eating?"

"Josh has already eaten. I did him a burger and chips and the girls ate with their mates, so it's just us. Fancy pizza or Chinese?"

Gail was happy to leave the choice to Dave. She didn't care as long as she didn't have to cook a meal that night.

"You decide. I'm going to have a long shower and change into something cosy, my feet are killin' me. See ya later."

She turned as she walked toward the door.

"Dave?"

"What?"

"Thanks."

"For what?"

"For believing in me."

"It'll work; you and Cass'll make it work."

She winked at him, and he winked back at her. She carried her wine glass to the bathroom calling out to her son as she passed his bedroom door, "Anybody belonging to me in there?"

"Hiya, Mum, see ya in a minute. Just watching the end of ..."

She didn't catch the name of the programme. She didn't care. Her family was doing normal family stuff and it was Friday night. She freed herself from the business outfit and stepped into the shower. Heaven.

Jo rang after nine to make sure she hadn't forgotten about their trip to Ballymena to the bridal shop.

"Do y'know I had forgotten."

"Liar. How'd today go?"

They exchanged comments on their day, but they were both tired. It had been rather an eventful week, all round.

"I'll pick you up around ten; is that alright?"

"I'll be ready, bright, eyed and bushy tailed."

"That's good, ya sound wide eyed and legless right now."

"Not quite, but I'm getting' there. See ya tomorrow, g'night, Jo."

"G'night, Gail."

Chapter 34

KIERAN ARRIVED ON JO'S DOORSTEP shortly before ten on Saturday morning. She was ready for him and his soft soap, but he took the wind out of her sails.

"Mornin', Jo, good news - I've got a new job. Same line, but more money. It's an ill wind, eh?" he lied.

"Great. I'm pleased for you. Corey's finishing off his cereal. He'll not be a minute."

Jo didn't give a damn who he was working for so long as he was working and he kept paying the maintenance

Kieran could barely contain his glee. He knew she'd been ready with an onslaught of abuse when she'd opened the door.

He looked at her, his attitude was bolshie and defiant, as she indicated for him to wait for his son in the living room. He then proceeded to tell her about the great party he'd been to the night before, with his girlfriend Suzanne. Jo hadn't heard about her before and she had to admit to herself that she didn't much care that she hadn't.

Kieran stood in the living room, wittering on about Suzanne and her great job.

"Yeah, she's a recruitment consultant with one of the big multinational companies, very ambitious, but then she's very young. You were probably that way yourself when you were her age."

She refused to rise to the bait.

"Here's Corey, there ya go. Towser, grab yer bag. Have a great day. See ya tomorrow."

Corey was sporting a red nose that she'd bought him yesterday for Comic Relief, he'd been keen to show it off to his Dad. Jo thought it wouldn't have looked out of place on Kieran. Kieran took his son by the hand, barely acknowledging his prized red nose.

Asshole, she thought. She kissed her son, and waved and smiled as she saw them out.

After she'd seen them off down the road, she stood with her back to the door, furious. She'd been feeling old enough, fat, forty and pregnant. You'd think the bastard knew. She fought the desire to make a voodoo doll out of her ex-husband, of both him and his little girlfriend.

She calmed down. What did she care, as long as this Suzanne had found him a job. Fair play to the wee girl; she was welcome to him. At least that was one worry off her shoulders. Kieran would still be paying maintenance. Now all she had to do was get herself sorted with a wedding dress to disguise her blooming figure. She grabbed her bag and slammed the door.

Gail jumped into the passenger seat, looking at Jo's expression.

"What's wrong, your face is like thunder?"

"Bloody Kieran!"

Gail thought, *Who else?*

"What's he done now?"

Jo proceeded to tell her about their exchange.

"Like I care about his pubescent girlfriend. Bloody moron."

"Jo, you'll never learn; has anybody seen her? She's probably a figment of his imagination, somebody he's invented to annoy you. He's got a new job, that's the only thing that should concern you. Have you seen some of those recruitment consultants in the agencies in the town? She's probably an oul spinster in her fifties with support stockings and an arthritic hip. He's always gone out of his way to wind you up and you've always fallen for it. I thought you'd gotten over that. Forget about him, we're shopping!"

Jo laughed in spite of herself.

"Yer right, it must be my hormones. He is an eejit though. Young girls at his age. Anyway, more to the point: 'the dress.' Make sure I stand firm. Yer woman, Harriet, was doing her best to convince me I'd be able to carry the sheath off in a bigger size; don't let me buckle under her persistence. I'm not getting married flaunting a huge bump for all the world to see. We're looking for discreet and subtle. Keep that in mind."

"Don't worry it'll be fine. She's not really that pushy, she's probably just afraid you'll go elsewhere and renege on my dress as well. We'll find something exquisite, I'm sure of it."

They'd barely time to step into the shop than Harriet was over gushing at them. She was trying to be discreet, but a few heads turned at the word 'pregnant'. Jo blushed and Gail felt she had to say, "She's not really used to the idea yet, she's trying to keep it to herself for now."

"Of course, Jo. Go through to the changing room. We'll find you something exquisite."

Gail followed her in.

"See, what did I tell you? *Exquisite*."

She was trying not to laugh at Jo's petrified expression.

Jo replied, "And when I say layers, we're not talking meringue!"

"Shush, here's she's comin', it'll be fine."

Harriet had three dresses draped over her arm.

"Try this, Jo. I guarantee you'll be stunning."

She pulled the plastic covering up and that was the start of it. Two hours later Jo had settled on an elegant dress in the softest of fabrics, with a delicate fold detail all along the front. It was perfect, simple and understated and it would totally disguise her blooming baby bump. The added bonus being, that the colour and style would ideally complement the dress they'd chosen for Gail. She was thrilled with her choice. Harriet, for all her pushiness knew her job.

They left the shop with both the dresses, tired, but happy.

Orla was in the middle of tidying up for her family's visit when the phone rang, it was an ecstatic Jo.

"You were right. Everything is working out fine. I got the dress!"

"Oh I'm so pleased. Did you decide on the same one or did you get something else?"

"No - a different one. It'll look much better with the bump and Gail got to keep hers. I just had to let you know, Orla, it's such a relief. Have your sister and her family arrived yet?"

"They're on their way. They should be here in twenty minutes."

"Enjoy your weekend, Orla. You're sure you can cover for me

on Tuesday?"

"Sure, I'll talk to you Monday anyway. Have a good weekend, Jo. Say hello to Gail from me."

"I will, bye, Orla."

Orla had agreed to swop days with Jo next week. She'd explained Aiden and she were invited out for a big family lunch on St Patrick's Day, so Orla would be working for her. Which suited very well, as Orla could look forward to her night out with Declan, and not have to worry about leaving early if it was shaping up to being a late one, then she could have a lie in on Wednesday morning, knowing Jo was in the shop.

She was happy as she worked around the house, lighting scented candles and putting fresh flowers in vases, the fire set with logs ready to light. It had been a long time since Aine and she had spent time together.

In the kitchen she checked the casseroles; they were almost cooked. Everything was going well. At the sound of the car pulling into the yard and Snapper's barking, she rushed down the hall to open the door, but not before checking out the camera. She would never get caught like that again. It was her sister and brother-in-law's car. She flung the door open and ran out to greet them. At the sight of each other, the sisters were reduced to tears. They clung to each other wordlessly, and then Rory spoke, "No chance of a hug for the brother-in-law, then?"

They were brought back to him and the excited children.

Orla wiped her eyes and buried her face in his jumper as he held her in a bear hug, then the children ran to her at once, screaming, "Auntie Orla, I love yer house!"

"Auntie Orla, can we see the animals?"

Aine calmed them.

"Do you think you can let us get inside first, there're presents to be given out."

"Did you get us anything, Auntie Orla?"

"Annie!" Rory chastised the poor child.

"C'mon in all of you, it's freezing out here. You must be starvin'. How was yer journey? Did ya find me alright?" said Orla, asking all of the stupid, obvious questions we all ask when visitors arrive after a long journey, happy and excited to see them all.

She showed them to their rooms to leave their bags off. Rory asked if it was alright to take the children for a walkabout to see the countryside, leaving Orla and Aine alone at last sitting in the kitchen.

"It's a great house, Orla, what a beautiful part of the country, you'll find peace here, I'm sure of it, I can feel it already within these walls. It's a happy house, with a lot of good vibes."

Aine got vibes about everything; she teased her sister about it, but Orla respected the work she did. People came to her troubled and left feeling better, renewed. Aine simply had the gift of healing. Orla didn't understand it, but she didn't question it either.

"I'm glad you like it. I would have been worried about the isolation, but as I told you, Jo's fiancé's family are all around me, so I'm never far away from human contact and of course I've their neighbours, the Dohertys, over the back fields. There's always somebody about the surrounding farms. It's been an oasis for me, I can tell ya. Yer lookin' well, girl, it's so good to be sittin' here with ya."

"You too, Orla, you look better than you've looked in years. We almost turned into the wrong laneway. There was a farmer out on his tractor. He asked us who we were lookin' for, and directed us up the next lane to you. Who's he? Late thirties/fortyish-looking man, with lovely twinkling eyes."

"That'll be the farmer from over the field; his farm is just across the way."

She didn't say it was Declan although she knew it was him. Orla hadn't told Aine about Seamus's visit; she hadn't wanted to frighten her off visiting, especially with the children.

"You'll be safe with him around. He has a good aura."

Orla felt a bit spooked, considering Aine didn't know about Declan and the events of last Saturday night.

"Oh, and what sort of an aura is that, exactly?"

She tried to make light of it, pouring her sister a cup of herbal tea. Aine looked directly into her eyes and replied, "Everything Seamus's wasn't."

They were both quiet for a moment.

"You knew all along?"

"Yes. But I've learned, even with family, you don't say what you see. What would you have said if I'd asked you point blank if Seamus was beating you, say this time last year?"

"I'd have denied it. I'd have denied it to you as I denied it to everyone, even to myself."

"If I'd been closer I may have intervened, spoke my mind, but at a distance it can be difficult. Sometimes the messages get mixed up, or you just read them wrong. Can I ask you something? Last Saturday I felt really bad, not really ill, but that kinda fluey feeling you get, hot and cold, shaky legs, headache. I went to bed after teatime and I had the oddest dream that you were in danger, but immediately I awoke the fever had settled and the headache had gone, I knew the danger had passed. I was so tired I went straight back to sleep and stayed asleep until the next morning. I knew you were safe that the danger had passed directly after the dream, so I didn't want to upset you by calling and telling you. It was around eight o'clock Saturday night. Did anything happen, Orla?"

"Yes. Yes, it did. I don't want to frighten the children talking about it now, though."

"It's okay. Rory will keep them out for a while. He knows we've a lot to talk about. Tell me."

She told her sister the full story, of her husband's visit, and about Declan and his father's intervention. How Seamus had been reduced to a blubbering heap and left the house like a scalded cat as Declan followed him, the gun still cocked. How she was sure he would never bother her again, even going as far as getting his solicitor to write the letter confirming his intention to leave the country.

"And that was Declan we met on the way up today?"

"Yeah, it would have been."

Aine reached out and held her sister's hand, and said quietly, "He's carrying a lot of sadness. Be good to him, Orla, he'll be good to you. I can see it."

Orla didn't say anything, there was nothing to say. Aine knew nothing of Declan's circumstances, none of her family did. Aine couldn't possibly know he had lost his wife, but she could see them together. Orla nodded; she wouldn't question it. She knew better.

Rory returned with the children and they all exchanged presents. Afterwards, Orla set the table with the goodies she had bought them for afternoon tea. Their mood was light and they enjoyed being in each other's company. The tea over, they all went out to walk in the countryside, the children squealing with glee at the animals all around them. They saw animals every day at home, but they insisted these ones were much better. Rory said it had to be down to the accents. Orla couldn't remember the last time she'd felt so at peace.

Chapter 35

THAT SATURDAY NIGHT, IN KATE and Andy's house, Jo and Aiden arrived for dinner as arranged the previous week. They all sat talking around the dinner table. Most of the conversation up until that point had revolved around the quest for 'the dress.' Jo was beaming, all thought of her run in with her ex-husband that morning forgotten.

"Now, that looks like the smile on the face of a girl who's just chosen her wedding dress," Kate announced.

"That's m'girl!" Andy said, grinning at his daughter's pleasure.

"It's been quite a week all round," said Aiden. "Kate, did Mum tell you about her coming across their old friend from years ago, while she was out delivering tickets for Activity Age, y'know that St Patrick's night do she's been working on?"

Kate and Deirdre had become friendly since they'd first met. Recently Kate and she had been organising for all of the women in the family to attend a fashion show, in aid of the cancer charity Kate was still connected to.

"No, I haven't really had a chance to talk to her this week; we've had so much on. What friend is that?" Kate asked, as she served the dessert.

"A man called Sammy Stevenson, used to live downstairs from Mum and Dad when they lived in the bed-sit in the university area. Sammy befriended Dad when…"

Aiden's voice was interrupted by the sound of the plate Kate had been holding in her hands crashing to the ground. It hit the tiled floor with an ear piercing bang, scattering into pieces all around Kate's feet. The three of them looked toward her.

"Look at me, butterfingers! Continue with yer story, Aiden, I'll clear this up."

Kate's cheeks were flushed with pink blotches.

Andy sitting nearest to her, jumped to help.

"Here let me."

"No, I don't need help, sit down!"

Kate's voice was uncharacteristically sharp. They went on talking as she cleared the mess, putting her outburst down to embarrassment.

Andy was saying, "Yes, I remember Benny telling me about that fella, the one who took him under his wing when he first moved up to the town from Derry..."

Kate put the broken pieces of crockery into the bin outside, using the time in the cool night air to control her erratic breathing and shaking hands.

She looked up to the dark blue, star filled sky, thinking, *Holy Jesus, Sam Stevenson! After all these years. What now...?*

Her thoughts raced back to that night before Christmas last year when Deirdre and Benny had invited them round to celebrate Jo and Aiden's engagement. The first time they'd, Andy and she, met them. The conversation had been flowing. They'd been talking about everything under the sun as you do.

At one stage they'd been discussing neighbours, as Andy and she had only recently moved house after forty odd years in the same street. Deirdre had related the story of the man in the downstairs bed-sit in Lawrence Street, Benny's neighbour, who'd been a lifeline to him in his early days in Belfast, Sammy Stevenson.

Kate had known immediately it was Liz's old lover. She'd looked at Benny and she'd seen in his face that he'd just put it together. Sammy must have confided the affair to him. Of course, Jo had always been the spitting image of him. Liz and she both knew it. But she'd always put Liz off believing the truth, telling her she was full of imagination, saying Andy was Jo's father, and that was that. She'd watched as Benny left the house for a short time on some errand, or the pretext of one.

When he'd returned he was calm and collected. He circulated around the company topping up drinks. Kate, realising she'd drank her wine too quickly, had said to Benny, as he replenished her glass, "I've already had three."

He looked straight into her eyes, saying with emphasis, "Don't worry, Kate, your secret's safe with me."

And she knew, beyond a shadow of a doubt, these few words

were his cryptic way of telling her, he knew, but he wouldn't tell anyone.

Now this.

In Derry, Orla and Aine settled the children for bed. All four of them in the one room and then returned to the living room, where Rory sat at the roaring fire. They'd eaten late, and as night fell the children had become sleepy.

"They'll sleep tonight, I'll sleep myself. Thanks for asking us to stay, Orla. It is a long drive, makes the visit all the more enjoyable when you can relax and enjoy it. Try some of this wine we brought you," Rory said, filling their glasses.

The rest of the night was spent talking and laughing, listening to music, while the children lay curled up under their cosy duvets upstairs, their voices dying out, then rising and ringing out in laughter every now and then, exhausted but desperately trying to fight sleep. Eventually, the voices were silent and as they checked on them, all that could be heard from the room was the sound of breathing.

Orla made a mental note to see more of her sister and her family. She had been neglecting them, as she had so many other areas of her life, in her years with Seamus.

She thought over Aine's words about Declan. Her sister never spoke for effect, she didn't need to. Aine had always been true to herself, never seeking other people's approval. She simply told it as she saw it.

Chapter 36

MIA JUMPED UP AND DOWN clapping as she saw her mother walking up the front path. Cass smiled at her granddaughter, she loved the child to bits, but inside she was jumping up and down clapping, too.

She didn't begrudge Lara the night out, but she'd had Mia a full twenty four hours now and her energy levels were starting to dip. And she'd still more interviews to look forward to tomorrow. Lara didn't hang around, wanting to get home and get organised for the week ahead.

Cass needed to wind down. She promised herself a complete day of being lazy, doing nothing. She searched through her DVD collection for something vacuous to watch for a Sunday afternoon. Quickly finding one that fitted the bill, she put the disc into the player and pushed the button on the remote, settling down on the sofa to enjoy it.

Dean appeared at the room door, he'd been in the kitchen putting together a late breakfast after a night on the tear.

"What are ya watching, Ma?"

She looked up at him with a sleepy grin, passing the cover over to him, "Car chases and bare arses."

He flopped down beside her on the sofa, "Aye, that'll do the job."

Monday was set to be another day of full on interviewing, by the end of it Cass had no doubt they would find more than the necessary quota of staff, they would meet up in Cassie's the following night to make their final choices from the shortlist of applicants, but right now she was off the air.

She pulled a cushion under her back and snuggled down beside her son, whispering, "Bring it on…"

That Sunday afternoon, as Orla stood in the front yard seeing her family off, Aine hugged her sister tightly and looked into her eyes, saying, "Don't forget."

"I won't. Safe journey; give me a call when you reach home."

Chapter 37

Monday, 16th March

DECLAN CALLED ORLA ON MONDAY night. She jumped on the sound of her ringtone although she had been expecting him to call.

"Well how'd the weekend go, I met your family on the laneway on Saturday."

"It went well. Yes, Aine said she'd been speaking to you. The kids had a ball too. I don't see them often enough. I'll have to start making the effort to go down to them more often. What about you, good weekend?"

"Quiet. The boys are at the stage where the house is more of a stop off point for them, than a place they want to spend much time, bloody teenagers! Nah they're not bad, I'm just jealous 'cos I'm an old fart now. My wild oats are well and truly sown."

"Yer not that old. Anyway, what about this do? Are we still on?"

"You bet yer life we are. I'll pick you up about eight. Don't forget yer fiddle."

"I won't. Should I bring my banjo, as well."

"Certainly, I'll bring my bodhran. Are ya working on Wednesday?"

"No, I swopped with Jo to help her out. Why will it go on late d'ya think?"

"Ye can never tell with these boys. It could be close to mornin' when they finally clear the place, so yer lucky you've a day off. See ye tomorrow night at eight then, I'll look forward to it, Orla.

"Me, too. G'night, Declan."

Chapter 38

THE HOTEL RESTAURANT WAS BUSY, being a holiday. Deirdre and Jo were there first with Mary, awaiting the arrival of the others in the family, together with Sammy and Ida.

Benny had suggested placing Sammy beside her mother as too many people confused Mary. She became a bit annoyed if Deirdre didn't give her enough attention; that would spoil Deirdre's day, so they agreed Benny would be placed on Mary's other side, to keep her included in the company, and take the pressure of Deirdre. Rosie, Kelly and their husbands arrived together. They sat waiting in anticipation for Benny and Aiden to arrive with Sammy and Ida.

Aiden had picked his Dad up and they had travelled up to Sammy's in relative silence, both excited and nervous for different reasons. Benny was emotional introducing his son to Sammy, and he could see as they shook hands, that they too were feeling the same way. Ida was also in Sammy's house; she was chatty and easy going and she made the journey down the road easier.

At last, they arrived at the hotel restaurant. Benny was buzzing with nervous energy. He introduced Sammy and Ida to everyone in turn, but as Sammy reached his hand out to Jo, Benny had to swallow hard to stop himself from gasping out loud. It was a memorable moment for both of the men, and for the others, merely the start of a great day out with their parents' old friend from forty years ago.

The place settings worked well, Benny had told Sammy of Deirdre's mother's dementia and the old man made a fuss of her, listening as she related tales of long ago into his ear. On her other side, sat Benny who joined in their conversation, making sure Mary didn't feel left out. It was going incredibly well.

The hotel was extremely busy with St Patrick's Day revellers, so after lunch they moved into the bar. All of the women, apart from

Mary, made their way to the toilet. Deirdre had just brought Mary back. Aiden was at the bar with his brothers-in-law organising another round of drinks. He called something across to Jo, as she reached the door of the Ladies' toilets with the other women. She stood holding the door for a moment as she called back her reply, then followed the others in. Mary, who had been following the group of women with her eyes, turned to Sammy, as Jo disappeared into the toilets and said to him, "And she's yer daughter then; she's the picture of ye." Obviously, forgetting she had met Andy and Kate many times.

Benny changed the subject, only he and Sammy had heard her remark. Benny looked around to check, no one else was within earshot, he thought, *My God, Mary couldn't tell you what she's just eaten, but she picked that up.*

As the others rejoined the group, Benny asked would they mind if he and Sammy made their excuses for a while, saying they wanted to go out into the air to stretch their legs. Sammy's friend, Ida, had hit it off with Deirdre. Both of the women sat talking animatedly in the centre of the gathering. They waved to them distractedly, understanding that the two men had a lot to talk about.

As they made their way across the lounge bar, to the front doors, they almost collided with another group of women heading to the toilets enmasse. Sammy turned to Benny and whispered, "Why do women do that?"

Benny grinned.

"They're afraid to be the one left behind; they know the rest'll talk about them."

They left the hustle and bustle of the hotel and walked across University Street, and made their way toward the street that housed the old bed-sits.

"It's been a helluva a day fer ya, Sammy."

"It's been a helluva week, Benny. She's a beauty isn't she?"

Benny nodded his agreement.

"Don't worry about that comment from Mary, Sammy, she was just trying to place everybody. I watch her doing it at family gatherings all the time, we'll all be sitting around the dinner table in whoever's house and I'll see her scrutinising all the faces. Of course, she knows Jo well, but in a big gathering she gets a bit lost, and she frantically tries to work it all out. This time she simply said what she saw, she put two and two together and got four. It doesn't mean anything, ask her now and she wouldn't remember she'd said it."

"God help her, she's not even as old as me, is she, Benny?"

"No, there'd be a few years in it. She was great until Deirdre's father died over a year past, but she's just gone downhill from there. In the main she's happy enough with her lot, though."

They walked on.

"I hope we don't meet up with the blue beg (bag) brigade, I saw on the TV last night they were riotin'."

"Too early for them; they'll still be in their beds sleepin' it off."

They reached the corner of Lawrence Street. Two young men stood talking on the corner, both on bicycles. As Benny and Sammy entered the street they surveyed the scene before them. Not a lot had changed in forty years. Anonymous doors and windows, the windows decked with curtains in various stages of repair, some heavy and completely pulled, others barely hanging on, their hooks having parted company long since, the obligatory discoloured nets, the whiteness they had once proudly displayed, a dim and distant memory. The odd bare light bulb, burning bright, from a centre flex, even though it was the middle of the day. Every so often, an inside window ledge with an object perched on it in a vain attempt to personalise the space.

Benny recognised one that his granddaughters collected, a small cuddly 'Tatty Teddy' with paws outstretched offering a red heart, proclaiming 'My Heart is Yours'. Another, precariously held, a pink plaque, announcing 'Only Boring Women Have Tidy Houses.' One grimy window embraced a pair of rotund stick-on Santa and Frostys, wishing 'Happy Holidays' to all and sundry, still.

Behind the closed, heavy curtains, it was certain, lay at least one, horizontal student in deep slumber, or sluggishly awaking from sleep, scratching his head, contemplating if he could be arsed getting out of bed to face the day yet. And, in the gutter, one lone, rain soaked, Adidas trainer. Flatland.

"At least Kate isn't present. That would have been just too much."

"Aiden and Jo were at their place on Saturday night for dinner, of course he shared the news. At one stage he told me Kate dropped a plate shattering it into pieces at her feet. I'm guessing I know at which stage."

Sammy looked at him dolefully, and then his face creased with

268

laughter. Benny joined him, the tension of the week finally exploding in both of them. They both stopped to sit on a garden wall to catch their breath.

"Oh, we shouldn't, it's not even funny, poor Kate, I can just imagine what was going through her head, "Is that bugger not dead yet?""

They gathered themselves, walked on up the street and came to a stop directly opposite the old house. The windows had been double glazed, but apart from that nothing much had changed. Both of them stood looking through the panes of glass, glimpsing the rooms that had once been home to them, in silence.

Benny could almost see himself sitting at that upstairs window, reading, listening to the wavelengths of the world on the big, brown, wooden radio, the radio which had brought him the voices and the music that had sustained him, through many a lonely night. The room where Deirdre and he had first made love, the room that had been their first marital home.

A taxi driver honking his horn brought them back to reality. They looked at each other and moved on.

As they passed one of the houses near the corner, music filtered out from an open window. Benny stopped and cocked his head to identify the singer.

Sammy spoke, "Morrisey. Used to be Bob Dylan; only the music changes."

Benny remarked, "Morrisey, in a bed-sit. Could you be more depressed?"

They continued on. As they reached the corner they both stopped for a final backward glance before leaving the street behind them.

"A lifetime ago, Benny Boy, but in ways it seems like yesterday. Life's been good to ye Benny, and I got my second chance. We've been lucky. She's like me, of course yer right, but she's the build of her mother. Liz was a looker, great legs too, like Jo. And oh my God, could she dance."

"Yer prepared for this wedding invitation, Sammy."

"Yeah, that would be a step too far. At least we can decline with good reason. You'll keep me informed how the day goes won't ye, Benny?"

"I'm not likely to lose touch again. You can come to the house

269

as well y'know. Kate and Andy aren't always around. We'll work something out."

"We'll see, Benny."

As they turned the corner back into Botanic Avenue, they were met by a group of young people walking arm in arm, some of them wearing tilted Leprechaun hats, slightly the worse for wear, but in good form, they greeted Benny and Sammy, "Happy St. Patrick's Day!"

Benny and Sammy returned the greeting, both looking after them, laughing.

"Not a care in the world," Sammy said.

Benny looked at Sammy, "Happy St. Patrick's Day, mate."

"Happy St. Patrick's Day, Benny Boy."

Chapter 39

TUESDAY NIGHT, FOUND CASSIE AND Gail sitting in Cass's kitchen, mulling over the application forms, matching the required paperwork to each applicant. If the documentation wasn't complete they set the forms aside. It was crucial that they got all these details right or it could sink them before they even got started.

Heads down, they worked together in comparative silence, only speaking to exchange information on each candidate. By nine thirty the task was complete, they had their pile of successful applicants. They divided the pile into two, agreeing to do the call backs the next day.

Tired, but satisfied they each decided on an early night. Tomorrow, they would fit the final pieces of the jigsaw. Their staff selected and their premises in place, their business was ready for operation on the following Monday.

Cass saw Gail to the door and their attention was drawn to a house across the street. All of the windows were open wide and the sound of Shane MacGowan belting out, 'The Irish Rover,' at full volume could be heard all over the street. Through the open windows, they could see a crowd of people dancing and waving their arms about, as they sang along to the music.

Gail looked to Cassie, "Party, on a Tuesday night?"

"It's St. Patrick's Night I think, isn't it?"

"Oh yeah, I'd forgotten that. I used to have the day off when I worked in the bank. Funny I'd forgotten completely, Happy St. Patrick's Day, Cass. G'night."

"Happy St. Patrick's Day, Gail. G'night."

Gail drove up the road, thinking it strange she'd forgotten the holiday. The holidays would be few and far between now, while they got themselves established.

She didn't care; she was more than ready for self-employment, she felt empowered, it was the chance of a lifetime and she was sure Cass and she were more than equipped for it.

Cass closed the door on the scene of revelling across the road, and headed upstairs to bed. She was exhausted, but happy after the weeks of planning, they were ready to go. She sank under the covers as the music from the party blasted out late into the night.

She slept like a baby, not hearing a thing.

By ten to eight that same Tuesday night, Orla was standing all dressed up and ready to go. She had agonised over what to wear, finally deciding on her favourite jeans and a cashmere jumper, with her new boots.

She felt nervous and edgy. Declan had said this was a community thing; it was just to introduce her to people. She was probably stupid thinking of it as a real date.

She checked the camera as the car drove in; it was definitely him. She opened the door and waved, to save him having to get out.

As they entered the pub it was already packed. She could see one lone man with a guitar sitting on the stage singing.

"I thought y'said it was traditional?"

"It's early days. There'll be a few turns like him, singer song-writer types, maybe a group as well, then the diddly dee kicks in when everybody's merry. Merry as newt's some of them'll be, no doubt. What'll ya have, Orla, a pint o'stout?"

Her eyes found his, they were laughing at her.

"Yeah, that'll be lovely and a pig's foot."

He laughed at her.

"I'm the boy would get it fer ye. What'll ye really have?"

"A glass of white wine, please. There's yer Mum and Dad - will we sit with them?"

"If ya don't mind. I told you it was a community thing."

She walked over to where Geraldine and Liam sat with their company, they moved to make room for them, as Declan introduced her.

It was a cosy, local pub, and Orla loved it immediately. It was a far cry from the elegant, tasteful, lifeless places she had frequented with Seamus.

The singer took a break for a while and music played out from the speakers around the walls. She recognised the voices, Brian Kennedy and Juliet Turner:

'Well I hope that I don't fall in love with you,
'Cause falling in love just makes me blue,
Well, the music plays and you display
Your heart for me to see...'

She looked over toward the bar. Declan was standing placing the drinks on a tray. He looked across and met her gaze as the song played:

'And I hope that I don't fall in love with you.'

The song continued to play out as he set the drinks down on the table looking directly at Orla. Someone told a joke and they all laughed. Orla smiled at Declan not hearing the joke. He returned her smile, an intimate meaningful smile.

It was a moment shared by the two of them alone, as the rest of the company laughed at the joke.

The song ended...

'And I think that I just fell in love with you.'

The moment passed, but it was bookmarked, there to be considered, by either, or both of them, when the time was right.

He took his place at the table beside her, joining in the conversation. As the night wore on, the place became louder and livelier as the alcohol took effect, the voices rising in argument and banter, finally joining together in song as the musicians took to the floor.

Orla loved it.

She told Declan so as he left her home.

"I really enjoyed it, Declan, but I'm glad I don't have to get up early, I think my head may be a wee bit sore in the mornin' - I drank far too much wine."

"Sure ye can lie in, ye've no work t'get up for. Would you like to go out for dinner on Friday night? I mean, I wouldn't like ya to think I'm a big culchie who thinks a few jars in the local constitutes a date. It's as well I'm sober, that's a hard word to say. Wha'd'ya say, Orla, Friday?"

"I'd love to, call me. Happy St. Patrick's Day, Declan."

She leaned over and kissed him lightly on the lips, and then she swung the car door open and was gone.

He called after her, "Happy St. Patrick's Day."

He waited until he saw her safely in, the dog scampering up the hall behind her, she turned and closed the door and switched on the lights.

Then he drove the short distance home, his heart was still singing when he reached his own front door.

Part Three

Summer in the City

'Come – on, come – on
and dance all night...'
Lovin' Spoonful

Chapter 40

Friday, 3rd July
THE INSPECTION COMPLETED, CASS TURNED to lock the front door of the last apartment. She was startled by the sound of a voice behind her.

"Hey, how's it goin'?"

She spun around to see Tony O'Connor standing there.

"Tony, it's you. I didn't know there was anybody about. It's going well, just finishing the inspection."

They were standing in another of his apartment complexes 'Call-a-Cleaner' had been contracted to clean. The work had been steady since Cass and Gail's first job in March.

"I was checking out some maintenance work. Power shower packed in for the third time in a month so I had to get a new one installed, wanted to see it going in with my own eyes. Ya can't trust these bloody plumbers."

"Or indeed, these bloody contract cleaners," Cassie quipped.

Tony had called round to inspect their first few jobs himself.

"No, not at all, Cassie, if your workers weren't leaving the complexes to perfection I wouldn't be paying you. Simple as that. There're no back doors in Tony O'Connor. I'm more than happy with the standard of work."

"Good. We're still doing the inspections ourselves so I didn't think you could find fault with any of the apartments. We are at the stage where we're becoming too busy to do it all ourselves. We'll have to appoint a permanent supervisor, but we'll still do spot checks, to keep on top of things."

"Never a bad idea; I've always been that way. Some people resent it, but t'hell with them, if their work is up to the mark it shouldn't bother them."

They were standing facing each other, Cass was about to say,

"See ya later." And move on, but Tony spoke again, "Would you like to have lunch with me?"

This was the second time in a month he had asked her. The first time she hadn't been sure if he was actually asking her out. She'd had to decline the offer anyway, because she was on her way to another inspection.

Today, she was heading back to the office, with no plans. She usually grabbed a sandwich for lunch and ate it at her desk. This was awkward, she really liked him, and she certainly didn't want to offend him, but she couldn't bring herself to accept. It would upset the business relationship, things were going so well, Gail and she were working long hours, but it was all working out. She couldn't jeopardise that.

"No thanks, I don't…"

He cut in, "You don't eat lunch, or you don't care to eat lunch with me?"

His eyes were playful, but she still had to be careful not to say the wrong thing. He smiled at her and said, "Okay we'll leave it. See ya, Cassie, have a good weekend."

She thought, *Oh Christ, I have offended him.*

He turned toward the car park, Cass called after him, "No, Tony, please, it's just that I've been on my own a long time. It's the way it is, you get used to it, that's all."

He looked at her sadly.

"No, Cassie, you don't get used to it. You forget, I'm on my own too. You don't get used to it. You just learn to live with it. Have a good weekend, bye."

With that he turned and was gone before she'd time to reply.

Shit, I should have gone to lunch with him. If he stops givin' us work Gail will never forgive me, and I do like him.

She drove back to the office, stopping for a ham salad sandwich in a garage along the way. It lay discarded on the passenger seat where she'd tossed it with disinterest. As she fought her way through the busy Friday afternoon traffic she was unaware that she was talking aloud to herself, "Seventeen long years without a man in my life, now that I've money and a business of my own, Prince Bloody Charming has to turn up. Well, I don't need him!"

She turned the radio up and joined Roy Orbison in the chorus of 'Only the Lonely', oblivious to the fact that both of her windows

277

were fully wound down, and her voice could be heard ringing out, loud and clear from the van, as she drove over the Albert Bridge, much to the amusement of the group of backpackers waiting for buses outside Central Station.

Kieran was meeting Suzanne for lunch, another lunch he couldn't afford, and he was running late.

He pushed his way through the shoppers, many carrying their wares from the Friday market in St.Georges, mostly elderly people. Kieran hated Friday lunch times; these old codgers only seemed to come out on Fridays. Busy Bus to the market, then they shuffled about with their bags of fish and fresh vegetables, cluttering up the town for busy people like him. Standing on the footpaths outside Isibeals and Blinkers and every other restaurant within a mile it seemed, reading through the menus, working out who was offering the best deals.

He wanted to shout at them, "Make a decision. It's only friggin' fish and chips, not friggin' life and death!"

He'd had a bad morning. His figures were poor, with little prospect of improvement. July was always slow with the Twelfth holidays to contend with, but this summer was something else.

Earlier, he'd heard a radio report saying Northern Ireland was likely to be suffering more than any other region in the U.K. during the recession. Taking into account, that many local property market areas had been priced on a par with London in 2007, Northern Irish homeowners and prospective buyers were feeling the effects of unemployment more so than their mainland counterparts. Kieran thought, *Tell me about it.*

If things continued in this vein, he would really have to consider upping sticks and moving to London. He arrived at the restaurant ten minutes late, and was annoyed to see Suzanne was not yet there.

She burst through the doors minutes later full of apologies, but it didn't wash. Suzanne was really starting to get on his nerves again. For a while, he had quite liked her. She was getting him interviews and they had fun together, he found she was growing on him. Even her whiney sing songy voice didn't seem so accentuated outside of her workplace.

He had been a bit concerned; at one stage that she was falling in love with him, though. And then she had come clean and confessed she had a boyfriend at university in Bristol, who was due home in September. She had shared their engagement plans.

Kieran couldn't have been happier, no strings sex for the summer, and then he would be shot of her. Hopefully, by September, she would have helped him into a position with a decent salary and more secure prospects than he had presently with the bunch of tossers she had landed him with. He'd asked her to go to Springsteen with him next week. No point in wasting the ticket and hotel room he had already paid for. But he was seriously considering the move to London. He may just be kissing her farewell, before September rolled around.

Suzanne was having a good day. Her daily quota of interviews was achieved by midday, and she had a job interview herself at twelve thirty. She had arranged to have the afternoon off earlier in the week. The interview had gone really well, more money and better prospects for promotion. Her hair had been coloured specially for the occasion, the previous night. The effect was pleasing; she thought it looked kinda Keira Knightley.

Kieran hadn't even noticed it, or asked how the interview had gone for her. Instead, he had been straight in about himself, brushing off her apologies for her lateness.

"Chill. I'm only just here myself. Any sign of any new positions on the horizon? Yis must get away with murder in that place, flogging the same few jobs to the punters, week in, and week out."

She was furious, but said nothing. He really was an insufferable prat at times. Thoughts of the Springsteen concert kept her tongue in her teeth. She'd never seen him, but had heard his shows were legendary. The tickets couldn't be got for love or money. On the day they had gone on sale, she and her colleagues had been on the phones and the internet first thing. Not a hope. They had gone on sale at nine and sold out by two minutes past. When Kieran told her he'd a spare ticket, she thought she'd died and gone to heaven. He may be an obnoxious 'know it all', but she wasn't about to fall out with him now, with only a week to go until the concert date.

To think, she had actually believed he would be devastated when she finally told him she had a boyfriend. Fearing this, she had confessed all one night, shortly after they had started going out. Admittedly she had been slightly drunk at the time. She now knew the woman hadn't been born who could devastate Kieran Hughes.

Just yesterday, Ian, her boyfriend, had phoned to tell her he had an interview in Belfast, next Friday. He said he'd decided to stay at his parents' house that weekend. Friday night, he'd arranged to meet up with some old school mates for a lads' night out, but they'd be able to spend Saturday together.

Her eyes had quickly flicked to the calendar on her desk, *"...next Friday..."* Friday 10th of July he had meant, the concert was the next day *"...spend Saturday together..."* he'd said.

She had been gutted; there was no way she was missing Springsteen. Of course, she loved Ian and everything, but no, she wouldn't be available on Saturday.

Immediately, her brain went into overload, she thought of an old friend Sinead, who lived in Dublin.

"Jeez, I'm sorry, Ian sweetheart, but it's Sinead's hen night in Dublin next Saturday. Did I not already tell ya that?"

He had fallen for it. His interview was with a leading law firm in the city, she knew his da must have set it up because legal firms were getting rid of staff hand over fist, at the minute. Under those circumstances, he would more than likely be successful, and that would be the end of her summer of fun. She had been planning on dumping Kieran soon anyway, but it would fairly curb the nights out on the town with the girls.

Every cloud has a silver lining, she mused; think of the engagement party, it would be gas. She smiled at Kieran, as he moaned on about his sales figures, placing her hand on his across the table, she said, "Ah never mind, sure ya never know what's around the corner for you."

Deirdre was sitting flicking through a magazine in Frankie and Benny's diner, waiting for Benny. She usually bought a morning paper, but today she'd opted for a magazine, something frivolous to take her mind off things. On breakfast news she'd heard there had been another death from swine flu. She had switched the television off, she couldn't take any more news like this today, not with all the nerves of the approaching wedding starting to build up.

With a week to go to the wedding, Jo was almost six months pregnant. Of course they all now knew that pregnant women were most susceptible to complications if they caught swine flu. Jo had only just discovered she was pregnant, when the news of the impending swine flu pandemic broke, both she and Aiden had been beside themselves with worry over it. One of the childbirth organisations was even advising women against getting pregnant, such was the degree of concern. Deirdre did her best to reassure them, but in all honesty, it was a completely new area to her too. She was worried sick about Jo. She had read recently that vaccine trials were about to begin in Australia. If they went well the vaccine would be available in the U.K. in the autumn. That was little consolation to Jo, who would either be in the latter stages of pregnancy by then, or would actually have given birth.

Minutes later, Benny came strolling through the doors. She watched him walk toward her, thinking that he was still a striking looking man for his age, he bent to kiss her.

"I saw that look. What is it? Do you think I'm wasting my money in the gym?"

"On the contrary, I was just thinking how well you look."

"Aye right."

"No really, can an old married woman not give her own husband a compliment."

She gave him her raised eyebrow look, as he settled down beside her.

"I see the Italian place has gone," Benny said.

"Yeah, I noticed that. Kelly said the food was lovely too, but maybe it was a bit pricey."

They had seen a few changes in the shopping centre since the start of the year, with some of the retail units closing up, in or around the centre's first anniversary. Even Benny's favourite music store had gone. She could see by the bags he had been shopping in one of the other music stores in town.

He handed her a small carrier bag.

"That's for you, open it and see."

She opened it to find an old Moody Blues album on CD.

"Remember?"

It had been one of the LP's she'd been renting from the record library the day Benny and she had first spoken. It had almost tumbled from the collection clasped under her arm when she had tripped down the step of the shop.

"Of course, I do, you'd just brought it back you told me.

Thanks, Benny, yer still a gem," she said and kissed him.

"Course I am. Well, what's new?"

"Ger rang. Apparently, she's taking Mum shopping for a new hat for the wedding later on today."

"Did you and yer mother not buy a hat for her outfit months ago?"

"Yeah, we did. It seems Mum was looking through a magazine and she cried out, 'That's it, Geraldine, that's the hat I want fer the wedding!' Geraldine was about to say what she'd just said, but Liam gave Ger a look and said, 'If that's the one you want, Mary, Geraldine'll make sure ye get it.' When she got Mum out of the way, she asked him what he was playing at. He said, 'It's like this, Geraldine - she forgot she'd bought a hat - but she remembered she was goin' to a weddin'. Just humour her for God's sake. If that's the hat she says she wants, take her out and let her buy it.'"

"He's right, that's what I said all along. You and Geraldine make too much of things, if it keeps her happy, yer better to work with her, go along with her."

Mary had gone back up to Derry to live with Geraldine and Liam for the summer months. So far the arrangement was working well, for all of them. Geraldine was better equipped to care for her mother after the four month break, and Deirdre had helped her find a nurse. Lorraine, from the agency, had contacted their branch in Derry, and they'd found a lovely woman, called Jenny, to work with them during the summer. And, Ellie was contracted to Deirdre from September again.

"I suppose yer right. We spend too much time arguing with her, trying to prove a point. At her age, what does it matter if she's one hat or twenty hats, if that's all it takes to make her contented at the time."

He nodded.

"Oh, I'd a text from Sammy look." He offered her his phone, the message read, *"Up, up and away!"*

"He's a case, isn't he - I take it they're in the air now then?"

"Yeah. No doubt I'll get another one when they land."

Sammy and Ida were setting out that morning for a month's holiday in Canada.

"Can you believe it's only a week tomorrow 'til the wedding, after all the talking and planning it's just crept up, hasn't it?"

282

The waiter came and they ordered. They didn't bother to look at the menu, they knew it by heart. They had been back into their Friday routine since June, after Mary went back up to Geraldine.

"Aiden's takin' cold feet over this stag do, I can tell ya. You know what he's like, a couple of pints does him. Some of those boys goin' tomorrow night would drink that fer their breakfast."

"Yeah, Jo thinks she's in fer a nice quiet night out in a restaurant, but she'll know all about it if our ones hit the cocktails. They were wild in their day those two. Kelly and Rosie may be settled now, but there was many a morning they came home with the milkman."

"Aye, I remember it well, is it any wonder my hair's white."

"It's payback time now, nearly their turn to go through all that with their own wains."

Deirdre was quiet for a few moments. Benny could tell by her demeanour she was annoyed about something. He interrupted her thoughts.

"What's bothering you?"

"Ach, I just wish Aiden and Jo had let us help pay for the wedding reception. It's such a huge expense for them when they've both just come through divorces. I suppose I'm worried about people assuming it's a free bar."

"Deirdre, Aiden was right to stand firm on that one. He knew it would offend Andy if we paid, he knows Andy's in no position to offer help financially. And fer God's sake look at the invitations they ended up sending out. Jo's family may be small and mainly teetotal, but my clan alone could empty a brewery. And that's only the seven brothers, let alone their seven brides! They both went through all that palaver the first time around, everybody goin' knows their situation, it'll be fine. When I was over in Jo's with Aiden the other night, she was watching one of those TV reality shows about weddings…Dear God, the things some couples spend money on would make yer hair curl. Ice sculptures, fer Christ's sake! What's all that about?"

Their meals arrived and the subject was dropped. Benny looked at Deirdre as she ate. He was thrilled that they were back into the routine they had developed when they had both retired, he didn't begrudge her mother the time Deirdre had spent with her over the past few months, but he was glad it was Geraldine's turn. And, for now, he had Deirdre to himself again.

"So, what are the plans fer this afternoon?"

"I have none. It's just such a pleasure to have nothing to do and all day to do it in. I could buy some new holiday clothes."

They were both planning on flying out to Portugal the week after the wedding.

"Like you really need them, Deirdre."

"Sure a woman can never have too many summer dresses. It's a shame Ger couldn't convince Liam to come out to us for a week or two; the sun would've done Mum the world of good."

Benny was secretly pleased they had declined. He liked his brother-in-law, but Liam had never left Ireland, and had no inclination to do so. He was a man who knew what he liked and in his own words had *"no desire to try anything new at this stage in life."* A holiday in Portugal would have been an endurance for him, and like a penance to the rest of them.

Each to their own, thought Benny.

He understood Deirdre's concern for her mother, but in truth, he thought Mary would be much happier going to Donegal, with Geraldine and Liam, as they had planned. Deirdre meant well, but Benny knew what the scenario would have been, had they agreed to the holiday in the sun. The three others, would more than likely, spend the time pretending to be enjoying it for Deirdre's sake and in reality be miserable in the heat, out of sorts with the 'foreign' food, and return home tired and stressed from the effort. He felt the whole concept, of the five of them holidaying together, defeated the purpose of the term 'holiday.' And the four months of looking after her mother had taken its toll on Deirdre. This was their time, she needed to get away from it all and completely relax, ready to return to her commitment of looking after the old woman, refreshed and energized, the batteries fully recharged for the winter months ahead.

"You can't fit a square peg into a round hole, Deirdre. A holiday in the sun would be Liam's idea of holiday hell. Let them go off and enjoy their summer the way they like to, and we'll do the same. We can think of takin' yer mother out in September, or October, when the climate would suit her more. Right now, you need to think of you. Give yerself a chance to soak up the sun and swan about in those summer dresses."

"I know you're right. Remember this?" she tilted her head, as the music playing out loudly, changed to one of their old Motown favourites. "1968 was it, or '69?"

They reminisced about the times the old song conjured up for them. Glad of the chance to sit relaxed in each other's company, before the weekend was over, and they were on the final countdown to Aiden and Jo's wedding, a week on Saturday.

That morning, Deirdre had left her car at home, accepting Benny's offer of a lift into the town. She'd spent the morning shopping alone, while Benny went to the gym and did his Friday morning stuff. Without either of them suggesting it, the two of them had found themselves walking through the shopping centre car park to his car, and heading up the motorway, toward Portstewart, one of their favourite places to visit throughout their years together.

The day was wet, and the rain was warm, as they arrived in the picturesque holiday resort. Summer in Northern Ireland. They walked along the strand and let the rain soak their faces, then drove back to the promenade and battled for a parking space. Even on the wettest of days, this promenade always attracted crowds, and parking spaces were as rare as hen's teeth.

Sitting side by side, on a pavement bench overlooking the beach, they ate ice creams from Morrellis, in the drizzling rain, contentedly watching the sea do what is does best, just be the sea.

Chapter 41

FRIDAY EVENING, FOUND CASS SITTING eating at her kitchen table, alone. A tuna salad, accompanied by a glass of water; *the excitement of it all*, she thought.

Jo's wedding was next Saturday, and she still had a few pounds to shed to fit into her dress neatly. Gail and she were going out shopping for shoes tomorrow, then they were planning on a meal with Jo and a few close friends and family members tomorrow night.

Jo had decided to forego a full on hen night, for obvious reasons. Cass had promised herself she would count the calories, all of this week, so that she could have a pig-out in one of their favourite restaurants on Saturday night. Dean was working until nine, so she would probably go out for a walk alone later, to burn off her sumptuous dinner.

Tony O'Connor's face had stayed with her all day. There was something about him she really liked him. Why did life have to be so unbelievably complicated? Here she was at forty, she had struggled alone on meagre wages to rear her two kids, then out of the blue she gets a lucky break, and she's in partnership in a rapidly growing business with one of her best friends. Life was sweet, for the first time in years. Couldn't fate just leave her alone to enjoy it for awhile, without throwing Tony O'Connor into the mix?

She thought of the properties they had worked on for him. He must be worth way over and above what they had first imagined when they had checked out his website. Of course, he wouldn't have looked twice at her when she was working as a cleaner, and could have done with a wealthy man taking an interest in her. Now she'd didn't need money, although the money in her bank account was a mere drop in the ocean compared to Tony O'Connor's bank balance.

One thing was for sure, he definitely wasn't after her money.

Her head turned at the sound of the front door opening. She

looked at the clock, too early for Dean. Her daughter's head appeared round the door.

"How ya doin', love, where's the child?"

"She's at that wee birthday party. Remember I told ye, the wee girl from playgroup."

Cassie was always glad to see her daughter, but she hoped she wasn't going to ask her to look after Mia tomorrow.

"Ya haven't forgotten I'm goin' out with Gail in the mornin', love, and then Jo's night out the morra?"

"No, I'm not lookin' a babysitter, Mum, I just wanted to talk to ya about something."

Cass rose to fill the kettle, to give herself a chance to compose her expression. This didn't sound good. She said a silent prayer, *"Dear God, please don't let her be having another child to Jake."*

"Jake and me have finished."

Cass thought, *Thank God, is that all?*

She wasn't unduly fazed by this information. Although Lara didn't usually talk to her directly about him, she was kept informed of the situation through Dean. Cass never expressed an opinion, but Lara couldn't have failed to sense her mother's disapproval of the way he had abandoned her, and her child, shortly after Mia's birth.

"Did yis have a fall out or what?"

"No, I finally came to my senses, that's all. I'm sure ye know, he's been back and forward like the Scarlet Pimpernel since you gave me that money. Well, the other night he was round, Mia was in bed and he was sitting watching the football. It was late, around eleven o'clock, he'd asked me to make him something to eat. I was standing in the kitchen, making him tea and toasted sandwiches, I'd just poured the tea and put the sandwich on a plate, when I just thought to myself, *What are you doin', girl?* It was like a light had switched on in my head. I went back into the living room, where he was sitting opposite the television, with his feet up on my coffee table. I lifted the remote control and switched the TV off and turned to him. He was about to ask me what I was doing, but I got in first, saying, 'I'd like you to leave now, Jake.' He replied, 'Sure the match isn't over yet, and what about my sandwich?' I said, 'I want you to leave now, and not come back. If you want to see Mia, of course I'll respect that, but you must call to make arrangements. I don't want you calling here unannounced again. Is that clear?' He was gobsmacked. He grabbed his coat and

287

then he says again, 'What about m'sandwich?' I marched into the kitchen, lifted it plate 'n' all, and handed it to him, as I shoved him out the door, shuttin' it firmly behind him! I haven't heard a peep from him since, the gutless bastard. He was only upsettin' Mia, dandering round any night he was at a loose end, if she never sees him again, she'll not miss him."

Lara was still standing in the middle of her mother's kitchen, hands flailing agitatedly, as she related her tale. Cass walked over from where she stood by the sink, and hugged her like a child. They both cried in each other's arms. It had taken a while, but like Cass herself, all those years ago, Lara had come to her senses. Cassie knew she had learnt her lesson.

No man would be taking Lara Gallagher for a fool again.

Later in the day, Benny and Deirdre bought fish and chips and ate them from the wrappers, sitting in the car park, above the ocean top cliffs, watching the sunset on the horizon.

Benny's phone buzzed indicating a text, *'Back on Terra Firma.'*

"Sammy and Ida. The eagle has landed. They'll have a right time to themselves in Canada. It's good to see them livin' it up, at their age isn't it? D'ye think we'll still be up holidaying together when we're in our eighties, Deirdre?"

His voice was light, but they both knew he was serious. The deterioration of Deirdre's mother mind had knocked them for six, totally compos mentis while her husband was alive and well, and only months later, as dependent on her family as a small child.

She reached for his hand and grasped it.

"I hope so love. But who knows? In this life you can only live one day at a time - and less of the 'at their age.' Ida would be mortified; remember she's quite a few years younger than Sammy. He's her 'older man.'"

They finished their chips, licking their fingers like children, the salt and vinegar stinging an indiscernible paper cut on Benny's finger, he winced, exaggerating the pain.

"Cry-baby," she grinned at his discomfort.

Deirdre drank down the cold fizzy drink greedily, the bubbles burning the back of her throat.

"Wanna go home?"

She nodded sleepily, and snuggled down into the seat, rummaging in her bag for the present he had bought her earlier. She slid the CD into the player and listened, as The Moody Blues filled the car, taking them back forty years.

Benny squeezed her hand, the car headlights lighting their path, as he drove the familiar road home, in the falling darkness.

Chapter 42

CASSIE AND GAIL WERE KNEE-DEEP in shoes. This was the fourth shop they had been in, and Cass still hadn't found the right shade for her dress. They left the shop and made for the next one on their imaginary list.

"We'll have to find them today or we'll still be shopping next Friday. How's Jo? I haven't spoken to her in a few days. Is she managin' to keep the nerves at bay?"

"Just about, from what I can gather, Aiden's worse. Of course the stag night's tonight. I think he's dreading it. Most of his mates are either younger or dedicated bachelors, so he may have a lot of pints to down, to keep up the pace. Jo's told him to stay out of her way tomorrow anyway. She says she's no time for people with hangovers when she can't go on the razz herself. Here, that's the shade isn't it?"

Gail pulled Cass toward a window displaying shoes that appeared to be exactly the shade they had been searching for.

"C'mon and we'll see, I bet they don't have them in my size."

Cass clutched the bag containing the dress. Inside, they found the shoes in her size, and she also bought another pair to wear with her outfit for that night, a better match than the ones she'd decided on. As the assistant handed them to her in the fancy carrier bags, she thought back to the state of the shoes she'd been wearing that day in January, when she'd bought the scratch card. Who'd have thought it?

Starbucks was Saturday afternoon busy, as Orla and Anne Marie sat opposite each other sipping their coffees. The meetings had become a once a month ritual by now, one they both looked forward to.

"So, no sign of a promotion yet, Anne Marie?"

"Not at the minute; they've got their full quota of team leaders in the store, and by all accounts Brown-nosin' Brendan is a right wee tyrant to work with, anyway. He's down on the staff like a ton of bricks for the least wee thing, all through his downline of course. I'm not sure I could do his dirty work for him. Have you ever noticed supermarket managers are always wee men with ferrety faces?"

"Can't say I have."

"Aye, I suppose you wouldn't. You're one of the organised ones who do an online shop at the same time every week, whether ya need to or not."

Orla looked hurt.

"I shop too, it just suits better to do it online, with the business, that's all."

"I'm just pissed off that it's eejits like me who have to process your orders. There must be something else I could do, but I haven't a qualification to my name. I'm not thick, but when I think back to the school I went to, it's a wonder I can even read and write."

"Would ya not consider goin' to college to do some kind of a course?"

"Nah, I'm too old, sure I'm nearly thirty. I'd feel stupid in the midst of all those youngsters with their heads full of smokin' dope and last night's sex."

"That's only in 'Hollyoaks'. You'd be fine, I'm sure there're plenty of people your age in college."

"I don't know. I mean, I'm not playin' the 'poor me' card, but I don't even know what I'm good at anymore. I remember being good at English and Art in primary school, but that all changed with the move up to secondary school. It was a crap school. The teachers treated us with disdain, barely made eye contact. It was such a shock after the lovely maternal teachers we had in primary school. My world, literally, changed from colour to black and white, overnight. I suppose I developed an attitude, 'couldn't give a shit' sorta style, but it was a defence mechanism. If you'd let those tyrants see you were frightened of them, they'd've devoured you whole. I was outta there at the first opportunity, couldn't wait to earn money and get a life for myself. I'd a Saturday job in one of the big retail chains in the town, they're still round the corner there," she jerked her head toward the window, "they offered me a full-time position with them, if I was leavin' school. *If I was?* I jumped at it. I was working full-time before I'd even officially left school. I loved it. I was no sooner there than they made me supervisor, then eventually shop manager."

"Well then, there's your answer. You're good with people, you've great organisational skills, you can handle responsibility and you've years of retail experience, you should do a management course of some sort, a BTEC or something."

"Maybe. I suppose it's all down to confidence, you've tons of it, but you came from a background where you were encouraged to be self confident. In our house, if you showed signs of self confidence, you were told 'self praise is no recommendation.'"

"When you say I've tons of it, just think back to the state I was in when we first met. If it hadn't been for you, I doubt I'd have managed to pick myself up again so quickly. You opened me up, made me talk, that's a skill in itself, Anne Marie."

"You forget I'd been there eight weeks by the time you arrived. I was as low as I've ever been in my life, when I walked through those refuge doors for the first time. Eadie, a woman you never met, she'd left by the time you came in, she sat with me many a night in that kitchen, pulled me through. I was only doing for you, what she'd done for me."

"We're both strong women, Anne Marie, we've managed to get back on our feet again, but I'll always be grateful to you, for spending that time with me."

They sat in silence for a time, no doubt, both reflecting on the circumstances that had brought them together. Anne Marie spoke first, "So, what about that new range you brought in, is it goin' okay for you?"

At the start of the summer, Orla had made a trip to a trade show in the NEC, she'd been introduced to a personalised gift range there. The sales of art were practically at a standstill by that time, she knew she'd have to find a product to sell to cover the overheads, or she'd be shutting up shop for good. It had been that bad.

Earlier in the year, Jo had suggested the card range and small line of silver jewellery to complement the specialist candles they carried. They were add ons, but not enough in themselves to make a difference. She'd decided to go for the personalised gift range, even though she knew Jo was less than enthusiastic about the idea.

"Unbelievable, they've been a life saver. I told you about the profit margins the distributor sold me on, they practically fly out the door. Jo wasn't too keen, although she didn't say as much. But, the goods are top quality if they're not exactly art, and something has to pay the rent."

"Good for you, you've done the right thing for now. I mean, this recession won't last forever, if you want you can do away with the new range when things turn around. Are you ready for the big 'comin out' at the wedding next week?"

"Well, all the family know about us by now, but it still feels a bit strange to go to such a public gathering together, y'know with my still being married 'n' all. Seamus is in Australia organising permanent residency. I suppose his brother thought he'd have a better chance of getting into the country permanently from that side. According to the solicitor, everything's in place for the divorce, now that the apartment's sold. It's just a matter of time. Even if he did know about Declan, I doubt he'd make an issue of it. He just wants to get shot of me and leave this all behind. That night at the house really put the wind up him. If there's one thing that matters to Seamus Delaney, it's his reputation. He'd have died of shame if I'd involved the police, not to mention the fact that it would have wrecked his chances of emigration completely."

"Well, you have a great time at the wedding with Declan. Keep me a piece of cake to dream on. I'll talk to you before Saturday anyway."

They finished their coffees and walked toward the door. Orla was leaving town early, to get dressed for Jo's night out. They parted company in Cornmarket. Anne Marie walked toward Donegall Place to shop for new jeans, and Orla walked toward the multi storey car park in High Street.

They turned to wave at each other.

"Enjoy yer night out."

"Have a good weekend, Anne Marie. Talk to ya later in the week."

Chapter 43

LATER ON THAT NIGHT, THE fateful day in January was to come back to her thoughts again, as Cass sat looking around her in the restaurant. It was the same one they'd been to, on the night of Helena's daughter's hen night, in January, the weekend she'd bought the lucky scratch card. Life had changed so unbelievably for her since that weekend.

She looked at her friends sitting with her. Gail had been told of her imminent redundancy that Friday, and when they had calculated Jo's dates with her, after she finally believed that she was pregnant, her baby had more than likely been conceived that Friday night.

Of course, everyone now knew Jo was pregnant; so much of the talk was of babies. Helena and Naomi, like Cass, had reared their families, and were all grannies. Aiden's sisters and Jo's sisters-in-law had families also, only Orla had no children.

Helena turned to Orla and Jo.

"Here, I was thinkin' about you two the other day, Jo was saying the art work isn't selling the best at the minute. My granddaughter was four the other day, and by word of mouth, we heard of a fella who does children's portraits from photographs, or from life. We took Grainne round to his house, and he did a portrait of her that's as true to life as you could ever get, you can nearly see her breathing. You want to see some of the ones of babies he has hanging up, they're unbelievable. He says he can't keep up to the work since he set up his website. He's lookin' for a pitch in the town, a permanent place to work from. It might be worth yer while contacting him. He could share some of the rent and you'd be getting more people through yer doors to look at the range of gifts you stock. No matter what happens in life, people will always be havin' babies, and money will always be bein' spent on gifts for those babies."

Orla looked at Jo.

"It certainly would work in well with the personalised gift range; what do you think, Jo?"

"Sounds like something you could think over."

She hoped her voice didn't betray her words, what was Orla thinking? The personalised gift range was going much better than even Orla had anticipated, but it was hardly art. Jo understood Orla was under a lot of pressure to cover the overheads, but she really couldn't see this idea working in with the atmosphere of the gallery.

"I'm wasted, I could pitch in the 'Dragon's Den,'" Helena laughed.

Orla asked her, "Do you have his number Helena? I think it would be an idea to have a look at, certainly."

Jo couldn't believe Orla would seriously consider bringing in a guy to sketch portraits in the gallery. God knows she herself had had reservations about the personalised gift range being introduced. Orla was probably just being polite, knowing Helena meant well. Someone called up to Jo, from the other end of the table, and she forgot all about it for the time being.

The night was a success. Jo had been a bit worried because it was to be the first night some of the women were to meet before the wedding, but after the initial few minutes, they had all been laughing and talking like old friends. The baby was lively, and as the night wore on, moved more animatedly, as the conversation grew louder, and she was firmly kicked with every outburst of loud talking, or laughter. The early worries about her dress and shape had calmed.

Jo couldn't believe she had really been that upset about a mere dress. Her weight increase was much as it had been with Corey. She was looking forward to next Saturday when she became Mrs Aiden Brannigan.

She watched in amusement as her friends became tipsy, thankful she wouldn't have the problem of a searing headache and 'budgies cage mouth' next day. Cass was in great forms, telling jokes at the other end of the table. Jo grinned at Gail, as she poured another cocktail from the jug in the centre of the table. What had she said about taking it easy?

Gail gave her the thumbs up, always a sign she was getting drunk. Jo returned the gesture, as she smiled wryly to herself, wondering how Aiden was bearing up.

Chapter 44

DECLAN AND ORLA WERE OUT walking that Sunday afternoon, the idea of the portrait artist was still in her head from the previous night. She had sensed Jo's reticence over the whole idea, but she was the one paying the bills.

"One of Jo's friends has given me an idea. She was telling me about a portrait artist she came across recently, he did a portrait of her granddaughter, a birthday present. Apparently, he can't keep up to the work, he's looking for premises to work from. Helena thought it might be something we could do, y'know to sell alongside the personalised gift range, charge him rent to work from the gallery. I've got his number. I'm thinking about it, it might help me cover costs."

"Portraits are always popular, I'm sure. I remember Molly gettin' the boys done when they were wee, but is it something you really feel would work in your gallery?"

Declan had been in the gallery once with Aiden before he met Orla.

"I'm no art expert, but surely the appeal of the place is the space, all that shining glass, the, what's the word, ambience? Are you not in danger of lowering the tone a bit?"

"I know Jo feels that way about the gift range, never mind this idea, but it's as simple as this: I need to find a way to make more money, or I won't survive this bloody recession. If it wasn't for the odd Jaguar driving Sugar Daddy, we wouldn't be selling any art works at all, at the minute."

"You'll weather it. Trust me, I'm a farmer, I know about these things."

Orla looked up at him, with a tight smile; she really wasn't so sure.

Aiden called his parents on Sunday afternoon.

"Any food up there?"

"Is it that bad, son?"

"Christ, I don't know how those boys do it every week, my head's bangin'. It feels like some bastard's climbed inside it with a Lambeg Drum. And my teeth are wearin' jumpers. I didn't even stay 'til the end, Tony O'Connor and me got a taxi home about one. It's anybody's guess where the rest of them ended up. Can I come up fer m'dinner, then? Jo doesn't want me anywhere about her with a hangover."

"Certainly, son, I'll tell yer mother to kill the fatted calf."

"Any chance of a lift up, Dad? I don't think driving would be a good idea today."

"See ya in a few minutes."

Benny hung up.

"That was Aiden, he's comin' up fer dinner, but he's not fit to drive, so I'll pick him up."

"Good. I dare say the girls will be lying low today, they're probably both in the recovery position right now. Jo's probably the only one out of the whole lot of them who can lift her head."

"Aiden reckons the boys were still goin' when he left, he couldn't stick the pace," Benny laughed at the idea of him bailing out of his own stag night. He lifted his car keys from the hall table and called out to Deirdre in the kitchen,

"Back in ten minutes."

"Okay, take care."

By four o'clock, Aiden had all but recovered, after one of his mother's roast dinners.

"That hit the spot exactly, Mum. I'm afraid my hell raisin' days are well and truly over."

"So where did yis go, or can you remember?" Deirdre asked.

He mentioned a few nightclubs in Belfast city centre, and she looked at him in bewilderment.

"I've never heard of any of those places. I'd need a road map fer a night out in Belfast now."

"Aye, Deirdre, it was all so much simpler when ye'd only the choice of the Maritime or Sammy Houston's."

297

"It was good enough fer us."

"I'm tellin' you it's a whole other world out there. I'd rather have a night in with a DVD and a pizza. Jesus my head still hurts."

"I'll get you a couple of painkillers, son, sure nobody looks after ye like yer mammy does."

Deirdre left the room to get them.

"Tony O'Connor has it bad for Cassie, y'know Jo's friend who won the money?"

"Aye, I remember, the girl who Gail set up business with. Where'd Tony meet her?"

Benny loved a love story.

"I gave them his number, thought he'd be able to throw some work their way. He did, by all accounts he's more than happy with their service, but he got a bit maudlin as we were on our way home, telling me he's asked her out to lunch twice, and she's turned him down. Y'know Tony, he's been bitten once, he hasn't bothered much at all since the divorce."

"Bothered much with what?" Deirdre arrived back in the room overhearing the conversation.

"Tony, he's taken a shine to Jo's friend, Cassie."

"Aye, I've met Cassie, Gail's partner, so what's happening then?"

Aiden related the story.

"Tony O'Connor's a catch in any woman's eyes, gorgeous and money."

"Exactly the same reasons why you fell fer me, Deirdre."

Deirdre rolled her eyes heavenward.

"That's the thing, as I said he hasn't bothered much since the divorce, I mean you remember how bitter that was."

Deirdre and Benny nodded. When Aiden had gone through his divorce, Tony had been a true friend to him, having experienced a similar situation himself, only a short time before. The two men, originally business associates, had become firm friends, as Tony supported Aiden, when many of his 'old friends' were nowhere to be seen.

"Tony had always been used to women falling at his feet, whether he wanted them or not, even when he was married. It seems Cassie doesn't seem at all interested. Normally, he wouldn't have said anything, but he was well gone."

"Did Jo not say that girl had been on her own a long time, rearing her kids by herself while she worked cleaning offices, or somethin'?" Benny asked.

"Yes, that's right, sure Jo was delighted for her when she won the money. Cassie's one of her old school friends, isn't she, Aiden?" Deirdre asked.

"Yeah, don't mention it to Jo though. She's enough on her plate. She's liable to say something to Cassie and frighten her off, then Tony'll be annoyed if I blow his chances. I think he's big plans for our wedding day."

"Good fer him, he'll be in like two men and a wee lad. Sure there's nothing like a wedding to get the juices flowin'," Benny was getting into it.

"Yer right, Aiden, don't say anything, just watch and see it unfold. This girl's gonna think all her Christmases have come at once, a big win and Tony O'Connor!" Deirdre chimed in.

"One thing's fer sure, she'll know he's not after her fer her money," Aiden said. "Jesus, the fella doesn't know what he's worth, but so far it hasn't brought him happiness."

"I'll be watching this carefully too. Oh I love a happy ending!"

"Will ya listen to yer mother, the fella hasn't even had the chance to ask the girl fer a dance yet, and she has them standing on a beach in Jamaica saying 'I do.'"

"And don't forget, Saturday is about our happy ending too!" Aiden was miffed.

"As if we could. Are ya getting' nervous, love?"

"Of course I am. That's why I'm working through until Thursday. I keep thinking something's bound to go wrong."

"That's all behind ya, son. Nothing's going to go wrong. Relax and enjoy the day, God knows, it's costing yis enough. Are ya sure you don't want a glass of wine?" Benny asked.

"As sure as I've ever been. I may never drink again."

"Is Jo still keen on 'The Doll on the Ball' photo shoot then?"

"Benny, don't be saying that. Jo hates it. It's 'The Angel of Thanksgiving'," Deirdre corrected him.

"Aye, whatever. All I can say is, Jo obviously sees something there I don't see. T'me it's just a mangled, mass of curved and bent steel tubes."

"She's been discussing it with Malachy, the photographer. He has been down to check out the angles and all that. It seems he'll have to do it in composites to get us, and the full height of the sculpture, completely into the shots, but he reckons it'll turn out well. He's even looked up the exact time of the sunset on Saturday."

"You've seen his website and you've both talked with him. The same boy won't let ya down, I'm sure of it."

"We're both really grateful to you and Mum for paying for him, Dad. I know Malachy has a great reputation and all that, but there's no way we could have afforded to hire him."

"Ach, never mind that; we're only happy to do it for yis. Sure money's made round to go round."

"Jo's so excited about this sunset session, but I'm afraid I'm with you, Dad, I don't see the big attraction in 'Nuala with the Hula.'"

"Jo's an artist, she sees things differently," Deirdre came back at them decisively, putting a full stop to the subject.

Benny chimed in, "Never mind the photographer, what about this band – they better be able to blast out 'Brown Sugar!'"

"First question I asked them, Dad. Sorted!"

It was a standing joke within the family; no do was ever complete until Benny had danced to 'Brown Sugar.' He only had to hear the opening strains and he was up. Deirdre, or any other available woman close at hand, would be hauled onto the dance floor. A mere appendage as he gave it his all.

Deirdre grinned and quipped, "Well, that's a relief."

Chapter 45

BOTH ORLA AND JO WERE in the gallery the next morning; Jo had a hospital appointment and had called into the shop for a quick chat since she was passing that way. A few minutes later, Dolores and Maxie came through the door. They walked straight toward the counter.

"Jo, glad we caught you, before the 'big day', this is just a wee gift from both of us, for you and Aiden."

Dolores handed her a gift wrapped package and a card.

"Thanks so much; that's very thoughtful of you both."

"How are the nerves holdin' up?" Maxie asked.

"I'm fine, well when I'm in here I'm fine. I actually finished last Friday, I just called in to see Orla. I'm on my way to an appointment. I'll not know what to do with myself over the next few days. I'm sure the nerves will kick in as I get closer to the final countdown."

"You'll be fine, and let's hope t'God this rain stops by Saturday. Don't forget what I told you about the prenuptial agreement. I wouldn't take on any man without one. Not that there's one on the horizon, but I live in hope! My next victim's out there, I just have to find him, that's all…it's not fer the want o'lookin' I can tell ya!"

Dolores threw her head back and laughed. Maxie joined in, Orla and Jo smiled politely.

"She's not jokin'. You wanna seen the cut of 'er on Saturday night in the 'Grab a Granny.' She'd make Tina Turner look like a Shrinkin' Violet, that one. Good luck t'er, I say. I wouldn't take on another man if his arse was studded with diamonds!"

They were off again, laughing like hyenas.

"Ah my God, a good laugh does ye good. We'll just have wee nosey before we leave yous in peace. C'mon, Maxie."

Dolores and Maxie tottered down the shop on their spiky heels, stopping to look at the large area Orla had designated for the personalised range. They hadn't been in since the new feature had been added. They commented to each other, in stage whispers, "Oh I don't know. A bit tacky, isn't it, Dolores?"

"Aye, yer right, Maxie, I thought I was in 'Poundcity' fer a minute!"

Their shoulders shook, always a dead give away that were trying to stifle laughter. At the front of the shop Orla and Jo, continued their conversation as they watched them, pretending they hadn't heard a word. But they had, loud and clear.

A few minutes later Dolores and Maxie left, calling out their goodbyes and good wishes to Jo. For the first time, since either Jo or Orla could remember, they hadn't bought a thing. Orla's face was tight with rage. She stood watching them wiggle down the road together giggling, hoping they would both take a tumble, and break their sprayed orange ankles.

"I better be off or I'll be late. I'll give ya a call later, Orla."

Orla smiled, but Jo could tell she was hurt by the comments. If Dolores and Maxie thought the products were downmarket, how many other good customers had they lost with the introduction of the new range?

Chapter 46

LATER THAT EVENING, ORLA SHARED the episode with Declan. "I mean they're by no means oozing class themselves, but they do know what they like and they spend plenty, so how many more of our serious art buyers have we lost, due to this range? Of course, I didn't mention the portrait artist to Jo after that. Jesus, I don't know what to do now, that range has been keeping us for the past few months, if we lose it, I may as well close the doors for good."

"Calm down, let's think it through. Maybe you've a good idea here, but yer just selling it in the wrong place."

"I've only got one place to sell it, unless I set up a stall in Royal Avenue."

"Ye could do worse. That's exactly what you want to be thinking about..."

"Hello?"

"No, listen Orla. You've found a range that's a good seller, it's making you money and ye know it could make you even more, with this portrait artist fella in residence. But, if you were to expand that side of the business, it could cost you the art gallery altogether, and if you don't, you could find you'll continue to lose art buying customers, as you have been, due to the recession, and you'll have to close anyway ..."

"Is this supposed to be makin' me feel better, Declan?"

"A mini market pitch, that's yer answer! Y'know, like one of those wee units, under the multi storey car park in the city centre. You'd have loads of passin' trade and the rents are lowish; I knew a fella who'd one of them a lot o'years ago. Separate the two sides of the business. Set up another shop to fund the gallery, exclusively to sell the downmarket range, while times are rough. I mean, I've seen the samples of the cuddly toys you've bought in, they're good enough quality, people love stuff like that..."

Orla cut in, "They're just not art."

"Y'know yerself they're not right fer the gallery. Put them into one of those units, combine them with the artist fella, if he's interested, and you're on a winner."

"Yeah, but I've only got so many days in the week. Jo's goin' off on maternity leave shortly after the wedding, I've got her sister-in-law lined up to cover her days, and I'll carry on doing mine, even allowing that I could run a unit in the days Siobhan works. Who's goin' to run a shop in the city centre for me while I'm on the Lisburn Road?"

"Ya can advertise. There're plenty of people outta work."

"It's a good idea, Declan, but I don't know. I'll have to think it over."

Chapter 47

ORLA HAD SPENT THE NIGHT tossing and turning, as the dilemma came between her and sleep. By morning she was still no closer to making a decision. The gallery was her dream, and it saddened her to see it being cluttered up with too much stock, too much of the wrong kind of stock.

When Jo had suggested they extend their gift range from scented candles, to cards and jewellery she had been unsure. To be fair to Jo, the jewellery was a small range of beautiful, exclusive silver pieces and the cards were a hand made, tasteful selection based on original art works. They blended ideally into the atmosphere of the gallery. Unfortunately they didn't bring in the return the personalised gift range had. The profits had been so bad at the time of her trip to the NEC she had been desperate and possibly made the wrong decision for the business long-term. Declan's idea sounded ideal, but who could she trust to run another business?

She ate her breakfast on automatic pilot, not really tasting it. As she drained the last of the coffee in her mug, she decided to talk to Jo. There had to be a solution to this problem, but for the life of her she couldn't see it. She glanced quickly at the clock, remembering Jo had told her she was going out with Deirdre and Kate today, to pick up her wedding dress. She'd still time to catch her at home. Orla dialled her number.

"Jo, how's it goin'? Eh, about Helena's suggestion on Saturday night, I wanted to ask you what ya thought…"

Jo who'd been waiting for this moment since the beginning of the week couldn't stop herself, "Look, Orla, I have to be honest with you, when it comes to retailing there's not much Helena doesn't know, she's worked in the same department store since she left school. I'm not being sniffy; she's an old friend, but what she knows about art could be engraved on a pinhead."

"I take your point. If I continue to promote the personalised range, it could cost me the main business, that's how Declan put it. I know it's true, I saw Dolores and Maxie's reaction to the range yesterday, if they walked out without buying because of it, how many others have done the same? I've talked it over with Declan and he's given me an idea. I'm thinkin' of opening a shop in the city centre to accommodate that idea…"

"You're not closing the gallery to sell that stuff," Jo said, referring to the personalised gift range.

"No listen…"

Jo sat nodding into the phone, as Orla explained Declan's thinking on the business plan.

"Well, that's interesting, he's not just a pretty face is he?"

They were both silent for a few moments, as Jo thought over the idea. Jo asked, "What about your friend, Anne Marie? You were saying on Saturday night she was unhappy in her job, she's the retail experience you need and you trust her, don't you?"

"God yes, Anne Marie, why didn't I think of her, but would she want to work for me?"

"Why wouldn't she? You get on well together; you can only ask her. Oh, here's Deirdre, I've gotta go. Think about it. I'll talk to ya later, Orla."

It was exactly nine thirty on Tuesday morning when Deirdre pulled up outside Jo's house. Harriet had encouraged Jo to take the dress home and try it closer to the date of the wedding, wearing it for short periods of time as her pregnancy progressed, to assess her comfort correctly for the actual wedding day.

Jo came rushing out of the front door, and flopped into the front seat of Deirdre's car.

"Deirdre, you're always dead on time. How's it going?"

"Fine, how are the nerves?"

"My nerves are in bits, 'cos everybody keeps asking that question!" she laughed.

"Sorry, love."

"It's alright. I'm just trying not to think about Saturday too much. Thank God I'm finished with work, I couldn't cope with customers this week. Not that there have been that many recently. Talking of work, wait 'til ya hear this…"

She proceeded to tell Deirdre of her conversation with Orla minutes before, about Helena's suggestion, put to Orla at the hen night, her own worries about lowering the tone of the gallery, and Orla's plans.

"Well, that sounds like it should work in well all round, what do you think, Jo?"

Jo explained to Deirdre about her suggestion that Orla approach Anne Marie, explaining how Orla and she had met up in the refuge.

"Good for you. Orla's a good head on her shoulders. She deserves to do well after the time she's been through with that husband of hers."

"It was Declan's idea originally. Oh have I blabbed; do you know about…?"

"It's okay, I know. Ger told me a while back, I know they were trying to keep things quiet in case yer man Seamus got wind of it. I must admit I couldn't picture it at first. I don't really know her, but I suppose I thought of Orla as a pretty, rich girl with all she wanted in life, before her husband's violence came out in the open. I couldn't even imagine her living in my old home, let alone falling for my big culchie nephew, Declan."

"I had her wrong, too, and I've known her much longer than you have. I didn't know she was reared in the country herself, until that night I took her up to see your mum's house. And as for Declan, he may be a culchie, but he's very attractive culchie, that lovely craggy face, the twinkling eyes, the sexy voice."

"Is he really? God, I must be getting old."

"You're just too close to him, that's all, Deirdre. No, Orla tried to keep it low-key, but I knew even before she'd told me she was head over heels in love with him. It started the night he saved her from Seamus. I teased her about it, I knew she was smitten. It was the way she reacted to my jokin' about it that gave her away."

Deirdre, who had strong suspicions that Jo had orchestrated the romance between Orla and Declan, before they'd even met, smiled knowingly at her.

"What?" Jo asked sheepishly, in reply to the look.

"Nothing, I'm just thinking it's all worked out well for Orla in

Derry, hasn't it? And I must say I'm delighted for them, especially after the way he was left when Molly died, he was like a lost soul. Your life can turn on a pinhead, eh? You never know what fate has in store. This is your Dad's isn't it?"

Jo nodded, glad of the diversion.

They were picking Kate up for the final dress appraisal, as Jo's Godmother she had been closely involved in the arrangements for the wedding. They planned on going for lunch after the dress was firmly placed in the boot of Deirdre's car. Kate climbed into the back seat, all talk of Orla and Declan forgotten as she asked, "Well ladies, all set?"

They discussed the final loose ends that had to be tied up before Saturday.

"It's such a shame old Sammy couldn't make it to the wedding, that would have been the cherry on the cake, wouldn't it?" Jo commented.

Of course, Kate had heard the whole reunion story from Jo and Deirdre.

"Aye, it's a shame." Kate lied, thinking, *"Yeah that would indeed have been the cherry on the cake!"*

Chapter 48

ORLA CONTINUED TO MULL OVER Jo's suggestion about Anne Marie. By nine thirty that night she thought, *Jo's right, I can only ask.* She picked up the phone and dialled her friend's number.

"How's it goin', Anne Marie?"

"Don't ask. That wee bugger Brendan is doin' my head in. He got one of the Team Leaders to tell me I had to help clear up the stock room before I left tonight, because they've a contingent of 'big bosses' flying in from Head Office in the mornin'. I don't even work in the bloody stock room! If I didn't need the money so much I'd've told him to shove his job up his arse sideways..." She ranted on for another few minutes then said, "What did you ring me for, by the way?"

"I was thinking of offering you a job, working for me."

"Ach now, Orla, let's get real here, I know we were talking about self confidence and all that, I mean I think I'm as good as the next person, but me in an art gallery, are ye serious?"

Orla couldn't help laughing. She could just see the question on Anne Marie's face.

"No, not the gallery. I've an idea for a wee business down the town."

She explained the basic idea to Anne Marie, who listened in silence.

When she finished, Anne Marie replied, "Yer never goin' to believe this, my sister just got one of those portraits done of the child. Cost her a packet, but she's delighted with it. Those bears cost a fortune, I've seen them in some of the shopping centres, but there never seems to be any shortage of people buying them. They do a Christmas line too, don't they? Oh my God yes, I think I could sell them alright. Let's be honest they'd sell themselves. Keep me informed. Oh this is brilliant, Orla. I might be able to tell Brendan where to put his job after all!"

Orla laughed at her, "Well don't be tellin' him yet, I haven't even spoken to this artist fella, I'll call you tomorrow night, sleep well, Anne Marie."

"You too, Orla. G'night."

Chapter 49

Wednesday, 8th July

WEDNESDAY MORNING SAW ORLA IN the shop. Today was her day to work, but that didn't stop her contacting the manager of the retail complex in the city centre, and arranging to see three of his vacant units that evening.

She rang the portrait artist, and enquired if he would be interested, giving him the impression that she already had city centre premises. He was keen to talk so she arranged to meet with him the following evening.

The day would be sure to drag until closing time. The Twelfth fortnight started on Friday, the traditional holiday period in many parts of Northern Ireland. If the rest of the summer had been slow to date she knew the coming two weeks would be dead. She would take the opportunity of this quiet time to research more products. If she was going to devote a whole shop to this kind of range, she was going to have to expand the lines she carried, accordingly.

The additional rent was an added burden, but if she was honest with herself, she could easily afford it. The sale of the apartment had supplemented her savings account somewhat, and she was paying a reasonably low rent to Geraldine and Liam for the house. No, this was a chance she had to go for, if she was to keep her art gallery through these hard times and help it to thrive again when the economy picked up, which of course eventually, it would.

The more she thought of employing Anne Marie to run the new shop, the more she liked the idea. Anne Marie was great with people. She would be an asset to any business. Also, she was her friend and Orla would enjoy watching her blossom in her newly created role of shop manager. And, Anne Marie would have the added bonus of being able to tell Brendan to shove his job up his arse sideways.

Benny watched Deirdre clean the kitchen floor for possibly the fifth time that day, and it was only mid-afternoon. All this planning was wearing him out, and he was merely watching. She had done the online shop last night, and today she had cleaned the house from top to bottom, and made up all of the spare beds. Surely, it must be ready now.

They had to get out of the house or he would explode. He made his way upstairs and sat down on their bed, reaching for the most recent Grand Opera House programme. He flicked through to this week and scanned the entries: *Wednesday the 8th of July*. He checked out the details of tonight's production, his eyes running over the cast.

"Yeah, she likes her, that'll do."

Benny wasn't much of a one for drama, but Deirdre liked it, anything, to get her out of the house. He fired up the computer and booked the tickets online.

Deirdre was polishing the coffee table when he re-entered the room.

"Deirdre, do you fancy a night out? I've booked us tickets for the Opera House, look you'd enjoy that wouldn't ya?"

He handed her the programme, she glanced at it.

"Yeah, that'd be good," she replied distractedly. "When is it?"

"Tonight."

"*Tonight!* Benny, we can't go out tonight, I've still so much to do."

"Yes, we can, and we're going to. You keep on pushing yourself like this, you'll collapse before Saturday."

"I won't, I'm fine. I just want everything to be right for them staying, that's all."

"Deirdre, it's yer family, yer mother, yer sister and her husband, maybe a couple of my ones. What's all this cleaning craic? If it's good enough fer us to live in, it's good enough fer your family and mine. Now that's it, it's not open to negotiation, the tickets are booked. We're going out."

"Alright. I'll just finish polishing this table, then I'll get ready," she said, resigned.

Cass sipped her coffee as she looked over the jobs they had taken in since the start of the week alone, and it was only Wednesday.

Gail had said last week, that Dave had asked her if she thought it would be worth their while opening up over the Twelfth holidays, as quite a few businesses shut completely for at least one week. Of course, Gail and she had no idea; they just had to play it by ear.

They were both surprised to find that it appeared some businesses took the opportunity of the quiet period to have a total clean up carried out on their premises. Gail was due to go off on holiday to Florida in a few weeks, and it was obvious to both of them, the time had come to appoint a supervisor. They had agreed to mention it to Louise, one of their permanent team. Cass and Gail both liked her, and knew they could trust her to deliver the best for the company. Also, she was a single parent, so Cass had a soft spot for her. They had agreed to talk to her next week.

Cass checked the time. She would rush round the shops after she closed up. She wanted new perfume for the wedding, she was booked in for a complete beauty routine the next night, and the hairdresser was arranged for Saturday morning. The door opened - it was Louise.

"Hiya, Louise, how's it going?" Cass asked; Gail who was on the phone, nodded to her, from across the office.

"Been better, how are things with yous?"

"Busy, surprisingly. We've a lot of work on next week, we were intending closing Monday and Tuesday, but by the look of this work comin' in, we may need you in. We'll pay ya public holiday rates of course. Wha'd'ya say, Louise."

"I say, bring it on. I'd work the whole weekend, and Monday too, if you offered it to me. I could be doing with any extra yis have goin', Cassie."

"That's great. We'll talk to the others when we see how many of a staff we need in. I'll give you a call on Friday to confirm the details. Money tight fer ya with the kids off on school holidays?"

"It's not the holidays; it's the bloody school uniforms. My youngest is startin' secondary school this September, and I've the whole uniform to buy, plus my second wee girl's going into third year, so that's more or less another complete new uniform, it's never ending. You'd love just to be able to relax with them fer a few weeks in the summer. Take them up to Portrush fer the day, and enjoy a wee bit of time with them, but they're no sooner off, than yer preparin' fer sending them back again."

313

Cass felt for the woman. This was her, a few short months ago. It was all still too recent to forget how hopeless it felt.

Gail looked at Cass from across the office, where she was still on the phone, they had been talking about Louise only a few minutes before.

Louise lifted the supplies she had come in for and placed them in her car, "Right that's me, I'll hear from ya later then. Bye."

"See ya later, love," Cass said.

Gail waved as she went out the door. As the door closed Gail finished her call.

"I heard that. Should we ask her to come in for a quick interview now, and discuss terms next week. It would lighten her load a bit over the weekend, what d'ya think, Cass?"

"Yeah, I'll call her back."

Cassie rushed to the door and called out to Louise, who was still in the car park.

"Louise, could ye come back in fer a minute, please."

Louise looked up, probably feeling pissed off that she had been called back; she was on her way to her last job of the day.

They explained to her about the full-time permanent supervisory position they wanted to offer her. She looked at both of them, and for a minute they thought she was going to cry.

"Would I be interested? Of course I would!"

Gail spoke up, "We were going to ask you next week, but we both thought it might cheer you up a bit today if we mentioned it. Now, as yet, we haven't decided on the exact terms and conditions. There'll be a company vehicle of course, and a salary increase. So, can we leave it that Cass or I will be in touch about it early next week."

"Thanks, really thanks, I won't let yous down. I'll talk to ya then, bye."

They watched her walk out, her posture already different, the burden almost visibly lifted from her shoulders.

"God help her, I thought she was going to cry fer a minute. That's what this is all about, isn't it? You feel in control of yer own life, but you can give other people a bit of a break too. I mean I know I'm not Mother Theresa, but it feels good doesn't it? You know yer treating people fairly, giving them a chance."

"It does, Cass. Somebody has to do the manual work, but if you know yer treating people well, somehow it seems right. I mean,

Louise, would be a cleaner anyway, but if she's working for us, she'll feel she's appreciated. That's the difference. We'll discuss the salary and all that at the start of the week, yeah?"

"Yeah, we'll have to decide on the vehicle a bit sooner now, but early next week will do. Nearly closing time; I'm heading round the shops to buy myself some nice perfume for the wedding."

"Oh, planning on capturing some luscious man on Saturday?"

"Sure, I wouldn't know what to do with a man."

"Oh, it would soon come back to you. They say it's like ridin' a bike."

"Never did crack ridin' a bike."

"Well you've two kids, ya must've been ridin' somethin'!"

They laughed together, the dirty laugh they saved for 'the girls', both in good form, looking forward to the wedding on Saturday. Cass almost told Gail then, that Tony had asked her out, but she thought better of it. Gail still hadn't mentioned to Cass that Tony O'Connor would be a guest at the wedding, Cass hadn't said anything, but she acted a bit strangely when he was around. Gail thought better of telling her as she suspected the attraction wasn't all one sided. She knew Cass well enough to know that she really hadn't bothered with another man since she had gotten rid of Gerry all those years ago. But she was still young, and she looked great, especially since she had won the money. It had given her a new lease on life. Why shouldn't she make a play for Tony O'Connor, if he was interested?

Gail decided to keep quiet. It wasn't as though Cass wouldn't be making an effort for the wedding; she would be drop dead gorgeous. And if Tony O'Connor was ever going to make a move on her, it would be at the wedding. Gail was sure of it. After all the years on her own, Cassie was understandably wary, and telling her he would be there, would only make her nervous. She would find out soon enough.

"See ya in the morning, enjoy yer shoppin' trip."

"Night, Gail."

The town was still rush hour busy, as Orla turned into the multi storey car park, although it was after five, the car park was still bunged. She thought of Declan's words about passing trade. How many people walked through the centre beneath every day?

She found the manager's office easily and he offered her a

leaflet on the shopping complex, as he picked up the keys. He chatted as they walked through the shopping centre, pointing out the various types of units.

"It's all down to the type of site you want. The three I'm showing you are all different, small, medium and large. Each one has a different customer flow, but in the main, you'll have hundreds of people passing your premises every day, no matter which one you decide on. Can I ask what line of business you're in?"

Orla explained her idea.

"Gift shops go well. We've a lot of different kinds, but nobody's doing that sort of range. I like the portrait artist idea, but I'd just say watch your prices. You'll get a lot of impulse buying in here, so if you don't mind me saying, you'll need to price accordingly."

Orla nodded.

After seeing the three units, she was almost sure she would go for the medium one. The guy gave her all of the site measurements, and she assured him that she would be in touch by Friday. As she drove home she knew she had to call Anne Marie. If she was free around this time tomorrow, she would arrange to meet her so that both of them could view the premises, then drop Anne Marie off before meeting up with the artist, Tom Hannigan.

Orla was buzzing with excitement, this could work, she was sure of it. She rang Anne Marie even before she'd eaten.

Anne Marie must have had another bad day at work as she answered Orla's call practically before the phone rang.

"Well did ya see the units, wha'd'ya think?"

"I like them. I saw three different ones. I've more or less decided on the one I think would work best for us, but I want you to see it first. Can you meet me around five tomorrow, or are you working late?"

"I'm on earlies tomorra, so that would suit me fine."

They made arrangements for the next evening. Neither of them wanting to talk much, both excited at the prospect of the new business, but for different reasons. The underlying feeling between them seemed to be, if we talk too much about it, it won't happen.

"Hey, Ma, how's life?"

"Bloody tiring, son, but not half as tiring as it used to be, when

I was doing the real work, rather than merely organising it. How's the job?"

Cass had hardly seen her son over the past week; they both passed each other like ships in the night these days. But she was glad to have it that way, it beat watching him sleeping through the days and drinking coffee through the nights, as he watched reruns of 'Jeremy,' pronouncing people, *"...scum..."*

The lowest common denominator they may well be, but if her son was watching them, what did that make him?

"Alright, I'm goin' out with a crowd from work tomorrow night, so I'll not be home. I'm staying at a mate's house."

"Oh aye, what d'ye call this mate?" she'd suspected for a while that he had a girlfriend.

"Just a fella from work."

"Aah hah."

"Emma."

"Sounds like a nice fella."

He grinned from ear to ear.

"She works in the store; she is nice."

"Good, just be careful, son, remember you've applied for university."

"I'm only going out with her, Ma. Why do all of you old people think all of us young people are having sex all the time?"

Cass thought, *because you are,* but said, "It's something that happens automatically when ya turn thirty, Dean, you stop having fun yerself and ya can't abide young people doing what you used to do. Daring to enjoy themselves. You become a begrudger; it's all part of growin' old."

"Yer not old, Ma, yer in yer prime."

"God no, my prime's just around the corner. If I'm in it already, what would there be left for me to look forward to?"

He smiled at her as he rummaged through the cupboards for biscuits.

"What's fer dinner?"

Chapter 50

LATER IN THE EVENING, DECLAN asked Orla what she'd thought of the units she'd seen. Orla told him briefly about the viewing not wanting to go into any great detail, sensing this, he changed the subject.

"I told you, my mother and father are staying in Aunt Deirdre's on Friday night, didn't I? Along with Granny, of course. They're heading up to Belfast early on Friday. I suppose to allow for the women still having bits of shopping to do."

"Well, you can never do enough shopping, Declan."

He grinned at her.

"Are you still set on driving back here on Saturday night, Orla?"

"Yeah, I'd prefer to."

He nodded. They had been over this many times in recent days. It was now almost four months since they started going out together, in that time they had grown close, but neither of them had said the word 'love', frightened to voice their feelings, for various reasons. For these same reasons, they had yet to sleep together. Orla and Declan both knew without saying so that the wedding would be a turning point for them.

To date, they had tried to keep their friendship low-key due to Orla's circumstances, just going out and about locally. Now, they were on the brink of coming out in the open about their relationship at last, making a public statement. Deirdre had asked them to stay with her on the night before the wedding, and the actual night, together with the others, diplomatically offering them a room each, but they had declined, explaining Orla was happy to drive.

Sensing the delicacy of the situation, Deirdre hadn't pushed it. Aiden had offered Declan's sons his apartment, since Jo and he would be staying in an hotel near the airport on the wedding night, preparing for their journey to their honeymoon in New York. That left Orla and Declan free to travel back alone, and to stay together, in either house, if they so desired.

The past few weeks had been loaded with tension. The presence of the family, especially Declan's grandmother had been an obstacle to them. Orla had felt strange about Mary returning to Geraldine's, just across the way, although she had always known this would be the arrangement. Geraldine had assured her it would make no difference to her mother, but Orla felt like she had taken over her home.

At first, when the old woman had returned, she had asked Geraldine should she invite her mother over for a cup of tea. Ger had explained that Mary was contented now with being in the care of her two daughters, a return to her old house would be too upsetting. Insisting, that as far as Mary was concerned, Orla was a family friend, who was looking after her house, so there was no need for Orla to feel guilty, her mother was happy with that arrangement.

The family aside, Orla and Declan both knew, the only real obstacle they faced, was their own fear of commitment. They had both been badly hurt, albeit in different ways. Once they had crossed that line, there would be no going back.

The Europa Hotel was busy, with after theatre supper-goers. Benny guided Deirdre toward the upstairs lounge. They sat at the window, looking out onto Great Victoria Street.

A scattering of droplets trickled down the hotel window pane, confirming that the threatened shower had arrived. The traffic was a constant stream for the time of day, and across the road, the Crown Bar and Robinson's were summer evening steady, with a regular flow of customers. Both hostelries still serving drinks to patrons sitting around in small clusters at the pavement tables. A couple of backpackers were in evidence, walking toward the city centre, the slightly bowed heads indicating the weights on their backs were getting to be too much, as the day approached its end, or possibly they were avoiding getting their faces wet. The tourists glanced curiously at the pavement drinkers, not knowing it took more than a bit of rain to shift the resilient Northern Ireland drinker from his outdoor pursuits, on a sanguine, summer evening.

Benny looked at Deirdre. "Well, did you enjoy that?"

"Aye, I did. It's nice to get out. Did you talk to Aiden about picking up the suits tomorrow night?"

"Deirdre, I thought we agreed that we wouldn't discuss the wedding."

"I know, but there's just still so much to do. I hope it doesn't rain like this on the day. It'll spoil the photos."

"At least in July the rain's warm. Remember, it rained the day we got married, cold December rain, we'd four Polaroids taken, a reception of a few sausage rolls and a couple of bottles of fizzy wine; did it do us any harm, Deirdre?"

"Ach, I know, Benny, it's just different nowadays…"

"No, really, it isn't. It's not the wedding that counts; it's the years after it. Now, stop this once and for all. It's going to be a great day, the sun will shine and the wine will flow, and if the clouds break what of it? Jo will still insist on standing smiling by 'The Doll on the Ball' and she'll be so happy, she won't even feel the rain. They're young and in love, Deirdre, and unlike us they both got it wrong the first time around, believe me, the details won't matter a damn. They've a lifetime together ahead of them, that's all that counts."

The waiter took their order, and at last, for the first time in weeks, they discussed something apart from the wedding.

As she lay in bed that night, Cass thought of her son's admission that he had a girlfriend. Despite his efforts to make light of it, she thought it must be serious otherwise he would have continued to deny it. And, he was staying in her house. He would know next month if he had been successful in his application for a university place.

All those months of hopelessness now he finally had the chance of turning his life around, and he had to find himself a girlfriend. Cass sighed deeply, as she lay in bed waiting for sleep. She had finally seen Lara get herself sorted; now Dean had to rock the boat. She tried to allow her thoughts to dwell on less stressful topics, but she kept returning to her family and her worries about them, thinking, *All this money, and I still can't stop them from making the wrong decisions.*

A voice inside her head told her to let go.

You can't carry them on your back Cassie. Let them loose to make their own mistakes. You've made plenty yourself, just be there for them if they need you. That's all any of us can do.

She had almost drifted off to sleep when she realised the voice was her long dead paternal grandmother's. She couldn't have been there, of course. It was just inside her head. But just to be sure, Cass opened her eyes to see. There was no one in the room but herself, but the smell of lavender was all around her. Cass closed her eyes and drifted off to sleep. She dreamed of the old lady, standing at her big sink, scrubbing clothes on the washboard. The smell of her lavender scent mingling with washing soap and steaming hot water. It was the aroma of comfort to Cassie, the smell of her childhood days, days long ago, when life was simple and the world Cassie inhabited was secure and safe.

She turned on her side, and slept right through the night.

Chapter 51

Thursday, 9th July

THURSDAY MORNING BROUGHT BENNY AND Deirdre back to the wedding again. Benny had awoken feeling refreshed after the night out. But the respite was short-lived.

Geraldine was on the phone by nine thirty. Benny felt for their Declan, if he ever took the plunge again Geraldine would have his head turned inside out, and sideways, by the time the date rolled around.

And so it continued.

The day had been spent answering the phone, either that or watching Deirdre talk on the phone. As Benny surveyed the scene like an onlooker, his thoughts went out to his mother-in-law, back in Derry, with Geraldine.

"Poor oul Mary," he muttered to himself, "she'll not know if she's punched or bored."

Deirdre's voice interrupted his thoughts, "Benny, Ger says, 'Ye haven't forgotten, Declan'll be up tonight for the final fitting?'"

He wanted to answer, *"How t'hell could I, with yer sister giving me hourly bulletins!"* But he thought better of it, and called back, with a cheerfulness he didn't feel, "It's all organised, I'd a text from Aiden this morning."

Deirdre conveyed the message and that was Geraldine happy, for the present, until the next, '"OH MY GOD!" moment', when she just had to reach for the phone, again.

Cass arrived early for her beauty appointment on Thursday night, she was going to have a full aromatherapy massage to indulge herself. Since the dream last night she had felt calmer, more in control of her life somehow. Whatever her children did was their own decision, she accepted she couldn't steer them one way or the other; she could just simply guide them, nothing more.

The smell of the aromatherapy oils met her nostrils. That aroma of lavender again, bringing her back to the strange feeling of her grandmother being present in her bedroom. She was still unsure what had happened last night, dreams didn't usually produce smells. Whatever was the explanation for the smell of her granny's perfume, she was sure her granny was simply offering her guidance too.

Cassie knew she had worried and fretted for her children for too long, it was time to lighten up and do some living.

Anne Marie and Orla both agreed on the medium sized unit, whether the artist was going to be involved, or not. Orla knew this was the best site for them to start their business from. She could have thought it over some more, but she knew she didn't need to. She signed for it there and then.

Anne Marie and she would get together over the holiday period to discuss their new venture.

"We can start moving the stock down from the gallery over the next week, and I'll do an online order for more tonight. You can give that message to Brendan anytime now, Anne Marie."

Anne Marie threw her arms around her friend.

"You won't regret this, Orla. I'll make sure this works!"

"I've no doubt about it, Anne Marie. We're in business."

Anne Marie grabbed her by the hands and they danced around in a circle, like overexcited children at a birthday party, high on sugary treats. They were attracting stares from passers-by in the multi storey car park. Did they care? Not a jot.

Orla dropped the ecstatic Anne Marie off at her street and drove on to meet Tom Hannigan in his house. The artist was a man in his mid to late sixties, sporting long greying hair and a grey/white beard. He had a gentle manner and a wry sense of humour. She could see him working away in the unit with Anne Marie. Surely, he would be a much, more preferable compatriot to her, than Brown-nosing Brendan.

Orla and he liked each other on sight, they agreed terms and she told him she would call him during the next week to arrange a meeting with Anne Marie, her shop manager. She rushed home to put the online order in.

Now that it was really going to happen, she couldn't wait to get started.

She had the whole night to herself because Declan was going to pick the suits up with Aiden. Declan was to be one of the ushers at the wedding. Orla bought a pizza on the way home and devoured it in minutes flat, then sat down in front of the computer to place her order.

That done, she began to browse through the website. Anne Marie wasn't wrong; they did Christmas products, and then some.

By late evening, Aiden and Benny had arrived back after the final fitting for the male contingent of the wedding party. Four of the suits were now safely hanging in Aiden's apartment, and Benny's was in his wardrobe, being scrutinised by Deirdre. Jo had been informed all was well, and Declan was now on his way up the motorway to Derry.

Deirdre called out from the bedroom to Benny, saying that the suit was, "Perfect."

"Happy Days!" said Benny, rubbing his hands.

On her return to the room, Deirdre reached for the phone to call her sister, the successful conclusion to this final pre-wedding fitting, another excuse for them to talk. Benny could take no more.

"C'mon into the kitchen, son, we'll have a beer."

They sat opposite each other, delighted to be in each other's company. Benny cracked open the bottle of beer, poured it slowly and watched it foam up the glass. In pensive mood, he asked Aiden, "Do you think it's a genetic thing with women? If men had to organise weddings, we'd just turn up in our best suit and favourite shirt, say the words, smile fer the cameras, and pop the champagne open. Job done. How complicated does it have to be?"

"What was all that about Aunt Ger on the phone first thing this morning?"

"Don't ask. It's all sorted now. And that call was only the first of many today. Christ, she's not even here yet and I can feel my blood pressure rising. Y'know I used to wonder why Liam said he didn't like to drink in the house, preferred to go to the pub a few nights a week. Jesus, if I was married to Ger, I'd expect my alcohol to be available to me on free prescription as well."

"Ach, God help her, she means well, she just has the happy knack of winding everybody up like springs," Aiden replied.

"Another?"

"Just a glass, Dad, I don't want to be getting done for drunken drivin'. Declan was talking to me about Orla earlier tonight; it's seems they've been goin' out now for almost four months."

"I think Geraldine's been tellin' yer mother as much, but she hasn't said a lot to me. I suppose with the wee girl still waiting for her divorce to come through and all that."

"I offered him a bed in the apartment, y'know for the night of the wedding, before I asked the boys, in case he just didn't want to give Mum any trouble, eh? But he said Orla would prefer to drive back up. Maybe, it's not just Tony O'Connor who's been bitten by the love bug."

"D'ye reckon?"

"Well y'know Declan he's close, but he seems very keen."

"Good fer Jo, maybe she sorted Orla out with more than accommodation, eh?"

"Orla hasn't really said much to Jo either, I'll maybe get more out of him tomorrow night when he stays over, but going by his comments tonight, it seems like Saturday is going to be their grand coming out."

"My God, it's all happening," Benny said as he sipped his beer.

Orla was still browsing the website when the phone rang. It was Anne Marie. "I can't settle, Orla. I'm like a kid on Christmas Eve. Am I disturbing you?"

Orla told her what she was doing.

"Have a look. You should have no bother shifting this stuff, look at their Christmas range."

Anne Marie clicked on the mouse and found the website.

"Look at their promotional posters; they'll attract the attention of passers-by big-time. Aren't they really effective? What about those stand up boards - can we display those outside?"

On and on, they talked. Bringing each other's attention to this product, that product, until finally, one of them realised it had gone midnight. They reluctantly said goodnight, both still bursting with enthusiasm for their shop.

Anne Marie couldn't wait to see Brendan in the morning.

Chapter 52

AS ORLA SUSPECTED, THE LISBURN Road was busy on Friday morning with people shopping for the holidays, unfortunately none of them were interested in her gallery.

She spent much of the time packing the gift range into boxes, ready for its removal to the downtown premises during the next week. That done, she remembered to choose a card for Jo and Aiden from the original art works range, the one she picked was beautiful, the inscription, a few lines from a love poem. Orla felt emotional reading it.

When she had first met Jo, through Gail, she was just recently separated, her eyes always looked sad and she constantly seemed to have a worried expression, especially after yet another phone call from her oaf of a husband. When she had met Aiden, it had turned her life around, then the stress of finding herself pregnant in the midst of all the plans had knocked her for six for a few weeks.

Orla was looking forward to seeing them get married. As she wrote the card, she couldn't help but remember all the cards with good wishes Seamus and she had received when they had gotten married. It had been a good day, Orla had been serenely happy, sure this was it, sure that her life was complete. How could she have known it would all go so dreadfully wrong?

By three o'clock, she decided to close up for the holiday period. She put a sign in the window of the front door displaying her holiday closing times and locked up.

She turned to cross the road, heading for a delicatessen across the way. Declan and she planned to eat together in her place that evening before he drove up to Belfast to spend the night in Aiden's, together with the other usher and best man.

Friday was chaotic in the office, and Cassie was alone. Both of them had agreed, Gail could have the day before the wedding off, but that had been before they had realised how busy they were set to be over the 'holiday' period.

When Cass finally closed the doors that evening, she was tired, although certainly not weary. She was elated to find they were having difficulty coping with the workload. They'd decided they would discuss interviewing for more casual staff, if need be. That was next week though, tonight she was going home to relax before Jo's big day tomorrow.

She walked into her kitchen to find her son preparing a meal for them both. Cass was pleased to see him home, and more pleased to find him cooking.

"Hey, Ma. How was yer day?"

"Great, how was your night out, son?"

"Good we went bowling. I'm just firin' a few chicken fillets into the pan, I made salad and there's bread and stuff on the table."

"What's all this in aid of, are you not rushing out tonight?"

"Just headin' round to Miko's later, thought you'd like this, y'know with Jo's weddin' tomorra and all."

He looked shy.

"I love it! What about Emma are ya not seeing her tonight?"

"She's just part of the crowd from work, Ma. She's goin' out with her mates tonight too - I'm not goin' to marry her or anything."

Cass smiled at him. She really did have to let him live his own life. She took her coat off and went upstairs to the bathroom to wash her hands, leaving her son to finish making the meal. He was more than capable.

On entering the front yard Orla, was greeted by Snapper, barking with excitement and running in circles round her heels. Inside the house she unpacked her groceries and checked her phone messages.

There was one from Geraldine.

"Orla, love, this is Geraldine, just to remind ye, young Ryan and Marc will be at home all evenin', so any problems, don't hesitate to call them. It's…" She called out to Liam, 'What time is it, Liam? Liam d'ye hear me?' Liam's response was muffled; Ger confirmed the time he told her, the whole exchange being recorded on the answer phone. A quarter past ten, right, thanks, Liam."

She then returned her attention to the message to Orla, "It's a quarter past ten on Friday morning, that's this mornin', so we're headin' on up to Dee's house now, in Belfast. Right then, so, see ye tomorra, em, right that's all then. Right, take care now love. Mind the roads, bye bye."

Orla smiled to herself; poor Geraldine she had told her that a dozen times since Monday. She was up to high doe, she could hear it in her voice, and it wasn't even her son getting married.

Of course, Orla knew the boys would be there this evening. Wasn't she driving them to the wedding, for God's sake? She decided to go for a walk, to pass the time before Declan came round. The tension of the past few months was starting to get to her and she needed to clear her head. Little did she know when she made the decision to leave Seamus that romance would be waiting around the corner for her.

Of course, she wanted to make a commitment to Declan, but now that the time had come, she was nervous and excited, and just a little bit scared.

The walk in the fresh air calmed her. On her way back, as she approached the laneway to her house, she smiled to herself as she looked across to Geraldine's, thinking back to her answer phone message. Declan had been telling her his mother had Benny worn to a frazzle with her daily phone calls throughout the week, in the run-up to the wedding, as she manufactured one crisis after the other. Orla was glad she wasn't spending tonight in Deirdre's.

Declan arrived around seven.

"Well are ya all set?"

"Aye, I can't wait, there's nothing a man loves more than havin' to don a monkey suit for a day."

"Sure you'll be lovely." She ruffled his hair. "How's Aiden holding up?"

"He seems fine now that he's got the stag do out of the way. That was stressin' him out more than the thought of the actual weddin'."

By eight he was ready to leave, checking her camera before he left the hallway.

"Remember now, the boys are in the house. They'll be there all night."

"I know, Declan. I'm picking them up in the morning, remember? I'll be fine. He's in Australia."

It was the first time all of the family had been away from home since Orla's dramatic visit from Seamus.

"Yeah well, take no chances. That's all I'm sayin'. See ya tomorra then."

She hugged him tight as they kissed. The intensity of his look wasn't lost on her. Saturday the 11th of July was set to be a memorable day, and not just for Jo and Aiden.

In the bathroom, she set out her most luxurious hair and beauty products. She ran a bath, tossing a scented bomb in, watching it fizz. Inside, her stomach butterflies fluttered, but in a good way not in the anxious tense way she'd felt when she had anticipated a special occasion with Seamus. It had taken her too long to find clarity in her old life, a life that was almost behind her now. Her new life with Declan beckoned. She was ready for it, more than ready for it. Orla was in love, and it was time to let Declan know.

By late Friday morning, everyone had arrived in Benny and Deirdre's. Benny had taken them all out to lunch, and afterwards, for a stroll around the Rose Gardens in a local park. Everything seemed to be going according to plan, but of course that was too good to be true. Within a few hours of their arrival back from the afternoon out, Geraldine was flapping about like a headless chicken, realising she had left her new pairs of tights in her bedside drawer. She said she always bought two packets for a special occasion, one to wear and one for her handbag, in case of ladders.

Apparently, they had to be in that exact shade or her outfit would be ruined, in her own words, "It'll be a bloody catastrophe! Ye can't buy that brand just anywhere...I know, I'll ring Orla."

Deirdre watched as Ger held the phone awaiting a reply.

"Her mobile's switched off. I'll try the house."

From where she stood, Deirdre could hear the phone ringing out, but it wasn't picked up.

"I'll leave Orla another message. She can get the key off Declan and pick them up. No, she mightn't listen to her messages. And no point in ringin' Declan, he wouldn't know what he was lookin' fer..."

Benny, who been surveying the scene between his wife and her sister, saw the opportunity to get Geraldine and Deirdre out for a while. The countdown was now on to the wedding, at 1 p.m. the next day. And at this stage in the proceedings, Benny wasn't entirely sure he would make it through without grabbing Geraldine by the throat and throttling her to death.

Mary was completely bemused by the whole night's pantomime, unable to grasp the significance of the 'catastrophe.' Benny had to say to himself, he was with her all the way.

"Go on, get yourselves into the town, sure the shops are open late. Don't worry about rushin' back. Mary will be perfectly fine with Liam and me. Won't ye, Mary?"

"Aye, I will indeed."

Liam shook his head at Benny, as the two women grabbed their bags and left the house in haste to drive to the shops, they were on a mission.

"Peace, perfect, peace." muttered Mary. And the three of them collapsed laughing.

Aiden called to pick Sarah up around five. His ex wife wished him well for the wedding the next day, but without much conviction.

They picked Jo and Corey up and they all had tea together. Jo was jittery, unable to settle; the conversation was strained. She was doing her best for the children, but Aiden knew she was feeling very nervous. As he dropped them all off a couple of hours later, he was glad Gail would be spending the night with her.

"Have a good night, love, see you tomorrow. You'll be okay when Gail calls up, the two of you should have a few glasses of wine to settle the nerves."

She nodded.

"Only a few though, and you too, don't be having another stag night, yer only just recovering from last Saturday night."

"Jeff and the lads wouldn't let me. They know I can't handle it. It'll be a few beers and a DVD, then nodsville."

He reached out to her as he spoke, hugged her to him, and then he was gone. Jo's gaze followed him as he drove away. She loved him so much.

"Mum, can we play the Wii?"

"Yeah, course you can, carry Sarah's bag up to her room first, Corey. Thanks."

They watched as Corey struggled valiantly with the small overnight bag.

As he disappeared round the turn of the stairs, Sarah looked at Jo uncertainly, the child seemed unusually ill at ease with her.

"Everything alright, Sarah?"

"Yes, it's just...Jo, will I have to call you Mum after tomorrow?"

Jo felt for the poor child, they'd been so caught up in the arrangements, they should have explained this to her.

"Sarah, you have a Mum, I'll be your step mum, but you don't have to change what you call me because of that. Jo, is fine now, it'll still be fine this time tomorrow."

The child looked visibly relieved, she rushed to hug Jo, and Jo realised, this time tomorrow she would be Mrs Aiden Brannigan, at last.

Chapter 53

A SHORT TIME LATER THE doorbell rang. It was Gail standing on the doorstep with a bottle of chilled wine. Jo was grateful, she had forgotten to buy a bottle, because they were going on honeymoon Sunday morning, she had shopped only for essentials this week.

"Right, I'm in charge! I'll look after the kids. You get yourself upstairs to have a long soak. I've just dropped Josh off at his mates for the weekend. Dave's taking the girls to Mum's in the morning; they're spending the night with her. Do you know they actually had the audacity to be annoyed at us, tried to convince us they wouldn't have a party if we left them in the house by themselves, I mean, Jo, I remember being their age." She indicated to the wine. "After your bath we'll crack this open, can't have you tossing and turning all night."

Jo felt the guilt creep in again.

"I didn't drink at all for the first lot of months. I'm sure a small glass won't do any harm."

"Didn't your doctor tell you that? It's not as though yer downing a bottle of vodka a night. Now, lighten up, Jo, you can even have a glass of champagne tomorrow. Relax, everything's fine, go on off with ya. I'm going in here to whip these kids on the Wii, I'm the expert. Then, when I've well and truly beaten them, I'll pack them off to bed."

"Remind me I have to check online for the weather forecast for New York next week. God, I hope it's not going to be too humid. Leave it to me, thinking I was scooping a great deal."

They'd booked the honeymoon in New York before Jo realised she was pregnant; now she was dreading the heat.

"Will you stop it. The hotel's going to be air conditioned and so are all of the shops, it'll be grand. Now shoo, go! Have your bath and relax."

Jo did as she was told. Gail was right; the bath did help her wind down. As she lay soaking her cares away, she talked to the baby inside her, telling it, in only a few more hours it would be Mummy and Daddy's wedding day. She was glad Kate and her Dad had decided to stay in their home in Islandmagee and drive up in the morning. After Corey and Sarah were firmly tucked up in bed, Gail and she could have a good talk. She would have been lost without Gail when she had separated from Kieran. Gail had been there for her every step of the way, despite the fact, that they had rarely seen each other while she was married. A once a year lunch around Christmas time had been the height of their contact, apart from the odd phone call. But the years before Kieran had kept their friendship strong. They had gone right through primary school and high school together, and now they were closer than ever.

The house was peaceful as Jo entered the living room in her robe and slippers, both of the children were fast asleep and Gail was sipping a glass of wine.

"How'd you manage that?"

"Years of practice, and I drugged them before sending them upstairs, of course."

She poured Jo a small glass and patted the sofa beside her.

"Hey, girl, you're nearly there now."

Jo sat down beside her.

"Thanks for everything, Gail, you've been a rock. I couldn't have done it without you. I mean, you've had all the worry of redundancy and starting up a new business, but you've always had time to listen to my problems."

"Don't mention it, mate. You can do the same fer me some day."

"Yer not thinking of leavin' Dave?"

Jo turned abruptly to face her friend.

"Of course, I'm not. I couldn't survive without him. Even after all these years, he still makes m'heart beat faster. Here, talking of hearts, I know it'll be understandable if you only have eyes fer Aiden tomorrow, but if you get a chance, have the odd skellie in Cass's direction. I'd bet money she'll not go home on her own tomorrow night…"

"No! Who?"

They were off.

Benny switched the TV off and walked toward the staircase. He glanced into the kitchen, where Deirdre and Geraldine were still sitting drinking tea at the table, he was about to call out, "goodnight" to them both when he noticed Geraldine had her head down and appeared to be crying.

Deirdre signalled for him to go on without comment, putting her finger to her lips. The expression on her face told him it wasn't life or death, so he made his way up to their bedroom, knowing she'd tell him about it later.

He'd almost drifted off to sleep when he heard her enter the room; he turned to face her.

"Everything alright with Ger?"

"Ach, she's just a bit emotional, that's all. She'd a bit of a weepy fit. I could see it coming for days. It's their Declan; the wedding coming up has made her sad for him, y'know thinking about Molly. I mean you know yerself, Benny, Molly was like a daughter to her, but now it seems Orla and Declan are an item…"

"Aye, so Aiden was saying…"

He related the conversation he'd had with Aiden the previous night.

"That's it, tomorrow will be their grand coming out, and Ger's delighted for them of course, but it's like all the grief she's been bottling up since Molly passed away is being allowed to be released now, God love her. That's why she's been like a cat on a hot tin roof all week. Liam picked it up first about Orla and Declan. Apparently Declan invited her to a St. Patrick's Night do in the pub, shortly after yer man Seamus called at the house; remember Declan stayed the night with her? I mean, I'm not saying anything happened, but anyway that night in the pub, the whole neighbourhood was in, ya know what Paddy's Night is at home? They'd a good night and Ger said to Liam when they got home that she really liked Orla and he replied, "Well that's just as well, she's yer future daughter-in-law!""

"At that early stage, he thought that?" Benny asked.

"Yeah, and well, that's a few months ago now. It seems they've been inseparable ever since."

"Leave it to Liam, talk about 'The Quiet Man.'"

"Like I said, Ger's delighted fer them, but its mixed emotions, y'know."

"That's only natural I suppose, sure Molly was running in and

334

out of their house since she was no age. All the same, it's great fer Declan and Orla eh."

"It is, of course, they're both overdue a bit of happiness."

Benny rolled over to get to sleep, then turned toward her again and asked, "You don't think Jo set it up, do ya, Deirdre?"

Deirdre paused from taking her make-up off at the dressing table, and turned to look at him.

"Benny Brannigan, you've still an awful lot to learn about women."

Chapter 54

The Wedding Day

ORLA WAS UP AND READY with the birds. She made her bed up with fresh white cotton sheets and placed some scented candles around the room.

She had cleaned the house thoroughly before having her shower, and by ten o'clock she was ready to go. It was still a bit early to leave, so she had another coffee. Finally, it was time to pick up Declan's sons. Ryan and Marc must have been pacing the floor waiting for her arrival, because they appeared at the door almost as soon as she entered the laneway, both looking handsome and immaculately groomed in their best suits.

Orla had never known their mother, but she was sure she was up there somewhere, smiling proudly down on them. The boys asked her if they could listen to a CD instead of the radio; Orla agreed happily. None of them were in the mood to talk, all three of them excited and nervous in their own way.

As they made their way from Derry toward the motorway, in different parts of Belfast the bridal party and guests were preparing for the day:

In Jo's house...

"Jesus, my ear!" Gail yelped, as she burned her ear for the second time that morning on the GHD stylers.

Kate was sitting at the dressing table with Jo, telling her, "No, Jo, you really don't need another shade of foundation, that's the one Gail and you chose together, all those weeks ago. It's perfect. Absolutely perfect."

And downstairs, while the children sat watching television in the living room, resplendent in their wedding clothes, Andy, unable to

336

contain his nerves any longer, reached for the brandy, drinking it standing up, for fear of creasing his trousers.

In Aiden's place…
Declan was padding about like a caged animal, while Jeff the best man, and Pete, the other usher, helped Aiden - Jeff with his tie, Aiden's own hands incapable of tying it due the uncontrollable shake they had developed, and Pete with his breakfast, he was in the kitchen making a second batch of tea and toast.

Declan asked them for the twentieth time that morning, "Are you sure these trousers aren't too tight, does this jacket look okay, Jeff?"

Aiden had told Jeff in confidence about Declan's plans for Orla and himself.

"Yer a bundle of nerves, Declan. You'd think it was your big day," Jeff replied, grinning at him, as Aiden gave him a look that said, Shut up!

In Benny's house…
Geraldine and Deirdre seemed to be cool, calm and collected. But that didn't last long, as Geraldine's voice cried out, "For the love of God, Liam, are they the socks you packed to wear? I told ye, dark grey!"

"Don't panic! Benny has plenty in that shade, I'll get them," Deirdre's voice rang out.

And in the conservatory, sat Mary and Benny sipping cups of tea, looking out onto the garden. Benny was glad he had suggested they get Mary ready first. The two of them had been sitting peacefully, listening to the Saturday magazine programme on the radio for the past two hours. He had thought it was all going too well; he'd hoped Ger had exhausted the hosiery 'catastrophe' situation the night before, but it appeared not.

He turned the radio up, to block out the exchange between Ger and Liam over the socks, and watched two magpies vie for supremacy on the back lawn.

Mary offered him the plate of biscuits and he chose a Jaffa Cake.

Nearly there, he thought, *easy does it.*

And in Dublin city centre…

Kieran and Suzanne were sitting in a pub, having their first drink of the day.

They planned on having a big lunch before setting out to 'do the pubs' pre-concert. They were in great form, the animosities of the past weeks forgotten; Kieran and Suzanne were going to have a ball.

Orla had timed it perfectly. They arrived at the church with half an hour to spare. Much too early for the service, but in exactly the right time not to set Ger off on one of her panic attacks.

Benny, Deirdre and Mary were on their way and Geraldine and Liam were already inside. Seated in the church with them were a few other early arrivals. Orla and the boys made their way inside to join them. Orla could see from the puffiness around her eyes that Geraldine had already been weeping.

"Hello, Orla love, you look gorgeous. I'll just go outside a minute. I can't get a breath; it's too warm in here. The walls are closin' in on me. I need fresh air. Oh, do these tights look alright. They're not too dark?"

Orla glanced at Ger's legs, then caught the look on Liam's face, they looked fine to her, but she sensed that's what she had to say, "They look fine, Geraldine. You look lovely, that outfit's really your colour."

"Thanks, love. Keep my seat won't ye."

Liam waited for her to get out of earshot, then he said in response to Orla's questioning look, "The tights…Don't ask. Fresh air? Sheer bloody nosiness - she has to be the first to see the bride. That'll give her another excuse fer a bawling session. She's the only woman I know who goes to a weddin' with a handbag under one arm and a box of Kleenex under the other. When you marry my son, do me a favour and take him away to some far off sunny beach to exchange the vows."

Orla laughed.

"He hasn't asked me."

"Oh he will, believe me, he will."

Orla was amused by Liam's remarks, and not a little curious. She wondered if Declan had said something to his Dad.

Cass was so excited she couldn't close her eyes again after first light. She'd been awakened by the sun streaming through the bedroom window at daybreak. She had her hairdressing appointment at nine, then she would have plenty of time for make-up and dressing, before Helena and Naomi arrived to pick her up. The three of them, plus two of Aiden's mates, were travelling together.

She had recently changed the colour of her hair and she liked it, it made her look younger. Little things, like a change of hair colour still gave her a buzz.

Throughout the years of struggle, she had been resigned to her lot in life being more of the same, never miserable, but never completely happy, just coping, getting by, making do, "mustn't grumble," but now, she was ready for happiness, like they said, "it's not a dress rehearsal." She was revelling in her new lifestyle and looking forward to the future, and all that it held.

The car arrived a few minutes late. She had been ready for ages and was beginning to panic. Thinking, *What if they've forgotten about me?* But shortly after, it appeared at her door.

She saw Helena beaming out the window at her, waving madly. Cass smiled her greeting in response. They didn't get out often, but when they did they knew how to party. God knows, it had taken Gail and her until Tuesday to come round from last Saturday night.

"Hey, girl, you look fantastic!" Helena cried as she swung her legs into car.

"Thanks, so do you two. That dress looks great on you. And I love the hair, Naomi, the shorter style really suits you."

"Thanks," said Naomi.

"Doesn't it," Helena agreed. "Cassie, this is Tom and this is Danny, friends of Aiden, Tom and Danny, this is Cassie."

"Hiya doin', Cassie? Do yous not like my hair, girls, I'm up from five this mornin' blow-drying' it?" the one called Tom asked cheekily, with a wide grin on his face.

They all chatted on the journey, the men looking slightly ill at ease, in their obviously new suits, no doubt looking forward to the reception, when they could undo the ties and fold them into their pockets, and get down to really enjoying the day.

When they arrived at the church, a few small groups of people were already gathering around the front steps, waiting in anticipation for the arrival of the bride. Gail, little Sarah and Corey, were standing inside the arched entranceway to the church, they waved at Cass and the girls as they stepped out of the car. Helena and Naomi stopped to speak with some of the other guests and Cass made her way across to Gail, to compliment her on her dress. She looked beautiful, the dress was perfection and her hair was stunning, all piled up at the back of her head, with one side falling into soft, Grecian curls, cascading around her bare shoulder. Sarah was practically bursting with excitement, not even hearing Cassie's comments about her pretty dress, jumping up and down in her new shoes, the small floral bouquet bobbing around in her constantly moving hands. Corey was walking round in circles singing, trying to remember not to scuff the toes of his shoes, well not until after the wedding anyway. He was delighted with his new clothes. Cassie said he looked like 'Little Lord Fauntleroy.' She ruffled his already spiky hair and he grinned up at her, looking slightly bewildered.

Gail said to Cassie, "You look lovely, Cass; that dress really does it for you,and the shoes are class."

Cass beamed, she felt good about herself too, in a way she hadn't in years.

"We came in the car with a couple of Aiden's mates, those two guys over there, Tom and Danny talking to that fella, the one who looks a bit like Tony O'Connor from the back. You'd almost swear that was him, wouldn't ya?"

Cass thought she must have it bad. That's what happens when you are a teenager in love; you see him everywhere.

"Cass, that is Tony O'Connor."

"What's he doing here?"

"He's one of Aiden's best mates, you know that."

Gail tried to sound casual.

"Aiden said he was a client."

Cass felt jittery.

"He is, but he's also a friend."

"Oh, I didn't realise he'd be here."

She could feel herself blushing like a schoolgirl, on seeing the object of her affection across the playground.

"Jo should be here any minute now."

Gail changed the subject, but she couldn't fail to see the impact Tony O'Connor's presence was having on Cassie. She thought, *I was right, the attraction isn't all one sided.*

340

"Was she organised when you left?" Cass asked, glad of the change of subject.

"Well she didn't have her dress on yet, said she was afraid of spilling make-up on it, but she'll be fine, Kate's with her. Andy was downstairs getting stuck into the brandy. You think Aiden's nerves are bad this week, Andy was shaking like a leaf; his hands were trembling as he poured the brandy into the glass. He offered me one, but I thought, maybe not brandy. I had a wee Martini, though. Settled the nerves," Gail observed; by the look of Cass, she could do with a brandy herself.

"It makes ya feel a bit emotional doesn't it? Knowing she's y'know…I hope it all goes well after all the agonising over the dress," Cassie said quietly.

Gail nodded, saying, "Oh God, here she is."

The guests waiting outside lined each side of the entranceway to get a closer look at the beautiful bride.

Cass could feel her breath catching, as Jo emerged from the limousine on Andy's arm, looking radiant. The dress was indeed exquisite. Despite her absolute refusal to cry, Cassie could feel her eyes filling with tears. She didn't look at Gail as she knew she would be tearful too. After all they had all been through hell and high water together throughout the years since childhood, Gail and Jo especially. She caught Helena's eye and she too was struggling to keep herself from crying, she could see the tears brimming in her eyes. Gail and the two children fell in behind Jo and her father.

At the front of the church, Aiden turned to look at her, their eyes momentarily meeting along the length of the aisle. Jo felt her heartbeat quicken; she remembered to breathe deeply, in out, in out.

Cass rummaged in her handbag, as she filtered into the pew beside her friends. Helena was pulling tissues out of her bag, discreetly handing them to Naomi and all around them was the sound of quiet sniffing and nose blowing, and a lot of foot shuffling from the men.

Cass was thankful she had remembered to wear waterproof mascara. And so, the service began. Aiden and Jo were really getting married.

Jo held onto her Dad's arm tightly and began the walk up the aisle to the rhythm of the music. On the first notes the baby began to kick, as though it were moving to the beat, Jo gasped audibly, the emotion of the day getting to her despite her efforts not to cry. Andy,

341

gripping her arm gently in his, whispered, "Think of yer make-up, girl!"

He had spent what seemed like hours that morning sitting downstairs while Kate and Gail helped Jo do her make-up, thinking, *Just how long does it take to put on a bit of lipstick?*

Jo breathed deeply, composing herself. She wouldn't allow herself to cry today. The baby picked up on her emotions; she mustn't be sad. She had told it all about the day, talking aloud to it as she showered that morning. A lot of people thought it was madness, talking to a bump, but Jo had communicated that way all the time with Corey and she had done the same throughout this pregnancy, keeping her child informed of their plans every step of the way.

"Your mummy and Daddy are getting married today, little Baby Brannigan."

When she spoke to it, the baby rolled around gently, she pictured it doing a little kind of wiggle.

She looked to both sides of the church as they walked, acknowledging the smiling faces, moving on to the next one, if she glimpsed a tear. When she came to her closest friends, Cass, Helena and Naomi she moved on quickly, they were wiping their noses, and desperately dabbing tears.

Jo swallowed, and again she felt Andy grip her arm, nudging her, saying quietly, "Easy, gently does it."

They were almost there. She caught a glimpse of Kate, her mother's oldest and dearest friend. The tears were rolling down her face as she looked at Jo, beautiful, on Andy's arm. If Jo could have read her thoughts she would have known they were along these lines, *I don't know who you are, Ida, but thank God for you and your granddaughter in Canada. Sam Stevenson at Jo's wedding...the very thought of it...*

Jo almost lost control as she looked at Kate, but then her eyes met Aiden's and she saw the love shining out of them and her heart melted, she was about to marry this lovely man. She forgot to cry.

At that precise moment, across the Atlantic, the sun was just rising in the Canadian sky. Sammy sat alone, on the front porch of Ida's granddaughter's house, sipping coffee. Checking the time on his watch, he whispered a silent prayer for his daughter, Jo, and Benny's son, Aiden, "God bless, Jo and Aiden, may their life together be rich with love and happiness."

By the time they reached Belfast Castle for the reception, Benny was beaming almost as much as Aiden. But he was dreading Andy's speech knowing what he knew about Jo. He prepared himself by downing a large brandy at the bar, while he ordered another.

During Andy's speech, he avoided eye contact with Kate, knowing she would be upset too. But the day was going well. Nothing was going to spoil it now.

The meal and the speeches over, the party started with the pre band disco, the mood was jubilant as the music filled the room, mingled with the hubbub of voices. Guests were talking animatedly at the tables, whilst others queued at the bar, and, of course, the small group of children present were practising their knee slides along the shiny dance floor, much to the consternation of the eagle eyed adults. By this stage in the proceedings Corey had given up on being concerned about scuffing his toes.

Then the band began to play, and Jo and Aiden took to the floor for the first dance, to their favourite song, a beautiful ballad by Christy Moore. After that, the dance floor began to fill with the wedding guests, everyone relaxed now, warmed up and ready to dance the night away, after the formalities of the day. Cass had a moment of panic as she saw Tony approach. She'd been nibbling a piece of wedding cake, which she hastily set down. He had nodded to her politely from the table across the room where he'd been seated for the meal, although they hadn't spoken as yet. He was beside her.

"Well, I see you do eat then. Do you take a drink at all?"

Cass smiled at him.

"I'll have a white wine, please."

Tony asked around the rest of their company, ordered the round, and paid for it at the bar. He didn't return to sit with them though, but made his way back to the table he'd been sitting at, on the far side of the room. Cass watched him ask another female guest to dance, and she couldn't believe how annoyed she felt. One of Aiden's friends asked her up, and over in Tony's company the pattern was being repeated - just two people at a wedding being sociable.

Benny nudged Deirdre saying, "Take a look at yer mother."

Her eyes swept across to where her mother and Michael, Benny's brother, were gracefully moving over the dance floor. Deirdre smiled, saying, "She's enjoying herself. She still cuts a fine figure, for a woman of her age."

"She does that, but it's her face I've been watching. Look at her lips, she's singing along, hasn't missed a word. Chorus and verses, she knows the entire song by heart."

Deirdre shook her head, sadly.

"Who knows what her memory still retains; it's a cruel disease, Benny. God help her. Today's a good day though. She's loving all the attention, what does it matter if she doesn't remember it tomorrow. Would you look at those two, Aiden wasn't wrong, eh."

Benny followed her eyes, to where Orla and Declan danced.

Of course, Orla and Declan had eyes for no one, but each other.

Chapter 55

LATE IN THE EVENING, AS Jo and Aiden prepared to go into the city for the sunset photo shoot, Declan announced to them that he and Orla were leaving.

"It's been a great day, but it's a long drive back, y'know."

Aiden knew, and so did Jo. They hugged them both tightly and watched as they walked out to the car park hand in hand, a couple in love, proud for all the world to see.

The limousine arrived to take Jo, Aiden and the photographer down to Thanksgiving Square. The wag of a driver couldn't resist asking, "Are we headin' round the boneys then?" He was referring to the eleventh night bonfires, which were about to be lit all over Protestant areas of the city.

The night was perfect, as was Malachy's timing. They arrived at 'The Angel of Thanksgiving' just on sunset. The colours in the city sky were rich and vibrant in oranges and reds, tremendous, as the Lagan beneath them sparkled in the rich glow of the summer evening. Jo had no doubt the photographs would turn out exactly as planned.

She was ecstatic, the day was almost complete.

Back at the reception, the band was in full swing. Cass was doing her best not to be disappointed that Tony O'Connor hadn't bothered with her since buying the drinks earlier in the evening.

Just as she had given up hope, Tony O'Connor was standing before her, asking her to dance. She didn't say no. As he swept her wordlessly around the floor, she knew there was no going back. She gave up her resistance and let him hold her tightly to him. She was his. Cass could have sworn she overheard Jo's mother-in-law say to her husband, "Don't they look well together?" as Tony and she passed on the dance floor.

But she must have gotten it wrong. Deirdre must have been speaking about another nearby couple.

Dave, who had gotten the rundown on the unfolding stories from Gail, was starting to feel overwhelmed by all the sexual tension. He thought of their empty, childfree house and decided it was time to go. The band was taking a break for a while to open the microphone to guest singers from the floor.

"Will we go home before the uncle sings 'Sweet Caroline'?"

"Which uncle?" Gail asked.

He shrugged, grinning, "I dunno, it's a wedding, there's always one."

"Okay, we'll leave as soon as Jo and Aiden go."

"We'll be waiting a while. Jo hasn't sat down all night. I think they'll be here until the band has announced the last dance. Aiden looks relieved that the singers are being called, she's only havin' a breather I tell ya, look at her feet, they're still tappin'."

"Yeah, I see what you mean. She's havin' a ball isn't she? Why not? It's her day, but is it not bad form, for me as a bridesmaid, to leave before the bride?"

"Jo's not goin' to care, she's on cloud nine. C'mon, I'll ring a taxi and we'll say our goodbyes to everybody, eh?"

"Alright."

Gail was thinking of their empty house too.

Across in the main foyer, Benny was texting Sammy, "Beautiful bride. Perfect day."

His reply came back, "I've been with you every step of the way, Benny."

Outside in the car park, as Gail and Dave watched their taxi approach along the winding driveway, they took in the splendour of the elevated view, the lights of the city shining over the expanse of the water, across Belfast Lough.

"There'll be a lotta lurve goin' on out there tonight. Would you do it again?"

"Marry you?"

"Yeah."

"In the mornin'. I love you, Dave."

"I love you too, Gail."

They climbed into the taxi, and travelled across the city, and home.

When Orla and Declan got out of the car at the house in Derry, she saw the flowers he had sent her sitting on the doorstep, beside them a bottle of champagne.

Orla scooped up the flowers, reading the inscription on the card as she opened the door and entered the house, the ever faithful Snapper following at her heels. Declan lifted the champagne, and walked into the hall after her, with a forceful push of the heel of his shoe the solid front door swung into place, slamming firmly shut behind them.

It had been a great wedding, a special day. And, of course, Benny had danced to 'Brown Sugar.'

Author's Note:

With reference to St. Patrick's Day rioting in The Holylands, mentioned in Part Two, page 221 -

This area around Queen's University of terrace house streets, many of them multi occupancy, is known as The Holyland because of the street names, Damascus, Carmel etc. The area is occupied by both students and families, in the main living peacefully together, apart from the occasional 'noise' issue. However in recent years in the period around St. Patrick's Day these streets of this particular area of Belfast have seen rioters break the relative calm of the city, rioters perceived by many as being students. Many students would discount these claims, blaming outsiders on hijacking the partying. Some would say the media have played their part in exacerbating the situation by hyping it in the days before anything has actually occurred. Either way, St. Patrick's Day rioting had become an annual 'event' in the named area at the time of writing this novel.

About the Author

Janice Donnelly was born and raised in Belfast, Northern Ireland; she now lives just outside the city in a small coastal town with her husband and two daughters.

Her debut novel - *Buying Time* – attracted five-star reviews when it was first published in 2011. She began working on *Trying Times* just as recession unfolded.

"I decided to bring the characters from *Buying Time* right up to date, to see how they would fare in hard times. Although the characters are each facing their own particular challenges, I wanted to create a feel good, upbeat story; and this is what I hope I have achieved."

www.janicedonnelly.weebly.com

Night Chorus
By Samantha J Wright

Amidst the excitement of Australia's gold rush and the emergence of Melbourne as a fledgling state, Lorna and Daniel have carved out a life of their own that they could only ever have dreamed of when first arriving on its paradisiac shores fifteen years ago.

But one day trouble rears its ugly head in the form of a Pandora's Box of secrets discovered by their wayward daughter Marion. Emboldened by her earth shattering discovery and put out by the return of an old family friend, she leaves home to pursue a life in theatre and in the process almost breaks her mother's heart.

After more than fifteen years of familial bliss, the flood gates to the past are now beginning to open bringing upon them a deadly tide of jealousy, scandal, illicit passions, betrayal and even murder. Can Lorna and Daniel piece their family back together again? Or is it time to move on and make a new life with what they have left, out in the wilds of Stamford Brook?

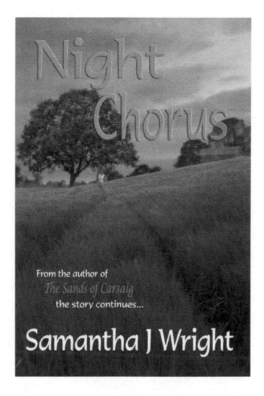

From the author of
The Sands of Carsaig
the story continues...

Samantha J Wright

The Sand of Carsaig
By Samantha J Wright

Raised on the Isle of Mull in the middle of the nineteenth century, Lorna McFadden is surrounded by change. Not only is the wild and beautiful coastline subject to constant variation, the economic climate is vastly unstable.

At the age of sixteen Lorna's pattern of life seems set on an unalterable course of hardship and poverty with no hope of anything better. Then one tragedy strikes after another, robbing Lorna of her beloved grandfather and threatening her family's livelihood.

Against the backdrop of famine and the highland clearances, Lorna battles the odds, seeking love and a new life elsewhere. They say that every cloud has a silver lining, but for Lorna it seems that tragedy may lead to something infinitely more valuable...

Find out more about Samantha J Wright at **www.samanthajwright.com**

Of Broken Things
By Lynda Tavakoli

It is 1920's Ireland and John Flynn is ten years old when his much longed for sister Stela is born at their isolated cottage. She is a beautiful child whom John sees as a gift sent to alleviate the harshness of his life with an alcoholic father Redmond.

Within a few weeks of Stela's arrival John is unexpectedly left to look after his mother and sister during a snowstorm after Redmond fails to return from one of his many prolonged absences. Stela grows strong under the protection and deep love of her brother but when she approaches her third birthday she inexplicably withdraws from the world. Unforeseen tragedy follows and slowly a web of deceit begins to unravel.

This is a story of divided loyalties and deception, of fear and mistrust, but also one of love and joy that will pull at the heartstrings until the very last page.

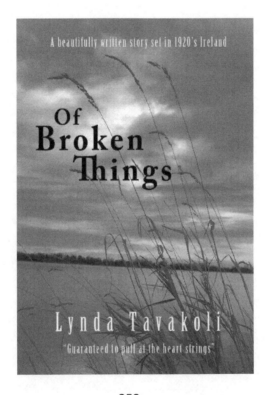

Wounded Heart

By David W Stokes

From the author of 'The Icelander,' WOUNDED HEART is the first in a series of three novels that tell the story about what can happen when the person you fall in love with suddenly starts hating you for no obvious reason.

We meet Euan: he's 40, has a grand house and no money worries. But he's a big loser in love. That's thanks to his wife Vicki. She thought she would love Euan forever - until her dark and secret past catches up with her. She needs to get away from him at all costs, which is great news for neighbour Trish. She's Vicki's best friend, but she also has her eyes on Euan. Big Time. And she always gets her man.

Euan's best friend William tries his hand at peace maker. When that doesn't work, beautiful psychologist Sarah is called on to sort them out. Then one day, events take an unexpected turn for the worst and life is never the same again. Set in Dublin, this is a sometimes funny, sometimes sad, sometimes tragic story of what happens when love and hate collide.

Printed in Great Britain
by Amazon.co.uk, Ltd.,
Marston Gate.